MACBETH

A NOVEL

The characters and events portrayed in this book are fictitious. Any similarity to real persons, living or dead, is coincidental and not intended by the author.

Published by Thomas & Mercer
P.O. Box 400818
Las Vegas, NV 89140

ISBN-13: 9781612183015
ISBN-10: 1612183018

MACBETH

A NOVEL

by

A. J. HARTLEY & DAVID HEWSON

Based on the play by William Shakespeare

THOMAS & MERCER

A Scottish autumn as bleak and bitter as the grave. Rain smears the gray sky. Lightning cracks, thunder shrieks over the drenched fells of the Great Glen.

A skinny, tall shape, a girl, young, yet not young, crawls through the bracken, the gorse, the cruel, sharp heather, heedless of her bloody knees stabbed by thorns. She stops, lifts her head, sniffs the air, listens to the wind and the sounds beyond. Mingled with the gale come the bleating cries of men in their death agonies, the screams of the wounded, the high-pitched whinnying terrors of desperate horses hamstrung and floundering in the mud.

She smiles and looks back at the other two. Sisters in name, though what they share is both more complex and more primitive than blood.

They crawl behind her, low figures in the stiff brown ferns. The farthest, most biddable, is ancient, her narrow, bitter face wreathed in gray matted hair, hands like claws, nails as long as her bony fingers. Filthy as an Elgin beggar, stinking in her sackcloth cloak and breeches. Crippled, she moves crablike on ebony crutches, as quick as a spider lurching forward with a malign stare, grunting and cursing. She was once someone's mother. Their own, perhaps.

No matter.

The second, flat on the turf, panting like an animal, is surly, six feet tall, broad, and muscular as any foot soldier. A shapeless habit, stolen from a long-dead monk, brown and filthy, covers her frame. Her face beneath its cowl is wide and heavy, a flat, stupid nose and dark, narrow eyes that peer constantly ahead. Her expression speaks of violence and a boundless anger searching for a cause. A break in the heavy sky sends a short shaft of sunlight to the ground. Caught in its wan rays, she seems for a moment like a cornered beast, ready to fight the unseen thing that hunts her. Younger than the crone by two decades or more, but as hideous, her black, stiff hair receding from her forehead to reveal white, bald skin, crisscrossed by a crimson blemish, a scar that runs across her temple like captured lightning.

The youngest turns and laughs at them. Next to this pair she is a beauty. Closest to the carnage beyond, watching avidly, drawn to the shrieks below, she's little more than some pretty child to the men she meets and taunts upon the road. Late at bleeding, though backward at nothing else. Special. Lithe and slender, as quick with her mind as with her knife. She wears a black wool cloak, quite clean, leather boots, a full, flowing dress that once was rich French velvet, the majestic gown of a noble lord's wife, as she went into the peat.

Too fine a robe for the dead, the girl said, and ordered them to dig deep and fast and hard once night had fallen and there was silence beyond the lych-gate.

The cloak still smells of embalmment, myrtle, and the thick, sweet fragrance of pine. Her hair is not clean or matted. Her face shines, washed in the streams each morning. Sometimes she bathes naked in the mountain burns or the great lochs that run from coast to coast, watched by the others, who are envious but afraid to say so. When she does, she swims backward, face to the sky, showing to the heavens the tattoo that spans her bony chest: the magical triquetra of a race now lost to these lands, three interlinked leaping salmon, two scaly shapes with dark, taut nipples for eyes, the third's depicted through her navel, their fins and tails reaching to her slender arms and down to the scant hair below. The form of the fish is indigo ink distilled from the Asp of Jerusalem, which the English call "woad," stippled carefully, dot by dot, each treasured precious wound stabbed into the flesh by her own steady fingers holding tight the quill of a raven, measuring the progress in the glittering mirror of a knight's cuirass. A year's work or more. The three symbols of the goddess are there, earth and fire and water, amid the carefully denoted scales of the strong wild fish that sport and spawn along Spey and Tay, free and fearless until her strong fingers grip their slippery underbellies and lift the thrashing bodies out into the bright, deadly air.

Sometimes men see this naked side of her, and a few—the lucky ones—run fast away.

There is, briefly, more for the fools who stay. Her eyes are shining, swirling pools as black as jet, the color of the deep lochs in autumn, fathomless, yet opaque, without visible pupils, yet seeming to see everything. Her mouth has small, even white teeth, sharp and keen like milk ones never shed. Her thin, gray lips are too wide, too active, as if she feels some hunger that can never be sated. No man can look at her and not want to touch, to feel, to know. She has understood this fact since the moment she could comprehend anything, knows how to use it, relishes the power that it brings.

"Move," she cries, and waves them on. There's a vantage point, a gap in the gorse and broom where she now sits, a happy spectator watching the savagery below, bare feet deep in the heather that is shedding its summer purple for the dry, dead copper of winter.

Men at their games again. Thanes and crofters, lords and peasants. Killing and being killed, with spear and knife, ax and sword, arrow and dagger, and bare, cruel hands. Much of a muchness when they're a bag of slaughtered flesh and bone bleeding out their little lives for the grateful worms in the peat.

She points a long, clean finger toward the battle, down the line of the saltwater loch that leads on to Mull, and says, "They call us witches, crones, and hags. And there I was thinking myself a god next to these beasts, such grand and self-regarding vermin as they are."

Her words are too old for her face. Older than theirs, perhaps, and sometimes they notice.

"Sister?" bleats a voice from her side as they lie there, crouched in the freezing heather, faces in the thorns, rapt, following the rank butchery on the field below.

Two wraiths in rags, stinking acolytes, snag-toothed and vile. One strange half child, elated, ecstatic.

"We will meet again?" asks the crone. "And soon?"

"The heath," says the giant. "When the fighting's done. And…"

She rubs her powerful hands with pleasure, her fingers writhe in anticipation. "Plunder. Men…the heath, I reckon…"

"Beyond the heath," the young one orders.

The crone offers no objection. The big one stares at the turf.

"We go east, the way they will eventually. Beneath the shadow of Ben Nevis, I'll meet you there. Men with murder on their minds are best avoided. Best let the blood cool a little."

"When?" asks the second.

"When the hurly-burly's done and the battle lost and won," the eldest murmurs as if this were some incantation from long ago, much used, much venerated.

"Tomorrow. Before the sun sets," the girl tells them. "Those left alive by then will be of one mind only. A grateful, fearful one. Fury spent. Time to repent and blub upon the soft and welcome breasts of female company."

She watches as they titter and caw like rooks over carrion.

"They kill in anger, then weep for their sins," says the giant. "Fools."

"Nevis's shadow," the young one repeats. "Tomorrow. To meet Macbeth. You shall do it."

Their filthy faces are stiff and stupid.

The crone lifts her right hand from the black stick, leans hard on it, cocks her ugly head as if listening, then says, "I hear Graymalkin. He calls me there."

The thing she thinks of as her familiar is a sleek and noisome cat. Left behind now, in a far-off hillside cave.

"I'm pleased he concurs," the young one says, then stares at the second. "And you?"

"Paddock sends me," she answers, nodding sagely. "I hear him as loud and clear as the screams of those fools below. You too, sister?"

The girl smiles, not kindly, and says, "It's not my good fortune to converse with toads. Your talents surpass mine, mostly."

And they are silent until she speaks again.

"Well…?" The young one unhooks the leather duffel from her shoulder, slung round there like a child's sack. She takes out a flask and some food, gulps at mountain water, eats dry berries, picks at hard rye bread, then bites off a lump of dry salt pork, chewing hard with her small sharp teeth.

They watch hungrily.

When she's done, impatient now for the dying of the day, she asks again, this time more curtly, "Well?"

Together, the two sing the little song that came to her that morning when she swam naked in the bright, sharp water on the moor, vowing to teach them every word.

"Fair is foul, and foul is fair. Hover through the fog and filthy air."

Something itches at her thigh. She pulls up the velvet dress, high enough so they can see her thin, white haunches. The leech lies tight to her flesh, like a fat black slug, full and sated.

"Feed on me, would you?" the girl mutters and rips the creature from her skin, holds the slowly wriggling form before her face, thinks, then places it between her teeth and bites hard. Blood runs over her chin. Severed in half, the worm's black slime slobbers down her front. The rest is mangled in her mouth, then chewed and swallowed in a single gulp.

The others stay stiff and silent, eyes upon her.

"Each thing tends toward its fate unknowing," she says, and wonders why. These drones do not understand and never will. "It would be impolite to refuse the call."

She leans forward and asks one last time. *"Well?"*

The pair scatter separately through the mist and thickets like malevolent ghosts, the crone low and swift on her black sticks, the other a tall, hunched, muscular figure, that of a sullen thief out for booty.

The young one stays there, hidden by the gorse and thistle, smelling the earth and the blood beyond, peering toward the battle and the tall, commanding figure in its midst.

"That warrior is in heat," she murmurs. "As am I. Macbeth. *Macbeth.*"

◈ ◈ ◈

"Macbeth."

The man didn't turn. He was listening. Some far-off sound caught on the cold, wet air, at the very edge of hearing.

"Macbeth!"

"Speak," he answered, wiping the blood and sweat from his face. Whatever it was, the words were gone, nothing more than one more fleeting illusion, a passing ghost in the midst of battle.

"There's a fleet landed down the loch," said the sergeant, a heavy man who always looked as if he'd spent the night in a ditch. "Vikings. Came under cover of night from the west through the Sound of Mull."

A raiding party, an unwelcome, though not infrequent, visitation upon Scotland, like pestilence or fleas.

"Where are they now?"

"The first boats are docking at Inverlochy. The men in the castle have fled already. There were scarcely twenty soldiers anyway. The rest are with the king. On the far side, almost at Loch Ness."

The absent king. Why had it taken Duncan so long to cross the Highlands from his eastern base in Forres and join the fight against the rebels in the west? Now there were two fronts, two enemies. The Scottish traitors and the Norsemen. Macbeth could picture the new battleground, Inverlochy, a handsome village in the foothills of Ben Nevis, fifteen miles and a short loch crossing from the insurgent castle at Ballachulish they now besieged. Thanks to that brief stretch of water, which Macbeth's boats commanded, they had a little time to spare between the present battle and the next.

He nodded and looked back to the hill fort around which his men had hunkered down, their eyes on its smoking battlements, set on an expansive crag of gray slate. The Great Glen ran like a diagonal sword slash across the neck of Scotland, from Inverness in the northeast to Loch Linnhe in the south, past purple and dun heather hills beside ribbon splashes of jeweled water. Macbeth and his men had spent the best part of a month chasing and killing MacDonwald's treacherous army the length of it. His soldiers were weary to be home and so was he. This fighting needed to be brought to a close.

MacDonwald's inside, thought Macbeth, his stomach clenching, jaw tightening. *This is his final stand. Inside and peering through a slit window with his dogs at his heels.*

"The Vikings must wait or do their worst. I've no time to deal with bandits. Once the rebellion's over—"

"My lord," said the sergeant.

He turned and caught something behind the soldier's eyes, a flicker of apprehension or dread.

"These are no bandits. Sueno, the king of Norway himself, is with them. They mean to stay." The man's eyes flickered and dropped to the rain-sodden heather, his face reddening.

"To stay? How do you know?" demanded Macbeth.

"They sacked a village on Mull. Left a single survivor to make sure word got out. They seemed sure they could divide our force, either side of Inverlochy. How…?"

Macbeth knew the beautiful island in the Hebrides and could imagine the devastation and death the Vikings would bring, as always. The ruined sheepcotes and shattered fishing boats, the smell of smoking thatches and chicken coops. Weeping women and spilled blood.

He turned into the stiff breeze and blinked before letting his gaze return to the rough stone tower with its crumbling curtain wall set on the gray-slate scarp.

"Then, first, we put MacDonwald to the sword, and after that, the Norsemen," he said.

A hasty, arrogant sentiment, one he regretted on the instant. The sergeant bowed and muttered as he left. He would soon be sowing panic and despair like barley. Wars turned on such moments, as did lives. Macbeth hurried after and stopped him with a hand on the shoulder.

"Find Banquo," he said. "Have him meet me here. In ten minutes, I want a report on the walls. We attack without delay."

"But..." The sergeant faltered, those shifty eyes flashing to and from Macbeth's face again.

"Yes?"

"We have no ram. No siege towers. Not even ladders. Our troops have been fighting six days in a row. I thought we were to starve the bastards out."

"There isn't time for that. Not now."

"We had word the thane of Cawdor would bring support from the south, through Glencoe. He will meet the Norsemen first..." said the sergeant, though even as he spoke his confidence stalled. "Can we not leave one fight to others? And..." He stared at the ground, refusing to meet the eyes of the man next to him. "And where in God's name is the king?"

Macbeth stilled his rising anger.

"Duncan is where he chooses to be. And Cawdor, a politician of the court, is not a Highland general. You would leave him to face Sueno alone, while we sit about the hillside like Whitsun revelers? We're men of the Great Glen. If there's a fight, it's our fight. Will you do my bidding or not? If you're afeared, go back to your bothy and sit sewing with your woman. We need men here, not quaking children."

Silence first, then doubt, then finally, and grudgingly, shame.

"Your orders, sir?"

Macbeth nodded toward a grove of windswept fir trees leaning over a tarn at the foot of the gray rocky hill. Patches of snow still lay in the shadows. Nevis, to the east, was cloaked entirely in white at the summit. "Have the men cut timber for ladders. Quickly. And find Banquo."

The wind had picked up, forcing the gray rain into gusty sleeting angles. The hills to the west behind the keep were purple, shading to brown, and streaked with ice and snow. The sky matched the color of the slate peak ahead of them. Below them, the narrow loch sat like a dark mirror, with Macbeth's boat guarding the narrowest point. They had only four more hours of daylight. Perhaps less. There would be bodies in the water before nightfall.

He watched a cluster of figures break away from the makeshift camp, unslinging their long axes as they trudged to the stand of pines. Moments later, the distant thud of their blades rang out across the valley like drums.

"So Sueno's come to join the entertainment?" said a familiar voice, deep as the ocean but suffused with warmth and grim humor. "A good time for looting, I imagine. He's a canny man if he can hear the wails of rebellion all the way across the sea in Norway."

Banquo. The one warrior Macbeth would wish beside him on a day like this. The biggest man in the field, a giant in armor. He held his helmet in his massive hands. The gray wolf pelt that covered it, lower jaw removed, the upper with its fangs gripping the shining metal brow, followed him like a train.

"He's here for land, not looting," said Macbeth. "How stand the walls?"

"Old and poorly maintained." Banquo was broad and muscular, with a long black beard, a weather-beaten Highlander's face, and speech that seemed to come from the pit of his vast stomach. "A dozen underfed women could drag them down with grapplers if those damned kerns didn't shower arrows and darts on anyone who went near. The Norsemen have come for something other than thieving?"

"So they say."

"Two enemies, then," Banquo muttered, playing with his beard.

"We deal with each in their turn. And the gate?"

"The doors are new. Solid. We'd need a ram."

"Ladders," said Macbeth. "Get men in, then open the gates from the inside."

"The troops are tired," said Banquo. "Readying the approach and preparing an assault will take—"

"MacDonwald is the rallying point of this rebellion," Macbeth reminded him. "This is his final stand. He has sold Scotland—our land—to foreign rabble. His Irish kerns and gallowglasses have mown our people like so much wheat, women and children burned like chaff before them. And Sueno himself will be here in a matter of hours, unless Cawdor can hold him off."

"I know, but we are not equipped…"

"One hour," said Macbeth.

Banquo cocked his head and frowned at Macbeth's hard, relentless gaze, then shrugged.

"You, my friend, are either the finest general in Scotland or a bloody fool."

Macbeth looked into his bright eyes and laughed. "But which?" he asked.

Banquo threw the helmet on his head, and the wolf's pelt followed like a cloak behind his back. "One hour," he said. "And then I think we'll know."

◈ ◈ ◈

The rain picked up and the sky darkened further. Ravens circled overhead as if sensing carrion. The ladders were no more than roughly hacked trunks, their branches trimmed to rungs. They would be slow and hard to climb.

The enemy watched their preparations idly, and Macbeth wondered how much they knew of Sueno's arrival. Plenty, he hoped, since that knowledge would give them confidence, and sureness made a man idle and weak. Surprise was as good a cloak for recklessness as they were likely to find, and he had tried to maintain it, keeping the men huddled as they readied their weapons instead of lined up, ready for an assault. Their scattered cavalry he had grouped and sent off to the north—give MacDonwald's lookouts something to watch—and a hundred foot soldiers had been arranged just out of the range of the archers on the western walls, where the fortifications were most ruined. These were diversions. The real assault would come directly from him, from the south, straight over the crumbling ramparts, using the rough-hewn ladders the men had disguised as best they could with cloaks and branches.

Macbeth strained for signs of movement on the ramparts, but he could see nothing. If MacDonwald knew they were coming, he wasn't showing it. Macbeth checked the handle of his shield once more and looked up to the sky as a great black raven soared shrieking overhead. The sight of it made the men around him wince. Superstition and soldiery went hand in fist at moments like this. He watched the black bird glide, buffeted by the wind, then drew his long sword and pointed it up toward its outspread wings, sighting along the blade as if he were shooting a bow.

His movement brought about a sudden nervous stillness in the army at his back. He felt it rippling through the ranks like their tightening muscles, the tension, the fear, and the wild exhilaration that began a battle. Behind him, Cullen, a loyal master of his family household, now pressed into service as a sergeant, muttered a prayer. Macbeth watched him. Macbeth had always thought Cullen a good and decent man, but he was struck by the strangeness of his words, by the idea that God might watch, might help, giving speed and strength to his soldiers, while splintering the weapons of the enemy. Priests might divide the world into good and bad. In battle there was strong and weak and nothing else.

High above, the raven called once.

Macbeth brought down his sword and the army roared into life.

They made a good thirty yards before the arrows began to rain down. The first volley was ragged and mistimed, but deadly all the same. A pale, thin boy was the first to fall, the shaft of a long dart in his neck, screaming as he stumbled to the heather and mud. But most of those around him had their shields above them, and the air was thick with the sound of iron biting leather and wood.

Macbeth made sure he was among the first to reach the battlements. For a moment, there was nothing to do but wait amid the hail of rocks and arrows as the tree trunks were lugged into place. He flattened himself against the cold, wet stone, then broke into the open and grabbed a rope, his shield slung onto his back. The man beside him was a bearlike figure, and as he strained to pull the massive ladder into position, an arrow snagged the flesh of his shoulder, opening a long, deep gash. It bled heavily, but the soldier never took his eyes from the top of the tree trunk until the wood fell heavily against the battlements. Then he stood beneath, holding it in place with massive arms as the men scrambled up, barely wincing at the ones who placed a boot on his torn shoulder along the way.

The rungs—such as they were—were slick with rain. Macbeth felt as if he were scaling the sky itself, open and exposed, propelled by the urgent thrust of those behind him. At the summit he took his right hand from the ladder and dragged his sword from its sheath.

At the top of the ladder, the man above Macbeth screamed suddenly. A huge kern had buried an ax deep in his chest. Macbeth did not give the kern time to wrench the weapon from his victim, but leapt over the wall and brought his blade down between the man's neck and shoulder. Sinews snapped, and with a single scarlet jet, the kern's legs buckled. Macbeth was past, shield swung round in front of him now, squaring for the next assailant.

The lowly kerns ahead were pulling back already, fodder for the blade: archers mainly, unprepared for close combat. Macbeth knew that if he could get enough men over the ladders that part of the battle would be won. The vicious mercenaries from the Western Isles, the men called gallowglasses, would be another story altogether, but he would deal with them when they showed themselves.

Three kerns, sharing their courage, ran at him. They brandished knives and axes with blades slim as picks. He stepped into their charge, shouldering one off the wall with his shield, then ducking beneath their axes. He came up hard, the tip of his sword driving up through the belly of one, his shield meeting the ax of the other. The weapon shivered in the fool's hand. The kern left it stuck in the shield, slashing desperately with his knife. Macbeth stepped back once, then twice, as if faltering, and as the man came at him again, reached suddenly with his sword. The point skewered his ribcage and he dropped, dead before he hit the ground.

There were two more at the top of the stairs down into the courtyard, but they fled before him. An arrow flew past and rang on the stonework beside his head. Macbeth bounded down the steps and into the chaos below.

The castle had a central keep with a flight of steps and a heavy oak door studded with blackened nails. As Macbeth watched, sword gripped hard in his sweating fist, he saw it open. The gallowglasses, the cruelest mercenaries any rebel leader might buy, were coming, and with them was a red-haired man with a two-handed ax and eyes the color of deep, cold water.

MacDonwald.

As the kerns scattered, the gallowglasses marched down the steps, their mail shirts and helmets shining in the weakening winter sun, swords and pole arms flashing.

"To me!" Macbeth bellowed.

His men drew up beside him, but the mercenaries came on undaunted, a wall of iron death barreling toward them. Macbeth curved his shield, then angled his sword above it. He held his breath, heart pulsing, as they came closer.

Twenty yards. Ten. Five.

Then only the fury and desperation of battle.

The clash of steel, the dull thud of severed bone, the rip of flesh, and the cries of anger and bravado, terror and death. The courtyard was packed with struggling bodies, the living, the wounded, all crowded in so tight that even the dead stayed upright. His men were trapped, packed in like sheaves of wheat, and the gallowglasses were the reapers. They wore crested helms with metal plates, which covered their faces with terrible masks so that only their eyes showed through. Their armor was thick. Not just mail, but metal plates laced together over heavy hide. Twice, Macbeth delivered what he thought was a killing blow, only to feel it stop and slide off the target.

And then, quite suddenly, there was room to move. A space opened and he climbed over the corpses slumped about him, turning to see Banquo and his men pouring in through the gates, smacking the gallowglasses side-on with their spears so that the enemy turned, shock and confusion in their eyes.

Heavy in their armor, the mercenaries tried to run. Some made for the keep, some fleeing for the hills outside. Macbeth scanned the slaughter and saw MacDonwald cutting his way toward the keep.

He crossed the courtyard and charged down the door, ran on through a stone hallway lit by pitch torches, then into a vaulted chamber that echoed with the shouts of those huddled by the great fireplace at the far end. There were doors and passages in the alcoves, frightened figures hiding in the darkness against the walls, servants, women, children. There were bodies, too, a few soldiers, but also others, struck down where they stood.

He stopped by a cowering group of women and switched the grip on his sword.

"Where's the traitor?" he demanded.

A cheer went up from outside. He knew that roar anywhere. Banquo, triumphant.

"We harm none who wish us well," Macbeth declared. "Where is MacDonwald?"

A boy stepped forward from beneath the skirts of one of the kitchen girls and pointed at the door.

Macbeth strode toward it and used his shield arm to twist the latch. A tight spiral staircase ran before him—a tower or a way up to the roof. The fighting here would be more difficult and confined than the courtyard, and if MacDonwald was above him…

It was dark on the spiral stairs. He had to feel his way with the knuckles of his sword hand, listening to his labored breath, his gaze fixed up ahead. He took three more of the narrow, treacherous steps, then stopped, straining to hear. The quality of the silence had changed. Beyond the sound of his own movement he could hear the thin whistle of wind in the tower. He was near the top. Three more steps and he could see light bleeding round the rounded corner ahead.

Stealth or speed?

Stealth. He kept the sword close so its steel would not ring on the stone and inched up the spiral with agonized slowness. Two more steps and he saw the leaden sky, felt rain on his face again.

There was no sign of the red-haired man.

Perhaps the boy had lied, lured him in here so the rebel could make his escape or trap him inside with the fearsome gallowglasses. He stepped out onto the turret, but before he could turn from the mountains laid out in front of him, he felt movement behind him.

"Still running Duncan's errands, Macbeth?"

He turned.

MacDonwald was standing against the crenulated wall of the tower. A broad, two-handed ax leaned against the parapet. He was training a short and powerful crossbow squarely at Macbeth's heart.

"I serve the king," said Macbeth. "I serve my country."

"Whereas I serve myself, you mean? That's a convenient way of looking at things."

Macbeth didn't answer.

"Put down your blade," said MacDonwald.

Macbeth didn't move.

"Show a little sense," MacDonwald went on, extending the bow slightly, his fingers tightening around the trigger, stock to his strong shoulder. The bolt was thickset, the point fluted and ugly.

Macbeth lowered his sword arm till the tip touched the stone floor, then let it fall. In the silence the crash of the metal rang out like shattering glass.

The rebel was a handsome chieftain from the north, with a thin, sardonic mouth that now broke into a smile.

"There's a sensible man," he said. "Now you'll come downstairs with me and we'll have a little parley with whichever of Duncan's errand boys holds the purse strings. Banquo, is it?"

"You're past forgiveness," said Macbeth.

The surprise was genuine.

"Forgiveness?" MacDonwald echoed, the smile returning. "What can I do with that? I want a horse and free passage." He looked Macbeth in the eye. "Or you beside me in this just cause. Macbeth, you're a fine warrior. A decent lord so far as I can tell. As am I. Do you think we raise rebellion lightly?"

"Treason's treason. I neither know nor care for your reasons."

"Then get your wits about you," MacDonwald cried. "Or it's your head next. Why not listen to me for one moment? Why not join us?"

"I know my place. I know my duty."

Anger flared in the man's gray eyes. "Duty to a cur like Duncan? A coward? A thief who'll steal the crown of Scotland for his own folk if we give him half the chance? When the king dies, *we* choose his successor. The nation's lords, the thanes. We do not hand it on a plate to any bastard Duncan happens to have fathered along the way…"

"What trickery do you throw at me now?" Macbeth barked back. "I know about Sueno, MacDonwald. I know he came for land, not booty, this time. What's the reward for the Viking's sword? What portion of our homeland have you promised him? Where's your patriotism there?"

MacDonwald shrugged his shoulders. "Desperate times demand desperate measures. Land that's taken now may one day be recovered. But give away the crown and the nation goes with it. A greater spill of blood ensues. Oh, Macbeth! Why is it you can see so much and yet so little?"

"Away with your nonsense. You talk as if you have won, but your army is broken and running, and Cawdor will hold Sueno."

"Ah, yes," said MacDonwald. "Cawdor." There was something new in his face. Amusement, perhaps. "When men pick sides, they should choose wisely. This shall be an interesting day for those who stand beside Duncan's throne."

Macbeth's eyes narrowed. The man's composure felt wrong.

"Enough of this. Down below," MacDonwald ordered. "I wish no quarrel with you. Stand down your men. I'll treat them fairly. But you must surrender. This moment, if you please. Then we will speak, and I will give you such reasons as will change your mind about the king. Come, man, your duty's to Scotland and to yourself. Not him. When he's gone, by rights, any of us might wear that crown, if his peers so wish it. Even you."

"I've never slain a lunatic before," Macbeth replied. "But there comes a first time for all things, so they say."

The insult was deliberate and well timed. It hid the way he watched the dark mouth of the spiral stone staircase and took a step toward it. MacDonwald bent slightly to pick up the discarded sword, and in that moment, Macbeth moved.

He wheeled, vaulting over to MacDonwald's ax, which still stood propped against the wall. The shot was rushed. Macbeth leaned and the crossbow bolt scudded through the space over his right shoulder. He turned, and MacDonwald had already halved the distance between them, sword at the ready, screaming.

Macbeth dropped his shield and came up with the long-shafted ax, swinging it in a wide, lethal arc, and MacDonwald hesitated, but only for a second. Then he came on, blade sweeping from over his head. Macbeth caught it with the haft of the ax, thrust its edge aside, and kicked at MacDonwald's stomach. The red-haired man stepped back, his smile now wolfish. His second rush was faster, the sword cutting the thin, damp air as Macbeth dodged and parried. Two steps backward and Macbeth felt the wall of the turret against his back.

MacDonwald switched his grip on the hilt, lowered his head, and lunged. Instead of parrying, Macbeth rolled right, let the ax head fall a little, then, as he completed the circle, swept his cruel blade up with a fearsome violence.

It caught the rebel lord just above the waist and kept going till it tore free beneath his chin. His body opened as he dropped, and Macbeth stepped aside, adjusting his stance just long enough to raise the ax one last time and strike off his head.

The regret was instant. This was a noble death. Not the hanging the man's foul sedition deserved.

◈ ◈ ◈

Duncan the First, king of Scotland, played with the heavy gold cross he always wore around his neck, tracing its edge with his thick fingers. The air in the tent was thick with smoke and the sourness of men too long in the field. He would have pinned back the canvas flap over the entrance, but the rain had picked up again.

The remains of an entire cock pheasant, taken on the rugged hillside behind Invergarry, stood on a silver plate in front of him. The bird sat heavy in his belly, its grease rank on his hands and face. Outside he heard the shifting of horses. There was still no news of the scouts who would bring tidings of the two battles, Macbeth against MacDonwald, Cawdor tackling the unwelcome and unexpected intervention of the Norse king Sueno. Time was running short.

So the king sat surly in his furs and gleaming ceremonial mail, distant from the fighting by his own design, now feeling slighted and outmaneuvered. The treachery of MacDonwald had been known but not its depth, and his reach beyond Scotland to Norway had been a most unpleasant surprise. Macbeth and Banquo had harried the turncoat to some ramshackle castle close to the loch of Linnhe and—in time—they would, no doubt, have his head. But while the king welcomed the thought, he would have preferred others to have brought the trophy. Those two were as useful as leashed wolfhounds were, but they were proving too popular, Macbeth most of all. And that could make trouble of a different kind. When it came to the kill, it mattered who gave the final blow. One of Duncan's sons might have been better. Malcolm or Donalbain. He would speak to a chronicler and turn invention into the artificial truth called history, but that wouldn't solve the immediate problem. He—and therefore the kingdom—owed Macbeth and Banquo a great deal. Too much, perhaps, for comfort.

Duncan watched his sons. The brothers lay sprawled on their beds. Donalbain, who was only nineteen, was asleep after another evening of toasting other people's victories. Malcolm, ten years older, was doing nothing as usual, lying on his back whistling tunelessly and watching a single sluggish fly move over the tent fabric.

The king frowned. Further victories from Macbeth and Banquo might complicate matters, but Duncan's grasp on the Council of Thanes remained firm, and the loyalty of his captains was beyond question. MacDonwald must have made some contract with the Viking. Land and money, perhaps some slaves. If the Vikings still proved strong, Duncan might settle a similar contract with them after MacDonwald's death. Then he would change Scotland forever, by making public what he'd privately been mulling for some months: the pronouncement of his eldest, Malcolm, as prince of Cumberland and heir to the throne by right of blood, second in a dynasty that would prosper for all time.

Such an action would require careful management. Succession was a perilous process, one Duncan treated with serious and measured care. By tradition, the Scots did not routinely pass the crown from father to son like the English, preferring instead to select from the lords among them a suitable king, chosen by the popular acclaim of his fellow thanes. It was, Duncan had decided, a dangerous and primitive practice, and not only because it left the nation in turmoil on the death of each monarch. The practice bred treachery and rebellion during a king's lifetime, for if a monarch was nothing more than some elected lord, might he not be replaced—by force, if necessary?

He would change this primitive habit and the thanes would have to live with it. With victory behind him, he was strong enough to force his will upon them, placing the line of Scotland firmly in his family's grip, a glorious jewel passed from father to son, by right, by God, by the sword, if necessary. There would be surprise, perhaps even resistance, but it would pass, and the mightiest clan lords—Macbeth and Banquo and MacDuff—would, with a little flattery and preferment, stand so strongly by him that none would dare voice their discontent. Their backing was the most vital and the trickiest to secure since, given the old ways, one of them might have considered the crown within their own reach. It would require craft, diplomacy, and no small play of secret cunning. But the path from beloved hero to drawn-and-quartered traitor was not so lengthy, and if one of those three should step an inch toward defiance, all the hellhounds of the state would rip their throats apart.

Then, with the throne secured, not just for himself, but also for his son, treachery such as MacDonwald's would be stifled like a throttled viper chanced on in the heather. Scotland would know peace. Duncan could be done with sitting about in damp fields while lesser men hacked each other to pieces.

The guard at the tent flap stirred, his hand straying for the hilt of his sword. The king stiffened in his chair, listening.

"Quiet," he snapped at Malcolm, who had resumed his whistling. His son shot him a baleful glance, then swung his legs over the edge of his bed and sat upright. He was good-looking, tall, and muscular, as his father had been at his age, if a little soft around the middle. But there was a hardness in his eyes and a sly, meticulous side to his nature. He never said or did anything without consideration. In practice that meant he rarely did much at all, but Duncan knew the value of caution, of deliberation. Impulsiveness was to be encouraged in warriors like Macbeth. It made them useful tools on the battlefield, though often of limited duration. Malcolm, like his father, was a planner, and that was a fine and useful talent in a king.

The guard stepped out. Duncan could hear running feet—the scout with word on Sueno's demands. If they didn't come to terms quickly, the Norse army would run into Macbeth, Banquo, and Cawdor, and how that encounter turned out would affect both those terms and Duncan's secret plans for Malcolm. The king rose, the hem of his vast mail coat dropping around his knees like a dozen tiny bells. White-haired, with an ascetic, intelligent face, he became in an instant the man they wanted, a monarch, calm and open, all calculation and anxiety melting away as if he had put on a mask.

The scout came in, dropped to his knees, face to the ground, panting, out of breath.

"Well?" said Duncan. "You are disrupting time I would prefer to spend at prayer."

Malcolm and Donalbain exchanged looks.

"My liege," said the messenger, face still down, "the king of Norway has sent an emissary to negotiate the terms of your…" He hesitated.

"The terms of my what?" demanded the king, his eyes flashing.

"The terms of your surrender," said the scout. "Sueno orders that you relinquish the Scottish throne to him and—"

He didn't manage the rest of the sentence. Duncan kicked him hard in the side of the head, sending him sprawling. Had he been younger and more agile, the king might have pinned the scout to the ground. Instead, it was Malcolm who landed on him, squatting like a cat, a long, leaf-bladed dagger in one hand, his eyes bright and wide.

"Orders?" repeated Duncan, looming over the prone scout, who had turned his head away and was whimpering like a girl. "Sueno orders me to relinquish the crown?"

"I beg your highness's forgiveness," the scout managed. "I only wished to warn you of what his own emissary will say."

"His what?" Duncan said, caught off guard. "He brought an ambassador with him?"

"No, my liege," said the scout.

"You'd better start making sense," hissed Malcolm, "or I will slit you a new set of lips and we'll see if they work any better."

The tent opened again. It was the guard. His eyes flashed over the struggling scout, then returned carefully to Duncan's face. Even so, he looked troubled, and not just by what he saw.

"Yes?" roared Duncan.

"Sueno, king of Norway, has sent…" The guard stumbled.

"His emissary?" Malcolm suggested.

"Indeed, sir," said the guard. "But…"

"Fetch him, man."

"But, sir…"

"Do as I say!"

The guard paused, gave a nod that might have been a bow, and stepped aside as Duncan turned back to his chair. In a booming voice, given as much to the field outside as the men in the tent, the guard announced, "The emissary from Sueno, king of Norway. The thane of Cawdor."

Cawdor?

Duncan froze. For a long moment he stared at the ornate gilt throne that followed him about the land, an icon of his majesty. Then he turned slowly. Standing inside the tent, armored from head to foot, his face showing nothing beyond a crooked, knowing smile, was Cawdor, a man he'd known since both were bairns.

Kings die in two ways only, Duncan thought to himself. *In battle, at the head of their failing troops, or through the artful, knowing treachery of friends.* He'd seized the throne for himself decades before and always sworn he'd never face that first eventuality again. Yet the second, crueler end, lurked always in the shadows, unseen, unknowable, like a contagion waiting on its moment.

Cawdor had turned traitor. There was no one now to stop Sueno and his Vikings from pouncing on Macbeth and Banquo's forces, however they fared against MacDonwald. The fight was lost. Those who had been loyal to the crown were as good as dead.

And so, thought Duncan, king of Scotland, *am I.*

◈ ◈ ◈

"The castle's a shambles," Banquo grumbled.

"That it is," said Macbeth. "Barely defensible."

"I'm not sure you're getting my point."

"Which is?"

"That being a shambles was fine when we were the attackers, but somewhat disturbing if we're the poor bastards inside."

The news had grown worse with every passing hour. As Macbeth's men took the slate castle on the scarp, Sueno's men had crossed the loch, slaughtering the guards who held the narrow crossing below. The Vikings had now pitched camp at the foot of the hill. They were taking their time and seemed to know it was theirs to squander.

"Sueno shows no sign of moving toward us tonight," Macbeth answered, gazing from the battlements down to the loch. "His men have marched hard. If they were mine, I'd grant them some rest before laying siege. It may be more than that. Perhaps he knows he's safe. How long do you think we can hold them off?"

"A few days at the most," said Banquo, spitting over the wall. "Probably less."

"That's what I thought."

"Time enough for Cawdor to get here," said Banquo. "If we can hold them off till then…Only a fool camps by the shore. They've the cold loch at their backs and we may yet push them back into it."

Macbeth scowled. "The Vikings are creatures of the sea. The ocean doesn't scare them and neither, I'm afraid, does Cawdor."

"He's a good man," said Banquo. "Not much experience as a warrior, I grant you, but he leads a mighty force."

"I'm just not sure we can count on Cawdor."

The conviction had been growing since MacDonwald's curious words before he died. They kept running round his head. Men lied, to others and to themselves at times.

Traitors more than most. But that red-haired rebel knew something, and it wasn't to Macbeth's advantage.

"What?" said Banquo. "Why not?"

"I don't know. Something MacDonwald said." He caught Banquo's eye. "Why did a thane, a lord we all thought loyal, turn traitor? What was this rebellion about?"

Banquo looked at him as if the question were stupid.

"We're Highlanders, you fool. Since when did a fight need a reason?"

"There must be one. Even here."

Those cryptic references, to Duncan and the crown, worried him. Macbeth was not a man for gossip, idle or otherwise. He preferred to be a good lord, to keep his tenants well provisioned and collect from them their annual dues. The chatter of the court bored him. If some secret plot were being hatched…

"Your duty's to Scotland and to yourself…"

"Why?" Banquo asked. "What did you hear?"

"Nothing. All the same, let's presume we're on our own. That we should not expect help from any quarter: Duncan, Cawdor, God himself."

"Then that changes things."

"It does," Macbeth agreed.

He turned to look down into the yard, now bustling with troops and supply carts. He called to a skinny, narrow-faced servant who was pissing against the side of his barrel-laden wagon. Fergus was his name, a vile thing, but one of his own. Reliable in the way that untrustworthy men were to the lords they served. A creature for the tasks his master would prefer stayed secret—spying, connivance, and a little bribery. Even the most honest of thanes had need of a villain from time to time.

"How much food and drink is there?"

"Can't you see I'm busy?" said the man, looking cross and crafty.

Banquo gave Macbeth a quizzical look. "You know this one?"

"One of mine," said Macbeth under his breath. "Every farm has its weasel. In this case, he's a porter with a mouth on him. But the man's got a talent for finding things where others fail. Though…" He shrugged. "It's best you don't ask their provenance."

Banquo coughed into this hand and pointed to another across the yard, the silver-bearded Cullen, busy tallying weapons. "I thought that was your right-hand man. A good sort, too. I like him."

"Cullen's a loyal, decent servant. Honest. A man with scruples."

"Ah." Banquo rubbed his nose and winked. "Scruples are admirable in principle. But in times like these—"

"You've got a question or what?" the porter below shouted up at them.

"How long will the food last?" Macbeth replied.

"A few days," he said, and patted the wagon. "A week if you only feed the healthy ones. After that…" He shrugged, then shifted from foot to foot as if he might fall over. "There's a village yonder and a few scraggy sheep on the hills. Not much else but weeds and mekilwort and we won't live long on that."

Mekilwort. Macbeth's wife, Skena, was no stranger to herbs and potions. Sometimes the apothecary even asked her advice. She was from the south and knew this common winding vine as belladonna. Deadly nightshade.

"That's a medicine of a kind, I think," Macbeth said out loud.

The porter gave him a knowing grin. "A medicine? Right. You're a smart one sometimes, lord," he said. "It is. Not one to feed an army, though."

"It grows here?"

"The castle grounds are infested with the stuff. The berries are everywhere."

Banquo looked interested. "I don't know which looks craftier," he said. "You or your skinny porter down there. What's on your mind, eh?"

"How many barrels of beer are left?" asked Macbeth.

"Twelve," said the porter, checking the wagon. "Not enough to keep out this cold night, that's for sure. If we're still alive in the morning, I'll find a village and get us more." He rubbed his fingers together, grinning. "It'll take a little cash, mind."

"Open the barrels," said Macbeth. "All of them."

"You're going to let the men drink knowing that we'll be having breakfast with Sueno's cutthroat Vikings?" asked Banquo, aghast. "What is this? A wake for the living? For surely we'll be dead tomorrow. Dead with hangovers, which may be doubly painful..."

"It's not for us," Macbeth cut in. "Fergus, set a guard on the wagon and send some of the kitchen staff to gather the weed."

"Fine," said the man below with a sigh.

Macbeth laughed at Banquo's bafflement. "Belladonna, man. Does the name mean nothing?"

"I leave gardening to women and servants!"

The porter was still listening, and he was quicker. His face went white and his hands went to his cheeks. "Not the beer!" he cried. "Sweet Jesus! Not the beer!"

◈ ◈ ◈

An hour later, when the rain had finally stopped, the porter drove his wagon south with much spitting and cursing. Banquo watched him leave, then turned to Macbeth.

"You're sure about this?"

Banquo had donned his helmet with the wolf's head grinning above it, fangs forever bared. The pelt came from a Viking he'd killed, one of the strange and merciless monsters they called the "berserkers." No other Scot owned such a prize or, if they did, would dare to wear it in Banquo's presence.

"No," said Macbeth. "But more sure of it than I am of Cawdor."

Or Duncan, he thought.

They'd found a local woman in the kitchen who knew of belladonna. A single berry might save a man from a spasm. Ten could kill him, half that for a child. The barrels of beer were vast, the calculation difficult. Too much poison and the men would taste it. Too little and at best they'd suffer a sore head. If the encounter could be resolved through single combat with Sueno or his champion, Macbeth would have been the first to volunteer, but this was war. He knew that steel and sinew and raw courage were not always the surest way to victory, even if he didn't like the alternatives. He left the woman to work out how many berries to add to each barrel, and when she came later to explain her decision, he waved her away, not wanting to know the details.

Now he stared into the deepening twilight and caught the shapes of three figures on the side of the fell that tumbled down toward Linnhe. Spies? He doubted it. These forms were too still, too obviously watchful. And though it was a good way distant and difficult to tell, he had the strange feeling that they were women.

◈ ◈ ◈

The porter returned as sour as when he left, but none the worse for his excursion. The Norse guards had swallowed his drunken tale of mistaking their camp for Macbeth's as easily as they would now consume the generous barrels of beer laced with soporific belladonna.

Macbeth gave the order after the moon rose. The men were tired and skeptical. It was a measure of their faith in him, Macbeth thought, that they got to their feet at all.

Banquo roared with laughter at the audacity of the plan, and though he had raised various objections and refused to be entirely persuaded, he had finally grinned and shrugged as if this were one more boyhood prank.

The army fell in and marched as close to silence as they could. They saw no sign of the enemy till they crested a long wooded ridge. Then, by the waterside, emerged the fires of Sueno's camp. Banquo led his company to the east, while Macbeth cut round to the north, each following the other's movements in the bright light of the moon. Macbeth could not say if they had been seen or if the enemy was waiting for them. But in his bones, he thought they went undetected. The camp was too quiet.

Finally, his lead scout raised a warning hand and pointed. The whole silent company shrank into the hillside and froze.

Ahead on a raised tussock stood a helmeted figure with a tall spear, silhouetted against the sky.

Slender black clouds scudded across the stars. The weather, for the moment, would be kind to them.

The man closest to Macbeth unslung a bow and nocked an arrow in its string. Macbeth stilled him with a touch and crept forward, stooping in the tall grass. He drew his sword silently, his eyes on the black shape of the watchman, trying to see which way the man was looking. A rough path of bent grass stalks, dark and gleaming with the day's rain, led right to him. *Made by deer, probably*, thought Macbeth, though his mind prickled at the memory of the three strange figures he had glimpsed on the hillside. The idea unsettled him and he stopped, glancing down to make sure there was nothing underfoot that would give him away.

When he looked up again, he was unsure whether the silhouette had moved or not. It was certainly motionless now, but for all he knew, the guard was staring right at him, trying to ascertain what he was seeing in the moonlight, poised to plunge that long spear into Macbeth's heart.

He took a careful breath, made one more step, and stopped. The man had made a sound. Macbeth hadn't caught the word but was sure the Viking had grunted something in an unknown tongue. A demand for a password? Macbeth did not move, but his grip on the sword tightened. He was about to spring forward when the noise came again, and this time he knew it for what it was.

Half propped against his spear, the Viking slept there standing, snoring like a pig.

It was all he could do not to laugh aloud. Macbeth rose silently and drew his knife. He moved close enough to smell the ale on the guard's snores, then moved behind him, the blade raised to his throat. There was foreign lettering stamped on the man's helm, a prayer, perhaps, or a family motto. Macbeth focused on the unreadable words, clamped his hand over the snoring mouth, and drew his knife across the Norseman's throat in one clean cut.

He signaled, and the army began to move again, following him silently past the still, sad corpse and down toward the camp. As they reached the enemy tents, it was clear the guard was not a solitary sleeper.

The entire army was insensible, or as near as made no difference. Even when the noise of fighting rang out, most of the Vikings failed to stir. Macbeth himself killed only two, both drunk with slumber and waving wildly with their spears and axes. It was barely a battle at all.

Sueno's army was counted later at more than seven hundred men. Half of them died that night, many as they slept. Macbeth—who preferred not to kill a man except in the hot blood of open combat—was unamused, but as Banquo reminded him, this was the way of warfare, especially for the Highlanders. Had the conflict gone the other way, the Scots would now be on their knees, sorry heads bowed, waiting for the ax to fall.

"This was a mighty force," he added. "Sleepy, I grant you, but more than we could handle had they been awake."

Those of ransomable rank were spared and bound, the better weapons claimed for plunder. The foot soldiers and any deemed a Viking slave through the oar blisters on their hands were taken to the loch and there lined up in a miserable, complaining line and beheaded like animals brought to slaughter. The lucky few died where they slept or in the foggy moments just after opening their eyes. There was probably a clansman or two among them, Macbeth thought. Not that there was time to look.

"War," shrugged Banquo, taking off his wolf's-head helmet, wiping the blade of his sword. "No one said it was fair."

They found Sueno waking in a bath of tepid water in a tent beside a fire.

Macbeth and Banquo walked in to see the king of Norway naked, shivering, fearful for his life. The man spoke in a language none understood. He was elderly, skeletal, with a ragged beard and mad, frightened eyes. Fergus the porter sneaked in behind to watch what happened.

Sueno stumbled out of the bath, fell across the tent, tumbled hard against his traveling chest, hands grasping ahead of him.

"If he finds a sword," Banquo murmured, "king or not..."

But the Viking's fingers fell on something altogether different. A crown. Ornate gold, covered in jewels. He came forward on his bare knees and offered it to Macbeth, finding a few words the men there could understand.

"Come!" Sueno bade him. "Gold! Take! Yours! Take!"

Fergus was in front of him now, waving a small, sharp dagger, grinning, snarling.

"My master's worth a better crown than some scurvy mongrel foreigner's." He glanced at Macbeth. "Am I right, sir? After the battles we've won today, you could mount the throne of Scotland yourself."

The porter's boot came up and connected with Sueno's groin. The Norseman howled. The crown fell to the dank earth.

"Shut up, Fergus," Macbeth ordered. "And leave him alone. He's an old man and a king. He'll fetch a damned fine ransom, too. Let him get dressed."

Macbeth bent down, retrieved the gold circlet. It felt warm and precious in his hands. Still, he offered it to Sueno.

"Take it," the Viking murmured, terrified. "Do not kill..."

The other two stared at Macbeth, waiting for an answer.

"We'll take what we deserve," he said. "But your crown's your own till Duncan says otherwise."

"Ach, Duncan," the porter muttered. "Where *is* he?"

As he moved, his purse chinked.

"I hear it's been a profitable evening for you, Fergus," said Banquo, scowling.

"I take no more than my share," said the porter. He stabbed a grubby, skinny finger toward the Viking king. "This one doesn't understand a single word you say. You want me to find someone who speaks this heathen tongue?"

"Yes," said Macbeth.

Fergus wandered out, but he cast a long and greedy look at the golden crown before he did so.

"That man of yours," Banquo began, "is a low and vicious cur. But not without his uses." He raised an eyebrow at his friend. "Or are you above such things?"

There came no answer. Macbeth helped up the shaking, naked figure and cast a cloak around his shoulders. They would treat the Norse king half kindly, even with a little respect.

That, thought Macbeth, *wasn't fair, either.* That was politics.

◈ ◈ ◈

King Duncan stood in the thin light of dawn, his cloak drawn tight around his shoulders, considering his options while the priest concluded the Latin prayers with which the court habitually began the day. These rituals bored him—today more than most—but he had long since decided that such things were important. It had been an endless night, talking, bargaining, pacing around each other like dogs thrust into the pit, Duncan with his wary, demoralized thanes, Cawdor smug and amused, with four of Sueno's housecarls standing grimly behind him.

He had courted the thane of Cawdor, encouraged the lord's fawning praise. But he'd never liked the man, he realized. Cawdor had always been too pleased with himself, too opulent of dress, too quick to command every room he entered. Duncan had felt a petty kind of contempt for him, never dreaming that arrogance might turn to treachery. He should have squashed him when he had the chance.

But now there was nothing to be done. Thanks to Sueno and his army, Cawdor had him backed into a dismal corner. The night's deliberations were little more than a show for the Scottish thanes, pretense at a defiance he could not possibly deliver in the field. Cawdor knew all this, which was why he stayed so affable, joking with the lords he had betrayed, toasting them with his cup while they stamped and bellowed like bulls.

Tamed bulls. They all were. Duncan, too.

Lennox, Ross, and MacDuff had begun the night full of high indignation and threats. But even they could see that, with the Vikings behind him, Cawdor held all the cards. The man would soon bore of this posturing and Duncan would hand over the crown and country to be divided as Sueno saw fit. And that last was a crucial detail. No one had threatened Duncan—not yet. They wanted his help, a peaceful abdication. There would be baubles offered: a coastal retreat, perhaps, a few thousand acres of his own with a profitable town under his lease, and a mountain or two of grazing land. As well as a place at Sueno's right hand, of course. The Viking wanted a kingdom, one he could run from across the cold North Sea. And that would be Scotland's future, to be nothing more than a vassal state for foreigners, run by Cawdor, with Duncan playing second fiddle to the thane whose betrayal had brought his monarchy to an end.

This was a moment for diplomacy, not threats, for biding time and stalling his enemy with lengthy negotiations. Duncan had wielded power too long to abandon it easily. He knew this country and its people in ways Sueno did not. He understood what the men, those still loyal to him, now thought of Cawdor, too. A little sly procrastination might extend his options.

And there's always England, he thought.

The pious king in London, Edward, "the Confessor" they called him, had left the Scots alone for most of his reign. Even so, he would not be happy with Sueno and his Vikings squatting on that porous border from Berwick to the Irish Sea. There might be a lever there if he could find a way to lean his weight upon it…

Complaining of tiredness, Duncan had asked that they break for private discussions. Now, with the priest's morning office concluded, he sat silent outside his quarters, watching a bright cerise dawn break over the eastern hills. Some shunned him already, making their dejected way to Cawdor's camp a short way opposite. Duncan could cross that short space and slit Cawdor's throat—or rather send some suicidal fool to do it for him. Though that would satisfy his pride, he knew it would bring Sueno down upon them. This endless and circular talking, however maddening, was at least preferable to that.

If only he had seen Cawdor for what he was sooner. If only there existed a talent to read the heart of a man through his face…A king could surely use that.

Malcolm emerged from his tent, yawning and stretching. Duncan gave him the smallest nod and his son came to stand silently beside him, considering the day.

"Did sleep grant you visions of a way out of this bloody farce?" Duncan muttered, his voice low and wry, his eyes fixed elsewhere.

"Can't say it did," said Malcolm.

"We can't keep talking forever," his father answered. "I'd give my right arm for Macbeth and that madman Banquo. The two of them would listen to this cant for an instant, then tear Cawdor's tongue straight from his head."

"True," said Malcolm. "But they're not here. So give Cawdor what he wants. Be amenable. The thanes, for all their bluster, know your hands are tied. We may live to revenge ourselves for this indignity. For now, concede to their demands. You have no choice. Sueno will not stay long, and when he leaves…"

"Then Cawdor will murder us all at the slightest opportunity," said Duncan, the words like a weight in his mouth. "He'll watch like a hawk and find excuses. Or invent them, anyway. I would."

"I don't doubt it," said Malcolm. "So when he's absent, we make sure he's got good reason. Old alliances might be reforged. Caithness and Angus will stand with us. So will MacDuff, Ross, Lennox, and Menteith."

Duncan turned to his son and asked, " 'With *us*?' "

"With you," Malcolm answered carefully, his eyes steady. "Cawdor may force their hands, but he won't rule their hearts. They still believe in the throne of Scotland. Which is rather what got us into this mess in the first place, isn't it?"

"And you?" said Duncan.

"I am your majesty's most faithful servant," said Malcolm, with the smallest hint of a smile.

"And his son," said Duncan, "which makes you dearest to my heart."

"And your only hope of dynasty," said Malcolm, the amusement still there.

"I did this for you, ingrate!" Duncan roared, whipping the back of his hand across his son's face. Malcolm's head snapped back, his cheeks colored.

He flashed his father a vicious look, then touched his lip where it was cut and bleeding.

"Your violence should be directed at your enemies, Father," he said. "Not me."

Duncan hung his head. He squeezed his eyes shut, then grasped Malcolm's shoulder, ignoring the way he flinched. The men on the far side of the fire had followed every moment.

"Forgive me," he said, embracing his son. "It's been a long night, and so much seems lost."

"Mislaid, for a time only," said Malcolm, wiping his mouth. "It may yet be recoverable. With patience."

Shouts came from the edge of the camp, and the clear drumming of horse hooves.

Duncan looked quickly about as soldiers blundered out of their tents, belting on their swords. His personal guard gathered round him hastily, spears and targets hedging him in. They seemed fewer than the night before. The stillness of the morning was lost in a rush of panic and confusion. *This,* he thought, *is how defeated kings who never take the field will always come to die.*

A lone horseman rode, barreling into the camp. He was a young man, his face vaguely familiar, though smeared with mud and blood.

"I come with news of Macbeth and Banquo!" he shouted.

The tension broke like an overdrawn bowstring, and in its place came dread and weariness. They had all known this was coming, but hearing the details of it, and in earshot of Cawdor with his Viking housecarl escort, was no way to start this difficult day. It would discomfort the men and end all negotiation. With a flash of anger, Duncan wondered if he had missed his opportunity. It was one thing to offer Sueno help before the final defeat was confirmed, quite another to do so afterward. He had been foolish to let the argument go on as long as he did. He saw MacDuff, Ross, and Lennox standing at the edge of the circle, dithering already, and he hated them for the swaggering, pointless defiance with which they had taken up the night.

"They're victorious!" shouted the rider. "MacDonwald is dead, and his force destroyed. Sueno's army was surprised last night and his army routed utterly. The Viking king himself is captive and already offering ransom for a boat back home, with his tail between his legs."

There was a silence in which no man breathed. Then, as the cheering began, the horseman slid down and recounted the victory in such great detail even Duncan came to believe him.

"Thanks be to God," said Duncan, crossing himself piously, but unable to keep the flicker of a smile from his lips.

Cawdor listened, horrified, his arrogant face bloodless and full of fear. In the moments that followed, he regained something of his old composure, though it was bleak and without hope. His housecarls were disarmed and dragged away. The thane stood where he was, unbelting his sword and leaving it where the scabbard fell. His eyes met Duncan's and held them, his lips twisted in a self-deprecating smile.

"I could have killed you and all your kin last night," the man said with a shrug. "I wanted a pact, not slaughter. That's worth something, surely."

Duncan peered at him and said not a word.

"It was about the throne," the thane added. "Not you." His voice began to break. "Monarchs serve their people, and the people choose them. That's how it's always been!"

The king blinked, but no other reaction showed in his face. "Malcolm," he said, his gaze still on Cawdor, aware that silence had fallen again and all eyes were on him. "Take this traitor's chain of office. The crown of Scotland is full of forgiveness for the iniquities of its people. Only that most grievous sin against the crown, against the state, lies beyond its mercy. Take him, my son, and show him justice."

Cawdor's gaze flickered and he opened his mouth as if to speak. But as Malcolm tore the silver chain from his throat, he seemed to change his mind.

"Bind him," Malcolm barked at Lennox, and as they did, he drew his long, narrow dagger and considered his reflection in the blade.

◈ ◈ ◈

"I never liked the men of Perth," the old witch moaned. "They reek of herring, bacon fat, and smoke."

There was lightning over the distant western sea and, not long after, the low, heavy moan of thunder. Merciless sheets of howling icy rain ran across the hillsides. Unmoved by the storm, the women had scattered separately through the heather like wild animals, before meeting at a cairn of rough, dark granite hewn into strange shapes by wind and time. There, they had, by chance, encountered a stranger on the path, a sailor, one of several messengers sent from the king to the troops in the field.

"He brought good news," the young one said. "Be grateful."

"Good, bad," said the hefty witch. "What difference does it make?"

They sat around a lively wood fire, meat turning on spears of gorse over the flames, snatching at the flesh as it cooked. Close by stood the only path through the low deciduous woodlands that ran along the southern bank of Loch Oich toward Aberchalder. No one would pass without their noticing.

"Knowledge may be the difference between success and failure," the coltish girl intoned. "It's more fitting to cast an incantation for that which a man desires than that which he abhors."

She glared at them and wondered, *Why bother? Did they ever understand? Even in the shady, inchoate place that was the beginning?* The years had reduced them to their pots and potions, chants and prayers, the mistaken belief they might achieve anything, if only the right substance or incantation could be found. They were, in their own eyes, little more than kitchen maids tending the bubbling cauldron of fate.

"To take a good man and find the minuscule seed of darkness within him…to turn chastity to lust on a whim…the loyal to traitors...sway the incorrupt to venality...exchange love for hate." She munched on the morsel in her hand and found the burned taste unappealing. "Therein lies true magic. The unmasking of the hidden self below the surface, the skull beneath the skin."

The old one sat in a heap on the ground, stabbing the fire back to life with her crutch from time to time, mumbling a few disjointed words. Morose as ever, the giant gnawed on a fatty morsel, then belched toward the embers.

The girl's naked leg and siren cry had lured the sailor into a dark cave, there to be stuck and poked with burning sticks until he told all. Through Macbeth's valor Duncan was triumphant, primped up with all the vainglory that was the privilege of those who won the battle without risking a single hair of their own heads. Against the odds, Macbeth had snatched victory from the hungry mouth of defeat, taking the Norsemen by surprise as they waited, drugged and drunk, believing no man alive would fight them with so small a band of warriors. Sueno had thought his foe would wait for reinforcements and knew they would never come. So, in his lazy leisure, he had taunted the Scots and fortune herself, believing he could put off till the morrow the slaughter he might so easily have had today.

Macbeth was brave, foolhardy almost, taking the Vikings in their sleep as they dreamt of plunder and women. Just a single Scot had died. The invaders counted their losses in hundreds. Sueno himself and all his surviving generals had been taken prisoner and would be conveyed to the coast for a punitive ransom that would keep the Vikings at bay for a while at least and add more riches to Duncan's rich and private coffers.

Now the king was returning to Forres in the east, victorious. Three enemies vanquished—the rebel forces, the traitor at their head, and the Vikings. And not so much as a bruise on his royal frame.

Rebellion and invasion had consequences, foreseen and unexpected, always. There would be a shuffling of the baronial order, the lazy losing favor, the treacherous their heads. And the king would be stronger, richer, more venal than ever, all the while presenting to the world the face of a white-haired saint on first-name terms with his Almighty.

The sailor had spoken most freely once they had removed his toenails. Duncan's cruel and ambitious nature was, she learned, common knowledge, even among lowly men. Yet still they persisted in the illusion of his sanctity, preferring to believe their monarch a holy paragon rather than recognize his rank corruption and let its stain fall upon themselves.

"Pah!" the big one cried and spat out the gobs of meat she was eating, choking and coughing as she did so. "The crone was right. He does taste of fish and smoke. Pah!" More coughing, more lumps of flesh fell upon the crackling fire. "Men are useless. Tomorrow I'll snare a rabbit, I tell you. Not eat this muck again."

The young one had found the taste vile from the outset and quietly sat there eating cheese and hard rye bread, offering them none. The sailor's right haunch still hung on gorse sticks, roasting and burning over the flames.

The two of them stared at her.

"Take the taste away with this," she said, and cut off two shavings of the sourest, oldest truckle in her bag. "We are creatures of the earth. This is the price of magic. We eat for reasons other than base hunger."

The old witch pushed the mess of gray hair away from her face, reached across the embers, and took the dry, half-rancid cheese, and then the other did the same.

"I know who I am," the crone spat at her. "I kept this from him!"

She reached into her tattered robes and withdrew something small and crooked. "A sailor's thumb is a magical thing," the hag declared. "I had one once before when we trounced that English pilot by Findhorn Bay, on his way to the royal palaces. Stripped him bare and stole his gold…" She threw back her head and laughed at the bright moon. "I went back after we stuck him. I took his thumb and, with it, cast a spell that gave some stuck-up priest a canker of the bowels that ate him inside out." More objects emerged from beneath her grubby shawl. "With this and antic potions and a little blood from my teat, I could blast that crow Duncan dead by morning. Watch me."

"You do nothing unless I order it," the girl said quietly, remembering now that night by the bay near Forres and the way the pilot had pleaded so meekly for his life.

"As for this latest man," the second interrupted, "I stole his lodestone. Since he said it was magic. Fool. What magic there? To point at nothing but the north, to ice and darkness. I can find those anytime. Some use—"

"I took his prick," the girl said, and that shut them up. "More pleasure than business, I thought. Although…"

She reached toward the fire and retrieved the long, thin branch of gorse she'd slipped onto the embers earlier without their noticing. The limp, cold shaft she'd speared with the wood was now blackened and cracked. She blew until the thing was cool enough to touch, then held it beneath her nose, sniffing, the way a man smelled a roll of blood pudding, full of himself, of hunger, too.

They watched and didn't move.

She raised the flesh to her lips, bit hard, took a lump, chewed, and swallowed. Then offered it to the crone.

"My teeth," the old one said, and scowled, exposing fangs as black and crooked as her crutches.

"Are good enough…"

"My *teeth.*"

The thing stayed in the girl's hands. She did not flinch.

"These men we deal with are powerful and determined," she said. "Not a halfwit sailor lost in the night. The hexes and invocations we need I know alone. You follow or I send you back whence both you came."

They shivered at that and the old one shrank into the shadows.

"Do this," the girl commanded, her voice full of anger and authority, "and I will forgive your impudence for now. There is necromancy here beyond your understanding. *Do it.*"

The crone reached forward, took the thing, bit, and choked only a little.

"Give me," said the second and snatched it from her. "I've no need of reasons. The doing's enough."

Well said for once, the girl thought. The doing was everything.

She watched the giant, manlike face munch hard on the piece of meat. Then she took the half-eaten thing from her, retrieved the secret items from her bag, and rolled the flesh in unguents and other substances from her bag. She thought hard, waited for the words to come, not knowing their source, not caring either, or that they were little more than strange nonsense.

The doing…

All this was nonsense, a dumb show for their sad amusement. And perhaps they knew it. Faith and superstition walked hand in hand. Even the priests from Rome had their share of something close to magic. Wine that turned to holy blood. A man who died and then was risen.

Belief was all. She threw the messenger's prick, dressed in its fresh finery, into the fire. There it spat and shrieked as if the sailor's dead voice struggled in the flames, trapped inside the ripped flesh and sinew of his manhood. When the noise died down, she held out her hands. The other two came closer, took them, formed a circle.

"Thrice to thine and thrice to mine and thrice again, to make up nine," the girl sang.

"Thrice!" the sisters echoed.

"Silence," she hissed at them. "Someone comes."

There was a sound then, not far off. The drumming of horse hooves on well-worn grass.

"Macbeth approaches," she said, and was up as quick and as lithe as a cat. "Scatter into the shadows till I call."

"Where are you going?" the old woman asked, anxious as ever at losing her.

The girl cupped her ears forward and grinned with her perfect white smile. "To listen, sister. Great lords are about to bless us with their presence. It's wise we creep and listen, to know what's in their heads."

◆ ◆ ◆

Macbeth was a big man, six foot, broad-shouldered, with a ruddy complexion, a trimmed black beard, and deep-set gray eyes. Banquo was larger still, a lion in the field, yet gentle in style, in words, and in manner, even with the wolf's pelt around his shoulders and the animal's fearsome jaws over his brow. Their friendship ran back into the distant years of childhood, hawking and hunting in the glens, taking salmon from a spinning coracle in the Spey, living off the land for days on end, free in the way that was open to the privileged sons of minor nobles, forever aware that one day they would be called to battle, asked to lay down their lives for whoever was the king.

There'd been moments in the previous few days when Macbeth believed his time had come. Banquo, too, had dodged many arrows, axes, and blades. The impact of the carnage lay upon them, dents in their armor, bloodstains and gore, man and beast, smeared upon their own muddy metal as well as the thick hide bardings and cloth caparisons that had protected their weary mounts in the fight.

But a complete report had to be brought. The king was owed it. So now the two men wound through the mist and rain of the hillsides, following the familiar path of the Great Glen from the head of Loch Linnhe in the west on to the long, dark inland sea of Loch Ness and then out to the coast and the royal palaces of Forres. Both men checked the sky and prayed they might meet a messenger from Duncan along the way, saving themselves a journey through the black night.

Foul times spark grim humor. Banquo, though nursing a deep and painful wound to his sword arm, rode a few yards ahead throughout, keeping up the pace, regaling Macbeth with stories of their boyhood, the perils and the pranks.

"Do you remember the time...?" his great voice boomed through the moonlit night.

"Enough remembering, friend," Macbeth interrupted after the fifth such tale. "We live now, not in an idyllic past. Which was not so idyllic, I seem to recall. Not always."

"Not so idyllic now, either, but men will be talking about it—about *you*—for centuries. To best MacDonwald and slice off his treacherous head...then fall upon that fool Sueno while he was in his bath!"

A king taken naked. That story would run the length of Scotland before the week was out.

The gigantic figure ahead shook with mirth.

"I wish I'd been there to see MacDonwald's end. The stinking traitor."

"I wish you had, too," Macbeth replied, but he was talking to himself. Banquo, who possessed a fine, deep voice, had launched into a bawdy Highland ballad, the kind of filth that soldiers liked when the fighting was done.

"Why do men always sing of love after slaughter?" Macbeth asked when the tune came to an end.

The man in front turned round. He looked puzzled. "Love? *Love?*"

"You know what I mean," said Macbeth.

"I surely do not! We spent today sending men to hell. What's more natural than to pass the night dreaming of procreating a few more to take their place?" He reined in his exhausted nag and slowed to ride by Macbeth's side. "Do you remember that time we took on those Irish pirates at Greenock? What? Five, six years ago? Here's the truth and I've told it to no man before. Duncan himself—our king—came home from that glorious rout and seized his queen straight to bed. After which, no more than an hour later, he took his pleasure with a Spanish concubine he kept on the side. After *which...*"

Banquo leaned into his side and whispered from behind a vast, mailed gauntlet. "Here's a revelation; keep it to yourself. After which, he visited the wife of that fool Wallace and spent midnight till dawn bouncing her from one end of the mattress to the other. Do your sums, friend. Before the year's out, the queen gives birth to twins, that Spanish trollop calves a daughter, and Madam Wallace finds herself blessed with triplets, each one a boy *with red hair.*"

He chuckled.

"You ever seen a Wallace with red hair? No. Me neither. What's good for the king is good for his subjects, I say. My lady knows what's coming. She'll be in her hip bath the moment I get home, dousing herself in perfume I bought from a French molly in Edinburgh not long ago, with this very eventuality in mind. And don't tell me yours won't be doing the same. That day...fifty Irish in the earth and six new Scots in return...We're in credit, that's for sure."

Macbeth remembered only too well. "Duncan left the field too quickly. I lost seven good men in skirmishes that night. While he was home leaping from bed to bed."

The broad, armored figure next to him went quiet for a moment. "He's our lord, Macbeth. It's his right."

"I know. I know..."

"The king is the land. The land is the king."

"Kings are men, and men will die," Macbeth retorted. "Scotland lasts forever. So long as we guard it well. So long as we are strong and rule with a firm, just hand."

"Yes, yes," Banquo replied quickly. "That goes without saying."

"It's not said enough. If we were strong and beloved of our people, how would treason such as MacDonwald's prosper? What foreign marauder dare invade a happy, prosperous land where every man's of a single mind and defends it to the hilt?"

"You're a dreamer, man," Banquo said, laughing. "That's paradise you're talking of and we got kicked out of there a while back. You speak as if this is a good world with a little evil in it. Rubbish. It's a hellish one where the best a man can do is put a little sanity back and look after his own."

Macbeth gazed at his friend and realized that most men he knew would think the same. Which confirmed, he thought, his point.

"This land deserves better stewardship than that," he murmured.

Banquo shook his head and the wolf's jaws nodded with him. "Well, it won't get it. A nation's not a child, for God's sake. You raise it well enough only to find there's a saint sitting by the hearth. It's like a wild horse you tame by breaking it. Or a fiery woman you slap till she sees sense and warms your bed."

"Your son might make a saint," Macbeth observed. "Fleance is a fine young man."

"Fat use we'd have had for saints today. Give me a potion that'll make that boy a warrior…I'd pay plenty for such magic, that I would."

He is a decent, loyal son, Macbeth thought wistfully. *Quiet and thoughtful—dreamy, even. Not like his father at all.*

Banquo sang another line of the bawdy ballad, then paused.

"If by chance we should be delayed," he whispered, "there's a widow I know who lives by Loch Knockie, as pretty as a picture, always willing to put up a gentleman for the night if he's kind. I hear it's good sport to go a-knocking in Knockie." A hard elbow nudged Macbeth's side. "Perhaps she's got a sister, eh? No. I'm sure of it. She does. It's a long ride home with nothing but me for company. I bore myself sometimes. Not often. Just now and again."

Macbeth laughed and closed his eyes, exhausted. "You're an evil rogue, Banquo. I wonder we were ever friends. Here we ride, doused in the blood of men, and all you can talk about is fornication."

"All? *All?* Priorities, man. If it weren't for fornication, there'd be nothing in the world but death. If sheep can do it so can I..."

Macbeth fell quiet. It was six years now since his own wife gave birth to a boy, the only child they'd ever had, the only one they ever would, a sickly babe who barely opened his eyes in his short life spent mainly suckling at his mother's breast. All of Duncan's court knew of this tragedy. None spoke of it, not in Macbeth's hearing, nor did he address the subject much, even with his wife. What was there to say? Bleak fate had spoken. After the bloody, prolonged birth, Skena's womb was judged torn and fruitless. There would be no line, no comfort in old age through watching a son or daughter grow from fond childhood to a knowing maturity. Like every thane, he was but a tenant of the king. So when he died, the name *Macbeth* perished with him, and his estate would fall to the monarch as was the crown's right. This seemed a cruel turn of fortune, undeserved. What made it worse was that he knew, through brief murmurs, glances, and quiet asides, that his wife felt the loss daily, more than he ever could.

A picture of her waiting in that dismal black fortress in Inverness rose in his head and refused to leave. He stared into the dusk where the broad, dark line of Loch Ness wound snakelike ahead, lit by the silver sky. The knowledge that it led straight home stirred a pang of longing in Macbeth's breast.

"Visit your mistress in Knockie, if you wish. The only sheets I'll ever long for are my own."

Banquo guffawed. "Come, come, friend. The Spanish have potions to cure that malady...What? Ho? Who's there?"

From the west there came a distant rumble of thunder. Macbeth pulled his cloak tighter about him.

Something moved in the bushes, flitting through the undergrowth. Voices. Female ones, one gruff and coarse, another musical. And laughter.

"Get out where I can see you," Banquo ordered. "We're tired and bloody soldiers and have no time for games."

The two men stayed immobile on their steeds. The rustling increased. Heavy black clouds drifted across the moon. When the silver light returned, three shapes stood before them, became clear in the bright evening, standing on the path ahead, blocking their way.

A bent and wizened old woman dressed in rags, leaning on a stick, stood closest to Banquo, head upturned, cocked sideways. Next to her was a figure in little more than a hessian sack running down to her ankles, tall and muscular, though it was her bare head that caught Macbeth's attention it was so large, the skull shining, half bald, half cloaked in long, black, matted hair, a zigzag scar across her temple, not quite man, not quite woman.

By the bridle of his own steed stood the youngest, a slender, lithe, and beaming creature in a full and half-fetching black cloak, which she held round herself with bare, skinny arms. Her face was both beautiful and shocking, the eyes so large and wide they seemed inhuman, the mouth a broad slashed gape showing even white teeth.

"All hail Macbeth!" cried the old hag in a cracked, hoarse voice. "Hail to thee, thane of Glamis."

The second took a step forward and curtseyed in front of his horse. "All hail Macbeth," she said. "Hail to thee, thane of Cawdor!"

He wanted to laugh but somehow couldn't.

The third stayed silent, staring at her fingertips, picking at a stray piece of skin there and nibbling it with her queer teeth.

"Do you have no nonsense for me, girl? Or are you dumb?"

She glowered, not at him, but at Banquo.

"Hail to you, sir. A lesser creature than your companion," the girl said in a sullen voice that came from elsewhere, the lowlands—England, even.

"What is this gibberish?" Banquo demanded. "Will you read our palms next, then ask for silver or else we're cursed?"

The young one came to stand in front of his mount. "Your palms are fixed, lord. And we own sufficient silver to last your lifetimes twice over. Whatever curses you carry come from yourselves, not us. You are both the lesser and the greater. Do you not wish to know why?"

The two men glanced at each other.

"We have better business than riddles," Macbeth said, and shook his reins. "Good evening, ladies. May I hope you escape the coming storm."

"We *are* the coming storm, you fool," the large one murmured in a gruff, deep voice.

"Banquo…"

The girl was whirling, changing in front of them. The black cloak flew through the air, became a midnight mist, and then was gone. The two men sat transfixed on their steeds. The child stood naked in front of them, a writhing, swirling figure, her front covered by a dark-blue tattoo that ran from her groin to her neck, three salmon interlinked, nipples and navel for eyes, fins and scaly flesh seemingly alive as she twisted and contorted lasciviously in front of them.

Then she stopped, placed a hand on her skinny hip, looked at him with a coquettish, come-on grin.

"What do you crave most, Macbeth?" the girl asked, grinding her narrow hips with a coarse and carnal rhythm. "A fuck or a future?" She stopped, as if considering the answer, then said, "I can assist you, lord, with both or either. The choice is yours."

"I fear you flatter yourself for the first," he said.

"What a fortunate woman is that lady of yours," she declared. "To share the bed of such a noble figure. You possess a majestic visage, sir. Too splendid for a thane. More fit for a baron or a pope. A countenance that is positively…" She hesitated, put a hand to her mouth as if struggling to find the word. "Majestic…That's the word."

"Thanes are ten a penny," the big one cut in. "Nothing more than peasants who know where to shit."

"If I were a lady in a fortress, I might covet that head of yours for myself," the girl went on. "Such a majestic face might cast the whole world in shadow." She grinned. "Had it the ambition to meet the opportunity, of course."

"Do you have something to tell me?" Macbeth asked, exasperated.

"And where's the magic word, sire?"

"I am tired. I beg you, child—"

"He begs, he begs," she cried, falling to her knees; the others, wailing, did the same. *"This one last time before his too-hesitant elevation Macbeth begs…"*

Banquo sighed, cast him an irritated glance, and said, "We've better things to occupy our time than these loons. My lady of Loch Knockie…"

"True," he agreed and lifted his reins to leave.

Her voice broke the night, so clear and loud and certain he could feel its force through the armor. "All hail Macbeth, thou shalt be king hereafter!" the naked thing shouted at him, grinning from the earth.

Macbeth became cold and still, remembering MacDonwald's words on the tower: *"Your duty's to Scotland and to yourself. Not to Duncan. When he's gone, by rights, any of us might wear that crown, if his peers so wish it. Even you."*

"All hail Banquo, lesser than Macbeth and greater," cried the crone.

"All hail Banquo, not so happy, yet much happier," said the giant.

The big man on the horse was silent at that, watching the third, who leered at him, her hands behind her skinny body, that tattooed bony chest sticking out like a dockside harlot seeking custom.

"Well?" he demanded.

"Oh, Banquo, Banquo," she in a lilting, laughing tone. "Tragic in the present, yet glorious in the future. You shall beget kings, though never reign yourself. So all hail lords. Both of you. Masters of this modest world. After a fashion. For a little while."

A sudden crash of lightning broke from beyond the nearest crag, its jagged fork of unearthly light stabbing down from the heavens to the earth. The white fire wrapped itself around a tree behind them, splitting the trunk in two, sending burning shards and embers down to the ground, sparking all around them. The horses cried and whinnied, the two riders fighting to still their terror.

The three women were on their feet. The crone and the giant shook with mirth at their fear.

The youngest glared at them. They turned quiet in an instant and, at her bidding, made to go.

"Wait," Macbeth ordered. "You will not say such things, then flee our presence. How can this be? I am thane of Glamis, by the king's kindness. But Cawdor...Cawdor lives, a good and prosperous lord with a fine estate, if"—his voice fell, remembering the gap in the ranks that day and MacDonwald's dark hints—"tardy to the battle. To wear the crown is so far from anything I could imagine. *Tell me.*"

He watched, unable to believe his eyes. It had to be the night, the strange light of the livid moon. They were vanishing before him, fading and flittering through the air like will-o'-the-wisps and jack-o'-lanterns that flickered over lowland marshes, dead souls, the credulous country people said, as elusive as the creatures of dreams.

"Tell me, child!"

Another fork of bright white light cracked above the hills. The searing light it brought seemed to swamp them, its fire so bright both men were forced to shield their eyes. When their vision returned, they found themselves alone, listening to nothing but the panting of their terrified mounts, struggling to control the beasts.

It was Banquo who broke the silence with one word. "Lunatics," he said. His voice shook a little and seemed to lack conviction.

"You think?"

"Yes! Lunatics! What else might they be?"

"Samhain was three nights ago," Macbeth said, remembering the ceremonies by the cairns. "The old priests say sometimes on that night the earth may cough up spirits from a place beyond our knowledge. That they may see—"

"Spirits? *Spirits?*" Banquo cried, leaping the burning tree with his horse, sweeping his blade through the gorse and rowan groves around him, finding nothing. "You saw them. You smelled them. Just as I. Foul hags, man. Nothing more."

He spat out a vile curse and made one last futile sweep with his sword, finding nothing but branches and leaves.

"They said—" Macbeth began.

"These gypsy bitches wander the glens and pounce on the innocent, feeding them mad ideas to turn their heads. Then run away and cackle at the consequences, waiting for the seed they plant to grow and bloom and belch its poison into the air. Let's hold onto what we can see and touch and comprehend, not the devilish tales these weird sisters offer."

Banquo was unsettled by what he'd heard, Macbeth thought. Just as much as he. Yet feared to show it.

"Your children shall be kings, Banquo! You heard them. Do you find this of no consequence at all?"

"You shall be king yourself. They said that, too. Does that interest *you?*"

"The throne lies in the hands of greater men than me," Macbeth replied. "But if they chose…I'd take it and be as good a monarch as Heaven allowed. Not fear any man or shirk a fight…"

Like Duncan, he so nearly said.

Banquo's eyes burned with something. Fury? Dismay?

The warrior muttered a curse and said, "Oh God, Macbeth. Were the throne open tomorrow, you'd have my hand and fist propelling you toward it before all others. But it's not."

There was a side to his voice Macbeth did not recognize. They never spoke of property, of betterment, of what gains might come to them in the future. Only service to the crown and the Council of Thanes. At home, in the dark chambers of Inverness, brooding with his wife, things were different with Macbeth. Inverness was a low prize. She thought he deserved better. He knew she merited a finer, richer life. But even these low, formless dreams were discreet fantasies, shared with no one. Was it possible they were visible on a man's face, clear as day to all but the bearer himself? Had the weird sisters seen this somehow?

Had Banquo?

That last thought unnerved him. He stilled the steed and looked the man next to him square in the eye. "The blood of these last few days has turned my head. I'm sorry, friend. To think I might gain a rich domain like Cawdor is so far beyond my ambitions. A crown…?" He laughed. "Ridiculous. I'm grateful for your hand, but it would be a solitary effort. There are other greater lords who stand in line before me."

"There's Malcolm, too," Banquo muttered grimly.

Macbeth wondered if he'd heard his friend correctly. Malcolm? The king's son was young and fey and lascivious. No council would choose him.

"Why do you say that?" he asked.

"It does you credit you avoid the drunken banter of your peers," said Banquo. "I wish I'd done the same. There's gossip that Duncan wishes to change the throne. To make the crown hereditary, as it is England. Which would, they say, give us a sacred king, chosen by a single lord." He nodded at the sky. "The one above, though how divinity squares with the issue of Duncan's fecund loins is, I must confess, beyond my simple brain. Still, there's your path to glory for Malcolm."

The words chilled Macbeth's blood. MacDonwald's cryptic warning finally made some sense. This was the source of the rebellion. Such a change would alter the nature of power in Scotland—the country itself—irrevocably and remove all chance of the ultimate ambition from every thane in the land.

"Is this true?" Macbeth asked when he'd found his voice.

"They say MacDonwald intercepted letters. Whether it's true…How would I know? We've been fighting for the best part of a month. The nation's been divided by sedition. Even if Duncan wanted such a thing, could he force it through the council?"

At just such a time as this, he might, Macbeth thought. *When the thanes were exhausted and weakened from fighting and he remained strong from doing nothing more than watching them bleed.*

Banquo puffed himself up in the saddle and said, "Let's bury this nonsense forever. We're what we are and all we are. And damned fine at that, too."

Macbeth smiled and said, "Aye. The only crown this world will offer me came from a naked Viking fresh out of the tub. Some prize that was!"

Banquo laughed, that deep, guttural sound that Macbeth felt he'd known and loved since birth. The brief mad moment of discord between them was over. Or perhaps they had both agreed in silence to keep it hidden from their faces.

"A man gets foolish in the night," Macbeth added. "Those mischievous bitches saw their chance. My hand..."

Two gauntlets met briefly between their mounts, metal and mail in friendship.

Then Banquo cried abruptly, "Holla! Who's there?" His hand flew to his sword, his eyes fixed on a point up the path.

Two men were approaching on horseback, their forms and faces shadows in the gloom.

No more fights, Macbeth thought, bracing himself. *No more bloodshed.* He wanted to be home, in his wife's sweet arms, to hold her, to comfort her.

"Who comes, I say!" Banquo roared, drawing his sword. "Name yourself!"

Two voices cried in return.

"It's Angus!"

"And Ross!"

Banquo's joyous roar broke the reverie, and Macbeth was aware for a moment that, had this been an enemy, his fight would have been absent, his body soon a corpse on the damp peat where the strange naked child, with her writhing tattoos, had taunted him only moments before.

"Rogues," Banquo boomed at them. "Buffoons. Identify yourself in the dark, or I'll spear you through the bowels next time. These are dangerous times, you fools. Don't make me blunt my blade on friends."

They were two good men, loyal and loving to Duncan always. No minds of their own in all truth. The kind the king liked to keep around him among his priests and servants.

"Oh, sirs," Ross declared in his fluting lowland voice as they came close. "Your fame shines so brightly we assumed you saw us miles off reflected in its brilliance."

"On a night like this? Flatterer," Banquo said, and slapped him so hard on the shoulder the man nearly fell off his horse.

"No," Ross replied. "It's true. Tell him, Angus."

"Every word. The king knows everything and sent scores of heralds out to track you in the night. It's our good fortune to be the first. To congratulate you on his behalf for your courage against the rebels and the Norsemen. Your cunning with the poison. How you fought for him without a thought for your own skins."

"For Scotland, too," Macbeth added.

"The same thing," Banquo said.

"Every report speaks of your valor, lords. The king's gratitude is boundless. The nation is in peace again, no small thanks to you."

"Tell Duncan we did our duty," Banquo said. He eyed Macbeth. "Home, then. To a warm, soft bed. I'll find my own way."

Angus and Ross smiled at each other as if sharing a secret.

"There is one more matter," Ross said. "Macbeth, the king decrees you are no longer thane of Glamis."

There was thunder again, more distant this time, all the more strange since no lights in the sky preceded it.

"Meaning?" he asked, and found his right hand had fallen naturally to the weapon at his waist. "I've fought hard for his majesty. There's no more loyal subject in the land..."

"Do not be so suspicious, sir!" Ross cried, laughing. "We joked. Nothing more. When you next meet—which he demands will be tomorrow evening in Inverness—he shall address you as thane of Cawdor, too. With Glamis. Two shires of the crown you tenant now..."

Banquo turned to stare at him, his face more deathly stiff and pale than ever it was upon the field.

"Cawdor? *Cawdor?*" Macbeth asked. "Why do you dress me in borrowed clothes? Cawdor lives, a man I'd like to ask some questions, true..."

"Cawdor lies in bloody pieces feeding salmon in the loch," Angus said brightly. "He was with Sueno and MacDonwald all along and thought he might usurp our rightful king through such treachery. Prince Malcolm has"—he scratched his beard and broke into a wry smile—"dealt with him in ways that might appear unseemly in other circumstances. That young fellow surprises us all at times."

Angus watched Macbeth carefully.

"Scotland rises like the phoenix from the ashes of duplicity and the covetous attentions of the Norsemen," he said. "The king marks his gratitude for your part in this, Macbeth. Cawdor's yours. A property of no small value. It strikes me you do not seem grateful."

"No, no...This was a long, hard day, friends, and there's too much news for my weak mind to comprehend. Bear with me." Macbeth leaned across to Banquo and whispered, "We must speak. Alone."

"Stay clear of this," grunted the man by his side.

Macbeth stilled a sudden fury inside and forced a smile at the bringers of this strange news. "Give us a moment, please," he said.

Ross shrugged, though his smile was uncertain, and Angus gave him a look. Ignoring them, Macbeth reached over, dragged Banquo's vast frame so close to his he could smell the staleness of his clothes, then guided their horses several uneasy paces down the path.

"They called Cawdor right and could know nothing of it," he whispered, feeling the coarse, dark beard rub against his cheeks. "They said you would beget a line of kings."

Banquo pulled back and caught his eye. "And that you would one day wear the crown. Yet we have a king, a strong and healthy one. Who succeeds him only the council shall decide. This is madness, Macbeth. I should have cut off those viper heads the moment we first saw them."

"Banquo—"

"Home!" the big man bellowed, breaking from him and turning his horse.

Hearing the din, Angus and Ross shouted back, rattling their swords against their armor, a soldier's cheer.

"I've a warm wife in a warm bed," said Banquo. "Enough of these black and bloody glens for one day. Farewell, friends." Then, in a lower voice, "Farewell, thane of Glamis and Cawdor. A worthy reward for your boldness and your loyalty."

That familiar, vast gauntlet stretched out again. Macbeth snatched Banquo to him and whispered, half choking, "You are my truest friend, my conscience, my compass in the tempest."

"Bah!" One final hard slap on the shoulder. "And you're the sentimental fool you always were. Go home and make yourself a son."

That last remark, both an unintended foray into his private torments and a reminder they were common knowledge, pained him, though he fought hard to hide it.

"Well," said Banquo quietly, seeing his unintended gaffe for what it was. "That's it, then."

He turned his horse around and retreated into the hills. To his castle in the north, Macbeth guessed, not his pliant mistress in Loch Knockie.

Angus and Ross waited for his orders.

"Tell the king my lady and I are honored by his kindness," he said, riding back as he watched the towering figure of Banquo disappear into the darkness. "I will see my wife tonight and make arrangements..."

"Do that tomorrow, Macbeth," Angus said. "The king wishes you first to sit in judgment on Cawdor's household, those men who came with him on this treacherous adventure. They're captive back near Inverlochy, freezing in the snows that now fall down from Nevis. These are your men now, so you must judge their fates. After that, return to Inverness."

His heart sank. The order meant long hours retracing the winding track they had just taken. He wanted to shout, to refuse and ride quickly home, but knew this was impossible.

"And will you join me?" Macbeth asked them.

They looked a little guilty. "We are to go to Inverness. On personal matters."

"Then wait a while, sirs. I would write my wife a letter and have you carry it to her."

Angus nodded.

"A personal note," Macbeth added. "Fond tidings and the king's kind news, nothing more."

"Sweet words never go amiss," Ross replied. "Write them, sir. We promise we won't peek."

◈ ◈ ◈

A few low cottages and a ragtag line of shacks and taverns and brothels for sailors apart, the castle was all there was to Inverness. It stood on a low, rocky bluff overlooking the winding dark line of the River Ness, now full with the floodwaters of the recent tempests, banks bursting to bring the water's chill presence into the paupers' hovels built by the shore. Skena Macbeth was a lowlander, born far away in Glamis in the southern valley of Strathmore, a warm and fertile sweep of land caught between the Sidlaw Hills and the Grampians, half a day's ride from the coast at Dundee. The castle there was modest, set on a low hill amid green fields, English in style—foursquare pale stone with towers at each corner of the tall curtain wall, one main keep that was living quarters for the thane. But Duncan was king, and they his subjects. He liked to keep his men close and so instructed Macbeth to spend his time mostly in the north, at Inverness, thirty miles inland from the royal palaces at Forres, where the monarch lived for most of the year in luxuriant splendor. Her husband was a native Highlander, a creature of the Great Glen. But he loved green Glamis almost as much as she did and felt her frequent pangs for that gentle, rich land, most of all during the desolate months of winter.

The property Duncan had forced upon them could scarcely be more different from the castle that came with Macbeth's title. It was a vast, brooding monster, a relic of years of constant civil war, with ten times more arrow slits than windows and twice the dungeons it had bedrooms. Warrens of dark and secret passages ran behind its grim, black walls, cold and damp and sinister places that allowed the incumbent thane to hide from assassination and his enemies to whisper and plot behind his back. From the ramparts, she could see the swollen mass of water that led to the Moray Firth and the cold North Sea beyond, an open invitation to avaricious foreigners like the Vikings, and one they'd seize at random, bent on rape and plunder and the capture of oar slaves for their longboats. Within, she felt a stranger, unwanted, a foreigner almost to a household that had served numerous thanes before this one, and hoped to outlive many more in the years to come.

Inverness was a citadel built on fear, not power or glory. A fortress that served to stave off death and despair and took on the traits of both for its pains. In Glamis, the lost babe had moved safe within her belly, a joyous discomfort, until, two months before he was due, Duncan had ordered them here. Not long after, she felt the small body grow sluggish inside her and came to dread the day of delivery. What followed was seared upon her memory: two desperate weeks in which she fought to feed the sickly child, pleading through her tears for it to suck the leaking milk from her breasts, reduced to desperate wails when finally the nurse took the tiny, frigid corpse away.

They said she'd held it to her, dead and cold, for a night and a day before relinquishing her grip, that she was, briefly, insane and lost to the world. Composure soon returned—and with it, a new vision of the harshness of this heartless northern world. She now detested every last gloomy bastion of this hideous fortress, amazed by how boundless her loathing of each stone of its dank, clammy walls had grown.

It was midnight when the messengers, Angus and Ross, arrived, looking smug and expectant of a warmer welcome later, doubtless in one of the whorehouses down by the port. Sleep had been impossible. She listened to their brief report and news of her husband's coming return, then took the letter from them. It still bore Macbeth's unbroken seal, and when she glanced at the first few lines, she was grateful.

"Gentlemen," she greeted them, placing the document in the pocket of her long black gown. "The kitchen will make you food and drink, if you require it."

She was a fetching woman and was not above using that. Skena had greeted them in the hall, fresh from bed. Her long hair hung loose around her bare shoulders, straight and lustrous, the color of barley the moment before harvest. Her round, bright eyes were the pale blue of the rare cerulean topaz they mined in Lochaber, as clear and all-seeing as a summer sky. Like most of her station, she felt no embarrassment about dress before servants and still had on the flimsy French-styled gown she'd worn beneath the sheets.

"Your husband survives, lady, on a day hundreds have perished," the one called Angus said with a sly, appreciative smile. "Was there a messenger here before us? You seem so unsurprised."

The question took her aback. "I have no need of runners to tell me my lord lives. Macbeth is as much a part of my body as my heart itself, sir. Do you think I wouldn't feel the moment he ceased breathing? Or doubt that he possesses the same faculty for me?"

"Keep quiet on those talents," the other one advised. "There are bishops around who'd call that sorcery."

"What?" she demanded. "Love? I feel sorry for a man of the church who regards such close and dear affection as witchcraft. The bond between husband and wife is given to them by God, or so these selfsame priests would claim. Who is mortal man to question it? Particularly such chaste churchmen as we have these celibate days."

The two of them chuckled at that, then, after turning down her offer to raise the kitchen staff, made their way out.

The night was vile, with squally showers of sleety snow making their way from the ocean, gathering force in the firth, then battering the walls of the castle like sword blows rained down upon a granite shield.

She clutched the letter to her, found the warmest coat she possessed, and rushed to the one place she felt secure from the prying, duplicitous eyes of the servants.

◈ ◈ ◈

The keep that enclosed the thane's household quarters stood on the land side of the squat black square of the fortress. At its summit, behind crenellated battlements a century or more old, she found some respite from the storms that raged within and without her febrile mind. Macbeth knew she loved this small place of escape and had ordered a cabin built on the summit, for shade in the summer and shelter in the freezing winter. On a clear day she could look west across the expanse of Beauly Firth to the rising foothills of the western Highlands, then south beyond Dochgarroch, where the waters of the river Ness broadened to become the long ribbon of loch that superstitious locals said was home to fiends and monsters. Somewhere along this stretch of lake Macbeth now surely rode, anxious through the dreadful night.

His letter was scribbled in a ragged, feverish hand, and not through hurry, either. In another man she'd have thought it madness.

> *Three strange creatures met me not long after the victory. Witches—one a crone, one a monster, one, the worst, a child. This sounds like madness. Perhaps it is. Yet thinking of it as I write I feel I saw a veil lifted upon myself, upon those joint ambitions we whisper about from time to time but dare not speak aloud. From what I saw in those few strange*

minutes I know there's more than mortal knowledge here. These fiends offered a certainty, some guarantee of a future we merit should we rise to it. Yet when I challenged them, wishing to know more, they vanished into the air. I stood there amazed, arguing with Banquo, who wished away this meeting as if it were nothing, though it had news for him, too. And then came Angus and Ross who hailed me as "thane of Cawdor," just as the weird sisters had saluted me not minutes earlier.

She looked up into the night, feeling her heart quicken. *Three weird sisters?*

No. It couldn't be. Yet his description left little doubt. The crone, the monster, and the child…

She began to read again, hungrily now.

How this is possible, I cannot guess. In truth, the more I try to understand it, the greater does my ignorance seem. How is *this possible? Know only that you are now the lady of both Glamis and Cawdor, and if these spirits speak the truth, queen of Scotland to be. By what means…No. This letter is peril in itself and you shall burn the parchment and scatter the ashes once its contents lie safe within your head. Know this also: however great your future, by whatever title you shall be known, there is one above all that is dearest and most precious to me in that it came willingly, freely given that day we married in the kirk at Glamis. Lady, dame, or queen, you are my beloved wife, my finer, braver half, and that is why I tell you these things. These* promises…*For that is what they are, gifts held out to us, prizes daring us to take them and unmask the hidden nature within ourselves. Somehow… Enough until we meet. Bury our secrets in your heart and now farewell.*

Skena sat and shivered in the cabin on the battlements, listening to the wind and the distant thunder capering beyond the snow squalls in the hills.

"Oh, Macbeth," she murmured into the dark. "From Glamis to Cawdor in a single day, and a fine king you'd make, too. If only..."

A sudden sharp moment of self-knowledge stabbed at her. Love was honest, open, frank, or else it was not love at all but merely blind infatuation. She knew this man, for better, for worse. The milk of human kindness ran too much through his good and valiant veins. His nature might lead him to crave the prize he deserved. But that same duty and deference would bid him to avoid its seizure through any quick and necessary means. Greatness beckoned, but the humanity he was born with would hold him back, a lost figure in the shadows, too modest to meet its demands.

The Scottish crown never changed hands without bloodshed. Not in her lifetime. And the innocent and worthy were as likely to perish in the maelstrom as the guilty and the wicked.

A southern phrase from childhood entered her head: "You cannot have your cake and eat it too." What must be done must *be* done, whatever the price, the cost, the pain. One day we all must walk through fire. Or he—they—would face the consequences of Duncan's wrath, for Macbeth was so guileless that one thought of disloyalty within him would soon make its presence known upon his cheeks.

She thought of white-haired Duncan, a wily villain posing as a saint. Thought of their own exile in this bleak fortress prison at the king's behest, the lost child dead and gray in the nurse's arms, nothing warm about him except that last trickle of her milk running from his still, dry mouth.

"If I could pour my spirit into your ear, husband, there'd be no hesitation, not for a moment. You'd wake up king tomorrow, and Scotland ours to love and foster. The crown, the crown..."

There was a noise from the stairs. She braced herself. When witches walked the earth and saw inside men's minds, there was no sanctuary for treachery, not even on a wild night high on the ramparts of Inverness.

It was the youngest servant, a boy of eight.

"One more messenger," he said, and yawned. "He woke me, mistress, though I'm glad."

"Why's that, Ewan?"

Child of the yew. The same name they'd given the sickly babe she'd tried to suckle behind these black walls.

"I had a dreadful nightmare. There was this strange girl, all bare and..."

Skena put a hand to his slender shoulder.

"Don't bore others with your nightmares, child. In times like these we've enough of our own to wrestle with. The messenger..."

He brightened.

"The king is coming from Forres tomorrow—in the afternoon, with his court and all the noble families he can rustle up. We're to prepare food and make sure his tasters get a sample before he touches it." He hitched up his britches. "Can I be a taster? Cook says she can get goose in from the firth. And salmon and lampreys and ptarmigan with fine spices."

"I'll see you get a plate," she said. "Now go back to bed, Ewan. Tell all the servants to do the same. Leave me here on the tower for a while. I like the wild night. It thrills me."

"Don't you get lonely?"

An open, inquisitive child, cheeky at times. Had their own boy survived, he may have one day been like this.

"Macbeth is with me."

He looked around, baffled.

"Here," she said, and held a hand to her breast. "Go, Ewan. You heard me."

She watched him leave, mind racing, full of possibilities.

The parchment burned in her pocket. She stood up and went to the western wall, by the crenellation, and stared down at the vast emptiness below, her tall, strong body buffeted by the gale. There she tore Macbeth's letter into shreds and threw them into the mouth of the gale, watching the pieces scatter in the moonlight, out toward the water. That was an element, too, like fire and earth. Their secret would be kept.

Three weird sisters. No strangers, Skena thought, *to me.*

Across the river, clear in the moonlight, ran the winding stone path to the lonely wind-blasted moor of Culloden and the strange circle of cairns at Clava—three mound circles of carefully placed rocks surrounded by standing stones that grew from the earth like gigantic frozen thorns. The locals avoided them mostly as a place of sorcery and bewitchment. Except for one evening each year, the ancient feast called Samhain, when fear more than anything drew them back to pay a form of timorous homage.

She had visited this bare, uncanny place repeatedly in the past during the day and, while she felt and recognized its power, had never found herself afraid. This year had been different.

Samhain was three days ago. With Macbeth absent, she had taken her horse there, following at a distance the gathering of peasants who'd come, from coast and hills, to walk behind the gray-bearded followers of the old rites, singing strange melodies every step of the way.

Samhain.

Most Scots stood beneath the Roman cross these days, even if an older pagan spirit still lurked inside their hearts. The priests of the pope called the same feast All Hallows, but whatever the god, the meaning was the same. This was a night when dying summer took its final breath and bade the world farewell, giving way to darkness, the cold, hard winter, a black time with little promise of renewal. The new religion spoke of resurrection and the eventual dawn of spring—for some, at least. The old faith was brutal, more real. It talked of a moment when the milky cataract that kept apart the living and the dead became briefly clear and fragile. In such an instant, the dead and other terrible things might slip through into the waking world, malevolent spirits intent on mischief and worse.

Fairy tales to send children to their fearful beds, she thought.

But at Clava, on that strange evening, curious to watch the locals at their rites, the idea did not seem so preposterous. Skena watched as the elders shook their staffs of ash and mistletoe and recited a series of sonorous prayers and incantations in what she took to be the ancient language of the Picts. She lingered a little after the rest left. They said these places were the burial mounds of a lost race so distant none could remember its name or begin to imagine what its people looked like, how they lived, what beliefs they followed. Next to the windswept heath of Culloden it felt an eerie, unworldly spot. Macbeth was away in the west, in battle, risking his life for the loathsome Duncan yet again. These strange obelisks suited her mood.

She left the horse tethered by the path and went to sit alone on a boulder beneath a yew tree close by the northernmost circle. After a few moments, she become aware of a sound from beyond a gathering of standing stones, toward the woods. There was a flickering light and voices, low and old, singing. She walked to see and found herself facing a squat wall of uniform rocks with a single entrance, a door to nothing. In the center of the circle stood two stiff figures by a blazing fire, one huge, like a farmhand, the other crooked and bent, leaning on crutches. The words of their chants were as impenetrable as those of the pagan priests, though different somehow. Then the peculiar melody came to a climax and they drew back, with cries of wonder and fear, and she saw another.

This third apparition was so strange that Skena wondered whether she'd fallen into a waking nightmare. Little more than a skinny girl, she pranced about the fire naked as a bairn, moved by the spinning, manic energy of an acrobat, twisting and turning around the first two as if she owned them.

Skena Macbeth took a step forward to see more clearly. A branch broke beneath her feet. The noise stopped them immediately. Before she knew it the bent crone had turned and half crawled, half leapt across the circle, propelling herself on those black sticks. The big one was by her side, too, so swiftly it seemed impossible.

"What's this? What's this?" the tall figure cried. "A spy in the night. They hang spies hereabouts."

"Pretty spy," said the crone, grabbing at her cloak.

They stank of smoke and dirt. She pulled back from them, blue eyes flaring, furious, not afraid for a moment.

"I am Lady Macbeth, wife of the thane of Glamis," she told them. "If there's any hanging to be done in these parts, it'll be at my behest, not that of some pack of beggars."

"Beggars? *Beggars?*"

It was the young one now, with a bright-burning brand from the fire in her right hand, dancing in front of her as the others shrank back. Skena felt the air freeze in her lungs. So thin her ribs stuck out, dark eyes like gleaming coals, no pupils and fathomless, the girl stood tall and full of sinister confidence. A twisting ornate tattoo in flowing Celtic lines the blue color of the moonlit sky ran across her front, from groin to chin, three salmon interlinked. The thing seemed to be alive, to move both across and beneath the pale skin into which it was etched.

"Kill her," the crooked hag spat.

"Kill her!" said the thuggish one. "Let me carve the bitch…"

The girl turned on them and they were silent in a moment without a single word of admonition.

Then she looked back at Skena, with a face that seemed both old and young, and asked, "Why call us beggars, lady? You're the intruder here. We demanded nothing. Besides… Before this week is out I expect Lord Macbeth will be begging from me."

She could only laugh. "And why would the thane of Glamis do that?"

"To help him find at home what he discovers so easily on the battlefield."

The sight of this strange, wraithlike creature made her flesh crawl, yet Skena felt unable to leave.

"Which is?"

"His spine, lady. Why ask me when you know the answer?"

She thought of calling for the servants who'd followed her at a distance, dragging these three to the castle, having them whipped and thrown into the deep dungeons. Yet they had committed no crime except insolence. And somehow this strange child seemed to know of matters, of private, secret difficulties and doubts…

"You presume too much…"

"Do you fear to tell him?" the girl cut in, holding the burning torch closer.

"Tell him what?" Skena demanded.

"That Duncan plans to steal the throne for himself and all his line. That your faint, yet feverish ambitions that way—his and yours—will become as fanciful as the daydreams of sad wee bairns. And all will be denied you, save the black prison that is Inverness."

"This is fresh rumor! It started after he'd left. Besides, my man's above tittle-tattle."

"More fool him, then. This is fact and soon you'll know it. Macbeth's been fighting. He has no idea. And still you'll hesitate to tell him, won't you? Why? Because you're a woman? Is your destiny such a small thing, then? To keep your legs open and your mouth shut?"

"You will not speak to me thus!" Skena retorted and drew back her hand.

Something stopped the blow and it took a moment to realize what it was. The absence in the girl—complete, unquestioned—of fear.

"Poor lady," the child said in a soft, strange, lilting voice. "Trapped behind your thick dark walls, mourning the only bairn you'll ever have…"

She shivered, watching the skinny figure so still and certain in front of her.

"How can you know…?" she whispered.

"There are no secrets." The thing smiled, showing a row of even, childlike teeth. "None worth keeping. Only the ones you hide from yourself, which are the most damaging and hurtful of all. Truth is truth, and lie is lie. Tell yourself one's the other and all the world turns kilter."

Sniffing the chill night air, she said, "This land has that smell about it now." A scowl, a glare. "Soon it must choose. The old ways or the new. And when that fearful moment comes, you'll blame us. You always do."

She turned and barked at the others in a language that was unrecognizable. They shrank back to the circle, one walking with a heavy, awkward gait, the other skittering across the turf on her crutches.

"What do you want?" Skena asked in a low, nervous voice that she felt belonged to someone else.

"Only that, in the days ahead, you find yourself and, in doing so, discover that which lies hidden in him, his true nature…" She hesitated, thinking. "A noble and ambitious one, I think. Or else…" The girl stopped and smiled at her, her strange distended face full of impudence.

"Or else?" Skena demanded.

The torch flew toward her face. She felt the flames singe her forehead, smelled the acrid stink of burning rags and oil.

"Or else go back to your bed, madam, and cry yourself to a sleep like a wee girl who's afraid of the dark. Wait on King Duncan to come and bestow his favor upon you, grunting in your face as he does with the wife of every other thane he covets. Find your mettle or go hide away like a bairn in terror of the night."

A light grew in her black eyes, and it was fury.

"You sneer at us as if we're animals. But what are you? With a nod of our heads and a kick of our heels we'll be out of here and away to the fighting in the west before daylight.

Free as the eagles, bold and alive. And this great lady?" She shook her head, and her long hair moved hypnotically as she did so. "Trapped in your fortress, powerless behind your stone walls. No man owns us. Courage comes from the heart..."

"Courage?" Skena cried. "*Courage?* You lecture me on courage. You know nothing, child..."

The torch flew at her again. She closed her eyes, her legs frozen as if turned to the same solid rock as the standing stones and cairns around her.

When she looked again, the tall, limber child let loose a wordless banshee howl that flew shrieking to the moon; then her skinny arms gripped the firebrand and ran the flame and embers up and down her pale, bare skin, not flinching, not crying or giving for a moment some single indication of hurt.

Her black eyes never left the woman in front of her, nor the smile on her face.

The girl stood there, dashing the flame over her too-smooth skin for a minute or more as if it were a bath-time rag. When she stopped, there was no mark on her, no sign of burn or scorch.

"Should you find the pluck to speak the brave, bold truth," the child said, "say it came from you, not us. If it happens, that will be true, I think. Skena is a fine name. An old one. Do it justice."

And then they were gone, the youngest flying into the night like a fox, the second grunting and falling into a soldier's steady march, the last, the crone, vanishing crablike, a bent figure on her sticks.

This strange encounter had revolved around Skena Macbeth's imagination, searching for reason, for three long days and nights. Now, seeing the path back to Culloden and the cairns beyond, thinking on Macbeth's letter and his meeting with these same weird sisters—they could be no other—a kind of answer finally came to her. It had lain in her head all the while, and made its presence known in her earlier unspoken admonition to her absent husband.

What must be done must be done, whatever the price, the cost, the pain. One day we all must walk through fire.

She was the daughter of a thane, a great and powerful lord himself, one who'd died through the anarchy and violence of civil war. An inner voice, long trapped and kept in harness, burst from its dark quarters deep inside her guts and broke furiously free.

"I do not fear a thing," she screamed over the battlements, oblivious to the beetling heights that stretched before her.

"Since Duncan's cruelty stole from me my child, I will be nothing but a vessel of hatred for him. Bring your witches, demons, hags, and all," she raged. "If Duncan steals from us all hope of destiny, then unsex me, fill me head to toe with cruelty. Turn my mother's milk to venom. Thicken my blood, remove from me the least temptation to remorse or decency..."

She ripped open the cloak and then the gown, snatching from the folds at her waist the short, sharp dagger she kept about her always.

"Hear me, crones...*hear me?*"

There was no one across the water on the meandering path to Culloden. She knew her words flew into empty air, and did not care. The moment of wild madness had passed. The festering wound inside, years of silent, bitter resentment, now was lanced and open.

"Hear me you did, wherever you are, whatever you be," she murmured, and felt a door had opened and closed somewhere, and with it, a milestone passed. "Should these tales prove true, I'll not let that villain thieve all hope from me and mine."

She waited. After a few minutes, a filmy sheet of cloud returned and hung around the moon. It sent a gray and mournful cast upon the land.

Those three must come back soon, she thought, the image of the thrashing blue salmon fast in her thoughts. *Return. Inform me.*

Do not tell him we spoke.

Yet it was wrong to wish for their return. The child's words rang true. The resolution had to come from within, not some artificial external force or an accident that stole away their determination and wrapped itself inside the comfortable name of fate.

She stared over the precipice, down to the rocky ground that led to the river below, feeling a cold thrill of sanity, a sudden shock of fear. She would as easily launch herself out into the empty air as kill a king if this would bring her man the destiny he merited.

A wan reflection appeared on the puddled rain along the wall. Turning, she saw a glint of light rising from the eastern sea beyond the firth. Morning approached—and with it, surely, her husband, riding steadily home.

Each day was a journey toward an unseen destination. To glory or the grave. What counted was action, not faint hope, a sense of purpose over patience, will over duty.

These they would embrace or fail together.

She retreated to the cabin and stared back into the west to await him.

◈ ◈ ◈

The sun had been in the sky three hours by the time Macbeth reached the sprawling, open plain along the southern shore of Beauly Firth. The weather had abated. He could see the green shoots of winter barley emerging from the fields of the farms they called the Mains of Bunchrew. When he was past the final mount of Craig Phadrig he could see a dark figure on the dingy ramparts of Inverness, scanning the route to the castle.

He had made better time than he'd hoped, not lingering with Cawdor's servants as they shivered beneath the cold breath of Nevis. A simple question was all he'd asked.

"Will you be as loyal to your new thane as the man who ruled before him?"

None said no. None asked the pertinent question, "And will that extend to treachery for you too, my lord?"

It had seemed an important point at the time. Now, with war behind him and home ahead, the question wished to scurry and hide in the shadows of his mind.

No matter.

He raised his standard and brought his exhausted horse to a trot. That soon became a gallop and then he was over the defensive ditch, through the gate, inside the courtyard, leaping off as the beast slowed, handing over the reins to a servant he didn't see, so desperate was he to race up the keep steps straight into her arms.

By then she had come to stand at the top of the tall flight of stairs, her pale face stiff with suppressed emotion, her long blonde hair pinned up, exaggerating her gaunt and angular features. Her bright blue eyes held him, sharp and knowing. The very sight of her filled him with awe and love and passion.

He fought with his leggings as he took the staircase two steps at a time. The hall was empty, sharp winter sunlight streaming through the single window and the side arrow slits. She helped him remove the last of his armor, berating him mildly for his impetuous nature. Then as metal gave way to mail, to fabric, and finally, to flesh, she led him to a pewter bath before the fire, kissing each cut and bruise, washing him down slowly, lovingly, her pale, fine hands working with a rag and soap, then musk, and for the wounds, ointment.

Silent in the metal tub, Macbeth reflected all the while on Duncan and Banquo and the three women in the hills.

His thoughts troubled him and there was one sure way to dispel them. He climbed out of the bath, reached down, and lifted his wife in his strong arms, carried her, half protesting, but only half, to the great four-poster in the bedroom, where he gently lowered her damp form onto the coverlet.

Her fingers ran through his soaking hair.

"Macbeth?" she whispered, not objecting. "It's morning. Time for breakfast. There's a summons from Duncan. The king comes. We must prepare…"

"Not yet," he said, and raised her gown, spreading his fingers across her belly.

"There are weightier matters than this," she whispered, though he knew that short catch in her voice and what it meant. "The words of the weird sisters…"

He lifted the soft fabric over her head, threw the dress to the floor, bent forward, kissed each nipple, then the navel.

"They can wait," he said, and took her on the coverlet, found the familiar position, felt his throat tightening as the two of them locked in place.

"Not long," she seemed to sigh, then moaned and kissed him, hard, tongue working into his mouth.

A brief and anxious coupling, the rising of desire—and with it, the doubts.

He was tired, exhausted. It had to be that. She felt for him. Touched below.

A dim bitterness rose in his head. So many times, so much effort. And one feeble body to show for it, the brief life of a boy.

He was failing again and she could not help but tell him through the familiar tears, damp and warm against his bristles.

"It's my fault," Skena whispered in that soft lowland voice that was the loveliest he'd ever heard. "You are tired from the fray. Macbeth..."

"No," he muttered, and tried again.

"Mine..." her warm mouth whispered in his ear. "I will make up for this, my love."

Eyes closed, mind reeling, he could not keep the battles and the encounters from running through his head like a bloody waking nightmare. The strange, dark night. Banquo's hinted warnings of great changes to come. Duncan's preferment, which now seemed tainted. The idea, long buried, that a nation made whole was a peerless state, a happy one, raised like a perfect child who knew only love and prosperity and chased away all fear.

And, more than anything, the three weird sisters who rose like spirits out of the loch or the peat, then disappeared into the cold, damp air.

A living image rose in his imagination: the youngest, naked and writhing in front of him like a succubus, a twisting, turning triangle of leaping salmon, eyes bright and inquisitive through nipples and navel, fins and scales animated all the way from her chin across a ribbed chest and tiny tits down to the hairless cranny below.

A fuck or a future?

The creature's lilting words came back to hang there in his mind, gently repeating like a dying echo in his mind.

"Fuck," he grunted, and something moved inside him, a fierce and urgent power bringing life to that which was dying.

She sighed beneath his struggling frame as he arched and pumped and roared above her.

Then in one sweet-sad moment of damp violence it was done and a long-elusive joy held fast between them, conjoining him to her, two creatures made as one. Her eyes, the color of Lochaber gems, were wide open, staring at him.

"What was that?" she asked straight out.

"Love," he said. Then, tentatively, "A gift. An offering, perhaps. God knows there's been sacrifice enough these last few days."

"You think so?" she said quietly. "Duncan arrives this afternoon. The rumor is he has an announcement to make. About his heir."

"The crown's not his to give."

"You know, then?" she asked, and seemed relieved.

"I know there's gossip. Where's the surprise there?"

"When does he leave, husband?"

"Tomorrow. Back to Forres."

Her voice changed; her eyes grew fixed and steely.

"And if these rumors prove true? That he will hand all to that brat of his?"

Macbeth shook his head and brushed the fine, fair hair away from her eyes.

"I should have brought a gift," he said. "Some bauble looted from MacDonwald or the Viking. I apologize..."

"Do not play that game with me! I thought from your letter your mind was rightly turning..."

"No, no, no," he groaned. "I wrote in haste."

Her hands went to his cheeks; her eyes, steely and hard, stared into his.

"Listen to me, husband, and listen well. Your face is an open book. When Duncan enters, have nothing but welcome in your eye, think nothing but the thoughts of a generous host. If he sees in your all-too-open features what I see now—"

"You see nothing!" he cried.

A long sigh racked his aching body. He pulled himself from her, rolled over on the soft linen coverlet, a cherished heirloom of hers from Glamis, woven from flax that grew no more than a mile from that castle's soft and welcoming stones.

She rolled back above him, straddling his waist, staring into his face, hands on his shoulders.

"It may please you to come home and play the part of conquering victor, bedding me like a slack-minded mistress. But remember this: you cast your seed on stony ground. My womb is as bare and cold as Nevis. You shall have no heir and no more station in this world than we can make for you."

"I am lord here. Do not forget your place."

She laughed at him, propped on an elbow, her long hair falling down to his chest.

"Oh, I know my place, lord," she said cheerily. "More's to the point, I know yours, too. And Duncan's. These sisters you met spoke true, spoke for all of us. They saw this land for the desolate place it would become if we allow it."

"What makes you so sure?" Macbeth asked.

"Because I know you," she replied quickly. "The man you are. What you deserve."

He thought of the king, with his mane of white hair, his saintly demeanor. Thought of the red-haired children Wallace raised as his own and that gap on the battlefield that should have been filled by the men from Forres, not the bodies of his own. Scotland was a fractious, insecure nation. It would not be long before war, civil or foreign, gripped the land again.

"What happened in the forest…the letter…the weird sisters," he said. "That was a kind of insanity."

Her face lowered until it was so close to his he could feel the sweet warmth of her breath.

"The world is mad, Macbeth," Skena told him. "Whose lunacy would you impose upon it? That foul brute Duncan's or our own?"

Then she bent down and kissed him tenderly on the cheek. This close, she smelled of primroses and lavender, and he wondered what he'd ever done to deserve such beauty by his coarse and brutal side.

"Now, take me again, lord, rough and quickly," she whispered, then nibbled his ear. "Or let's get about our business. Which you shall smile through and leave the working of to me."

◆ ◆ ◆

Banquo watched as they began to arrive midway through the cold morning, thanes in furs, their wives with gold wound into their hair and dresses hitched daintily over the frozen mud. Every Moray household of note was here, summoned at brief notice, along with all the lords from the armies who'd fought against the traitors and the Vikings. The men bore the weary, hunted look of soldiers who had traveled difficult country in dangerous times. Even the glowering darkness of the castle came as a welcome respite after the wilds, and though they swaggered about, talking too loudly about how utterly they had crushed the rebels, there was a lingering sense of anxiety that hung about them like smoke. They had dressed for the occasion and were relieved to put the walls of the castle between them and whatever scattered remnants of MacDonwald's and Sueno's forces might be skulking outside. Banquo could not help but notice how they unbelted their swords reluctantly and scanned the eyes of every man they met inside.

The day was bright and brilliant, with not a cloud in the clear blue sky. It was as if the heavens wished to witness everything there was to see.

A pecking order had quietly emerged, Macbeth at its summit, MacDuff from Fife as second fiddle. He was a quiet, thoughtful warrior and had now come with his wife and three children from the eastern battlefield where they'd mopped up the last of the rebels in Moray. The oldest boy, a wild-eyed child called Gregor, joined some play fighting with the boys in the courtyard, wielding wooden swords, till one of them split his lip and buried his head in his mother's skirts. Banquo watched MacDuff's disappointment at his tears and felt a pang of sympathy—the young today. His own boy, Fleance, though older, was no better with a weapon.

MacDuff's wife, Ailsa, was black-haired and pale-skinned, her limbs lithe and strong from work. A formidable woman, she had hard gray eyes, and as she hugged her injured son, they flashed over the others with a warning fierceness.

Banquo embraced them all and accepted their compliments—Angus, Ross, Menteith, and the rest—with a hearty laugh. The rebellion was over and this was to be a day of feasting and celebration.

What else? He wasn't sure.

The memory of the weird women lingered in the sharp mind of the Highland warrior, however much he tried to shrug it off. The castle felt brooding and cheerless in spite of all their efforts to make it otherwise. Fleance had arrived at dawn with a guard provided by Macbeth. The boy had been tired and a little wary of his father, who had been fighting in the hills for more than a month. Banquo, never the easiest father, had misplayed the meeting, roaring and shouting like a berserker with overacted joy and bloody tales of battle. He didn't know why. Fleance had always been a dreamy, solitary child, his quiet and sensitive manner taken entirely from his mother. There was a wall between them. Love, though, that was never questioned. The moment he saw the boy ride into the castle Banquo's relief had been so real, so complete, that he had forgotten himself and had run to him, arms wide, the hint of tears in his steely eyes.

By way of thanks, Fleance had winced at his embrace, and when Banquo had finally persuaded him to speak, the boy had merely looked up at the black walls and said, "I don't like this place. It stinks of death."

His father laughed heartily, but that was for the benefit of those around. The boy's manner and his preoccupied, credulous nature were ever more alarming.

Father to a line of kings? Best not think on that. Or what else the sisters said. Besides, from the gathering whispers, Duncan had ideas about that already.

Macbeth, he guessed, felt much the same wariness. This man was his friend, none closer. The love between them was old but forged mostly of late in battle. It was one thing to stand back-to-back hacking at the legs of an enemy in the field, another entirely to stand by the banquet table making idle conversation with revelers who had never wielded a blade. Banquo was a man of combat, uncomfortable away from conflict. Macbeth fought like a lion, but preferred quiet amity to war.

Skena was entirely more sociable when a smile and small talk were needed. She swept among her guests, gracious and welcoming. Her smile was open, guileless, and Banquo found himself envying his friend a little, and not only because he would have someone to keep him warm in what was bound to be a long and bitter night. She ensured that everyone's cup was full from the moment of their arrival and was constantly flitting among the throng, ordering the sour old porter to haul up more beer from the cellar, pointing kitchen maids with pitchers of steaming mulled wine in the direction of anyone who set down an empty cup.

Duncan, it was said, had stopped in sight of the castle an hour before, taking time to prepare the order of his triumphal entry. At three o'clock, the sentries announced his trumpet had been heard, and everyone—thanes, wives, dignitaries, soldiers, and servants—flocked to the walls to cheer the king's approach. He wore a golden crown and sat astride a massive white stallion, barded with leather and mail, his own armor burnished till it flashed like lightning in the pale sun, the absence of scratches and sword marks all the more obvious. His sons, Malcolm and Donalbain, rode on either side. At the head of the column was a priest with a tall cross. Duncan never went anywhere without one, something that pleased his people, though a few of the thanes thought this mere superstition, while others, the ones who knew him best, dismissed it as political theatre. Behind the crossbearer came a massive man dressed in a vast bearskin, his face and hands painted with blood. He bore a golden mace before him, and on its spike was the blackened head of MacDonwald.

The rest of the honor guard rode with bright swords drawn. None of them had seen combat.

Still, Banquo thought, this was a show, a spectacle, and for that, impressive enough. As they neared the walls, the fanfare rang out again. Macbeth appeared on the turret by the gatehouse, Skena at his side.

"Glamis and the people of Scotland welcome Duncan," he called, his breath smoking in the cold. "King and savior of the nation."

The crowd shouted their welcome and applauded. If any felt Banquo's own wry amusement at the words, they did not show it.

Duncan's warhorse did not like the castle's cobbled courtyard and almost tipped the king from the saddle as he attempted to dismount. Macbeth rushed to steady the beast and offer his shoulder for support as the old man clambered awkwardly down. Banquo thought he caught Malcolm smirking, but the son lowered his eyes too quickly for anyone to be sure.

Then, a little breathless, Duncan made a brief and well-turned speech about victory and national pride and friendship, half smiled to himself, and concluded with a remark that set the thanes glancing among themselves with nervous excitement.

"There is no fitter time," he said, "with the rebel threat vanquished, the foreign invader repulsed, and the nation whole again, to think on the future, and that I will address this evening."

What the hell did that mean? Banquo wondered, his heart sinking. Some food, some drink, a little tumble with a willing maid. That was all these men about him wanted mostly, himself among them. Not more politics, with all the dangers that could bring.

With what small diplomatic skill he possessed, Banquo determined to press for opinions, quietly, subtly. An hour later, he found himself with a huddle of his peers, drinking and talking in an anteroom off the banquet hall, the walls hung with heavy tapestries depicting a stag hunt. These men had gathered informally, drifting together without apparent purpose as the rest of the castle bustled in the activity that surrounded such a bountiful feast. They had spoken of trivial matters: where they could get their boots resoled, the state of the garderobe privies, and how far they would be traveling once the festivities here were done. But there was a watchfulness about them as they skirted the subject at the forefront of their minds, and all knew it.

Ross, a gullible acolyte at the best of times, was vocal in his opinion. The king, he predicted, meant to embark on a new chain of fortifications—once a pet project when he had been a younger man. The broader consensus was more troubling. Many had heard the constant gossip that Duncan meant to announce an heir as he had sometimes threatened, bypassing the traditional voice of the Council of Thanes.

MacDuff, in particular, a hard and stubborn lord even in more peaceful times, scowled at that thought.

"So," said Banquo, resolved to break the tension, "I'm guessing we'll have a new prince of Cumberland among us before bed. It's like a game for children, isn't it? I wonder who will pluck the prize from Duncan's sack."

MacDuff shifted, brows creased, uncomfortable.

"This is idle talk," he said. "Duncan can choose who he likes. Any prince will need our voice if he is to become king."

"That's true enough," said Banquo, "and there's no reason to think Duncan will not hold the throne for many a long year yet. He seems well in body and clear in mind as ever."

"Why shouldn't he be?" muttered MacDuff, with a hint of bitterness. "The long arm of battle never reaches him."

Ross gave him a sharp look.

"And nor should it," MacDuff added quickly. "His majesty is the head of the nation. We are nothing more than the weapons of his purpose."

"Exactly," said Angus. "Perhaps one of us will be rewarded."

"You mean Macbeth?" asked Banquo.

"I don't think it an accident that we are gathered here," Angus replied. "And saving your good self, there is no man who has risked and won more for Duncan than our host."

"A brave and valiant patriot," said Banquo, nodding, raising his tankard. "And a worthy man. If he's named prince of Cumberland, I for one would be proud to see him wear the crown when Duncan's days are done."

An awkward mood had fallen on the conversation. It was in exchanges such as this that rebellions and the bloody nightmare of civil war found their roots.

"All this may be true," said MacDuff, "but I would rather such matters were left to the council when the need arise. Naming heirs in advance forces our hand. Now you must excuse me." His dark eyebrows rose at each of them. "I believe I am alone in having wife and family in tow."

"Bad timing," Angus said, and winked boldly. "There are more than a few pretty faces in these parts."

"At times like this," the thane of Fife said, staring at him balefully in return, "I prefer my family around me. Look after your own, friends. That's my advice. A wife and bairns are worth more than any strumpet."

They fell silent and gazed into their drinks.

When MacDuff had left, Banquo shook his head and said, "A stern and moral man. It's growing up by the sea that does it."

"That wife of his…" Angus grumbled.

"Happens to be my cousin!" Ross objected.

An awkward silence, red faces, men coughing into their hands.

"But you're right," Ross added, mock seriously. "She's a shrew and scares the life out of me. My friend MacDuff might make a king, but it would be a cold and tedious nation if those two should clamber onto the throne. Give me brave Macbeth and that pretty wife of his any day. At least you could have a smiling face on what few coins you own."

Banquo roared with laughter and, though not a sensitive man, was aware his voice was a little too loud, a little too enthusiastic.

◈ ◈ ◈

They were in their bedroom, a brief respite from the crowds below, the only place they felt safe together.

"Banquo says I may be king-to-be before the night is out," Macbeth remarked, watching her as she changed into a formal gown.

"Duncan has given me a gift already, husband," Skena replied. "Direct from his fond and roaming hands."

In her delicate fingers was a diamond brooch, an ornate foreign design, not Celtic. Silver, with a bright diamond at its center.

"Duncan passed it to me in private when he arrived. With a twinkle in his eye. We may not know what plans he has for you. But I recognize that look. I understand what he desires of me..."

He took the brooch, turned it in his hands, passed it back to her.

"Wear it on your gown tonight, smile, and avoid his gaze. He's king, not God. This is my castle and you're my wife. If you were willing, he'd accept it. If not, he knows better than to press his case too strongly."

"He's a gracious monarch, you mean?"

"He's a politician above all else. A man like Duncan doesn't keep the throne through making foes easily. Not over such a small matter as a bedmate..."

"Thank you," she replied, and cast her head to one side as if in thought.

"I meant..." He came forward, pressed the brooch to her breast, kissed her tenderly on the cheek, ignoring the small pressure of uncertain resistance there. "Small to a fool like him."

"Some fool," she muttered. "Safe on the throne, without risking a hair of himself or his own. Now leeching off us once again and giving nothing in return, save this..."

She held the brooch before him. He watched it sparkle in her fingers, then took the thing once more and carefully pinned it to her dark velvet gown, above her heart.

"Patience…" he began.

"Is a virtue for the dead alone. We are trapped in the mechanisms of a device made and run by others, Macbeth. Do you not feel it?"

"I feel…" He shook his head, without an answer.

"If Duncan names you Cumberland tonight, he does so for one reason only. To gain time, to halt you at the foot of his throne with an empty promise that will surely be dashed aside the moment one of his own garners sufficient support to usurp you."

"Malcolm and Donalbain are little liked…"

"They're vicious, striving, younger versions of their father and will happily murder one another to snatch the crown themselves. Listen to me!"

There was truth in her words and he knew it.

"If I am next in line…" Macbeth began.

"You're a corpse-in-waiting. And if not, the same. Listen to the gossip out there. You are the boldest, strongest, best-loved man in Scotland. If Duncan died this night, they'd crown you before the cock crows…"

"Wife," he sighed.

"If Duncan's gone, there's none in the land who'd seek to place another on the throne. Wait…" She took his hands now, held them tightly. "Wait and he will scheme to cast doubt in their minds, weaken your forces, and find the chance to bring you down. Then your head will sit on his berserker's pike, as MacDonwald's does today, and I'll be counted lucky to be one more harlot in his whorehouses. Those weird sisters you met…"

"Witches," he spat. "Had I never seen them..."

"Nothing would be different at all! They told you the truth, husband. We rise or fall on our own courage, nothing else. This cozy heaven you seek at home is no more than an illusion. The world moves on, and either we travel with it or lie trampled beneath the feet of others."

"I will listen to what the king says, then make up my mind."

Her subtle fingers fell to his cheek. "And in the meantime I shall manage the household. As the lady of the castle should. Your trick with Sueno...Nightshade is a powerful weed. A common one, too."

The memory of that amused him, though its relevance was lost. "So?" he asked.

"Nothing, lord. This is churlish on our part. We have guests below. Whispering in the shadows."

He held her slender body to his. "I'd stay here forever, if only that were..."

Skena dragged herself from him. "Possible?" she asked. "It isn't. Come, Macbeth." She linked her arm through his. "There's a king to heed and work to do."

◈ ◈ ◈

Duncan carved the boar himself. Not just the first ceremonial slice, but the entire first round of servings.

"See," Banquo whispered to Macbeth, "I told you he could wield a blade."

Fleance overheard and Macbeth caught the boy's shocked look.

"Your father's just joking," he said. "Duncan is a great man. A father to us all."

Banquo picked up his cup and toasted the idea, then drank down the ale, spilling it into his beard and belching so loudly that the nearest lady, MacDuff's wife, covered her mouth and looked askance.

The king's priest said the blessing and Duncan paused, eyes closed and face upturned, an attitude of pious devotion. The hall responded with an "Amen" and the feast began.

Skena—at Macbeth's insistence—had stopped ministering like a serving girl and taken her place at the opposite end of the table, facing him. Duncan sat in the middle, smiling and chewing, spitting gobbets of gristle and fat onto the rush-strewn floor. He knew they were waiting and was amusing himself by drawing out the evening. At the start of the feast he had said a few short words, then spoken of his gift to Skena, the diamond brooch from the English court. She had avoided the king's gaze when he came and admired the gem on her gown, took one step back as his prying fingers reached out to touch the jewel on her breast.

A modest smile, a blush. The king had shrugged, a gesture not lost on those around him. Duncan was used to taking favors from the ladies of his lords from time to time, but only with their assent. Nobility conferred a little privilege.

After this brief, tense moment, Macbeth sat with the rest of the men, but still he could scarcely take his eyes off her. She seemed so beautiful, so serene, and gathered those around her in polite conversation, listening to each with the patient skill of a diplomat, finding interest in the tedious and mundane. The ladies seemed agog at her composure, the grace with which she behaved as if nothing could be more normal than the presence of the royal court. They knew what such visitations cost, how crippling it could be if a king decided to bless you with his presence, not for a day or a week, but for a month, even an entire season. Yet Skena showed only a sublime and placid contentment. *She was made for this,* he thought. *No, something better.*

There were jugglers and jesters, dancers and musicians, and food enough for several armies, not that the average soldier would recognize what overflowed the best pewter plates Skena Macbeth could find. After the boar came pies; capons, grouse, and ptarmigan; larks and woodcock; salmon, herring, and lampreys—all accompanied by potage, breads, salt pork, bacon, and cheese. How she had managed to arrange it all at such short notice, and with the roads unsafe, Macbeth had no idea.

It was long after dark when the king rose to his feet. The man had been drinking steadily since he arrived, except for the half hour they had spent crammed into the tiny family chapel, giving thanks for their victory. Still, he looked poised and in control, like an actor who had played the same part so often he became the mask he wore. Duncan placed both hands on the table and waited for silence to fall. The harpist stalled, the clatter of utensils stopped, and only the crackle of the massive hearth served to distract the assembly from the king's words. However dulled with food and drink they had been, they were keen as knives now and all eyes were turned toward him.

"We begin," he said, smiling, "with gratitude. First, to God, the father of justice, peace, and victory. Lord of the world and of our humble, but beauteous corner of it—Scotland. Second, to the founder of the feast—MacDonwald!"

He nodded to where the berserker, a Viking mercenary lured by Duncan's gold, stood ramrod straight by the fire with the head of the traitor impaled on the royal mace.

There was a shout of laughter from the room as Duncan toasted the dead rebel.

Macbeth stared at the bloody prize he'd brought to the king. Two days before, MacDonwald had nearly taken his life. Now the man whose name had made their blood run cold was no more than a sideshow prop for mockery and laughter. The mighty had a long way to fall.

"Next, and most sincerely," continued Duncan, with the same easy and expansive smile, "to our kind hostess, whose beauty is rivaled only by her kindness."

Another toast, and Skena rose, inclined her head graciously to the applause, stroked the brooch on her breast, and sat down again without ever meeting Duncan's eyes.

"Lastly, to our most worthy captains, the architects of our victory."

Duncan turned, his smile widening still further.

"Banquo! And Macbeth!"

Both men stood to acknowledge the cheering with solemn bows.

"These have been troubled times," said Duncan, in his element now. He gazed around the lamplit chamber, taking them all in, confident and composed. Macbeth felt a reluctant rush of admiration for the man. There was a profound and well-honed talent here. "Dark times," the king went on. "And it is only through great courage and sacrifice that we have moved beyond them into the light of a clear, new day. We have given thanks to God, and to those men among us who were His instruments, but still the serpent of treason lurks within our midst. We must head it off before this vile and bloody snake rears its venomous head again."

Here it comes, thought Macbeth.

Duncan paused, and the spitting of the logs on the fire seemed unnaturally loud in the stillness.

"Death comes to all at last," he went on. "Even to kings. But it need not bring chaos and civil war at its heels. Therefore, after much prayer, to clarify our purposes in the hearts of our people and prevent future strife on the inevitable day we depart this life, we hereby invoke the ancient privilege of Scottish monarchs to name their chosen successor prince of Cumberland."

Macbeth forced himself to watch the king and ignore the glances straying now his way.

The tall, silver-haired figure at the head of the table paused, smiled again at the room, and—in a booming, level voice that echoed around the chamber—he called, "Arise, Malcolm, my eldest son."

A deafening silence. Ross's sister gasped. Menteith's face split into a broad smile that only caught itself from turning into a laugh at the very last second.

Malcolm?

So it was true.

Macbeth stared at Duncan, his face frozen. The king, oblivious to the shock in the room or resolved to ignore it, removed his chain of office and took two steps over to where his son was now standing stiffly by the table.

Malcolm, it seemed, was the only one not caught off guard. He dropped to one knee, a practiced gesture, and received the chain around his neck, head bowed. The priest moved quickly to his side and pronounced a few bell-like Latin phrases, ending with a theatrical sign of the cross.

"Arise, prince of Cumberland," Duncan boomed. "The throne of Scotland shall be yours."

There was a strange, fixed smile on Malcolm's face. He glanced at the crown on his father's head and said nothing, not a single word of thanks.

It was Ross who began the applause—and that, slowly. Skena followed suit, rising smoothly to her feet. As if coming out of a trance, the others followed, their chairs clattering back as they rose quickly, their eyes troubled, none daring to glance at his neighbor.

A few looked slyly at Macbeth, frozen to his seat.

"Come, brother," Banquo whispered, taking his arm. "Don't look so glum."

He forced a cup upon him and the two men rose.

"God save the king!" roared Ross. "Hail Malcolm, prince of Cumberland! King to be!"

◆ ◆ ◆

She found him on the eastern battlements, alone, staring back to the low line of the river and the distant firth, gleaming like streams of molten silver beneath the open sky. There was not a cloud to be seen, only the bright full moon and an endless panorama of stars set like jewels against soft velvet. Frost had turned the fields and paths from Inverness a ghostly white. The earth would freeze tonight, and any straggler left outside would most likely die a cold and lonely death.

The harshness of these beautiful yet barren lands continued to astonish her. In the south, the rolling flat pastures of Strathmore, the verdant, fertile fields produced a landscape made for the needs of man, generous and welcoming. Here was a country created for wild animals, for wolves and eagles, crows and wildcats. And creatures like Macbeth, warriors, hard and cruel. It was his misfortune to possess a shard of conscience inside his Highland breeding, from where she couldn't guess. This was one more reason why she loved him, but such a trait left her husband disordered, owning the strength and will to overcome his enemies, but hamstrung by his conscience.

"What are they saying about me?" he asked, watching her.

"About you?"

"There's another subject?"

"Of course. Malcolm. The prince of Cumberland. Heir apparent."

Macbeth shook his head, then said, "We shall be vigilant. I'll keep my troops around me, forge alliances. If they come, I'll be prepared."

Skena strode over to stand by his side.

"Should it come to that," she told him. "They're saying much about Malcolm down there. That he's ambitious. That this pronouncement of Duncan's stems as much from the son's threats as the king's own will."

His dark brow furrowed in bafflement. "They say that? Threat? What threat?"

She sighed and gazed at him as if he were a child. "It's a measure of your humanity, husband, that these intrigues are beyond you. Malcolm is an ambitious fox. Can't you see it in his face? They say he's anxious for the crown and half expected Duncan to announce the date for his coronation. An abdication of the throne. A passing of the nation from father to son, as if it were a family bauble."

"Death makes kings here, nothing else. That and the council."

She took his hand. It was cold, hard, and calloused. A soldier's. Still, she wound her fingers lovingly in his. "With a little assistance from the living, sometimes."

"Malcolm should consider himself lucky. Duncan's spoken!"

"He's next in line, not monarch. None trust him, even his own father. Every man in there knows he's unworthy next to you. If your name were Malcolm now...What would you think?"

The prospect of fresh conflict focused his mind immediately. "That his enemies would rise against him, and I'd be at their head," Macbeth said.

"Quite," she agreed. "So perhaps it's best he steal the crown in haste, or lose it—and his life—in leisure."

"They think such things?" He pointed back to the hall. "The thanes?"

"They do now." She smiled at him. "Oh, Macbeth. There's more than one way to skin a cunning cat like Duncan. Your peers are as easily moved by their mood as a wee girl waiting on her lover. A few canny words may turn an army north to south, make friend enemy, pluck victory from the gaping jaws of catastrophe. Men believe what they wish. What suits them. And at this moment, they wish that wily young thug ill."

She placed her fingers on the dagger at his belt.

"One swift and well-timed blow and Scotland's ours. You know that. And..."

"And Malcolm takes the blame," Macbeth murmured, a finger to his lips.

He turned and took her shoulders.

"I was not made to be a murderer, Skena. I do not have so cold a heart, nor do you."

Her face hardened and she stared at him. "You feel the temperature in this place as well as I do," she replied. "You dowsed those embers well, my lord, but still they burn and will one day soon return. Rebellion. Bloody civil war. One blow against the old man and how many women and children out there in the land would thank you, for they will go unwidowed, their bairns still with loving fathers? Peace over war. Justice over this stinking corruption."

Her blue eyes held him.

"The greater good depends on a single, swift, decisive act, one Duncan would deliver to any of us without a second thought. If you will not think of Scotland, think of me. And if we walk away from this last opportunity? How long, husband, before Malcolm and his friends are outside those walls, howling for our heads? Best die striving for conquest, not scurrying from these mongrels, regretting what we might have been."

She stared into his calm, decent face, held both his hands, and said, "Together. Always. I will be with you."

A flicker of hesitation, a moment in the balance.

"I have no talent for this scheming," he murmured. "In battle I see things, prospects, gains, and openings. In my own home…" He cast a sour glance at the ramparts. "I look for welcome and love and respite from this bloody world."

"A woman's place is by the hearth," she told him, laughing lightly. "Fear not. I am mistress of all arrangements for this day. Return to your guests, as shall I until the later time when the men seek entertainment of your own. Then I depart to go about a good wife's business." Her eyes narrowed. "Duncan's grasping fingers shall not trouble me again. He'll find other prey, I'm sure. Then later"—she leaned into him, kissed him once quickly on the lips—"find he's prey himself, and his damned son soon after."

Macbeth stood there, face turned from her, in shadow.

His resolve might waver, but it would not break. She'd see to it, and more, besides. He was distant from the ways of politics, but not ignorant of them. Their choices now were narrow and none easy.

"Our guests are waiting, husband," she said, and took his hand to lead the way. "Good hosts must never disappoint."

◈ ◈ ◈

An hour later and the evening was as she'd forecast—more pleasant, even.

"Which do you like best, Ewan?" she asked.

Skena Macbeth sat on the four-poster bed in the thane's quarters. The boy knelt in front of her, the wooden platter on his lap, his fingers greasy and smeared with food, a happy smile on his animated face. From the hall below she could hear the rumble of men's voices, loud and boisterous through drink. She'd left not long after the pretty girls from the west arrived, all scanty dresses and flashing eyes, dancing, playing their fiddles and flutes, crooning ancient Gaelic airs. The performance swiftly became so bold the noble women in the room departed, eyes averted, as was expected of them.

Now any man, single or married, who fancied company would be choosing partners from among those blank and beautiful faces, taking them into the many winding corridors of the castle in search of a bed or a dark corner that might serve as an excuse for privacy. Such was a lord's hospitality. It was always this way.

She could picture the evening coming to an end. Servants marching along the narrow stone hallways of the castle, ignoring the couples pressed sighing against the walls, extinguishing the brands that lit the winding, freezing passages. Night would enfold Inverness, and sleep and drink and fornication would take its toll on most within its walls. With the midnight peal would come opportunity.

"This is the best!" the boy said, and picked a small carcass out of the mess of bones in front of him. It was a modest-sized bird, the flesh gone, devoured down to the pink breastbone.

"Black grouse, I think?" she said with a smile. "Ewan, you have refined tastes. Here…"

Skena walked over to the cabinet by the window and drew the long tail feathers, shiny and black, out of the pot that sat on the top. She wore these things in her hair or on a hat sometimes. They were fashionable in the Highlands, a kind of badge, a sign of loyalty to the hard beauty of its glens and fells.

"This is what the cock flourishes when he wants to find himself a fancy lady," Skena told him, returning to the child and placing the feathers carefully into the soft blond hair that lay thick at the nape of his neck. "They could do the same for you."

"I hate the lassies!" Ewan cried, snatching the quills from his head and clutching them in his tiny fists. "They boss you and tease you and pinch you and make your life a misery!"

"That we do," Skena observed, stifling her laughter.

Three pewter flasks—one of wine, one water, one empty—stood by the bed. When Macbeth told her how he'd conquered Sueno's forces, she knew straightaway this was a stratagem worthy of salvage. That afternoon she'd gathered berries of belladonna from the frosty banks of the River Ness, then crushed them in a small pestle and mortar in their room. When she poured them into the sweet red wine they sank straight to the bottom. This was a powerful drug, one that could kill in excess. Too many berries had gone into the wine, she thought. They needed Duncan's guards to sleep, not die. She would dilute it and pray the proportions would be right to let the men slumber just enough.

"I didn't mean *you*!" the boy cried, suddenly afraid.

"Oh, Ewan," she said softly, stroking his head, then taking the black grouse feathers from him and placing them on the bed.

The younger castle girls could be vixens. It had never occurred to her they would taunt him remorselessly if they saw those things in his lustrous blond hair. She had so wanted to be a mother, yet at times like this, she asked herself why. It seemed so hard. To be responsible for a small bundle of humanity not yet formed, shapeless, seeking guidance, searching for a shining light to follow through the dark. And from what kind of woman? One with black aspirations in her heart and murder on her mind.

"Truly, lady," he said, his eyes wide with fear, "I didn't mean..."

"I know," she said, and kissed his forehead, which was warm and clean. The boy was an orphan, taken in from one of the bawdy houses down by the port. The kitchen maids adored his cheerful, guileless nature and kept him clean and fetching, always in the best clothes they could afford. They showed him real kindness, Skena thought, a generous, selfless form of care. Hers was the easy sort, a pleasant word, a gesture, a brief caress when she happened to see him. A plate of fine food ordered up from the kitchen, spare pickings from a banquet meant for none but those drunken lords in the hall below. "You meant nothing at all. And besides, not all girls are the same, now, are they? Cook gave you that rich food for the king…"

"Only because you told her."

Her fingers caressed his soft, warm cheek. "You should have seen the smile on her face when I asked her to do so. And I think those lassies in the kitchen—Maira and Elspeth and Subhan—they love you like one of their own. Now, don't they?"

"Aye," he murmured, his eyes downcast. "Maira *is* one of my own. My sister. They pulled her out of the same whorehouse down the port when they took me. She says our mam was a—"

"No, no," Skena said, and placed a slender finger to his lips. "What's gone is gone. Your family's here now. Ordinary bairns just have the one mother, the one father. You've got a castle full of them, high and low, all of who love you like a son. Count your blessings."

"I do," he whispered, staring at the stone floor.

She put her hand beneath his chin and raised his face to hers. "Now, young man. Will you do me a favor in return? A secret one? You mustn't tell a soul. Not even Maira."

"A secret's a secret," he murmured, still looking a little afraid.

"It's more than that," she added. "It's a bond. A *contract.* Like a promise between friends. You're my friend, Ewan. I'm yours. Friends keep promises to one another, always. Don't they?"

"I s'pose…"

She poured half the tainted wine into the empty flask, then filled it to the brim with water.

God make this right, she thought. *Send them to sleep for a little while, no more.*

"Lord Macbeth has been given a great gift by the king today," Skena told him, holding out the pewter vessel.

"I know," he said brightly. "Glamis *and* Cawdor…"

"A *great* gift. It's only right that all should share his joy. Not just thanes and their knights. Servants." She stroked his cheek. "Wee boys, too."

He held up the carcass. "I had my grouse!" he said. "It's only fair."

"Quite." She patted the tankard with the tainted wine. "This is not for young laddies. It's wine from abroad."

"Where's that?"

"Somewhere warm. A place the flowers bloom all year long and apples and pears and grapes grow on trees everywhere so you may pick them when you walk through the fields. And all that sun and warmth goes in here"—she tapped the flask—"to make a drink that's got the breath of summer and fruit and those fragrant foreign lands all trapped inside it."

His eyes were as wide and bright as the loch at full moon.

"This is the wine of kings," she went on. "Special and so costly none but the greatest should ever drink it. But tonight—"

"Is that why you watered it down?" he asked, sharp as ever.

"That's one reason," she said, amused by his quickness. "There's another, mind. I want you to take it to Duncan's guards. Those two soldiers outside his bedroom. They protect the king of Scotland. They deserve our thanks, too. But with water in their wine, don't you think?"

He nodded.

"Don't want *them* going to sleep," Ewan said.

"Certainly not."

"I'll be a soldier when I grow up." He threw the wooden platter onto the bed, leapt to his feet, and made the stance of a man with a sword, feinting, stabbing. "I'll kill Vikings and the Irish and the English…and…and…anyone the king tells me. Like this…"

His face wasn't handsome anymore. It was distorted by hatred and violence. *They pick this up,* she thought, *so easily it might be an invisible disease floating in the air.*

She placed her hand on his arm and he became calm again, looking a little guilty for his outburst.

"There's no hurry," she told him, trying to imagine the boy eight, ten years hence, out on the battlefield, blade in hand, fighting for whosoever gave the orders. "You could be a farmer. A priest. A clerk. A bright boy like you would make a fine lawyer."

"Me?" he laughed. "I'm the wee bastard turning the kitchen spit. That's what they call me."

"None of us chooses the nature of our birth."

"Or the day we die, either, cook says." He glanced at the pewter flask with the wine in it. "I'll be a soldier and get to see the world. Somewhere warm and sunny where you can take apples straight off the tree."

"Will you pick one for me?" she murmured, suddenly dismayed.

The question puzzled him. He was a precocious child, but a child all the same. "If that's what you want, lady. I'm a servant. You do the asking."

"Then take this," she ordered, handing him the flask and the two leather cups. "Tell those two guards it's a present from Macbeth. A thankful reward for their dutiful care of the king."

"Aye," he said. "And I'll tell them to keep their big gobs shut, too."

"Do that."

"And then?" he asked.

"Then..." She found herself wanting to touch his gentle head again and remember the child like this, before the coarseness came. "I think it's time for small boys to go to bed. Don't you?"

He stared at his empty plate and said, half meekly, "I'm still hungry..."

"You've had enough rich food for one night, boy. I have to meet Macbeth," she said. "Downstairs. We must discuss arrangements for tomorrow. See that things are in order for the king's departure. Well?"

"Well, what?"

"Well, away with you!" She reached forward and squeezed his lips together. "And you keep your little gob shut, too. Secrets between friends..."

She held onto his arm.

"I thought I was supposed to go," he said uncertainly.

"There's one more favor, Ewan," she said, and whispered in his ear.

The boy went white and shook his head. "I'm not the one for thieving, lady. Not for nobody. I seen what they do with the light-fingered round here."

"It's a game, Ewan," she said, smiling, holding onto him. "A jape, a jest. No harm in it and none will come to you." She stroked his cheek. "I swear." Skena smiled at him. "But you're just a child. If you're afeared—"

"I'm afeared of nothing!" the child declared. "If you say—"

"I do," she interrupted. "Now on your way, young man." She bent and kissed his hair one last time. "And be discreet about your business. As silent as a mouse."

◈ ◈ ◈

The two of them left the bedroom together, downstairs first, to the place she showed him. Then, when that small deed was done, he returned above, along the stone staircase that led to the guest quarters at the summit of the keep.

Visitors here were few, distinguished ones even rarer. Ewan couldn't remember the last time any lord of repute had stayed long enough for a banquet. Inverness castle was, his sister said, a cold and foul-smelling hovel, built for nothing but to lure the Vikings away from the king's rich palaces along the Moray Firth at Forres, a place as beautiful as Inverness was hideous.

The guards were two gruff foot soldiers in breeches and leather jerkins, swords in their belts, caps perched on their massive heads, seated beneath a burning brand. The first had the reddest hair he'd ever seen, the second the reddest cheeks.

"Sirs?" he said, meekly offering them the flask and the mugs.

They were by the curtain at the door into the bedroom, one holding the fabric aside, both peering slyly through. They had a certain demeanor he'd come to recognize among men in the castle at times, anxious and expectant, as if there were a fight or something equally pleasant about to be had.

"Sirs?" he repeated.

"Shush," whispered the redheaded one, placing a large, stinking hand over his face. "Can't you see the king's at prayer?"

The other sniggered and said, in a low, wicked tone, "Let the boy have a look for himself, brother. It's best he gets to know his monarch, don't you think?"

They chuckled at that and the hand moved from his face, gripped his shirt, and propelled him into the doorway.

It took a moment for his eyes to focus, and even then, he wasn't sure what he saw ahead in the half-light of the candle by the bed. In the center of the room, close by a tall four-poster bed, stood the man he knew to be King Duncan, tall and erect in a nightshirt, silver hair falling down his back, face up to the roof. A girl in the pretty flowered costume of the dancers from the west knelt in front of him, his hands on the back of her head.

She was bobbing up and down from the neck, in a constant rhythm that made her blonde hair sway and fall in front of her, raising and lowering Duncan's nightshirt with each measured motion.

The king crooned and sighed as if singing a strange, wordless melody, one that seemed to be approaching a kind of climax. Then it was done and a faint, sad cry emerged from his throat, a noise that made the two guards titter and punch each other on the arm.

"What's she doing?" the boy asked the redheaded one.

"It's called giving homage," the soldier said, and slapped the second when his laughter grew so loud it seemed impossible the king wouldn't hear.

The boy watched as the girl stayed there, kneeling. Sobbing, he thought. When finally she turned to look away, he saw her face and it was as miserable as any he'd ever seen. She wiped her mouth with her sleeve. Then the old man above her snapped something, rapped her once around her pretty head, and clambered onto the bed without so much as another word.

She got up and his heart stopped, remembering how she'd danced and sung in the hall. She was the youngest of the girls. No more than twelve or thirteen, he thought. Slim and as beautiful as an angel. Her eyes were glassy with tears; her shoulders racked with sobs. She half walked, half ran to the door where they stood, dashed past them without a word, and disappeared into the darkness. He heard her weeping and the sound of her spitting or spewing, he wasn't sure which, or whether it was both. It seemed an odd noise for an angel to make.

"The older he gets," the ruddy-faced soldier said, "the younger he likes them."

He patted the boy on the shoulder.

"You want to go in and say hello to his majesty yourself, boy?"

"No, thank you," he whispered, suddenly afraid.

The king was the king. It was beneath great people to close doors on servants. They would eat and sleep and shit, do anything in front of them, just as easily as they would with a dog in the room. Duncan now seemed to be asleep on the coverlet, snoring like a common drunk.

"Your gift," he said. "From Lord Macbeth. To thank you for your work."

The red-faced one took the flask, poured two mugs, and passed one to the other.

"Slàinte," he said, then, eyeing the boy, added, "Fancy a sip, young'un?"

"Lady Macbeth said it was for you, sir, not a child like me," he answered.

They didn't argue, but pulled up two stools by the door and gulped at the wine.

"Bah," said the redhead. "It's watered."

"Better than nothing," the other retorted. "Shut your moaning."

He could hear sobbing from below the stairs, a young, hurt voice.

"I can tell you like a fine joke, sirs," he murmured, slipping the thing she'd told him to steal beneath the grubby pile of bags they carried with them.

He left them and wandered back along the corridor, then down the stone staircase to the floor below.

The girl dancer sat curled in a heap beneath a solitary burning brand by the wall, head in her knees, shaking, weeping. He tried to think of something to say but could think of no words.

Sleep, the lady said. Go to bed. That was what children did. But the boy called Ewan couldn't think of closing his eyes, not after what he'd seen and done. Not for a while, anyway.

◈ ◈ ◈

There was someone in the courtyard, a tall, slim figure, awake, with a brand in his hand. *It has to be dark,* Macbeth thought. *Everywhere.*

He walked down the keep stairs, back into the cold night, pulling his cloak around him, falling close to the exterior wall, determined to see who was still awake.

When he was closer, hand on his blade, feeling more trepidation in his own castle than he'd ever known facing MacDonwald or Sueno in the field, another shape moved out of the gloom ahead of him and a familiar voice boomed through the night, directed at the figure with the torch.

"How goes the night, boy?" Banquo demanded, his bearded face suddenly caught by the moon, the wolf pelt about his shoulders.

"I haven't heard the bell," said a young, yet certain voice.

"That means it's not yet midnight," his father said patiently.

"It feels later," Fleance answered.

"Feels, feels, feels..." Banquo snarled. "You cannot spend your time in endless dreaming."

Macbeth walked out into the center of the yard, making heavy, audible steps.

"Sword!" Banquo ordered.

"No need of a sword in my castle," Macbeth said as he joined them. Father and son in the moonlight—one old and grizzled and battle worn, the other a handsome, fresh-faced youth of fifteen. "What game is this, Banquo? Playing soldiers in the home of a friend?"

The big man laughed a little too heartily. "Fleance is still a child in many ways," he replied, throwing his arm around his son, gripping him in a brief bear hug. "He needs to learn the art of being a humble guard. No man goes straight from bottom to top." He scratched his beard. "We didn't, did we? I remember some scrapes back when we were his age..."

His son looked none too pleased by the attention.

Macbeth smiled at him fondly. "Your father's right, Fleance. This is a dangerous, difficult world."

"I know that," he answered. "I see things sometimes. Things you don't—"

"Not now," Banquo snapped. "Not here."

"It's late," Macbeth added. "I beg of you. This was a long and eventful night. For pity's sake, go to bed. The king has—"

"He seemed unusually pleased with himself, I might say," Banquo observed. "And very generous to you and Skena in one way, at least. That diamond he gave her…"

"Was unnecessary. The king owes us nothing. I, on the other hand, owe him everything. And you, too." He put a hand to Banquo's arm, then Fleance's. "To bed, friends."

The bearlike figure glanced toward the vast towering keep. "Never seen this place so dark," he muttered. "Give me the light any day."

"Morning will soon be on us. The sun always rises. Your boy looks exhausted."

Banquo leaned and whispered in his ear, "He's not the only one who dreams. I had those three weird sisters in my head last night, and all that strange nonsense they spouted. Did you?"

Macbeth thought for a moment and said, "The witches? No. You were right. Lunatics on the heath. And see how wrong they were?"

"Not about everything. Those lunatics knew you were about to become thane of Cawdor."

Macbeth nodded and said, "I thought of that. They heard about it before we met them. Mischievous bitches playing tricks. What other explanation can there be? This didn't concern you last night. Why does it matter now?"

Banquo shook his head. "I can't get it out of my mind. Cawdor. The king and that foul son of his, handed the throne as if it were some present." He glanced at Fleance. "The idea that in that meek boy of mine might lie a dynasty—"

"Friend, friend!" Macbeth cut in. "I commanded you by rank in the field. Here, in my courtyard, we are equals. But be sensible. Put these fanciful ideas to one side, as have I. The king is asleep. He's spoken his mind about the succession. I heard no voices rising in argument."

"As if they'd say it to his face…" A brief, wry smile broke on his face. "I wonder what kind of monarch a man like Malcolm will make. They say he almost flayed Cawdor alive. Duncan would never have done that himself. Just asked someone else while he watched and smirked." He paused, seemed hesitant. "A brooch instead of the promise of a nation. No man would blame you if you felt a little cheated, friend. There's plenty inside who'd rather the prize had gone to you."

Macbeth guided him to the steps. "I'm fortunate with what I have. Tomorrow we will talk of this if it still concerns you. But now…forget about hags on the heath. Take your son and get some sleep. In a few hours the king will be on his way and we may all return to our business."

"Sound advice!" Banquo declared, and took Fleance with him up the stairs.

It was a naked lie, the first Macbeth had ever told his childhood friend. There had been a dream, though whether it was a waking one or the product of a brief slumber that evening, he'd no idea. He had found himself in darkness, in a winding corridor of the keep, following a light that chased and beckoned before him, the source never quite visible until that last moment when he stood outside the room where Duncan would sleep soundly in the grand wooden bed.

A dagger, a stabbing weapon made for soft targets, lay ahead of him every step of the way, hovering in the dark, its hilt toward him, radiant and shining with a strange unearthly light. A familiar blade, though he couldn't place it at that moment. Jewels ran down the handle to the guard. Blood and gore stained the sharp edge and dripped in gouts and gobs down into the dark below.

He'd woken not long after, but somehow that image would not leave him; the weapon, hilt outstretched, blade stained, seemed to beckon. When he glanced at the disturbed sky, clouds fast scattering across the dark expanse of stars, the constellations seemed to reform before him, their familiar patterns shifting until each resembled a pointed weapon, ready to stab and hack at each other as if the universe were at war with itself, filled with some deadly, malevolent hate.

"Must I do this?" he murmured to himself. "Murder an old man sleeping in his bed? Steal the throne of Scotland like a cutthroat bandit robbing an innocent upon the road?"

From beyond the curtain wall came the long, slow howl of a wolf hunting in the hills, and it seemed a kind of answer. This was the world he was destined to inhabit, the only one. What horror it contained existed before him and would endure long past his transformation to dust. The brief flickering flame of existence was defined, made real by a man's courage and willingness to seize the opportune moment and make the best of it, a best that would be more just, more decent than any Duncan and his ilk might deliver. It was either that or ignominy, defeat, disgrace, and death once Malcolm's skinny fingers tightened their grip upon the crown. And that could happen anytime—tomorrow, even. There was no space for prevarication or delay.

The low, metallic voice of the watch bell boomed from the tower by the gate.

Midnight.

Sleep tight, Duncan, he thought. *For this is a knell that summons you to heaven or to hell.*

Macbeth closed his eyes, and once again, the dagger rose gleaming in his imagination. When he looked again it was there once more, real this time, outstretched on a slender arm that emerged from the gloom.

He realized now why he recognized it, why—there could be no other reason—his feverish mind had invented this image for the blade in that waking dream. The thing was a gift, him to her, not long after their wedding. A lady's knife taken from a dead Viking, who'd doubtless stolen it himself somewhere along the way. Skena's now, and it was her hand that raised it before him.

She came out of the shadows and stood by his side, face hard and resolute, but pale as a specter in the darkness.

"The guards are drugged and sleeping," she whispered. "I sent the means, then crept to Duncan's chamber myself to see them snoring away like pigs." Her eyes flickered toward the moon. "I could have done the deed. I will, if need be…"

His hand went to her cheek. "Go back to the bedroom. Stay there. This is man's work."

"Is that why you linger here alone, muttering to yourself like some loon?" There was a fierceness to her tongue, and on occasion, he deserved it.

"Perhaps," he said. "I've never…"

"What?" she snapped. "If you are to do the deed, you should be able to say it."

"Murder," said Macbeth. The word hung in the air between them like a spell. "I have never murdered a sleeping man before. Let alone a king."

She took his coat with her two small hands and pulled him close. "You must now, Macbeth. We have no choice. Duncan's no fool. In the morning he'll see in your face the doubt that's written there now. And when he does, he will put both of us to the sword as easily as he did Cawdor. Deceit does not suit you, and for that, you have my love. But once the seed of ambition is planted within your heart it shouts its presence from your features as readily as if you spoke the treacherous words yourself. For our sake, husband..."

Beyond the walls the wolf howled again. He thought of the pelt that covered Banquo's shoulders, the cracked jaw above the shining berserker's helmet, the yellow fangs, the last thing many an enemy would see. Life and death were soul mates, walking hand in hand.

The dagger gleamed before him, tight in her white and delicate hand. From the courtyard below came the screech of a barn owl, dropping victorious on its prey, and the squeals of a rabbit or rat as the bird's sharp beak tore into its living flesh.

He grasped the weapon, felt the warmth of the leather hilt and the soft, cold glassy surface of the precious stones set into its length. This was no dream, some fancy flitting through the head of a pensive child. This was his world, as real as real might be.

◈ ◈ ◈

Duncan slept in the farthest reach of the stone fortress of Inverness, a place that seemed dark as a subterranean cave.

Caution led Macbeth to carry nothing more than a single candle as he wound his way through the gloomy corridors. He paced slowly, watching the shadows leap and fall on the black walls.

The king's suite lay on the uppermost floor of the keep, atop a long and gloomy spiral staircase where water dripped perpetually. Macbeth climbed it slowly, one hand holding the meager candle aloft, the other stretched out ahead, fingers splayed. In the tight stone stairwell it seemed he could hear the throbbing echo of his racing heart.

If someone were to enter below him now, he would have nowhere to go, caught with his dagger drawn as he skulked his murderous way to Duncan's chamber. Twice, he paused to listen, sure he had heard movement ahead, but there was nothing. He was alone, with only his own fear as a companion.

Close to the chamber, he paused again, listening, eyes tightly shut. Then, in the silence, he moved lightly up the final stairs, as quickly as he dared, and inched his way onto the stone landing, setting down one soundless foot after the other.

The guards were dimly visible, asleep beneath a single sputtering torch, heavy, unconscious snoring forms on the slabs before Duncan's chamber. He bent down gingerly and removed a cheap field knife—the kind they called a bollock dagger—from each man's belt and tucked them into his own. Evidence would be laid—and with it, blame. After that, Macbeth would see swift justice handed out, before too many awkward questions could be asked.

There was a fainter noise from the cold chamber ahead—the biggest bedroom in the castle, the bleakest and most remote, too, a good walk and half a landing away from the nearest, his own. He listened to the slow, weak wheezing of the old man there, then advanced, Skena's sharp dagger in his right hand, the candle in his left, his mind awhirl with thoughts and fancies.

How many men had he killed over the years? There was no way to count them. He was a warrior, a foot soldier once, now a great general in the field when needed. When war came, death was his job, his duty. But those savage encounters happened in the heat and madness of battle, out in the sharp, unforgiving light of day. Even the slaughter of MacDonwald had occurred without much forethought or preparation. Like every other life he'd taken, that act was filled with personal risk, one equal against the other. His corpse could as easily have lain on the gray slate of that distant castle in Ballachulish as the traitor's. In combat there was a balance between winner and loser, an unspoken pact, a sense that something—the elusive element called chance—might smooth out the most unlikely odds from time to time. It had happened with the mekilwort and Sueno.

Here...

The dim light of the candle revealed a shape before him. Macbeth halted by the bed. The man beneath the heavy winter coverlet coughed in his sleep and turned his silver-haired head from right to left. He was approaching sixty, thinner than a few years ago, perhaps consumed by an interior sickness that might take him in a year, a month, a day, even.

And then...Malcolm. His heir, not by the choice of the thanes, but through nothing more than blood.

The constant, historic struggle for power and supremacy that had come to define the free and valiant nature of Scotland would be swept aside to make way for the progeny of one man's efforts in the bedchamber, with a miller's daughter, rumor had it, not even the queen.

"You argue this for yourself," Macbeth murmured, by way of self-reproach, moving forward to stand close by the coverlet, the dagger now within reach of the wrinkled, whiskery neck beneath him. "You try to make murder a virtue."

I want this for my own ambition, he thought. *For us. Because I will be a better king than he or his foul offspring.*

As quietly as he could, he placed the candleholder on a stand by the pillow. The sound of his movement made Duncan stir. Macbeth shrank back a step, his will failing.

Even if the greater part were true, he told himself, *could there be virtue in the murder of an old, defenseless man asleep in the dark in his host's castle? What might be righteous slaughter on the battlefield was cowardly assassination off it. Yet if one man's death, however heinous, brought peace and fortitude to an entire nation…?*

He felt lost, confused, even frightened, standing there, blade in hand, close over the shape beneath the sheets.

The body before him shifted, roused from slumber.

Macbeth glanced back to the door and the drugged guards. There was still time to flee.

Then a voice—familiar, tetchy, magisterial—barked, "Who in God's name is this? Who dares disturb the king?"

◈ ◈ ◈

The choice of Duncan's bedroom was no accident. Set alone, at the summit of the keep, reachable only by that single set of stone stairs, it was a prison of a kind, easily controlled, simple to monitor.

Now she waited one floor below, in an antechamber at the foot of the staircase, along the corridor that led to her own quarters. She'd not been there since watching Ewan leave to take the drugged wine to the guards.

The castle was quiet, swamped by the inky night. She'd walked its many floors in subtle silence, candle in hand. Earlier there had been feeble wanderers, most of them drunk, looking for a place to sleep for the night or to find some dancing girl still willing for a partner, but they were gone now. None would stir until the alarm was raised. The gloom seemed so intense she wondered if they knew who or what they'd partnered in the dark.

Above her, the owl in the roof shrieked and squealed once more. Small sounds of its feasting drifted down from the eaves.

Macbeth is about his business. Let the drugged guards not wake and disturb him, she prayed. *Let this dread business be done with.*

There'd been no sign of Ewan in the kitchen when she'd visited on one last circuit of the castle before hiding in the antechamber. This was curious. He was in the habit of sleeping on blankets near the fire.

No matter. He was a small man in the making, as he himself had made clear. What business the boy had found in Inverness this raw night was his and his alone.

She had walked the length of the kitchen, listening to the castle dogs outside feasting on the leftovers cast onto the garbage heap. It was lit by nothing more than the embers of the cook's fire. The dying orange from beneath the ashes reflected in the silver jugs and pans on hooks against the wall and the line of implements—knives and cleavers and saws—that lay ranged along the bowed oak lintel that ran ten feet or more from side to side. It was a place of deep shadows and stank of rich meat and animal blood. Shivering, she'd unlocked the door to the cellar, checked in there for intruders, found none, and out of fear herself, uncorked a bottle of the bold French wine they'd bought in honor of Duncan's visit—and poisoned for his guards.

Not a drop had passed her lips that night. But then…

With trembling fingers, she swilled it from the neck, like a hovel drunk from down the port, thinking all the while of the two unconscious guards above her, waiting on their deaths.

What makes you drunk makes me bold, she thought. *What quenches your life gives mine fresh fire and sets the world ablaze.*

The owl shrieked again. There would be no bell until daylight, no means, crouched hidden in this bare corner of the castle, to measure the time.

Yet Macbeth was gone too long. She knew it, felt it, as cold in her bones as the night.

◈ ◈ ◈

The king glared at him in the faint, smoky light, his teeth yellow, set in a baffled snarl. The jeweled dagger slipped from Macbeth's fingers and fell rattling to the floor—through fear or cunning, he'd no idea.

"I didn't know you were awake, sire," he mumbled.

"Macbeth?"

"My lord."

"I wasn't," Duncan replied, sitting up in bed, shaking himself. A slender shaft of moonlight from an opening in the wall caught his face, the only illumination in the room save for Macbeth's candle. "Not till you barged bumbling in here. Is there trouble? Where are the guards? I…"

He looked befuddled for a moment, no monarch, just an old man trying to find his reason.

"I remember a pretty child from the west," Duncan said, not looking at him. "A fetching young thing. Do not let her leave before me. I may take the girl for myself." Then, shaking his gray locks, "Age. God, I hate it. What *is* this?"

"I was concerned," Macbeth said in a quiet, humble voice. "I wished to make sure you were safe."

"I'm in the castle of a man I trust. If I'm not safe here…" A sly look crossed Duncan's gaunt features. "Unless there's something I don't know."

Macbeth stood there, saying nothing, holding out his hands, fingers spread, palms open.

"Why do that?" the king asked.

"A gesture. Nothing more."

"A gesture of what?"

"Of…friendship, sire."

Duncan sighed and said, "You have a guileless, open face, Macbeth, incapable of pretense. More's the pity for you. A king must learn to read his subjects. Sometimes I think it the most important talent we possess." He shrugged and reached beneath the pillow. "It failed me with Cawdor, I'm ashamed to say. Yet you rescued me from his clutches. And here you are…"

He smiled and withdrew from beneath the bolster a long and slender blade.

"With mischief written across your face in letters so bright and bold they might have been drawn by one of those clever English monks from Lindisfarne."

He held the knife before him, its steel as cold and hard as his eyes.

"Glamis and Cawdor. Was I not generous enough?"

"Sire, sire…you make no sense."

"A man who thought he might be gifted the throne himself enters my bedroom at midnight, stands trembling by my sheets. How much sense do I need?"

"You mistake me..."

The knife stabbed once toward him.

"Quiet, fool! I have no wish to hear. The torturers can drag it out of you, and then I'll send you to the ax."

Macbeth shuffled backward.

"Do not move, man," Duncan barked. "Guards! Guards!"

The king's voice echoed round the empty chamber.

"I've faced off better enemies than you," he spat. "I've—"

Macbeth reached out and pinched the candle flame between finger and thumb. The glow of light around them disappeared, leaving only the faint shaft of silver from the sky, which fell on one of them alone—Duncan. The king let loose a frightened, high-pitched shriek. Macbeth took one step forward through the darkness that hid him, snatching through the air with his right hand. His huge fist closed round Duncan's skinny hand. The dagger shook in the king's grip. Macbeth squeezed hard, a terrifying grip, and felt no great pleasure when he heard the cracking of bones and the pained, faint sigh of a soft, agonized scream rise from the throat of the king of Scotland.

"You do not own the nation," Macbeth said, "to pass on to your bastards as if we were some trophy."

The king's knife fell upon the sheets. Macbeth punched the old man hard in the face, then as he fell back moaning, seized the weapon and stabbed down once, deep beneath the bed shirt, into the scrawny breast below him. The knife stuck there, trapped between his ribs, and Duncan's skinny fingers fell to the hilt, struggling to drag the blade from his flesh.

His lips opened and closed like those of a beached and dying fish. A thin and fragile voice murmured once again, "Was...I...ungenerous?"

Macbeth said nothing.

He seized him by the gown, seized the blade from his bony chest, stabbed upward again, boldly, desperately, and finally held the man to him as he thrust the point as far beyond the ribs as he could.

This position—an embrace, almost—he held for one long, still moment, until he thought he heard a grim rattle work its way from the mouth that fell warm and moist against his neck. Then silence. Macbeth let go and allowed the bloody mess in his arms to fall back on the sheets.

There was a moment when he felt his own heart stop, as if its witness of this scene removed from it the will to beat again. Never had he seen so mournful a sight, an old man stabbed savagely in his bed at the hands of one he thought a loyal servant.

I did this, he told himself. *I had no choice.*

He strode to the door, checked that the guards slumbered on, returned with the brand, lit the candle by the bed, looked at his handiwork: Duncan stiff and still, chest welling blood, no sign of movement.

A bridge crossed, a moment passed.

He waited, thinking of what might happen after. The questions, the process, the sly and curious interrogations that would follow.

But first, there would be alarums.

They must talk and plan.

He stumbled down the stone steps, bloodied, mind racing, the brand flickering in the drafty gloom. Her hand reached for him at the foot of the staircase, and the two of them hid, whispering in the antechamber, eyes bright and fearful in the yellow cast of the torch.

"It's done," he said. "Did you hear nothing?"

"From here…only the owls and my own heart. You're sure he's…?"

"I told you. It's done," he repeated. "You heard *nothing*?"

"No."

He loathed the way she stared at him, as if something of his person disgusted her, and not just the blood and the violence that must have stood upon him.

"Where are the sons?" he asked.

"Malcolm and Donalbain remain on the floor below. No one's near except us. We may choose when we raise the alarm. A little while yet…"

"Look at me!" He raised his red and sticky hands. "A sorry sight…"

"Take hold of yourself. There's no murder without blood. Macb—"

"I heard a voice inside my head cry, 'Sleep no more! Macbeth murders sleep.' I heard…"

She came closer, touched him, her eyes still glazed, and said, "Be strong. Get water and wash this blood from your hands. We must master these next moments and make sure the blame falls on the guards."

He barely listened. "It said, 'Glamis has murdered sleep, and therefore Cawdor shall sleep no more. Macbeth shall sleep no more.' We—"

"Husband," she cried desperately. "Don't let your mind turn on these waking dreams. Be wise…"

He raised his hands. One weapon there, an ornate, fancy blade. The two guards' daggers still stood clean in his belt, not a drop of blood upon them.

She took a step back and stared at him. "Whose knife is that?" she demanded.

He sighed. "The king's. He woke and knew my purpose."

Her hands flew to her mouth. "You took my dagger," she said. "Where is it?"

Macbeth groaned. "By the bed. It fell. Duncan spoke to me. He *spoke.* And did not die easily. I'm not made for this foul subterfuge."

She took the king's blade from him and looked up at his face. "You must go back. Smear the guard's weapons with the king's blood and leave them there. Get my own blade from that chamber. Or we're undone…"

"No," he murmured, shaking his head with a wild violence. "I'll not enter that room again. The voice I heard… the *voice…*"

"Was your imagination! The dead are dead. They speak to no one."

He trembled.

Skena took the bollock daggers from his belt. "I'll do it, then," she said. "Wait for me here."

"I heard…" he whispered.

"Macbeth!"

He looked at her, wondering. Was this the same wife now? The same world?

And the selfsame thought ran through her head, too, at that moment.

"Our lives are suspended here on matters as flimsy as a spider's thread," she told him. "Wait on me. We'll see this through. They'll blame Malcolm…"

His eyes flashed wide with trepidation. "For God's sake, why? A son, however much he covets the throne he's promised—"

"They'll blame the son!"

The force and conviction stilled him.

From outside came another noise this time. Real and urgent. A loud, persistent knocking at the castle gate.

"That's a man, not a ghost," she hissed at him. "Macbeth. Dispose of Duncan's blade securely. And then you wait on me."

◈ ◈ ◈

Like a guilty child, she climbed the steps and crept past the slumbering guards, candle in hand, its flame a tiny beacon in the vast sea of night ahead, steeling herself to enter the cold chamber, the men's clean weapons in her belt.

It was as Macbeth had said. Her own jeweled blade lay on the stones by the bed. Duncan's left arm hung limply by it, as if he had struggled to reach the thing and failed.

"Miserable creature," she whispered as she approached, and wondered why. Then some dim memory returned from childhood. It was the time the English had raided from across the border, seized Glamis briefly, murdered all they could. She'd hidden with her mother in a secret cellar, stayed there for days on end, waiting, praying for relief. It came in the form of a bloody battle that happened over their heads. The marauders were dispatched. The men from the Highlands proved victorious. When she was released, she found her own father there among the dead. A mature man, not as elderly as Duncan, but white-haired, too, with a kindly face, that of a landlord, not a warrior.

He fought among the fiercest clan lords and died bloodily, not knowing whether his wife and children lived or not.

A better man than this thing had ever been, more deserving of a noble life.

"You are not my father," she murmured, looking at the torn, still figure on the bed. "You would vanish in his shadow. You shall not haunt my dreams or those of my beloved."

Something, the memories, the strong wine from the cellar, stirred inside her. She picked up her own clean dagger and placed it in her belt. Then she placed the candle by the bed and both her hands went to the cheaper blades Macbeth had taken from the men at the door.

She leaned over Duncan, whispering in his gray and whiskery ear, "You hear me, man? You are nothing now and were nothing before..."

His eyelids opened. The icy eyes, full of hatred and violence, came alive and glowered at her. Duncan's long, bony fingers rose and clawed at her throat, the nails biting deep into her flesh. Words emerged, unintelligible, with blood and saliva from between his purple lips.

Duncan's grip held her so tightly it seemed impossible, unnatural, beyond all sense. She screeched and screamed and tried to tear his clawlike fingers from her. Then the daggers in her hand found life, stabbed at him, his neck and face, his scrawny arm.

More curses, half heard and foul, spewed with the blood and bile from his throat. The silver knives rose and fell, stabbing, slashing. With each wound, he cried and shrieked.

Then, at last, she tore his talons free and fell back, staggering, crying, panting.

Dead, she thought. *He must be dead.*

There were men at the distant gate, noises outside. The castle was waking.

She stumbled back to the bed, stared into his keen eyes, knew he breathed still, like some immortal monster. The dagger in her right hand she plunged deep into the hollow of his wrinkled neck, ripped sinews there and flesh, and watched his face contort with each agonizing turn.

"Live if you wish," she said. "Like a damned thing from hell. You shall not speak!"

Duncan didn't move, though, and nor for a moment could she. The man was dead, his throat a bloody, gaping gash. And she was now bound more closely with Macbeth in the deed.

She stumbled out the door, flinging the bloody daggers at the guards.

A hand caught on her ankle, kept her, held her tight. She fell against the wall and cried with pain.

"What game is this, woman?" asked a low, coarse voice from behind, the intonation slurred and hazy. "Are we seeking company?"

She turned and looked. To her horror, the other was waking, too. The first, the closest, let his hand fall from her ankle and clutched instead at her dress.

The dagger in his lap clattered noisily to the floor.

"I smell blood here," mouthed the other. "I smell—"

"The king," the second cut in, and dragged himself upright, his hands hard on her gown.

The candle still remained within. She found her gaze drawn back to that dread room. Duncan lay there cruelly torn upon the gory sheets.

"The king," the man cried. "The king!"

Then turned and gripped her by the throat.

◈ ◈ ◈

There was a muffled thud, then another. It came from the gatehouse, and even in his drunken state Fergus knew what it was. Someone was at the door.

"At this time?" he sputtered. "As if I've nothing better to do. I should be asleep!" He blundered down the steps, conscious that the knocking on the door had become a steady, rhythmic banging. In the thirty years he'd served at Inverness he'd come to know every stone beneath his feet, but in a night as dark as this he still trailed one hand against the wall as he emerged into the courtyard. Somewhere an owl hooted. It had been squawking off and on all night. The banging at the gate was getting louder.

"Hold your horses," Fergus bellowed, fumbling at his belt for the keys. The cobbled courtyard was slick with ice.

There were voices out there with the knocking, irritable, curse-laden mutterings about what would happen to him if he didn't get the door open quickly. Fergus slowed down deliberately. See how they enjoyed being outside in a Highland winter.

He opened the little wooden window in the gate and asked, very sweetly, if they would mind telling him who in the devil's name they were, waking him at this hour.

"Envoys to the king!" snarled one of them. "Open the damned door."

"Name?" said Fergus. "You could be rebel…scum… assassins, for all I know."

This was a lie. Fergus would know that stringy beard and the scar down his cheek anywhere.

"It's Lennox, man!" he said. "You know me. Open the—"

Fergus whistled softly, "Can't see you properly. You'll have to wait till sunup."

"What?" roared Lennox. "I've been riding all night! It's freezing and I have orders to wake the king."

"Lennox?" said Fergus. "He's here already. Been here all night. You'll have to do better than that."

"It's me, man," shouted Lennox, his face pink. "Look at me! When I get hold of you…"

"You'll do what?" asked the porter, his face up against the little wooden window. "Think carefully. It's hours before dawn and likely to get colder yet."

There was a muffled curse and then silence. Fergus waited.

"I don't have much with me," said Lennox, with a sigh.

"Not a problem," said Fergus, pushing his hand through the window. "I wouldn't deprive a man of what he cannot afford."

More grumblings, then he felt the slap of a small purse in his hand. He pulled it back, sifted through the coins inside, took half, and returned the rest. He turned the key, threw the latch, and pushed the gate open wide.

"Enter, Lennox," he said. "Welcome to Hell."

The man came in and uttered several low curses. "This is a cheerless hole," he grumbled. "Why Macbeth lets a cur like you insult his guests…"

"I told you it was Hell," the porter said. "And I but one of the master's humble demons."

From the keep above came a shrill and chilling sound. It was a woman screaming, a high, sharp note like the shriek of an owl. "Murder," she cried. "Murder!"

Lennox drew out his sword and raced for the steps ahead.

◈ ◈ ◈

There was no hesitation on Macbeth's part. Whatever grim forebodings Duncan's chamber held they were nothing next to his fears for his wife. Two steps at a time he took the stone stairs back to that place of slaughter, sword in right hand, burning brand in left, blade sparking off the stone walls as he ran.

There was more light there than he recalled. A second torch was lit on the wall. He kept back in shadow for a moment, breathless, panting, blind with dread.

"Who's that?" yelled one of the soldiers, weapon bright and threatening, pointed his way.

Skena struggled in the second one's arms, eyes wide with fright.

"This bitch has slain him," the second guard yelled.

"Not so! Not so!" she cried, wrestling beneath his arm.

"Traitorous whore!" said the first, and slapped her with his hand.

Full of rage and panic, Macbeth leapt forward, skewered the first with one single upward thrust, then slashed at the head of the second. It was a high and forceful blow that crashed into his skull and sent him screaming back against the stones.

Skena threw herself free and fell shrieking to the floor.

Noises below. Footsteps getting closer, shouts and alarums, and in her eyes the clear presentiment of terror.

Think.

Both guards still lived and struggled, wheezing, cursing. He leapt upon the first and then the second, flailing, slashing, cursing.

There came a rush of bodies from behind, and still Macbeth wrestled with the guards, roaring, his eyes streaming.

Then arms gripped him, strong and forceful and resolute, and he loosed the bloodied blade and let it fall upon the floor.

"Macbeth?" said a deep, familiar voice.

Banquo, his face a mask of confusion and horror.

Skena sat in a pool of yellow light, distraught on the cold black stones, next to the baggage of the guards and their two slashed corpses, sobbing, casting her eyes around her, glancing toward the chamber beyond.

They were all assembling now, the thanes and their men. Lennox, Ross, and Angus. None of the king's family, though.

"I heard the saddest sound," Skena cried from the floor. "A child, I thought, in distress. Not wishing to wake my lord, I came here and found…" Her hands went to her mouth as she looked into the chamber and the shape upon the sheets there, dimly lit. "These two monsters, bloody handed, and a third who ran away. My lords…"

Her shoulders shook, her breast heaved.

"They have murdered Duncan and would have slain me, too, had not Macbeth fought them. Oh…" The tears were real and glistening on her cheeks. "If only…"

Macbeth bent down, held out his hand, and helped her to her feet. She clung to him like a lost child.

"Their daggers are bloody," said Ross, squatting by the bodies on the floor.

"A third?" Lennox demanded. "Where is he?"

"He ran, sir," Skena replied. "I do not know where." She breathed, then added, "He dropped something. I heard…"

They followed the direction of her gaze and scanned the ground. Close by the guards' baggage, an object glittered in the gloom.

Lennox picked it up and raised the thing aloft.

An ornate, leaf-bladed dagger. An unusual weapon, expensive and exotic.

Macbeth held her, unwilling to cross the threshold of the chamber. "This shame," he murmured, "that he should die inside my walls…It will never leave me. Nor sleep come easily again."

The rest had walked into the chamber and stood around Duncan's bed, some crossing themselves, others with murder in their own eyes.

Only Banquo did not go with them. He eyed Macbeth, the bloody corpses, the bollock daggers stained with gore.

"It's a shame you killed them," the big man said.

"My rage," Macbeth replied. "They slew the king."

Skena clung to him more tightly.

"These villains would have killed my own dear wife had I not intervened." He glared at Banquo. "Would you have done otherwise?" Macbeth demanded.

There was no answer. Banquo seemed distracted. He ran his feet across the cobbles, damp with blood and the spilled remains of a pewter flask beside the door.

Wine from the smell. With dark spots inside, like berries.

◈ ◈ ◈

Before long the chamber was full of muttering thanes. Even the slain king's silent, dark-eyed sons. Lennox put his head in his hands, suddenly weary beyond words. It was still dark, but the castle was awake. After the panic and horror of the discovery of Duncan's body and the bloody events that had followed it, an uncanny stillness had descended on the place. Servants crept up to the room with pails of water, though no one had been able to decide who should wash the king's body.

Malcolm had turned away from his father's corpse with revulsion, and Donalbain, the younger of the two, had vomited. They had stood there in silence, their faces subdued, but unreadable, and Malcolm could not stop his gaze, straying from his dead father to the crown, which had rolled as if forgotten into the corner of the room.

"This," said MacDuff, "is, I think, yours."

He handed Malcolm the strange, leaf-bladed dagger. The young prince's hand flashed first to the empty scabbard at his belt, and then a series of sly, worried thoughts flashed through his face.

"It is your weapon?" MacDuff persisted.

"The thing was stolen from my room. I meant to raise this with Macbeth. If a man cannot sleep safely beneath the roof of his host…"

The thoughtless response, too quick to be any kind of denial or accusation, hung in the air.

"Where did you find it?" Malcolm asked.

"With the guards," Lennox cut in, watching the prince's face for signs of guilt or fear. Grief seemed unlikely. "The lady said there was a third man…"

Macbeth kept silent. *Perhaps wondering about his wife,* Lennox thought. One of her household had led her from the room, weeping, shaking. A good woman, he felt, cruelly treated by the murderers of the king and lucky to escape with her life.

Malcolm's face was set like stone. "The dagger was stolen from me," he insisted and took the clean, slim knife from MacDuff's fingers.

Donalbain stared at him, then turned on the assembled thanes.

"You're saying this was us?" he demanded, his voice high and childish. "Why? Our own father?"

"No one is saying anything," said Macbeth.

"Just returning your brother's property," added MacDuff.

"Look among yourselves!" Donalbain screeched. "One of you killed our father and placed this knife here to lay the blame on us!"

"Brother…" began Malcolm cautiously.

"No!" exclaimed Donalbain. "You see their game? What they've done? You must punish them, brother. You're the king now. The power is yours."

It was a ridiculous, presumptuous challenge. The intervention of a young fool. This was no time for Malcolm to test his power and all knew it except the impetuous Donalbain. Malcolm stood his ground, defiant, a slim, arrogant figure, with sufficient self-control to keep his temper. But the fury was there and they all felt it. He wanted no talk of crowns and rule. That only made him look more guilty. *Still,* Lennox thought, *a time would come, within hours.* There were troops below, with loyalties to buy, through promises, favors, and gold.

"He named you Cumberland!" Donalbain persisted, tugging at his brother's elbow. "Take up the crown and arraign these traitors."

Two young and inexperienced princes, one scarcely more than a boy. A room full of warriors pressed around them. No one drew, but Macbeth felt them bracing for combat.

"We will discuss this matter later," Malcolm said finally. "I am too grieved to speak of it now. We will retire to our rooms. At first light we will conduct a service for our king and father in the chapel, then send him for a monarch's burial on Iona, as is his right. After the service..." His eyes turned on his brother. "Then we'll talk of crowns and justice."

No one spoke.

The pair left in silence, though the younger cast a last look at his dead father as he strode out.

The warriors in the room breathed as the two departed. The air was heavy with unasked questions.

"He didn't deny it was his dagger," Menteith muttered.

"How could he?" asked Banquo, but his voice was gruff and thoughtful, not accusing.

"Could two sons, even ones such as these...?" began Ross. "Why? Duncan was an elderly man. He couldn't live forever. And then Malcolm would ascend the throne rightfully."

"Had we allowed it," said MacDuff, his voice barely above a whisper. "Duncan may have lived for many years. His son may be prince of Cumberland now. Who knows how long the father would have kept him in that title? He may have wanted a dynasty, but God knows he barely liked the boy..."

"That's enough," Macbeth broke in. "We will not discuss this in the presence of our dead sovereign."

"There's a body to be dealt with, not that Malcolm seemed much interested," Banquo said. "Duncan's no foot soldier. We can't just dig a hole and throw him in."

Macbeth's face creased in pain as he looked at them all in turn. "Blame me for this man's death," he said. "He came here as a guest and was cruelly slaughtered beneath my eaves."

"The man who stabbed him bears the blame!" Lennox cried. "Not you, sir. You are a true and loyal servant."

"Skena and I will wash the king ourselves. Duncan died in our keeping. It's only fitting."

"I can help," Banquo offered.

"No," said Macbeth abruptly. "Thank you," he added, managing a half smile. "Take those two dead scum outside the door. Drag them down to the courtyard and have the servants dispose of them as the garbage they are. Find Skena, and if she's well enough, ask her to come to me."

Banquo gave Macbeth a long, searching look, seized one of the slaughtered guards by his ankle, then dragged him out of the room and down the stone steps. Lennox followed with the other, the two hauling the bloody bodies down the black stone steps like sacks of grain.

Outside, dawn was breaking over the Moray Firth. A bright winter sun heralded the day. No clouds, no snow, no rain. A brilliant blue sky would shine on Duncan as he made his final journey to the holy isle in the west where Scottish monarchs rested after death.

They laid the corpses of the guards next to each other on the cobbles. A woman servant began sobbing and wailing over one of them. Ross barked at her, lecturing her, saying he was a traitor not worth the tears of any loyal subject. She screamed in horror at this charge.

"We found the bloody dagger in his hand!" Ross shrieked at her.

The woman screamed. He struck her hard with the back of his hand, and then she scurried away, crying loudly.

Overhead, the ravens wheeled, and the thanes watched them in silence.

Banquo nodded at the bodies. "Deal with these for me. I will find Lady Macbeth."

◈ ◈ ◈

As Banquo reentered the keep, there was wailing from upstairs. It was the shriek of a woman, loud and anguished. There was something fresh and tragic about the sound, a note to it he found disconcerting. No one cried like this for a king, none except his wife, and she was in distant Dunkeld.

He took the steps quickly, aiming for the source, and found himself entering the quarters of Macbeth himself. The bedroom was crammed with red-faced, bawling women, young and old, the entire castle household as far as he could make out, cooks and maids in plain, coarse clothing, faces racked with despair.

"What is this?" he demanded, pushing through.

One, an elderly woman in a white, floured hat, turned and glared at him as if he had no place here. Still, Banquo pushed on, and finally, he saw.

At the foot of the bed, Skena Macbeth sat on the stone floor, hunched and miserable next to the prostrate body of a child. A young boy, seven or eight, no more. Blond hair tumbled around his narrow shoulders, face turned to the window, pale and still. His slate eyes were open and filled with fear and pain. From his open mouth trickled a line of reddish vomit, falling to the floor.

Banquo walked forward and pressed his foot through the puddle of sick. A pewter flask lay upturned close to the dead child's right hand. The last dregs of its contents—wine, no doubt of that from the smell—had trickled beneath the bed. It was full of what looked like crushed fruit and he had no doubt about the kind.

"Skena?" he said.

She clasped the boy's fingers between her hands, her eyes lost in the most abject sorrow. His heart went out to the woman. This was more than normal grief, he thought, and then, with bitter self-recrimination, remembered the child, another boy, whose loss had, gossip said, unhinged Macbeth's wife for weeks after.

"I need to know what happened," Banquo began. "I need—"

"Are you stupid, man?" screeched the woman in the cook's hat. "Does your high position make you blind? The same devil that murdered the king also wished to kill our lord here, and his lady. Put poison in their wine and left it by their bed."

"A knife and poison rarely mix," he murmured, thinking. Why slaughter Duncan with such cruel force and seek to kill another by subterfuge?

"Ewan asked for food and drink from the banquet," Skena said in a soft, high voice that stilled his words. She was speaking to herself, he thought, so focused were her face and manner. "I said…I said…"

"What?" he asked.

Her eyes fell on him, wild and restless. She swept the tears and the damp hair from her shining face.

"I told him later. *Later.*" Her hands kneaded his dead fingers. "And forgot an instant after. He was a kitchen boy." She glared at Banquo. "Not a thane. If this was meant for us, I wish I'd come here earlier and supped it. I wish I might breathe life back into his sweet, small body…Oh, Ewan."

"Do not blame yourself, lady!" cried the cook.

They hurried round her, clucking, crying, holding shoulders, weeping for the child. Trying, with little luck, to pry her fingers from him.

No place for a man, he thought. *No time for questions.*

And there were plenty.

"I leave you with your sadness, ladies," he said. "The death of a child, whatever his station, is a crime against us all."

Skena Macbeth's eyes flared. He took a step back, alarmed at what he saw.

"There are dead bairns the length and breadth of this land!" Macbeth's wife bellowed. "Murdered by the Norse and English. Slain in the battles you and your like wage as if they were games."

"War is war," he said half meekly. "Duncan did not die in battle. Nor did this boy. Your lamentations do your credit, but there's another worthy of it, too. Duncan lies below. Macbeth bids you meet him with the body. This is your castle. The king—"

Her head rose suddenly; her hands released the child. Two women swiftly, gently, worked their way toward her and slid him from her grasp.

"The king?" she asked sharply. "What king? Of whom do you speak, sir?"

"Of Duncan," he replied, shaking his head in confusion. "Who else? Of…"

A moment passed between them. A look rose in her eyes. He wondered what he saw there. Madness? Bewilderment? Even the faintest presentiment of guilt?

"Your lord requires your company," he repeated. "I'm sorry for the child, but there are matters here that go beyond a single life." Banquo paused. "Beyond that even of a king, perhaps."

She got up from the floor, wiped her face with the long sleeve of her gown, stared at him. Banquo had thought he knew Skena Macbeth. Now he was not so sure.

"I know my duty, lord," she said. "Tell my husband I shall be there presently, when I have washed away these tears, for Duncan and this child."

"I'll do that," he murmured, and was glad to leave the room.

◈ ◈ ◈

One hour later, the two began to wash Duncan's torn and bloody corpse in the chamber where he died. The water was holy, blessed by the priest, ladled from the leather pail used to fill the font.

Birth to death, beginning to end.

Skena wept throughout, not for the man whose body they now tended, but the boy. As she sponged away the blood from the old king's pale flesh, her tears fell on his skin and she wiped them away with her hair. Macbeth said nothing, his eyes wide as he watched her stroking Duncan's stiff cadaver, wider still when she began to hum the plaintive tune of a familiar lullaby.

He tore away the bloodstained sheets that had crusted to the skin below, then sent them to be burned. She brushed the old man's locks as if she thought him someone else. When they were done, she sat there, looking at the body with her head tipped slightly on one side, her thoughts strange and unreadable to him. Only when the dawn bell chimed did she come back to herself, starting and staring at the waxen corpse with sudden horror. She stared at her hands, which were stained with blood, and began furiously washing and rewashing them, scrubbing at her nails, smelling her fingers, and calling for more water, hotter each time. The last was so scalding he was afraid she would burn herself. But she held her hands in the steaming water, teeth set, eyes locked with pain, and when she took them out, they were a bright and painful pink almost to the elbows.

When the sun was higher, they wrapped the white and scrawny carcass in a winding sheet. Duncan was so light of frame that Macbeth managed to take him down the steps slowly, thrown over his shoulder, as if the dead king were an infant being carried gently to bed. The servants watched teary-eyed, the thanes hung their heads and melted into the corners as he passed, and all the while the bells continued their mournful chime. Finally, they laid the frail, torn corpse on a table in front of the altar of the tiny chapel and anointed his neck and face with unguents that smelled of spice and rose petals.

She stared at the pale flesh and whispered, "I need more water. I must wash my boy."

It was a flat, mundane comment, the kind a woman might utter at her work.

He checked they were alone, then came to her and took her arms. "As you see fit," he said. "The child was not your fault, Skena. Do not crucify yourself..."

"Not my fault! *Not my fault!*"

His hand was on her mouth. There was a bleak set to his face. "Fetch us both an ocean, then," he said in a breathy, faint voice. "Fetch two. This is our joint endeavor, but we've embarked upon it, hand in bloody hand. We shall not fail each other now. Oh, love..."

Eyes streaming, lovely face racked with sorrow, she looked just as she had when their own child died, still and cold in her loving arms.

"Do not do this to yourself," he whispered, holding her close in his arms.

"We sought to rid the world of a fiend," she murmured. "Not put two more in his place." She pulled away from him.

Macbeth gazed into her gleaming eyes. "Listen to me, wife. What we did, we did for good reason."

"Ewan..."

"Was a sorry victim of these cruel times! His death shall be a reminder that we are sinners, too."

She pushed away from him and cried, "You think I need reminding...?"

"We both do, Skena. And if we escape this perilous corner, let it make me a wiser king and you a more virtuous queen. If this nation knows justice alongside its strength, then none would blame us, even if they knew..."

Her bloody hand went to her mouth. "Oh, husband. I have turned a gentle soul into a murderer..."

He gazed at her and said, "And I've served you likewise. So we are equal. You my bulwark, I yours." Macbeth placed his hands tenderly on her shoulders. "Nor would I have it any other way."

She looked him in the face. The tears had ended. Some sanity had returned. "The temperament in this place," she said in a low and worried voice, "seems to me as uncertain as the quiet before the storm."

He laughed a little at that.

"Aye, love. What do you expect? Think of our boldness. We've slain an avaricious tyrant. And now our fingers touch his vacant throne. This is not an idle moment in a drab hole like Inverness."

She reached out and stroked his cheek. "Then we play out this dumb show, husband. We act the grieving mourners until others see our sorrow and piety and let it fire a righteous anger of their own."

The dreamy sorrow came upon her in an instant.

"And I shall bury Ewan, after this villain's bones are gone from here for good."

"The sisters promised me—" he began.

"The sisters aren't here. Nor do they bear weapons or ambition."

Whole again, her grief confined, she held Duncan's pale, cold hand up to him as if in greeting. The corpse was turning stiff. Time passed, always.

"Let us not be strange to one another," she said. "I need your—"

The door opened. She let go of the bony fingers in her grip. The bishop entered. His eyebrows rose. Perhaps he'd heard something. The dead were meant to be buried, not argued over.

Without another word, others followed behind him, bringing the ceremonial instruments of regal death, pennants and priests, choristers and bawling women. Macbeth, Banquo, MacDuff, and Lennox lifted the king onto the massive leather shield of a slain Norse warrior and replaced the body on the trestle before the altar. The chapel soon filled with standing warriors. The mood Macbeth recognized. It was as tense as the grim moment before the start of battle.

Then the man with the crook and the cross began to sing in Latin, swinging the boat of incense as he chanted, filling the tiny, bleak room with the foreign fragrance of worship.

And yet, Macbeth thought as they listened to the holy, unintelligible words, *I smell him still.*

The sons were absent. All eyes now were on one man, the strongest, fiercest warrior recently in the field.

Midway through the interminable rites, Ross came running in, sword in hand, fury in his face.

"Gone! Gone! Malcolm and Donalbain!" he shouted, his voice shocking in the chapel stillness. "They've taken to horse and fled! The bastards!"

An angry murmur rose and changed into a bellowed tumult.

MacDuff, his face alive with fury, was the first to reach the altar. In front of the body on the shield, he raised his sword and bellowed like a charging beast. The bishop stood there frightened, lost for words.

From God to vengeance in short order. This was the field now, a place Macbeth could call his own.

He walked before them and stood in front of the roaring crowd, his hands high till they all fell into a murmuring silence. None called to give pursuit and they knew why. The game was on the table, and Scotland itself would be the prize.

"The king had need of better sons," Macbeth declared. "Let it not be said he deserved better thanes, too. With decorum and graciousness, I beg you, pay your due respects. Afterward, there are matters to be decided. But first, let us treat with our noble dead."

A fleeting sense of shame came over them. He beckoned to the bishop to go on. Haltingly, the interminable service continued, then broke around midday for food. As darkness began to fall, the monks and nuns from monasteries and convents all around gathered to make up the party that would bear Duncan's body across to the west and Iona, along the Great Glen, past Loch Ness and Ben Nevis and the place where the sisters had ambushed him and Banquo, setting in train the deed that now, he knew, would come to shape his life.

◈ ◈ ◈

Skena absented herself most of the day, dealing with the weeping women of the kitchen and the funeral of the child. The thanes gathered separately, whispering in small groups. Macbeth watched from his window as Fergus and Cullen quietly spread gold and silver among his troops to keep them loyal and alert, and more among those he knew less well, men whose allegiance was unsure. There was a council here, of a kind. Enough lords to decide the crown, if necessary.

No firm word came of Malcolm and Donalbain, nor did Macbeth dispatch riders to follow their trail. They were two weak and hated princes, gone forever. The line of Duncan was at an end, whatever followed next.

As he watched, a tall, strong figure crossed the courtyard, hand on beard, lost in thought, vast arm around the slender shoulders of his son, Fleance.

Banquo…

"Tragic in the present, yet glorious in the future. You shall beget kings, though never be one yourself."

The sisters' words were burned upon his memory. Those in particular. It seemed ridiculous that a line of Scottish kings might flourish from that slender, innocuous child, Banquo's only son.

Perhaps, he thought, *they joked. Or failed to read the runes they cast.*

As a pale, wan sun set behind the mountains, Duncan's bier, wrapped in long white shrouds, began its final journey, heralded by the trumpets of his court.

No thanes left Inverness; not a soldier quit the castle. Every one of Macbeth's men stood quiet and ready for the fight.

Then, an hour after the royal funeral party had departed, there was a knock at the door.

Macbeth checked his sword, rubbed his reddened eyes, and bid them enter. MacDuff, Banquo, and Lennox, all armed, stood there grim-faced.

"You have food enough to keep your guests another night, sir?" MacDuff asked immediately.

"That I have. All men deserve a wake—kings more than most."

"Duncan's dead and gone," Lennox said, and spat into the fire. "Would that he'd fathered better sons—"

"I doubt he'd argue with that," MacDuff cut in. He looked across the room. "Though a man passes down something of himself in his offspring. So perhaps he should bear the blame. No matter. This hiatus is dangerous and must be brought to a swift close. We need another king. A better one. What power and unity this nation possesses at this moment it owes to you, Macbeth. You brought Duncan a traitor's head on a pike and killed the man yourself. You bested that marauding Viking Sueno, and we'll all be filling our treasuries with his ransom in the years to come."

He held out his mailed hand.

"I would like to say we'd talked this over, long and hard. But truth be known, there wasn't much to discuss. The crown of Scotland fits one head above all others at this moment.

Meet us at Scone a month hence. Then we'll crown you with all due pomp and glory, and swear our true allegiance for all the time we have."

Macbeth felt dizzy, lost for words. This went on too long.

"Say something, man," Lennox broke in, laughing. "We never confirmed Malcolm as the heir. Perhaps that was why he killed his father, after all. This cannot come as a surprise, sir."

"Surprise? Surprise!" Macbeth cried, suddenly furious. "You think I sought this? You think I somehow…ever in my strangest dreams believed…?"

They withdrew a step, except for Banquo, who stood there, steadfast, his familiar face watchful.

"You will be at Scone a month hence?" his friend asked mildly. "Or must we look for another? Though…" He scratched his mane of hair, his eyes not quitting Macbeth's for one moment. "Quite who…"

Composure, Macbeth told himself. *We have done well today, but a few innocuous words might bring this fabric of lies down about us.*

"I apologize, my brothers," he told them. "These strange and calamitous events have discomfited me. Duncan's death in my care weighs heavily on my mind. If, in a month, you still wish to place me on the throne, it will be my life's most cherished honor to accept. Should you find a better, I will happily swear my allegiance to him."

"There is none better!" Lennox cried. "Your good temper and equanimity have been the admiration of us all. Not just today, either. Though, you mourned Duncan more than his sons, and there's no one here who didn't notice."

Macbeth took a deep breath. "This is the judgment of you all?"

"Everyone, and those who are absent do not matter," MacDuff said. He shrugged. "Besides, this is your castle. We are in the arms of your men, have no great claim ourselves, and in all honesty, would rather spend this evening getting drunk and praising our new king than mourning the last one. The crown carries with it a burden of duty on its subjects, but that does not demand fondness on our part. We knew that man for what he was. Good and now—let's say it—bad. Lord knows he had plenty of that about him."

He gave Macbeth a frank look.

"Every last one of us loathed the way he let you fight his battles for him. Enough of this chatter. You start to sound like a wee girl trying to talk her way out of handing over her virginity. We all know what's coming in the end. You lose it, man!"

"Aye," Banquo added, grinning. "You do."

"Very well," Macbeth nodded, smiling. "Thank you. I will repay this generosity."

"That you will," said Banquo, slapping him hard on the shoulder. Then, with a wink, he added in a whisper, "And soon. I'll let you know."

As they all cheered and laughed, Macbeth caught Banquo's eyes and saw in them something shrewd and thoughtful. It lasted only a moment, but for a while, it took the edge off Macbeth's joy.

◈ ◈ ◈

A month was not enough to bury an old king or anoint the new. Winter saw to that, though there were other disturbances that set the world of Scotland on edge, almost from the moment Duncan's bier departed for the west.

Fair skies gave way to foul. Howling gales roared in from east and west, in turn. The snow became so deep that all the mountain passes, north and south, disappeared in drifts too treacherous even for the hill folk to move through them. No ships sailed down the Moray Firth for fear of blizzards and stray ice. The holy party for Iona was trapped for weeks on end beneath the gaunt shadow of Nevis, seeking respite from the season's vicious breath.

Curious events occurred that sent rumor and alarm skittering through the land, shared around hearths great and humble, producing the same anxious questions. At the foot of Inverness castle, beneath the frozen waters of the Ness, a pod of dolphins wandered, trapped and drowning below the cap of ice. A band of soldiers tried to free them, smashing the surface with their axes. The creatures, fond signs of life in the Moray Firth in summer, simply beached themselves upon the sharp shards, thrashing till their silver sides were shredded, moaning for one long day and half a night. The following morning, the bend of the river before the keep was awash with blood on snow, and the dolphins dead in their own gore, their carcasses sad, stinking meat.

In the frozen mountains, horses turned on one another, biting and shrieking. Over the castle battlements, a barn owl fought with a golden eagle and, after repeated vicious sorties, downed the great bird, dispatching it to a bloody end upon the stones in the courtyard, the selfsame spot, the soldiers said, where Duncan's body lay before the journey to Iona.

Food ran short. In public, the miserable porter Fergus bewailed the paucity of ale and whiskey; in private, the lack of secret commissions from his newly elevated master. Women grew fearful, men surly. Most blamed the disappeared sons, Malcolm and Donalbain. The world was out of sorts through the foulest murder of all, patricide compounded by regicide. What little news came through from beyond the Great Glen suggested the two brothers had fled to England, seeking refuge and support. They could stay there—two mean, untrustworthy villains, too sly even for the English to love. Besides, the weather was master now and affected all alike. No army could countenance movement in such conditions. No campaign could begin to contemplate assembly or provisions, let alone the distant sniff of victory.

This small, white world became Macbeth's kingdom, a dominion bounded by the visible limits of the firth. While those beneath his private apartments howled and cursed the season, for Macbeth, the weather proved a respite from the world beyond. This opportune exile saved him the earnest admiration of MacDuff and Lennox, and Banquo's studied watchfulness. His friend had said nothing more than that bland remark about repaying their gratitude, but Macbeth sensed something coming, a request, perhaps, though for what, he could not guess. Nor did he know why the possibility of such a favor gnawed at him like regret. Banquo was his friend. Had Macbeth not yearned for the day when he could shower Scotland's bounty on all who stood fast by him? What could Banquo ask that Macbeth would not grant?

The sisters' words had proven true. He was king of Scotland now in name and soon would own the throne through formal coronation. Yet the burden of the crown—its duties and responsibilities—were spared him by the blizzards. Safe behind the bleak black walls of Inverness, he was free to wrestle with his private doubts, his waking dreams, and bitter self-reproaches.

Duncan was not forgotten, but in the artificial paradise of exclusion his memory, and that of the old king's end, stabbed at his successor from a distance. A closer reminder would return. Of that Macbeth was sure. The inner voice that first spoke the night of Duncan's death was still alive, loudest always in the dark, whispering that no happy days would follow. Yet, after a fashion, it lied. Skena wore a perpetual smile now, forced a little, he thought, and perhaps a shade strange. But the dead boy, Ewan, was buried and never mentioned out loud. And her delight was visible in the strange, bright state that now was theirs. Never had she been so kind or biddable. Even at night—especially then. The evening the old king's corpse left their care, she warmed to him, demanded his close presence, spoke of how the antidote to death was and always would be the heat and fury of life itself.

Most times they went to bed early, rarely to sleep, instead to fall into each other's arms, hotly moving, one within the other, repeatedly, till exhaustion took its toll and brought with it a fleeting, snatched hour of sleep.

"My lord," she whispered, late of a passionate evening, panting, sweating in his tight embrace. "If this womb were not barren, you would have sired an army for us both by now."

He laughed and kissed her. Scotland was theirs. And yet he could not help but notice that each and every time they gripped one another, naked, thrusting, screaming beneath the sheets, her tears flowed free and salty against his bristled cheeks.

"Why do you cry?" he dared to ask one time.

"For joy," she said straightaway, and worked with her fingers to fire him anew.

He moaned, and no more questions came. In these hot and feverish couplings they hid their fears and doubts, striving to believe with each encounter, every ardent thrust, that they might bury their dark remembrances.

After a month of this strange and trancelike bliss, the skies abated. Clear blue replaced dank gray. Word came from the thanes across the Grampians, the north, the lowlands. A date was fixed for Scone. One week hence.

The evening the heralds started to arrive, they flew into each other's arms with greater desperation than ever before.

Four days later, they set sail in a small flotilla of ships to travel around the coast, south to Perth and then by horse for the short ride to Scone.

Macbeth would take the throne of Scotland on the day the pagans called the Winter Solstice, close to the Christian feast that followed in its footsteps—Christmas. It was fitting, the kitchen women said. A moment when the world renewed itself afresh through the coming of a new king. The turning point at which the days ceased growing shorter and slowly lengthened, beckoning fair summer to rise again.

None knew that the party making for Iona had also escaped the season's clutches and had reached the distant isle in the west. Or that even as Macbeth rose to mount the Stone of Destiny, a new monarch crowned in Scone, Duncan's chill and decomposing corpse was lowered at last into Iona's cold, dark peat.

◈ ◈ ◈

It seemed an insignificant place for such a momentous act, no more than a symmetrical grassy mound now covered in hard hoar frost and surrounded by a vast crowd of men and women shivering in heavy winter clothes, silent and full of awe. The Romans had reached this far centuries before, briefly turning the hillock into a puny fort from which they hoped to subdue the northern tribes. When the Picts came back to fight and fight again, the centurions fled, leaving behind a strange altar to a distant Persian god called Mithras, a deity the crude, superstitious tribes came to dread. So something foreign remained in this curious spot, not far from the snaking waters of the river. Afraid to despoil the simple temple there, the Picts, an itinerant people, embraced it instead, making the village nearby one of several capitals for the kingdom that became known as Alba.

During an interminable civil war, a monarch called Nechtan found another god the Romans had brought and converted here to the Christian cross, forcing those who came after to follow the same faith, at least in the light of day. After that, the modest grassy swell became known as the Hill of Credulity, acquiring a mystical, otherworldly quality as a place where one man could become, for a brief moment, an earthly god himself, gaining power, however fleeting, from its sacred turf and stones.

The three sisters, unremarkable among the lowing ragtag crowd of peasants and paupers, soldiers and thanes, around them, found a vantage point on a dry stone wall close to the ceremony, dispatching four youths who first occupied it by dint of foul-mouthed threats and promised curses. There, they made themselves comfortable on the freezing stones, watching the ancient rites begin in the narrow circle at the center of the multitude. The farthest edge was formed by all the principal thanes gathered in a row, Banquo a stride ahead of them, the silver crown of Scotland in his hands, the wolf skin on his back.

In front of him sat Macbeth in a long, dark robe, the sleeves and collar trimmed with ermine, perched awkwardly on a slab of ancient gray sandstone, his face impassive, in his right hand a golden staff with a lion rampant at its head. Behind stood his lady. *No crown for her,* the young sister thought. Dressed in fur over an ankle-length sky-blue gown, her long blonde hair falling loose and brushed around her shoulders, she wore a faint and fanciful smile as if none of this were real.

All were silent—bored, mostly—listening to a red-hatted cardinal, crook in hand, deliver a tedious sermon that began with a long-winded account of how God made the cosmos and everything it contained, among its plenteous riches the blessed kingdom of Scotland.

"Idiot," the giant sister muttered. "Every fool knows the universe was forged from the boundless sea of Lir—"

"That was the Celts' world," the young one said. "You think there is but one? Even the Romans had different gods."

"Then which world is his?" the old one asked, pointing a skinny finger at the stiff man on the stone whose eyes strayed constantly to the burly figure of Banquo and the silver crown in his vast hands.

"All of them and none," she answered, staring at the rock on which Macbeth sat. The Stone of Destiny, they called it. The pillow on which Jacob laid his head that distant night in the east when he dreamed of a ladder reaching all the way to Heaven, with God and his angels descending it, speaking as they came.

The two of them grumbled by her side. She barked at them for silence. There was a moment in this ceremony, one quickly approaching, that she always anticipated.

The girl briefly closed her eyes, and in that sudden dark space knew she was elsewhere, far away in the northwest amid the howling gales on Iona. Her inner self watched the coffin of Duncan descend into the desiccated bog in the grounds of the abbey where king after king now lay, with more to come, few dead of old age, many in slaughtered pieces. Tradition counted even among beasts. When a monarch was killed in battle or through deceit, still his murderers buried their victim's bones there.

In the green and fertile lands of the south, they made kings. On the wind-blasted pastures of Iona, close to the ancient abbey of Columba, they returned them to the earth. There was a fitting symmetry here, even if none but she might appreciate it. And three others, she remembered—Macbeth, his wife, and Banquo. Two of whom would wish to forget the torn corpse now entering the distant ground, if only they could.

And the third? She watched Banquo, the big and brutish man, wolf mane on his head, fire in his eyes, the crown in his hands, held with a feverish and clumsy desire.

"Tragic in the present, yet glorious in the future," she repeated to herself. "You shall beget kings, though never reign yourself." The girl laughed and watched him standing there, pompous and nervy, torn between duty and desire, like them all. "How that last must hurt."

A single word—Jacob—brought her back to the ceremony. The cardinal had raised his crook and now recited the words the Hebrew prophet heard all those centuries before, his head upon the stone where Macbeth waited for the prize he coveted.

In a fine and sonorous voice, the priest intoned, "And behold, the Lord said, 'I am the Lord God of Abraham your father and the God of Isaac; the land on which you lie I will give to you and your descendants. Also your descendants shall be as the dust of the earth; you shall spread abroad to the west and the east, to the north and the south; and in you and in your seed all the families of the earth shall be blessed.' "

The women beside her tittered and covered their mouths, half trying to hide their laughter.

A few in the crowd around them turned and dared to stare.

The burly sister leaned forward and said to a surly, scowling peasant, "They promised that to Duncan, too, fool. And now he's dead, while his offspring cower with the English, fearing for their lives. Plenty of dust. Not much of it blessed, eh?"

"Cower as regicides and patricides rightly should," the young one added with a smile.

"Macbeth will be a better king than Duncan," the man retorted.

"He could hardly be worse now, could he?" answered the old one.

"A man of the people," he insisted.

"He's a man no more," the young sister replied. "A king now. Above you. Beyond you. Bent on whatever destiny your magical stone has given him." She leaned down, eyes sparkling. "And if he disappoints, he's gone. You shall devour him, like all the others."

The tall sister chomped her jaws, biting, making crude, disgusting noises. "Nothing tastes better than a monarch," she spat at him, and the fellow shrank away into the crowd, leaving them alone.

The sermon was over. Banquo approached bearing the silver coronet. A small group of musicians, harp and flute and pipes, struck up a dirgelike drone from nearby. The red-hatted cardinal came forward and sprinkled water on Macbeth's bare head, chanting Latin dirges in a singsong voice.

"Oh, magic, magic," the girl crooned. "If so many fools believe it so, how can they be mistaken?"

She turned and gazed at the two women next to her and thought again, *They do not—cannot—understand.* The sacrament being played out in front of them had nothing to do with holy water, with an ancient stone, or Latin rites any more than their own incantations and potions depended upon an otherworldly power to wreak their damage. Magic came from within, from turning a secret key that lurked inside, waiting for the words to set it free.

The warrior in the wolf's mane came forward and placed the crown on Macbeth's head. The priest splashed yet more water on the anointed. The girl closed her eyes and, in her mind, saw clear as day a picture of distant Iona, peat being sprinkled on a closing grave—flowers, too—and the driving force of icy rain.

"Like Ouroboros, the serpent that devours itself," she murmured, smiling. "These creatures renew their agonies afresh with each new dawn."

A cry rang out. Then the crowd took up the chant.

"All hail Macbeth! *All hail Macbeth!*"

She laughed—and so did the other two—at that.

"All hail Macbeth," they shouted for a second time, though the man himself seemed muted and unmoved by all this noisy clamor about him, and his wife stood behind him as straight and rigid as a frozen corpse.

Servants began to wander through the crowd scattering coins and bread and meat among the mob.

The girl slipped down from the wall and bade them follow, handing the crone her crutches, watching as she sidled along the ground like a spider seeking prey.

"What next?" the tall sister demanded. "These fools bore me."

"We wait," she said.

"For what?" the crone wondered.

She nodded, laughing, and said, "For the king to seek an audience."

The girl watched the tall, strong figure in the wolf skin, standing now with the other thanes, talking to them in low voices, all of them apart from the two figures at the heart of the circle, one seated on the Stone of Destiny, the other silent by his side.

"They have risen above the rest already," she noted. "No longer thane and lady. King and queen, anointed by their god."

She hitched up her skirt and took a step across the tall and frosty grass.

"A day. A week. He'll want our company before long. Two creatures apart, detached from their humanity. He'll search us out. As like seeks like."

◈ ◈ ◈

By midday the elaborate public ritual had run its course. After came the private ones—whispered meetings, reports, promises of preferment, vows of eternal friendship from men Macbeth scarcely knew. The size of this new kingdom, stretching from the lowlands to the northern extremity, which not long before was property of the Norsemen, astonished him, as did all the beetling elements of the state—

courtiers and diplomats, financiers and merchants, finally assembled inside the ancient, comfortable palace of Scone, each ready with information and advice.

In Inverness his role was clear: defend the territory, maintain the king's rule, collect his tithes. Here, in the gentler, more complex territory of the lowlands, not so far from the English border behind which Malcolm and Donalbain now waited, doubtless plotting, he came to appreciate the complexity of monarchy and question his own ability to manage the task. Cullen, the head of the household, both diplomat and servant, and—though a little old for it—occasional warrior, was his right-hand man in this. An honest soul, parsimonious with the purse, polite and distant with all the many seeking favors. It had come to Macbeth long before Scone that this man would give wise, dispassionate counsel always. He had no land to defend, no fortune to enrich further. He was happy merely to serve.

With Cullen by his side, he endured two hours of these meetings, then, head hurting, retired to the private quarters in the palace to think, perhaps even to sleep, not that there'd been much of that lately. That same morning, after breakfast, Banquo had approached him, looking uncharacteristically nervous.

"You want to talk?" said Macbeth. "I crave a moment's peace, friend. This was a day and a half."

"When you're ready," Banquo replied.

"In brief," he said, "what is it? Tell me and I'll sleep on it."

"A favor," said Banquo, with a shrug. "A small matter but perhaps it merits more conversation than you're disposed to give it now. It will keep till you're more refreshed."

"As you wish," said Macbeth, working to keep the unease out of his face. "I will do what I can for you, Banquo. You know that."

"Aye," he said with a smile. "For old time's sake."

Then he left him without another word.

A favor.

Which meant what? Gold? Land? A military post more prominent than that he already held? All these he could grant without qualm. So why did the idea worry him so much? There was a wariness in the man's eyes that Macbeth was unused to. What could Banquo possibly request that his boyhood friend and comrade in arms would ever wish to refuse?

And if he *did* say no…what then?

The door opened without so much as a knock and a brusque voice said, "My Lord?"

Macbeth turned and saw the grizzled porter, already half in the room.

"The door was open, sir," he said. "I trust you don't mind…"

"What is it, Fergus?" Macbeth asked, head heavy, wondering if this was true or whether the man had simply entered unannounced.

"Might you have a moment, sir? A little time to chat?"

Macbeth scowled at him. "Chat?" he repeated. The creature was intolerable. Even before the coronation, no one else would assume such familiarity with Macbeth, except perhaps Banquo. The porter had been a part of the household so long that he seemed to have forgotten the differences in rank between them. That or he saw through such things.

"It seems to me," said Fergus, with his odd, knowing smile, "that with your newly elevated position, you may be in need of people you can trust."

"Are there people around me I should not trust?"

"I'm sure the greater part of your…subjects," he couldn't suppress the flicker of amusement as he said the word, "are, in most things, trustworthy. Yet in some matters—"

"I have the court. My wife. Cullen."

"Your wife's a wondrous woman. And Cullen…" He scratched his nose. "A capable individual, if a little dry and…judgmental, if you take my meaning."

"No, man, I do not."

"A man like that is welcome when it comes to affairs of state, my lord. Those things that occur out in the open light of day. But you are king now. Sometimes there will be private matters. Deeds your highness may not want the world to know."

He smiled and showed his blackened teeth.

"After all, sire, there were occasions when you needed my special talents as a thane. Surely a monarch, a man who rules over such a large and intemperate kingdom, requires them more, not less. On occasion."

"If you're angling to be bawd for the serving girls…"

Fergus spat with contempt. "Please," he said. "Women are distractions for lesser men."

"So you wish to be…what? A counselor? A steward?"

"I wish to spend the rest of my life doing things other than opening doors and lugging barrels."

"That I may appreciate," said Macbeth. "And instead you would be?"

"Cullen's prodigal brother, as it were. Your left-hand man."

Macbeth looked at him, lean and sly as he was. The porter gazed back, his lip curled between smile and sneer, his eyes as incisive and hungry as a weasel's.

"You are an impudent cur," said Macbeth, his voice low. "Little better than a common criminal."

Fergus laughed. "An *un*common criminal, please. In truth, I'm the most honest soul you'll ever meet. For others will tell you what you want to hear, while I say only what you need to know. The truth." He came close and whispered, "Good kings must sometimes sanction bad deeds. Cullen will howl and shriek at such a prospect. And while I defer to the queen's sage words always, I think there will be times when you would wish her ignorant of the details."

"And you will be my instrument in these?" said Macbeth.

"I have many talents and friends in low and obscure places."

"In return? Money? Status?"

"Ease," said Fergus. "Leisure. The right to keep my counsel and leave the fetching and carrying to boys and fools."

"No more than that?"

"They say virtue is its own reward," said the porter archly. "Loyalty to one's king is virtue, is it not?"

"Even if the deeds themselves are…?"

The question hung in the air between them.

"Less than honorable?" concluded Fergus for him. "I'm a humble man, sire. I leave morality to others who are better placed to judge."

Macbeth nodded curtly and looked away, but not before he caught that smile again.

"For your sake, my liege, and for love of Scotland, I would hazard my very soul."

"You still have a soul, then?" Macbeth murmured.

"They say the eyes are the soul's windows," said Fergus, stepping so close now that Macbeth could smell the beer on his breath. "Can you see it?"

His eyes were as black and empty as a burned-out house, as deep and fathomless as those of the girl witch who refused, even now, to quit Macbeth's imagination.

The king turned quickly away. "I have heard your offer," he said. "No more."

"I only mean to say—"

"I heard. Have someone build a fire in here. The water pitcher has frozen solid."

The man stood there for a moment, as if expecting more.

"Well?" Macbeth said, voice rising.

"I will do your bidding always, sir," Fergus answered, then bowed and left the room.

◈ ◈ ◈

In the small and richly decorated palace chamber, with its view out to the Hill of Credulity, Macbeth felt alone and detached from the court around him. He slumped into a chair and his eye fell and lingered on the silver crown, which sat on the trunk at the foot of the bed. A piece of ornate metal, nothing more. He picked it up, then sat again quite still, looking at the way the light played over the whorls of silver, feeling the weight of it in his hands. For this he'd murdered Duncan. For this he'd forfeited the simpler life that went before.

The chamber door opened again and he set the coronet down on the table hurriedly, snatching his fingers away as if caught doing something shameful.

"Come back in an hour," he said, only turning to the door when the words were out of his mouth.

It was Skena. She stood there, stung, and then moved to leave.

"No, no!" said Macbeth, rising. "I'm sorry. I thought it was the maid come to make the fire. Don't go."

She stood there, quite still, watching him.

"Come," he said. "Sit. It has been a long day and it's still not half past."

There would be more meetings, individual ones with the thanes who craved an audience. Then, in the evening, a banquet to mark the inauguration of his reign. Would there come another time when he might ride the Cairngorms, friends by his side, Banquo among them, hunting stags and hare? Another bright day on which he could race down the river netting salmon? These pleasures had been his since childhood, a part of his birthright, taken for granted since they seemed so mundane. Yet now, knowing they eluded him, he yearned for them all the more. Next to those few glorious hours, a circlet of silver seemed a trinket, nothing more.

Yet, still, he thought as she walked toward him, slender and erect in her pale-blue ceremonial gown, *I have a wife.*

Skena's eyes moved to the crown on the table. Her hands went to her hair and she removed the slender coronet they'd given her after the ceremony, placing it next to his. "You wear the thing as if it's foreign," she said, coming close to him. "It's a habit you must lose."

"A crown's a symbol," Macbeth replied. "A token of our new position. I'll be a king through ruling justly, wisely, not through a lump of silver."

Her hands went to his gown, brushed away some dust from the collar. "They need their symbols, husband. You must look the part."

"Scone is a strange place," Macbeth told her. "This is a strange time. We will return to Forres and settle there for a while. When I smell the air of the Moray Firth and we assemble around us our court, then I will be content."

He reached out and fondly touched her cheek.

"We will be happy."

A moment on a sunny afternoon. Once, they would have thrown all cares aside, undressed each other, fallen on the bed, spent an hour locked tight together. This thought, this remembrance, was running through her mind, too. He could see the fleeting idea on her face.

Yet nothing stirred between them at that moment and he wondered when it would again.

"These ladies-in-waiting of mine suggested I take up needlepoint," she remarked, as if searching for something to say. "I don't know what queens are supposed to do. It seems churlish to lock myself away, but I'm sick of being stared at. At least if my hands are busy…"

It was a curious statement. Quite unlike her, or rather it sounded as if she were talking to someone else. A stranger, a guest, perhaps.

"Skena," he murmured, and tried to take her hands, only to find she slipped back out of his tender touch.

"Banquo's anxious to talk," she said. "He says your long friendship should put him first in line for an audience. Somewhere private."

She looked around the room as if avoiding his eyes.

"There it is," she added, crossing to her side of the bed. From the window seat she picked up a circular wooden frame like a tabor with a piece of muslin tacked across it. She had embroidered a pair of turtledoves with colored silk. The stitchwork was clumsy. A needle still with thread was stuck through a half-finished flourish of leaves. She withdrew it and, as she did so, pricked herself. She stared at the tiny bubble of blood at her fingertip as if it were something foreign, hated.

"What does he want?" asked Macbeth, feeling once more the nagging anxiety in his guts.

A favor…

She licked the wound, rubbed the red spot, and kept on rubbing even after the blood was gone. "I think needlework does not suit me," she said icily. "Banquo didn't say. You know the man. It might be rumors of foreign invasion or just as easily a drunken yarn about your childhood. He says he wants to speak with you. Alone. That's all I know. He was trying to spar with that sad, dreamy-eyed boy of his in the yard beside the stables. The man seems…distracted." She looked at him directly. "Banquo is our guest tonight, isn't he? We need him at the feast. You must keep your court close about you, husband. That is the kingly thing to do. He's your friend, too, and a monarch should value those since they may be hard to find."

"Banquo will be there, along with all the thanes." He held her slender shoulders, tried to stare into those bleak blue eyes, and thought she shivered at his touch. "This disturbance in our lives is temporary. Bear with it a while and all will become…peaceful once again."

This is not the time, he thought. Skena's mood seemed febrile and disturbed.

"Will you walk down with me?" he asked. "The court will expect to see us. Together. Man and wife. King and queen."

"I'll stay here," she answered swiftly, staring at the gauche embroidery. "Since we came here my sleep has been…" She shook her head. "I'm tired."

"Skena, if there is something—"

"Forget the court. Go see your man," she urged. "He's waiting on your presence."

◈ ◈ ◈

"Rivers," Banquo said. "They always remind me of when we were young. Coracles and gleaming fish. Not a care in our wee heads. Or much of a thought, either."

That great hand came out and slapped Macbeth's shoulder. It was early afternoon. The Hill of Credulity lay behind them, empty now. Four members of the royal guard stood watch, strong men in armor, as they walked along the flat and frozen bank of the Tay.

"Am I being overfamiliar, sire?" the big man asked with a broad grin. "I'd no idea I played those japes in the presence of a future monarch. Forgive me. I was always the stronger, the louder, the brassier. It's in my nature. While you…"

They watched two whooper swans glide past above the water and settle on the sandy island midstream. Banquo seemed fascinated by the sight.

"They say those creatures mate for life," he murmured. "More morals in them than most men, eh?"

A wink, a smile.

"But not Macbeth. Not even now when you might take any lady in the land."

"My name's not Duncan," he replied.

The birds had settled and now nuzzled one another in the reedy grass.

"No one liked that man," Banquo said, still captivated by the swans. "But he was the king and a king's not there for affection." He stroked his long beard. "Admired. Respected." He glanced at Macbeth. "Feared. All those things. How fare you with them, friend? The first two you won long ago as a general on the field. I had the privilege to watch—"

"I had the privilege, the honor, to have you help me."

The big man dragged the wolf's mane closer round his shoulders, laughing. The wind was bitter and biting. The booming sound of his voice sent the swans scattering, white shapes flying against the pale winter sky.

"See," he said. "There you go. Gracious, generous, deferential to your peers, who are, of course, your subjects now." His face turned stern. "Monarchs do not prosper on such qualities, Macbeth. You know what they call the English king, Edward? The fool who now shelters Malcolm and Donalbain as if they were his sons, not those of an enemy?"

"What?"

"Edward *the Confessor*! A priest who wears a crown! They reckon that when this pious old fool dies—which will not be long, from what I hear—the pope will uncover a hidden miracle and canonize him in short order." Banquo tapped his red and fleshy nose. "England may be ruled by saints, but this is Scotland. A land of warriors. My advice? Do not seek to emulate him. Saints belong in abbeys and monasteries, not royal palaces. Those boys of Duncan will be back before long, and it won't be for a sermon. You'll need your thanes around you then. No doubts in their minds about their choice today."

Banquo fetched him a baleful stare.

"*No doubts*. For they must fear you as they love you. With all their hearts."

"I will consider your words, as always."

Banquo sniffed the air and grunted, "The south. It smells different. Give me the Cairngorms and Laggan any day. Mountain air, eagles, and good deer to stalk. You go home soon, I hear?"

"You hear much," Macbeth noted.

"This is the royal court. There's so much hot air spoken hereabouts I wonder these frosty banks don't melt beneath the heat."

"We return by Perth and boat a few days hence. Skena and I, and the household."

"Not to that black dungeon in Inverness, I trust?"

"To Forres."

Banquo beamed. "Ah, Forres. Flowers and trees and the prettiest girls in Moray. Those lovely views down to Findhorn. I'd choose to live there myself. Were I king, that is." He sighed. "Which I will never be. The weird sisters said so, didn't they?"

Macbeth halted, instantly on his guard. "I am busy. There is the feast tonight. The guests, the protocol, the meetings..."

Banquo said nothing.

"You will be there," Macbeth asked, "won't you?"

"I'm a wild beast of the mountains. I hate these fancy banquets. Laggan's the place for the likes of me."

Macbeth took his arm, gazed into his fierce eyes, and said, "You will be there."

"The king commands?" He seemed amused.

"As a friend, I request it. Not a king."

"Then, as a friend, I have something of my own to ask," he said, and there was a new note of gravity in his voice. "The favor I spoke of. It cannot wait. We must speak of it now, or you will become so lost in your crown you'll not listen to your old, dear friend."

Macbeth's heart sank as he asked, "What favor?"

"You need an heir. All monarchs do, even if their offspring never reach the throne. Skena will not provide you with a child. I know you well enough to understand you'll never get rid of her and marry another. If you will just—"

"No bastards in this line!" he snapped. "No shabby coupling on the wrong side of the blanket. We lost the only child we had. How can you throw this subject in my face?"

"Truly, you rewrite the rules that govern monarchy," Banquo responded, smiling as he spoke. "I speak of it because this subject must be raised."

"Do not presume on friendship," Macbeth told him, "to broach such personal matters at a time like this…"

"You're a king now, Macbeth! Nothing about you is personal anymore. And I presume on nothing." He came close. "I only wish to help. I have an heir for you. A fine one. Young and strong." His eyes flickered to the river. Then he added, "My own son…Fleance. Take him as your own."

Macbeth's mind spun. For a moment, he was back in the Great Glen, that dark and fateful night they met the sisters. "Fleance…" he murmured.

"Adopt him into your line and do it with my love. You're king and will get the blessing of the pope, if need be. Such practices are common among the foreigners…"

Macbeth could scarcely believe his ears. "He is your son! Not mine who's six years dead and none can replace. How do you think my wife would treat such an idea? You know how she felt over our own child."

"Your wife's like you," Banquo answered. "A part of the state now. She must put the common good above her own feelings."

"What have I done to deserve such thoughtlessness? Demand something I might deliver. Something that's not so close to my own pained history," Macbeth pleaded.

The man next to him stood silent, thinking. The swans returned. The river ran sluggish and eternal, the way Macbeth supposed their friendship always would. He could see now that Fleance was not far away, a slim, young figure along the bank, glancing at them furtively. This was planned from the outset, and that knowledge stirred his anger.

"What have you done?" Banquo asked in the end. "The sisters said you would be king. Of me…" He shook his head. "They called me poor for reasons I do not follow. But from my loins would run a line of kings." He took Macbeth by the arm, stared into his face. "You heard that, too. *You heard that.* Give me this small piece of my due, and then we'll speak of it no more."

"I am one day on the throne and you seek to gain such great advantage?" Macbeth dragged himself away, now furious. "This audience is at an end. Go tell your son to earn his place among his peers. As did you. As did I. As will all good Scots who seek preferment. By duty, sacrifice, and labor…"

"Not daggers and deceit, then?" Banquo roared. "Not murder in the dark?"

The pair of swans scattered and with them rose other white shapes from the reeds. Macbeth's blood ran as cold as the gray waters in front of him.

"Speak to me in a measured voice," he said, his voice as hard as stone. "If those guards should hear your lunatic rantings, then I must take this further."

"Take it wherever you may choose," Banquo retorted, though he was quiet now and grim.

"If you have something to say…"

Banquo shook his grizzled head. "Not yet. Not easily. Make Fleance your heir…"

"I cannot."

"You're the king!"

"I will not."

"Do not make me do this, Macbeth! Some things are best unsaid."

The guards behind them came closer. One gripped his sword and asked for instructions.

"We're Highland men," Macbeth told him. "We talk this way. Go back to the palace and wait for me there."

When they'd left, he turned and gripped the man beside him, fingers tight in the warm wolf fur of his mantle.

"Speak now and this one time I listen," Macbeth told him, eye to eye, so close that even Banquo seemed a touch afraid. "But guard your words."

"The boy—" Banquo began.

"The boy is yours! Not mine! My son is dead. I shall have no heir. When the crown becomes vacant, the thanes decide. The old way. The way it should be done. The way I fought for…" The words died in his throat. His face flushed.

Banquo grinned. "Fought well and bloodily in the dark, too," he said. "Oh, come, Macbeth. We're friends. Let's not lie to one another. The child in Inverness. The servant dead in your quarters. The poison on his lips. Your wife grieving more for his death than for Duncan's. Mekilwort, man. Belladonna. As you used on Sueno…"

"What nonsense is this?"

"And Malcolm's dagger clean as a razor. Even in Laggan we have eyes to see. This world is like a mirror and you would have us believe the reflection, not the original. The lie that Malcolm sought to poison you, then crept into his father's bedroom with those two guards so conveniently dispatched..."

"I slew them for their treachery!"

Banquo paused, allowed himself the briefest moment of laughter. "Oh, dearest brother. It is your misfortune to own the most transparent, most guileless of all the faces I have ever known. You cannot profess your innocence without screaming your guilt out loud. You need to learn to lie with conviction. Otherwise, avoid this mask of candor among those who do not love you..."

"And you love me?" Macbeth shouted, pushing him away. "Who accuse me of murder? Of regicide?"

Banquo shrugged. "No one mourns that bastard Duncan. He got what he deserved." He opened his arms, pleading. "Now let me have what I am owed. The prize the witches promised, nothing more. Not for me. For Fleance. For my line. What is it to you?"

"Consider yourself lucky you have a son!" Macbeth roared. "These vile lies—"

"The guards were drugged," Banquo cut in with a sneer. "I found the same berries in the dregs of their flask as lay on the floor of your room by the side of that wee child. Your lady is a cunning one. I imagine this was her doing. You are too honest and upright to kill a man in bed easily. Or two half-conscious guards. Because I know you, love you, I understand why such acts must cause you pain. Ease it now with a generous gesture. Fleance—"

"I will not be pressed to aid the son of one who slanders me."

Banquo nodded, as if understanding something. "I see the reason and, because I love you, understand it. To give me what I ask, you must first acknowledge the deed you have committed and face your guilt. This is a sore predicament. To want the throne so badly you will kill a king to seize it. Then to lament your ruthlessness with such sorrow you seek to wash the necessary evil from your hands and believe they were never ought but clean. What you have done has separated you from yourself," he added mournfully. "I understand that now. To give me my due requires that you reconcile your actions with your conscience. Yet why? Duncan slew many and never lost sleep over a single death. He would have killed any of us and dined on the story the same night. Yet you...You have my pity."

"Pity?"

He pulled the wolf skin tighter round his shoulders and said, "You heard right. Understand, Macbeth. None but those two foul sons will hunt you down for slaying Duncan. That death haunts you alone. But prove a bad king, weak and cruel and willful, and they'll have your head. Lennox. MacDuff. Ross and Angus. Every thane who kissed your hand today and swore undying loyalty. That's the way of things."

"And you?"

"Give me this one small thing," Banquo begged. "A meager favor. Fleance is a decent, honorable boy. Intelligent and loyal. He'll bring nothing but praise and glory to your house. We need never speak of this again."

"I will not suffer such extortion..."

Banquo frowned and said, "If there was no black deed to begin with, where's the pressure that I bring to bear?"

"Be gone. Sit silent at my banquet, then take you to the hills!"

"No," Banquo said. "I go home to Laggan now, with a heavy heart. You have a week to give me satisfaction. After that, I will tell them—MacDuff, Menteith, Angus, Ross, the whole of Scotland, all I know." He turned and his eyes were misty, raw with sorrow. "Your position is not as well founded as you think. It was a piece of silver I placed upon your head today. The keys to this kingdom must be earned, and there you have still to prove your mettle." His face was grim and miserable. "I never wished this, truly. The sisters gave us both a promise. All I ask is you allow me one small part of it for my own..."

"Enough," Macbeth murmured.

That great fist fell upon his shoulder one last time.

"Remember what I said about the throne," Banquo said. "Men will forgive many things in their king, cruelty and avarice and venality among them. But weakness and a humanity so gentle it deceives itself..."

He turned and called for his horses and his son.

"Send me a messenger in seven days to say you've seen some sense," he said. "If not, I'll sing this bloody tale from the highest hill I find."

◈ ◈ ◈

Macbeth watched the two of them leave. The anger was gone now. A cold and hollow dread stood in its place.

He wanted to go after the man who had been his friend, to protest, to plead, to apologize...

No. To lie, a weak and pointless exercise. Banquo saw through him as easily as if he were made of glass. If there were a way a man might take back a single deed, change the past...

What Banquo asked was impossible, cruel, and impudent. Skena's mind had almost shattered when they lost their child six years before. How could a man he once called a friend try to foist upon them his own son as some substitute? What kind of man…?

But Banquo knew. Had seen through all their organized guile.

A week. Was that how long this hard-won kingdom would last before it began to unravel beneath him? Could all the good he meant to do for Scotland disintegrate so quickly?

He stood alone in the chill wind, his breath coming in great smoking gusts, his jaws clenched.

When he turned, he saw, across the lawn, leaning in the shadowed portal of a tower door, the porter he'd spoken with earlier.

My left-hand man.

The thought revolted him. Fergus was watching, considering him frankly. Then he walked out into the light and strode purposefully across the frozen grass.

Their eyes met, king and servant.

"Loud voices even for Highland men. Banquo seems less friendly than of old," said the porter.

Macbeth gazed at him and felt as if he were in some strange dream.

Fergus looked at his hands for a moment, then glanced up at the sky as if looking for snow.

"He's a trusted thane and a very old friend," said Macbeth. "You were listening?"

"I would not dare to eavesdrop, sire," said Fergus, sidling up to him and glancing out across the fields. "No. But intemperate voices carry on the air. Time changes all things. Even a week, I think. Or so he said."

"My faith in him is beyond..."

The porter's half smile stopped Macbeth's words.

"May we be honest with one another?" asked Fergus, his voice lilting as if he were speaking kindly to a child. "This is no way to begin your golden reign. Kings must be honest, with themselves above all others. A man's face is a map and there's envy written clear on that Highland lord's foul mug. Think of it. Imagine. His boyhood comrade, his brother-in-arms as thane of Glamis? He rejoices. Then Cawdor, too? He wonders...And where's the prize for me? I fought MacDonwald, and Sueno, too. Yet nothing. And now? Now you are king of Scotland. Do you wonder this rapid elevation sticks in his craw?"

Macbeth opened his mouth to deny it, but he heard Banquo's words in his head: *"If there was no black deed to begin with..."*

The porter was quiet for a moment, then, without looking at him, said softly, "Enemies are like sickness. Cut them out when they're a spot and all you have is a scar that fades. Leave them to fester and you lose a limb. Fool yourself there's nothing wrong at all and then..." He opened his arms in a gesture of emptiness. "A wise monarch deals with his foes the moment he perceives them. All problems can be faced and solved. Some can simply be made to vanish. The sooner, the better."

Macbeth's heart felt as if it might cease beating. His sad face buckled, and for a wild and terrible moment, he felt tears start to his eyes.

Where were the words? He took a long, cold breath as if drinking in the air, then asked, "How?"

Fergus scowled. "How? What's how to you? You're a king now. Not a general. A king says do it and walks away. The means are up to me."

Macbeth took him by the scruff of the neck and snarled, "This man is my oldest friend. Do not make light of what you tempt me with."

The thin and sharp-faced man pulled back, a little scared, not much. "I tempt you with nothing, sire. If it's your wish, I'll go back to running errands, fetching beer. In truth..." He scratched his head. "That's a sound suggestion. I think I'll take it. Fare you well, lord..."

He turned and started to walk away.

"Stop."

The word said itself, Macbeth thought. No conscious will on his part summoned it from his throat.

Fergus came back slowly and looked at him, turning his head in a sly sarcastic gesture.

"Sire...?"

"I want an end to division and conspiracy," Macbeth told him. "A chance to build this kingdom. A time of peace and justice."

"As do we all," the man responded, nodding vigorously. "A welcome sentiment, I'd say. One your nation will echo. See..." He indicated the line of mountains leading north. "There's such wicked scoundrels abroad. Thugs and bandits. Robbers and murderers. Banquo's a landowner, and a man of property attracts foes as a candle gathers moths." He paused. "It is to be hoped his journey's a safe one. Though sometimes a tragedy may, by accident, do us service."

"Us?"

"You, my lord," said Fergus. "And the country. Who are now one. Where exactly is he going?"

"Home to Laggan," Macbeth replied without a thought, but he felt like a base informer, feeding news to the enemy.

The porter laughed. "Those mountain passes are more perilous than the rest—in winter, especially. I wouldn't wish to ride them with nothing but a boy for company."

Macbeth breathed again, then nodded. In his head were memories of the river and the glens, deer and salmon, laughter, love, and amity.

All gone. In truth, they died that night in Inverness, though he had not known it then.

He offered his right hand to the porter. Fergus smiled his crooked smile and extended his left. Macbeth faltered, then shook it.

"The boy, too," Macbeth murmured. "Make sure of that. It's important. Father and son. Both."

The porter shrugged, but Macbeth looked quickly away as if half wishing the words unsaid.

"I have three good men from Perth at my disposal," Fergus whispered. "Cutthroat sailors as good as any—"

"No!" Macbeth cried, waving his hands in horror. "No. Do not tell me. Do not…" His hands fell to his ears.

Fergus blinked, then stood there, stifling his amusement. "Of course," he said, then bowed and left.

◈ ◈ ◈

It was a bright, cold, windless day in the mountains. The clouds were pregnant with more snow. The drifts from the night before had an icy crust and even the powder beneath their horses' hooves crunched as Banquo and Fleance rode. A mile back they had seen a merlin swoop across the track and into the trees, but otherwise, nothing. The world was silent, frozen.

His wife would have called it beautiful. He smiled to himself, but a glance at the boy on the roan mare beside him banished the thought. They weren't out to admire the scenery. The last thing Fleance needed was a prompt to start writing poetry in his head about the glories of the mountain passes.

The boy had barely spoken since they left Scone. He had that brooding, dreamy look his father hated. Sometimes he hummed to himself or mouthed silent words, lost in a world only he could see. Banquo had talked to fill the silence, tales of blood and battle, most of them real. But Fleance wasn't listening, and as Banquo's frustration built, the stories grew more violent and disturbing.

"...so I take him by the throat like this," he said, snatching at Fleance's woolen cloak, "and I put the tip of my sword right here..."

"I dreamed of this place," said the boy, sitting up and looking around.

"What?"

"Two nights ago, I saw this path while I slept," said Fleance, somehow not sensing his father's swelling anger. "Not exactly like this, but—"

"We've been this way before. We always use it when traveling south."

"Yes, but I dreamed of it."

The boy looked suddenly hunted and uneasy. Banquo recalled his own nightmare about the witches and felt for a moment the cold bite beneath his wolf-skin coat. He had never wanted to make that ultimatum to Macbeth. It was rash, spoken in anger. It would be withdrawn and never used. Not that he intended to let the king know that for a day or two. Perhaps he might see sense and take Fleance back into the court some other way.

"What kind of dream?" he muttered.

"There was a crow and then an overturned hay cart, an accident, but somehow *not* an accident..."

"And?"

The boy looked uncertain. He shrugged.

"Dreams!" spat Banquo. "When are you going to pay attention to the world around you? To reality? You're a man nearly, or should be. But when you're not huddled in your room with a book, you're talking about dreams and premonitions like a doe-eyed serving wench. You don't practice with your sword..."

"I do, I just—"

"Don't lie to me, boy! I've watched you. The moment I go you put the sword aside. Yesterday you were supposed to practice for a half hour before dinner. And went off wandering by the river. When we get back, I'm going to find boys your own age to spar with you. Once a day, every day. And they won't go easy on you like I do."

"They won't do it," said Fleance, looking at the track ahead.

"They will if I order it."

Fleance looked sullen but said nothing.

"Why won't they do it?" Banquo asked with a sigh.

"They don't like me," said Fleance.

"Because you show no spark! You've a reputation to live up to. A family name to follow. They don't have to like you if they respect you."

"They don't."

"Then make them," said Banquo, fiercely. He seized Fleance's shoulder and glared at him till the boy nodded and looked down, his face flushed.

"And stop all this nonsense about dreams," he added. "I'll speak to your mother about it when we get home. She's been too soft. What were you doing yesterday, with the waiting women in the palace?"

"When?" asked the boy, his eyes evasive.

"You know when. When you were sitting by the fire in the great hall just before you went to bed."

"It was just foolery," said Fleance. "A game."

"What kind of game?"

"I was telling their fortunes," he said, flushing even more. "Reading their palms."

Banquo's eyes narrowed. "Why?"

"To pass the time and," said Fleance, a tiny note of defiance rising in his voice, "because they say I'm good at it."

"Good at it?" roared Banquo. "What are you, a gypsy girl at a country fair making up lies for a few coins?"

"Who said it was lies?"

Banquo wheeled his horse in front of the mare and stopped them both. "Now, listen to me," he said, one massive fist clamped around his son's wrist. "I don't want to hear of this again. It does not suit your family name to be playing with such stuff and besides…" His voice fell a tone. "It's not safe. People scare easily, especially at times like this. You've heard the rumors and the whispering. The last thing we want is for them to point at you, muttering about strange gifts. They might think it amusing now. But one day you'll cross the line and find yourself turned out on the moors, trading charms for a crust of bread and trying to stay one step ahead of the hangman."

"Is that what the weird sisters do?"

Banquo felt numb and stupid. "The what?"

"The three women you met with Macbeth."

"Who told you about them?" Banquo demanded, his grip now vicelike but unsteady.

"You did, Father. Last night, the night before. Tossing and turning in your sleep. You spoke about them to Macbeth. Talked to the women, too. You said—"

Banquo slapped him across the face so hard that the boy rocked sideways in the saddle and would have fallen if the grip on his wrist had been less secure.

Immediately, he was struck with guilt and a darker, vaguer panic. He pulled Fleance close and held him.

"I'm sorry," he whispered. "Nightmares are things that come to taunt us..."

"So you dream, too," the boy said, close to tears.

"Stay away from them, Fleance. There's only misery there. People will..."

But he couldn't think of what to say next. A breeze had picked up and Banquo felt the first kiss of snow on his cheek.

"Come on," he said, drawing the wolf hide tighter about him. "We have a long way to go."

He urged on his horse. Fleance drew alongside, eyes cast down. For several minutes they rode in silence.

The pass through the mountains tightened, the rocky outcrops at their sides became like cliffs. A series of ragged waterfalls were frozen hard to the rock, the stone flashing like glass in the sun. At the foot of the scarp was a stream, sluggish with ice, and a grove of slender rowan trees, the kind that Banquo's father had cut and hardened for spear shafts. He pointed them out, but as he began to speak, a startled bird rose cawing into the pale sky, its black wings beating only a few feet from their faces.

Banquo laughed at his own surprise, but Fleance's face was pale.

"Crow," the boy said softly.

As they swung around the grove of trees, Banquo realized that his son's attention had shifted from the bird and now was focused on the track ahead. A cart sat there blocking the way, one wheel splintered beneath it. Three men were working on it, one a massive, hulking brute. Banquo gave Fleance a look.

"We should go back," said the boy in a low, flat voice.

Banquo stared him down, then turned deliberately to the carters.

"You need assistance, friends?" he bellowed, sliding easily from the saddle.

"That we do," returned one of them, a broad-shouldered fellow who was piling spilled straw with a long-tined pitchfork. "We can repair the wheel, but we have to get it off first."

Banquo strode over. "Seems you already have a giant working for you," he said, slapping the biggest of them on the shoulder. "Still can't shift it, eh?"

The massive figure in coarse sackcloth shrugged and nodded.

"Cat got your tongue?" asked Banquo, laughing.

The giant turned and gaped at him. His mouth still had a few broken and blackened teeth, but where his tongue should be there was only a pale, fleshy flap with a straight edge as if made by a knife.

Banquo stepped back, the skin on the back of his neck prickling.

"You have my apologies," he said, then turned to the man with the pitchfork. "I know your face from somewhere, do I not?"

"I doubt that, sir," he said, eyes flashing over to the bushes.

It was a lie. Banquo would have known it without that telltale "sir." And as he squatted to look down at the wheel, he realized several other things at once: though the snow had frozen hard, there were footprints all around the crippled wagon, which meant they had been there a long time. Two of the wheel spokes were, indeed, shattered, but the breaks were clean and one of them showed a notch—the mark of an ax.

This was no accident.

He stood up and turned slowly back to his horse and, more importantly, his sword, but as he walked away, he saw the third man properly for the first time and knew him.

Fergus. Macbeth's skulking porter. A man for sly and wicked deeds.

His heart sank, but his senses quickened. If this was to be Macbeth's handiwork, then Fleance was as much a target as he was, perhaps more.

He reached the horse and casually dragged his heavy sword free, as if it was to be no more than a tool they might use to free the wheel. As he did so, he spoke softly into the beast's flank.

"Stay on your horse, Fleance. Be ready to ride. Don't wait for me." He hesitated, sensing the way the three men had left the cart and were coming closer. He looked up into his son's wide-eyed face and grinned wryly. "I love you, boy. Trust that. Trust no one else alive."

Then he turned with a roar, the sword scything out in a broad, vicious arc. The giant had a rough-hewn cleaver in his great fist, the porter a short stabbing sword. Both gave ground immediately, but the third lunged with the pitchfork and Banquo stepped first right, then forward. The long tines of the fork jabbed into the air where his head had been and Banquo closed fast, piercing the man's belly with a single thrust.

He grinned at the other two wolfishly as the man slumped bleeding in the snow.

Then there was a snap like a broken tree branch up in the rock wall to his left. Banquo didn't see the crossbowman till the dart found his side. It went in hard and cold between his ribs, and the flare of pain nearly knocked him down. Then they moved, one coming from the other side, a skulking, spindly fellow with a leather cap and a long knife, making for Fleance.

Banquo roared his defiance and slapped at the mare's hindquarters. The horse started and skittered so much the villain hesitated.

"Fly, Fleance! Fly!" Banquo bellowed.

The animal reared and retreated a yard, no more. Standing unsteadily on his own two feet, he found the stabbing wound turned hot, and the breath seemed to leak from out his lungs. He gasped, fell back, slapped at the mare again, and this time it took a few faltering steps. The boy looked back at him. Banquo yelled at him this one last time, "Go!"

Then Fleance spurred the mare. The animal bolted, slipping as it leapt forward, Banquo stepping into the space it left, swinging his sword, roaring like a beast. His ribs cried out with the effort of his reach; his heart beat the rhythm of a battle drum. Then the blade caught the knifeman at the elbow, severing his forearm.

The assassin shrank away screaming, clutching his wound, his eyes wide with fear and astonishment. Banquo turned from him to face the other two, and the crossbowman who was sliding casually down to the track, now with an ax in one hand.

"Get after the boy," shouted Fergus to the one with the crossbow.

Banquo managed three lumbering strides toward him, clutching the spot where the shaft stuck in his side. Turning his back on the others, he slashed wildly at the ax man who feinted and danced away, grinning, stalling.

One more lunge, his great strength failing. He swung a last time, stumbled, sinking to one knee.

"Fleance," he sighed, casting around him, seeing nothing, only a clear path, satisfied the boy was in the hills.

When he looked up he saw the giant with no tongue leering grimly at him, the pitchfork in his hands. One hard stabbing blow and the long iron prongs went straight through Banquo's chest.

He knelt now, breathless, bleeding. Two huge hands came down and snatched the wolf skin from his shoulders.

A memory flashed through his mind: taking that great fur trophy from a slaughtered Viking after a long and vicious fight.

"I killed that man in battle," he murmured, feeling the warm, salty liquid rise quickly in his throat. "I…"

But the air would not reach his lungs, nor the words his lips. The bright flashing edge of the ax blade was flying toward him, and in that brief moment, Banquo felt a final new emotion, one he dimly recognized as fear.

◆ ◆ ◆

Night fell, owls screeched, men whispered in the dark. Skena wandered the palace like a lost soul, surrounded by faces she scarcely recognized, searching for her husband for hours on end. Finally, not long before the feast was due to start, she found Ross, quiet in a corner, seated on a bench, alone and broody.

"My husband...?" she said. "Where is he? And Banquo?"

The man eyed her awkwardly and waved to the door of the chamber by his side.

"Banquo has gone riding with his son," he answered, though he seemed embarrassed. "Your husband and him had words, I hear. Now Macbeth is within, alone and...truculent."

"Is something wrong?" she asked.

"What should be wrong?" Ross replied with a shrug.

There was a roar of anger from beyond the door, a cry from a familiar voice. Skena's eyes flashed to Ross, who got hurriedly to his feet, avoiding her eyes.

"I need to get ready for the feast," he muttered as he made his exit.

Skena took a breath, then entered and found Macbeth there, wild-eyed and furious, a bottle in his hand, hair more awry than the wildest of Highland warriors, berating the world and himself.

The smell of strong spirits hung on the air. He rarely touched the whisky the Irish called poteen. But now he stank of the stuff, as did the small, cold chamber.

"What is this?" she asked. "I thought my husband was in here, the king of Scotland, about to greet his subjects. Instead, I find a crazed beast, half a man..."

"We scotched the snake and didn't kill it," he muttered, then swigged at the glass neck, found it empty, and staggered to the table to grab some more.

With her right arm, she swept the bottles there to the stone floor and heard them shatter. The noisome smell of strong drink rose from the ground in a fetid cloud.

"Why are you alone and in this state?" she asked. "This is a time to stifle what rumor and gossip remain. Bury it once and for all with certainty and confidence. Not fire more loose talk through this strange fury."

"Why strange?" he asked.

She put her hands on his chest and came close, ignoring the fumes of drink. "What's done is done, Macbeth."

"That's true," he muttered.

"Then let's leave Duncan in the grave. What we cannot change should not concern us. You're king now, with a court and subjects, both looking to you to hold the throne with dignity. Not"—she took the empty bottle from his hands—"this..."

He stood there, silent, distraught over something she could not begin to fathom. There was a water jug and basin in the corner. She went for them, poured a little freezing liquid, found a rag, began to wipe his troubled face.

"Come on," she pleaded. "Be gentle. Shrug off these fiery looks. There's a feast out there and guests who want you to be bright and jovial."

"Duncan sleeps and I cannot," he muttered.

"Forget him!"

His eyes were dark and mad. "Can you forget that boy?"

The tears started in her eyes and she opened her mouth in shock as if he had slapped her.

"The dead should think themselves fortunate," he ranted. "Nothing, no treason, no steel or poison or domestic malice may touch them further. Yet we eat and drink in terror, fearing to sleep for dreadful dreams..."

"Husband!" she cried, her hands upon his tangled, damp beard, cupping his face. "Hush now! Be calm. Be brave and noble, as you truly are. Let me wash you, dress you. Let me make you whole again."

"The vessel's broken," he murmured. "Not a million hands may put it back together."

"Do not say such things! We've come so far and taken so much blood upon our souls. Let us put the black past behind us and beg forgiveness on our knees, of God, of the pope, of anyone. In the summer. Not now. You are king for a day only and must cement your reign. Act the monarch tonight and stifle all these murmurs of disquiet. Be friendly with Banquo, too. They say you argued with him, the man you've loved since you were boys…"

His eyes flashed with suspicion. "Who said that?"

This hard, inquiring look of his was new. Her husband had always been so open and so trusting. Now he seemed to see dangers lurking in every shadowy corner.

"It's of no consequence," she told him. "Come to our apartment now and let me dress you."

"Banquo's line will rule this land through Fleance. We slaughtered Duncan more for them than for ourselves," he croaked. "And in return—"

"What does it matter once we're dead! Live now, Macbeth. Enjoy your kingdom and your fame. Think of me, husband."

Of me, she thought. *Just as guilty.*

"Be kind and loving to Banquo this evening. He's been like a brother to you all these years. You need your friends around you…"

"Friends? *Friends?* A king has none. Subjects only." His voice was frantic, broken. His demeanor unfit to be seen.

"The feast shall start a little late," she said, and stroked his face with a fond concern. "I've work to do on you."

"There's other labor being done," he mumbled darkly. "Before this night is out…"

"What, husband?" she asked, suddenly tense.

He stiffened, looked a little more sober. Sly and regretful, too, as if he'd said or done something unworthy. "The business of the state," he said.

"We are complicit in this together, man and wife! What work?"

"Nothing you need know about. But be happy with the consequences."

"Macbeth!"

His right hand came up and his fingers wrapped around her jaw, sealing her lips together so tightly she fought for breath. His eyes were wild and monstrous and there was something in his face so close to hatred she scarcely dared witness it. "I am the king!" he said through gritted teeth. "And I demand your silence."

In all the years they'd known each other, sharing the same bed, the same skin it felt like sometimes, he'd never struck her, scarcely said an unkind word. She'd thought herself the only woman in Scotland who could have said such a thing about her man. And now…

"Where are my robes and coronet?" he demanded, staring round the foreign chamber. "What is this place?"

His hand came away. He stared at his own fingers as if they belonged to another.

"My mind is full of scorpions," he said more softly.

"Oh, love," she said, still struggling a little for both breath and composure. "Come with me, lord." She reached out and touched his arm. He scarcely seemed to notice. "I will take you to your apartment and prepare you for the night."

"The night?" he laughed, bright all of a sudden. "That's spoken for already."

"Come," she said again, and finally led him from the room, finding herself fighting back the tears.

◈ ◈ ◈

An hour later, he lurked outside the banqueting hall, steadier in body, clearer in head, thinking, thinking. Possibilities, dangers, and fears assailed him from all sides. He was haunted by memory of his wife's reproachful look when she had guessed he was keeping something from her. His beloved Skena, his dearest partner in greatness. But it was better she not be a part of what Macbeth knew. Her mind was already infected by their bloody deeds. He sensed her sorrow, however much she put on this show of composure and contentment. They had washed Duncan's blood from their hands, but could not unsee what they had seen or forget what they had done. And the face of that dead servant boy still haunted her. This was pain enough. Spared the knowledge of his deeper sin, she might one day recover.

Did a part of him not also take some cruel delight in keeping secrets from her, punishing her for this course she had—to some extent—set him on? Perhaps. There was a distance between them now, one that seemed to grow hour by hour from the moment he put on the crown.

But this was no time for idle contemplation. He was the king. So he brushed away his thoughts and listened to the gathering throng. The noise from beyond the curtains sounded like the wordless murmur of a crowd for a contest or entertainment, a bear baiting, a hunt, an execution.

As he stood there, hesitant, a body brushed against him in the dark. Macbeth's fist reached out and grasped it. The porter's face came back at him in the diagonal light of a nearby brand.

"Do not dare enter that great hall," Macbeth ordered. "You've blood on your face, fool."

"He was a strong, brave man. Without my companions..." His eyes were stony, unfeeling, his voice grim and bleak. The man was dead to everything but opportunity.

"Banquo's dealt with?" Macbeth asked.

"No, lord. He's here." He extended a hand toward the raucous feast. "Go see for yourself."

"Do not try my patience!" Macbeth hissed at him.

"I brought you proof. And yes, he's dead. I cut his throat myself, ear to ear through that great beard. Not an easy task, but I did it for him. And for you."

Macbeth let go. "Tell me you did the same for Fleance and I'll crown you king of the cutthroats. And give you silver enough to take you so far hence that I may never see your hideous face again."

Fergus shrugged. "Fleance escaped."

Macbeth's hands flew to his neck. The porter retreated.

"Banquo was a bear in battle, fighting for his cub. I thought he might kill us all. Do not be ungrateful, sire. There's not one of us who came out of that encounter without hurt. Never have I faced down such a savage."

"Savage?" Macbeth echoed, and fell back against the cold stone wall. Had Fleance fallen alongside his father, then the witches' words would have died with him. Still, the boy lived. Now Macbeth felt himself hemmed in once more, confined by constant doubts and fears. He fought for breath and, feeling the floor swim toward him, braced himself on the porter's shoulder.

"You're sure that Banquo's dead?" he whispered, finding the notion almost unimaginable.

"Left in a ditch with his throat smiling bloodily and twenty gashes to his head. I put them there and none escapes me."

"None except the son."

"He's a stripling," the porter said. "He won't hide long. I promise…"

"The cuckoo's dead but leaves his egg to hatch and expel me from my roost," Macbeth sighed. He glanced at the skinny, sharp man in front of him. "These thugs of yours are trusty?"

"As loyal and silent as a priest at confession. And one is mute, his tongue cut out by Vikings. You have no need to worry." He smiled and stared. "About us, anyway."

"Then get about your business."

"Sir…" Fergus stood there, half frowning, half smiling, his hand extended. "Trust is bought, and those who earn it would be paid."

"You'll get your money later," Macbeth spat at him. "Go wash his blood from your vile features. I'll see you in the morning. Then—"

The curtain opened. Fergus scurried into the shadows to hide his face. Skena stood there, glaring at the two of them.

"What is this?" she asked. "A king in whispered congress with his servant. Absent from his coronation feast? Your guests await you, Macbeth. Do not disappoint them."

"Not Banquo?" he asked uncertainly.

"I haven't seen him," she said, shaking her head.

The porter mumbled an apology and scurried off into the passageway behind, but not before he had cast one last knowing look at Macbeth, grinning as he left. His face was twisted in the torchlight, silhouetted like a gargoyle in the church.

"I don't like that man," said Skena. "There is something in his eyes. I don't know why you favor him. You'd think he was a decent servant, like Cullen. Not the drunken porter…"

"A king needs many servants, of different kinds," Macbeth replied.

"Your guests," she repeated, extending her arm toward the chamber beyond.

He walked into the room, watching as they rose, lords and ladies, finely dressed, smiling, then clapping, some cheering.

A pretty girl was by his side in an instant, offering drink in a fine silver goblet. There was music and a little merriment. An atmosphere he recognized, too. One of expectation. This was like a waking dream, one that only sleep might dispel.

"Go lightly with the liquor," Skena whispered as he reached out for the wine.

Every eye was on him. He scanned the room, saw nothing there to fear.

"You hear my wife!" he roared. " 'Go lightly with the liquor!' "

They shrieked with mirth and raised their cups.

"This is the day of my coronation!" Macbeth cried. "Tomorrow…"

He grabbed Skena roughly, kissed her once on the cheek with a sudden, frank coarseness.

"Tomorrow I listen to women." He winked. They hooted. "Perhaps. Tonight I drink!"

She smiled and freed herself from his strong arms, walked slowly across to the two chairs set by the head of the table, and waited.

◈ ◈ ◈

They sang, they danced, they listened to stories old and new, laughing as they always did. And all the while the women watched, stifling yawns, wishing they might retire and leave the men to play as some of them wished at the close of such riotous evenings.

Macbeth, a little drunk again, was on his feet, his turn to recount a tale.

"Show us how you killed MacDonwald!" Angus cried.

"Behave like a king, not his jester," Skena whispered underneath her breath. "Like the man I know and love."

And now am losing, she thought with the quick, painful stab of revelation.

It was no use. The tale began.

"Then…*then*! I slew him," Macbeth bellowed, flying across the stones, spilling drink everywhere, cutting the air with an imaginary sword. He stopped and placed a thoughtful finger on his lips and said, "At least I *think* that was MacDonwald. So many enemies of late."

"And now you are with friends," MacDuff declared with a shrewd smile.

Skena Macbeth watched that man with care. He drank little and thought much. Few of them were fools. None, perhaps, as canny and observant as the thane of Fife.

"Aye," Macbeth said. "Friends. Friends…"

His eyes drifted to the far side of the room, no focus in them, no sense. She wondered what the men and women around these tables felt. Pity? Concern? A silent inner contempt? Or the scent of ambition for themselves? Men got drunk—kings, even. But not like this.

"My lord," she declared, smiling, rising to her feet. "The evening is late. The day long. Tomorrow you have many meetings…"

"Friends," he said, still staring into the darkness, waving her down. "There's one I thought I'd see here. The greatest friend of all. My savior and my rock. Oh, Banquo…" He scratched his head. "Where *are* you, man?"

"His absence is a shame," Ross said. "The man has only himself to blame for missing so glorious an evening."

"Where are you…? Where…I cannot…"

The king's voice died into a soft and terrified howl and the room fell silent, hushed by his terrified countenance.

"My lord…" Skena said, gripped by a familiar and frigid apprehension.

"Do you not see?" he cried, pointing beyond them into the dark corridor beyond. "Ross? Lennox?"

The two men glanced uneasily at each other, and Lennox said, "I see your subjects and servants, sir. Nothing more…"

"Which among you did this?" he thundered, turning to them, staring red-faced at the seated figures around the tables.

"His highness is not well," Ross said, rising. "The queen is right. It's time we all departed."

"Do not judge him," Skena said quickly, rushing to his side. "The king suffers from a minor malady, a fit, nothing more. He's known these since his youth. In a moment he will be himself, I assure you."

She took his arm. Still, Macbeth stared ahead into the darkness where the servants lay, moving between kitchen and hall, though none came now.

"Gone?" he muttered. *"Gone? And yet I saw—"*

"Husband?" she said out loud, then more quietly in his ear, "Macbeth, my lord. Act like a man, not a frightened fool."

"A man? *A man?*" His voice was as light as that of a girl and so detached he seemed lost to her. "I am a man and dare face that which would appall the devil. But not that fiend…"

She held him tight and close and murmured, "This is drunken lunacy. Like the dagger you saw in the air at Inverness. Like the voices you heard. All dreams and fancies, an old woman's story by a winter's fire. Find reason in yourself and I will lead you out of here."

A gentle kiss on his rough, bristly cheek, a squeeze of his cold hand. She took the drink from him and looped her arm through his, trying to fix on his wild and darting eyes.

Macbeth shook his head and stared at the room with all its silent, puzzled faces. "I apologize, most worthy friends," he said. "Do not be concerned. As my lady says, this is a malady from my youth. A strange and temporary infirmity, nothing to those who know me. Come!" He picked up the nearest tankard and banged it on the table. "More wine for you, though…" He glanced at her and winced. "I shall be sober from now on, as you and my wife deserve. A toast…"

"To Banquo!" cried Lennox and others after him. "To—"

A sudden, shocked silence. Sweating, cursing, Macbeth tore from her grip, wild-eyed and shrieking yet again, pointing back toward the corridor opposite.

"Look there!" he cried. "For God's sake, see!"

She followed the line of his finger and made out a figure in the shadows beneath the arches, beyond the balustrade. A gigantic shape, shoulders as wide as those of two ordinary men, a face unrecognizable for blood, a beard and hair disheveled like that of a corpse upon the battlefield.

Around this apparition's shoulders stood something silvery gray, and on its scalp a mask like the head of a wild creature, long fangs falling across his grimy forehead.

"What is this…?" she whispered, frozen with sudden fear.

"Do not shake your gory locks at me!" Macbeth cried. "Keep your corpse in the charnel houses and graveyard. Do not offend the living. Crawl back into the earth!"

She left him, took two steps forward to see this thing better.

"Banquo?" she murmured, and approached a step closer.

The creature was trying to speak, yet uttering no words that any knew, only a series of raw, inhuman moans, no language in them, merely pain.

The massive figure took a step into the light and MacDuff said, so loud and clear all heard, "I'd know that wolf's mane anywhere. But what's the beast that wears it?"

The vile porter who hung around Macbeth too much scurried into view from behind the stumbling, troubled figure.

"Apologies, lords," the man cried, eyes wide with fright. "This poor, dumb soul was lost within the palace and stumbled in here, confused and sore in mind."

MacDuff was on his feet.

"He wears Banquo's cloak!" the thane cried. "With blood upon it. Who is this man? And who his master?"

"Some visitor from the north," the porter replied, pushing the giant in the wolf skin back into the shadows.

"Banquo?" Lennox shouted.

Macbeth stood there, frozen to the spot, seemingly as dumb as the shambling figure in the animal skin before him.

"There has been a tragedy on the way to Laggan," the porter cried, arms outstretched, voice breaking. "Robbers attacked the lord and his son as they rode into the hills. This man came upon them and sought to help. He was wounded in the fray himself and found his way here after. Do not blame him, I pray you..."

More unintelligible sounds found their way out of the creature's throat and now Skena could see the strange truth: he had no tongue.

"He is dumb, sirs," the porter said. "A brave Scots soldier mutilated by the Vikings for his courage. He brought the skin to show us the truth he cannot speak and has been wandering these dark passageways in great distress..."

"And?" MacDuff demanded.

The porter spread his arms wide in apology. "Three guards found the good lord in a ditch. The boy is gone. Where, no one knows." The tears stood in his eyes, so full of bleak sincerity she wished to scream. "Lord Banquo's dead. They hunt the mountain rogues who killed him now..."

A breathless sigh ran round the hall. Macbeth stood there, speechless, rooted to the spot.

"Banquo?" MacDuff said, his eyes narrow and suspicious, casting round the crowd. They came to a halt on the silent figure with the crown staring at the strange and bearded man in front of him, as if he, too, saw a ghost. "Murdered?"

There was a long silence. Ross gazed into his cup while the woman opposite him began to sob quietly.

Skena broke the tension, stood in front of her distraught husband, and pleaded with them, "Lords and ladies, kindly give my husband room for grief. He and Banquo were the dearest of friends. You are witness to his keen distress. Retire to your rooms. There, mourn our great lost lord. Tomorrow, in the daylight, let us see what news of this dire event may be found, and hope that we can track the boy Fleance and keep him safe from these vicious mountain rogues."

"Tomorrow," MacDuff said, "I go home to Fife. I mourn Banquo there—alone. If need be."

He set his tankard quietly on the table. There was a finality to the act, and when he looked around the thanes close by him, Skena followed, watching to see who met his eyes. Lennox, Angus...they kept their counsel.

"What say you, Your Highness?" Ross asked boldly.

Macbeth could not remove his eyes from the creature in the wolf skin.

"Take this bloody man away!" she ordered, and quickly the porter obeyed, leading the mute giant from the hall.

Still, the king stood there silent, locked on the darkness ahead of him.

"I pray you," Skena answered, "do not ask more questions of my husband. Questions only serve to stoke his illness. Good night! Don't stand upon the order of your going. Leave now, I beg you."

Lennox got to his feet and smiled feebly, looking at Macbeth. "Good night. And better health attend his majesty," he said with a brief salute.

It was more than they got from most. There was a storm of chairs and benches, then an eerie silence as everyone left the chamber, some exchanging dark looks, some with streaming eyes, all speechless. Within a minute the hall was empty and the two of them stood alone in silence and the flickering yellow light of the torches.

"They say blood will have blood," Macbeth muttered, his eyes still on the spot where the creature in the wolf's mane had stood. "This fight has not yet run its course. What time is it?"

"Late," she said. "Too late."

"MacDuff suspects us. I see it in his cunning face."

She rounded on him.

"Suspects *us*? Suspects what? Did you give him reason?"

He looked away, as if her presence was unimportant, scanning the tables, with their half-finished plates and goblets. "I'll put money into all their houses—MacDuff and Lennox, Ross and all. So not a one of them lacks a servant in my pay. They'll tell us what these traitors whisper in the night, and then I'll deal with them."

"Macbeth!" she cried, clinging to him. "What have you done? Banquo?" She recalled the strange talk earlier. "That was the deed you spoke of? To murder your childhood friend and his meek and powerless son?"

"I did not seize this realm for them. The witches told me—"

"Not to kill them!"

"The sisters said from him stemmed a line of monarchs…" His eyes turned dark and thoughtful. "And for me a crown alone. I must see them soon. Those women. I will know the worst, whatever it pains me…"

"Enough!" she whispered, choking back the tears. "We killed Duncan for the crown. To take it from a tyrant and place upon it a man who was worthy of it. Not…this!"

It was as if he were deaf to the sound of her voice.

His index finger stabbed the dark air as he murmured grimly, "I am so far steeped in blood that if I chose to wade no further, then returning would be as bloody as to proceed. There are things here"—he pushed a finger to his temple—"that must be acted upon before the likes of MacDuff know it. Banquo told me my face is a map, open to the world. Let them read it well." He raised his hand before her. "From this day on, I treat those who love me with kindness and the rest with the iron fist of my swift justice. Tomorrow we make for Forres. Then—"

"Husband," she said in the faintest, weakest voice. "You must sleep. These cares, these troubles, wreck your reason." She took his arm. "Come with me. Come to bed."

"Bed?" His stark eye held her. "I will sleep when I am ready. We're still young in deed. There's mischief yet to come. More than any know." He gazed at her and for one brief moment seemed sane. "Even I."

◈ ◈ ◈

The night was strange and restless. Macbeth wandered the palace halls, his blood thrilling to every night sound, incapable of rest. When he finally entered their chamber, he saw his wife was awake, staring at the ceiling and quite still. She did not move, did not look in his direction, when he entered. After a moment watching her, he left and found a blanket on the floor of the great hall.

Dawn broke over the distant hills, revealing a palace in disorder. MacDuff was gone by the time Macbeth rose, his head hurting. The others followed not long after, a few making an attempt at politeness, others vanishing without a word.

In his mind, he saw his kingdom now, a vast and diverse land of mountain, glen, and pasture, inhospitable coastline, vibrant, prosperous ports. From the English border by the Tweed at Berwick to the contested lands of the far north to which the Vikings still laid claim, the nation stretched before him, daring him to master it.

He knew now why Duncan was such an itinerant man, moving from palace to palace, Stirling to Dunkeld, Forres to the grim fortress on the southern rock of Edinburgh. This ceaseless caravan kept him safe from discord, spread his presence and his authority from thane to thane, keeping all in check, close and familiar, drawing every local warlord into the shared conspiracy that bore the name of the state.

Before he seized the crown, Macbeth was thane of Glamis, forced to live in Inverness as Duncan's lieutenant overseeing Moray, one knight among many upon the chessboard known as Scotland. Now he was the player, not a piece, and the complex range of gambits, stratagems, and sly alliances that lay before him stretched beyond his knowledge and imagination. He was a general at heart, a warrior who saw the world in black and white, not a diplomat or politician used to treading between so many shades of gray they seemed like nightfall slipping from a fading sky, crossing the gamut from bright sun to black through every hue between.

Those skills were Skena's when she chose to use them. Yet now she was as distant as any of the blank-faced nameless courtiers he found around him, inherited like furniture from the king who went before. Even Cullen seemed more distant, as if that loyal, decent man had seen a shadow in his monarch's face and taken a step backward.

None said a word when he ordered them to quit Scone for the north. It was left to Cullen to tell him the weather was closing in, making the journey back by boat to the Moray Firth unwise.

That only left the hard way, through the Grampians and the Cairngorms, taking the mountain passes by horse and mule, an entire household in his train.

"If we waited a week, sire...Scone is not so unpleasant," Cullen suggested.

It was afternoon by then and the palace was empty, the Hill of Credulity covered in the first flecks of the coming snow.

"We strike for the north in the morning," Macbeth ordered. Then he told the man what he knew of the three sisters, their appearance, their manner, and asked that they be found.

"You have no names?" Cullen replied, amazed.

"None. The youngest, little more than a child, has strange eyes. Black. And a tattoo upon her chest, from below the navel almost to throat."

The man blinked, lost for words.

"She's a bairn," Macbeth snapped. "And I am not Duncan. I have good reasons you should find them. Do that. Tell her we must speak."

The following morning, they left on horseback, a party of more than sixty riding toward the peaks. The sky was black with snow, each man and woman, courtier and soldier, wrapped in such heavy winter clothing they seemed anonymous as their mounts trekked ever upward, past the lowland forests, then into the bare passes that led through the highest, bleakest ranges.

Laggan was this way, he recalled. Not that he raised the idea with Fergus, no longer porter, now steward and paymaster for the journey as he wished. Banquo had been right: some things were best left unsaid.

At the end of that first day, they passed a frozen mountain burn next to a rowan grove, the kind the pagans thought holy.

A simple wooden cross, freshly cut, rose from the virgin snow around it. In the ice by the river stood the unmistakable signs of blood locked beneath the surface. Something—a wolf, perhaps—had scratched at it for meager sustenance in the vicious cold.

Fergus glanced at the spot with a grim and knowing look as they passed. Macbeth stopped and stared and let the party struggle on through the screeching gale.

After a little while, Cullen made his way back and came to the king.

"Sire," he said, struggling with the gale. "There's shelter ahead. A hamlet. We will take the houses, and the folk there will happily sleep outside, such is the pleasure they will feel at your presence."

"A sudden and unexpected honor," he murmured, unable to take his eyes away from the simple makeshift cross of rowan branches. "One so great they will bestow it without foreknowledge. A king is fortunate to have such readily loyal subjects."

A shape moved in the dark fir trees behind, a crablike figure, and behind it, another, skinny and fleet of foot.

"The sisters I spoke of..." he began. He should have known they'd find him first. They had the power of inner sight, of arcane knowledge, that he craved. They'd know he needed them.

"We continue looking," Cullen answered. "Without a name. An idea of where they come from—"

"No need," Macbeth said, waving him away. "Leave me."

"I'll send guards," Cullen replied.

"Send no one! Those are my orders!"

The man didn't move. "It was here that Banquo fell," Cullen said. "The robbers who killed him may still be close."

"I fear no robbers!" Macbeth barked. "I cower at nothing that walks and breathes upon this blasted earth." He nodded toward the line of horses, now stationary a short way along the path. “Go with them. Say I wish to mourn my comrade where he died. I shall meet you at this hamlet and sleep in a tent like all the rest. Do not evict a poor and harmless farmer from his home for me.”

“Sire…”

The man fell silent, seeing Macbeth’s face, then left.

When the party had disappeared from sight, he dismounted, walked to the cross, stared at the frozen burn, Banquo’s blood locked inside it.

“They said you fought like a bear,” he murmured. “How else?”

The rowan bushes parted. The three were there, one tall and muscular, one hobbling spiderlike on her black crutches. The third, the youngest, most slender, erect and smiling, black eyes gleaming in the dying sun, a fine wool cloak pulled around her.

Macbeth withdrew his sword and said, “If Banquo’d had his way, we’d have slain you back in the Great Glen that night and been the happier for it.”

“Oh, sir.” The child laughed in a bright and girlish voice, coming straight to him, dashing out her thin fingers to touch the silver edge of the blade, then recoiling, feigning shock, surprise, a little excited fear. “You give us too much credit. What have we done? Nothing. We tell of possibilities only, wispy fortunes that may be. It’s for others to make them happen, if they please.”

“Your magic—”

“Is illusory,” she interrupted. “A shiny ribbon on a gift you give a loved one. Appreciated but nothing like as priceless as the thing itself.”

She touched the sword again.

"The thing itself being you and yours. How is the queen? As resolute and strong-minded as ever, I trust?"

His hand was there to slap her. The smile stayed fixed upon her face.

"Stay away from her," Macbeth muttered. "And do not trifle with me."

"We never have and never will," she said, peering into his face. "You should know by now. I see so many questions in your eyes…"

"I need to know…"

"Not here," she said, and silenced him. The girl nodded to the hill behind. "Somewhere a little warmer and more fit." That light look of amusement again. "Will you take a drink with three weird sisters and let us say our piece?"

She reached into his coat, her slender hand searching, found a pocket in his breeches, grasped, fumbling within, and took a coin.

"This time, though," the child cried, grinning, "there's a price that must be paid."

◈ ◈ ◈

Beyond the rowan grove, halfway up the steep hill, the cave mouth opened like a fissure in the earth. Inside, the air was warm from the smoky fire of damp branches and, it seemed to him, the very atmosphere itself, as if this gloomy channel reached all the way to regions lost far below, deep down, even to Hell itself.

Something—a hare, perhaps—stood on a charred spit over the fire. The tall one reached out idly as she passed and snatched a chunk of flesh from its burned limbs. They bade him sit on a low, cold rock and gathered opposite, the old one seated, the big one crouching on her haunches, the young girl perched on a rock, all eyes on him.

He glanced around the walls and saw there strange figures, sticklike men and animals that bore no resemblance to creatures he had ever known. "What is this pit?"

"A temple," the girl responded. "To gods so bored with this mean world they slumber." She stared at him, her black eyes gleaming. "And yet they know things, should you call them…"

The old one prodded the embers of the fire with her crutch and crooned, "By the pricking of my thumbs, something wicked this way comes."

She looked up, stabbed the crutch at Macbeth, and hooted, "Ach! It's there!"

"What are you?" Macbeth murmured. "What is your business?"

"Simple women who walk the heaths," the girl said. "Our business? A deed without a name, not one you'd fathom, anyway. What do you truly seek, Macbeth? You're king of Scotland, as we foretold. Our interest here is surely done."

"A crown is nothing of itself…"

"Simple women who walk the heaths," the girl repeated with a sudden impatience. "You have all the knowledge we possess. For more…" The hag crooned a strange incantation beneath her breath.

"A price, you said." He threw before them all the contents of his purse.

The girl gazed at the coins as if she despised them. "You've nothing more to hear from us," she replied. "Though, our masters—"

"Call 'em. Let me see 'em," he ordered.

They went quiet at that, and then the tall one rose and, with both hands, opened her long sackcloth coat. Ranged along the inside stood small glass bottles, eight or more each side, all stitched and secure within the fabric as if she were a mendicant quack.

The brute of a woman pointed to a violet-colored vial and said, "This would raise the dead for one who knew the words to make it work." Her fingers ran to an amber bottle next to it. "And this suck out the breath of the strongest, healthiest man alive and turn him to a corpse, all in a single heartbeat."

"I want no poisons..." Macbeth hissed.

"Poisons and medicine...what's the difference?" she asked. "Those guards you fed with mekilwort would have woken with clear heads had you not stuck a blade into their guts."

"I want—" he started.

"This," the girl said, retrieving a black bottle from near the tall one's breast, "will take you straight into the bosom of our rulers and ensure they tell you nothing but the truth." She shrugged. "Though you may not like the journey..."

"I have been through hellish times..." he murmured. "Do not treat me lightly."

She strode over, came close, and held it before him. Her face was pretty, clean and flawless, the skin so smooth it seemed unreal. The girl's breath carried the scent of strange fragrances—aniseed and flowers. Her perfect teeth, those of a babe, ranged white and even, none rotten, none misshapen, all the color of fresh milk. The black vial was tight in her fingers.

Her fine and slender hand went to his matted hair, her mouth rose to his ear. Macbeth recoiled at her unexpected touch.

"Do not shrink back from me, sir," she whispered. "Not if you wish to know. Take this potion and you'll hear such things that might never reach even our own ears." She uncorked the bottle and sniffed the contents.

"What is it?" he asked.

"Mountain herbs and the distillation of a certain mushroom that grows in southern pastures." The girl shrugged. "A man I once knew called it the Phrygian Cap, but then, he was a foreigner."

She waved the black bottle before him.

"Nothing strange. No sow's blood, no grease from a murderer's gibbet or bat or lizard. I told you. We have so little magic in our hands. But this"—she nodded, raising the bottle—"is nature's brew and will lead you where you wish. More"—her pale features creased in a frown—"we cannot do."

"Give me," he said, snatching the bottle and drinking down the contents in one swift move. The liquid was as thick as treacle and tasted like an exotic musty fruit blended with poteen.

They watched in silence, and then the hag said, "Had you listened, man, she'd told you to drink but half the thing. I spent a year distilling that concoction. And now some Highland fool..."

He didn't hear. A booming noise was rising in his head like the sound of a distant ocean growing to a winter fury. The room was closing in, the dark walls shifting as if the rock itself beat to some infernal heart that brought to life the stick men and their quarry, turning the scribbled drawings there into an active, bloody hunt.

Then a fast and screeching form of sleep came on him—for how long, he didn't know. When he woke, he was on the far side of the cave, close to the fire, half propped up on bags and blankets, back against the wall, a slumped and inert figure, legs and arms like stone, heart racing, mind awhirl.

The skinny girl was close upon him now, her lips on his face, her words in his ear. He tried again to move and couldn't, so potent was the working of the drug.

"Oh, Macbeth," she said, her fingers tugging at his coat. "Where are you, man? Your brow is sweaty, your skin as hot as the coals of Hell, your eyes as wild as a rabid dog. Let me loosen your clothes a little and make this brief, ecstatic journey halfway pleasant and memorable…"

"Do not touch me, you black and midnight hags," he slurred. "I asked for secrets…"

He could hear the roaring, pulsing of the blood rushing through his veins, the myriad chatter of the insects in the gloom. She touched him, cold, smooth flesh against his, and brushed her lips against his cheek.

"What would you give to know these mysteries?" Her voice was cunning, low, assured. "If storms might bring down churches, if gales might wreck your fleet, if castles topple on the heads of warders and their children, and all of nature rot and sicken…"

"I'll live with that. So tell me," Macbeth mumbled, watching his vision shrink until it became nothing but the vast pinhead of her black eye, his own face a pale and pained reflection in its mirror.

She giggled and said, "Or something closer to home."

Her fingers strayed to touch him.

"Think on this," she whispered. "After slaughter, your soldiers take women as easily as wolves take sheep. No please or thank you. No need or hunger on their victims' part. Yet men…"

He felt her thin and bony body shuffling ever nearer, breath coming in tense and anxious pants.

"…must stiffen their…resolve for the occasion. How works that, sire? You are a good and faithful husband. A would-be saint. Yet with my deft fingers and a simple potion, I may overthrow that flimsy thing you think of as your conscience…"

He felt like running, retching, but could not move. The eyes of the other two, dark and glittering, were on him, brightly avaricious, keen as knives.

"Ah! Like the sun, he rises," the girl cried in triumph.

Ribald cheers and clapping from beyond the fire. His mind turned, twisting, seeking reason.

"Which wins within you?" the girl cried in his ear. "The lamb that whimpers for less or the mindless lion that roars for more?"

"Leave me, witch…" he pleaded.

"Too late," she said, and straddled him like a beast upon its prey. "We are as one."

Two thin hands gripped him, forced him, took him where he never wished to go, and still, he lacked the power to argue or resist.

For one brief moment, he felt himself unconscious. When he woke, her arms were round his head like vises, her lips forced hard into his ear.

"Whatever you are," he moaned, "tell me…"

"Be silent, mortal!"

That was the voice of another, a man, dark and low and malevolent. The guttural words rose from deep inside the throat of the creature wrapped around him, writhing, the speech of some god inside her, as was he.

Her head twitched again; she sighed and rocked and whimpered, "He knows your thoughts, my little love. Hear him out and say naught, do naught, except move with me…"

The lilting tone vanished. She sighed, two long and bottomless moans.

"Macbeth! Macbeth!" the dark voice roared from deep within her. "Beware MacDuff. Beware the thane of Fife."

"I hear you," Macbeth murmured, swaying and hating every movement, "and thought as much..."

"Be quiet! Be obedient!" It was her again, limbs tight around him, arching, squirming, squealing, hissing.

He closed his eyes, wishing to wake from this sharp and infinite nightmare, and when he opened them, a naked, bloody child hung scarlet in the air ahead.

Its gory mouth opened and the thing sang through teeth like fangs, "Macbeth! Macbeth! Macbeth!"

Its voice was childlike, high and bitter, and came from the throat wrapped round him.

"I hear thee..." he whispered, eyes locked on the naked, bleeding form.

"Be bloody, bold, and resolute," declared the squealing tone, so close it chilled his spine. "Laugh to scorn the power of man, for none of woman born shall harm you."

His right hand went to the damp, soft nape of the head, pushing, heaving hard against his neck. A gesture of unconscious, unmeant gratitude, it could be no more. The lion, not the lamb.

"Oh," he groaned, mind racing, shapes and urges gathering in his body, forces he could never conquer. "Then live, MacDuff. Why need I fear you?" A sudden stabbing thought, a conviction as hard and firm as that now growing in his loins. "Yet you shall not live. I'll sleep fearless of a night and never count the cost. If..."

The blood and heat rose in him, and as it did, the scarlet babe faded. In its place rose another, a glorious child, five, six, no more, with shining yellow hair, upon it a crown, in its pale right hand an oak tree, growing, leaves and acorns, roots and all.

"This is the offspring of a king," he muttered.

Her voice was at him, nagging, relentless.

"I told you to listen, lord," it croaked, a good tone deeper than before. "Say nothing. Hold me. Move me, man…Ah, lord…"

Her tone rose wildly, a stream of imprecations flew like spittle from her lips. Now she had the clearest, sweetest voice he'd ever heard and said, "Be proud and take no mind who plots or frets or gossips. Macbeth shall never vanquished be until Great Birnam wood walks to Dunsinane hill against him."

A walking wood, he thought. *If this is true…*

The thing upon him caught wind of his distraction and clenched him harder, scratching, biting, screeching, spitting, warm saliva on his throat, vile grunts around his head.

"Banquo?" he cried. "What of Banquo? Will his issue rule this land?"

"I told you keep your peace, man," the sister shrieked, and as she spoke, the child flew backward, toward the endless gloom that lay beyond the fire.

Shapes formed there, figures, grand and noble, glowing with a bright unearthly light. A line, a procession of regal forms, crowned and sceptered, in long and graceful gowns. They walked past, each a visible king, and last of all strode Banquo, throat cut, beard bloody, eyes burning, pupils like fire, staring out at him, laughing.

False lust and passion died at that moment, and in their place came a fatal, all-consuming shame. The strange potion withdrew itself and took what meager energy he owned.

Eight kings from Banquo. None from him.

"No wonder!" cried the thing besetting him. "What use are you, man? What dynasty comes from wilted, sterile loins? I wonder your woman got a bairn in her to begin with. You think it's yours?"

So weak, so drugged, yet still his loathing of her brought with it a feeble show of strength. He pushed her back, looking to see the three blue salmon writhing, twisting, on that smooth, pale torso he'd first witnessed from horseback next to Banquo in the glen.

His fingertips touched rough skin and wrinkled flesh. The hag, the crippled crone, straddled him, laughing through a snag-toothed rotten mouth, foul breath a miasmic cloud upon his face.

Macbeth howled and shrieked, frozen as he repelled her skeletal frame from his. Cawing like a gigantic crow, she scrambled on the ground to find her crutches and crawled back toward the flames, where the other two sat seated, still and watching.

"What in God's name are you?" he murmured, and tried to stand, stumbling toward the cave mouth.

"God hasn't got around to us yet," the girl said flatly. "He's enough on his hands with the likes of you. I thought you might have noticed." She reached out and ripped a piece of meat from the burning branch before her. "What are *you*, Macbeth? There's a question of more moment."

"No more, no more," he moaned, feeling filthy and corrupted, the self-loathing rising in his throat like bile. "If I should see your ugly faces again—"

"Be confident of this," she cried. "As you may be of all else you've heard. You shall not see us hence, Macbeth. There's other work to do."

He struggled upright, half fell, half crawled toward the moonlight beyond the door.

"Don't forget your breeches, man," called the hag, and fell to cackling. "A king without his trews is nothing more than a man."

He snatched the clothes from by the rock and fell out into the freezing night, then spent an unknown time upon the ground, shivering, puking, weeping, wishing himself free of these frightful memories—dead, even. Quiet in an everlasting sleep.

That never came.

Dawn was breaking by the time he found the hamlet and the tent where Skena sat upright, pale and shocked.

It was the briefest of conversations. She saw the marks on his neck and face, smelled something strange and physical. Her face hardened as she looked at him, became puzzled, distant, hateful.

"Do you wish to tell me?" she murmured, nothing more, when he was naked, shivering in the bath, splashing water over himself constantly, teeth chattering, head shaking.

"Ask no questions, woman," Macbeth snapped. "You do not need to hear."

◈ ◈ ◈

Banquo's son was a boy of fifteen when Macbeth's henchman slew his father in the mountain pass on the way to Laggan. He turned sixteen at the close of the year, not that he knew the date, since by then he was shivering in an empty peasant's bothy forty miles south of Laggan, wondering how long it would take to die.

Tall and skinny, more used to talk than combat, he had known from the outset he was no use against the villains who flew at them that grim afternoon. His final memory of the ambush was of Banquo screaming at him to fly for home as quickly as his horse could take him.

Fleance obeyed. He always had. A loyal son, doing Banquo's bidding without a second thought, so fierce and incontrovertible was the voice of the man who'd raised him, loved him, tried to teach him the hard ways of the Highlands. It was only later that the horror of what had occurred began to dawn in his young mind. With a grim heart, he rode back down the glen to the point at which the men had set upon them. In his head, his father was so strong, such a roaring force of nature, that it was impossible to believe him dead. A part of Fleance fully expected to see Banquo there, seated on the corpses of the men he'd slain, laughing as he swigged from a hip flask, wolf skin round his neck, great fists smeared with their blood.

Instead, he found his father's sad and mutilated corpse and sat by it, weeping, wishing himself dead, too, killed alongside Banquo, their common blood mingled on the heather, frozen in the icy burn.

Then there were more voices from down the pass—men from Macbeth's court, from what they said—shouting out for Fleance, calling out their rank.

They did not call his father's name at all.

Something Banquo had said as he went for the villains, sword flailing, came to him: *"I love you, boy. Trust that. Trust no one else alive."*

He took his mare and scuttled back to the hills as quickly as he could, so anxiously that a mile on his mount stumbled, breaking its front right leg. There, he abandoned the animal and walked, through the driving snow, through blizzards, frost and fog, all the way to Laggan.

When he found the small house near the loch, his mother ran upstairs in floods of tears. His uncle, never a kindly man, weaker than Banquo but now with an eye on his land, questioned him repeatedly, more interested in the politics of the new court and Macbeth's power than the details of the murder or who might lie behind the deed.

That night, Fleance tested his bedroom door and found it locked. A guard was snoring heavily outside. None of this was right.

The following day, his mother, still red-eyed and racked with grief, took him to one side in the kitchen, slipped him a dagger, looked him in the face, and said simply, "Flee south, Fleance, and don't delay. The Highlands are Macbeth's now. They're safe for you no longer." She clutched his hand. "And if we never meet again in this harsh life, know I love you more than anything else that walks these great green hills."

When he went out to the latrines that evening, he never came back. Men on horses hunted him across the snow-capped peaks, following his footsteps, chasing him with dogs. But Fleance's legs were long and swift. Fired by the furious glint in his mother's loving, teary eyes, he found a flinty form of courage and determination, a steel he'd never guessed lived inside him.

Trust no one. Not even those you think you love and who love you.

All kith and kin around the lands of Laggan he shunned from that moment on, hiding in the empty bothies left by shepherds, seeking shelter from the snow. He remembered how to snare mountain hare and rabbit, turned snow to water with the warmth of his own body. When kindle and a flint failed, he ate the flesh of game he caught, raw and bleeding, crying with each bite. But not for long. Within a few weeks he was as rough and dirty as any mountain savage, a grubby beast with half a beard, a wild eye, and little in the way of speech for any that he met.

Fleance, the son of Banquo, a great and noble thane, was now invisible, dead to all who sought him. And seek him they did. Of that he had no doubt.

He'd no idea what way he took through the vast white peaks and valleys that lay before him. Each day seemed the same: wait till sunlight, fix the east, then turn a half circle right from the point of the rising sun and aim for that direction. A week, two, a month, more, passed in this grim and freezing manner, taking food and drink when best he could, stealing from the hen coops that he passed, swallowing down the eggs raw and whole to keep alive.

A point came at which he thought, *No more.* Death was better than this miserable, lonely existence. And in death, at least he'd find his father.

Though what that fierce and bearded man might say... That thought spurred him on for one more day, until starving, thirsty, he lay down in an abandoned sheep pen somewhere close to the peak of another rolling, snowy crag. There was sufficient shelter for his skin to touch frozen heather as he lay, mind roving, fully expectant that, come the spring, a wandering shepherd would find his corpse here, ravaged by wolf and eagle, as he had taken sustenance from the lesser creatures his knife and snare had found.

Sometime later, he woke and found himself rolling, turning away from an unexpected sensation, one he fought to remember, and only found its name—warmth—with difficulty.

There was a fire melting the ice on the frozen heather, sticks and hay crackling with a busy glee. The bloody skinned corpse of a mountain hare hung above it on a blackened branch. Its winter fur, white and stained with gore, sat in a bundle by the doorway in front of three dark shapes, one young and slight, one muscular as a man, the last a crone on crutches.

Fleance shuffled upright, racked by sudden fear, grappling for the knife he kept tucked inside his belt.

They didn't flinch.

"I kn...know you," he stuttered, recalling that last conversation with his father.

"We're your guardian angels," the young one said with a smile, and offered him a flask with sweet water in it, a hunk of bread, some sausage, then a piece of hot and welcome meat.

He ate and they said nothing, merely watched.

"You're the sisters," he declared when he was done, glad he felt no fear at all. "The ones who spoke to Macbeth and my father after they defeated Sueno." He hesitated. It had to be said. "The ones who started this. All of it."

They laughed, each of them, one voice high and young, the second low and masculine, the third an ancient cackle.

"Yes," said the crone, wiping her rheumy eyes. "Without us this land would be paradise. Unicorns and all."

"How do you know of us?" the young girl asked, ignoring her.

With a little reluctance, he admitted, "I dream." Fleance watched her as he spoke, then added, "Or perhaps you came into my head and showed yourselves—while I slept, that is."

They stared at him.

"Who are you, really?" Fleance asked.

"I told you. Guardian angels," the girl replied. "Our wings are elsewhere with our golden hair. Here..." She handed him a purse. There was more money there than he'd ever owned.

"You need a better knife than that," the big one added, throwing him a vicious, curving blade.

"And names," the hag said, passing across a paper full of writing. Places. People. Even a map that showed the path all the way down to the lowlands, then out to the coast by the Firth of Forth.

"Go south along the frozen burn," the girl said. "Avoid Dunkeld and Perth. Aim for Fife. When you see the blue waters of Loch Leven by Kinross, you may speak to men and ask the way to Crail. Do not say your name to anyone, nor your business. Keep your counsel till you reach the gates of MacDuff."

"And when I'm there?"

She smiled. Her teeth were white and even, like those of a bairn.

"Then consider yourself safe, for the time being. This weather lifts soon, Fleance," she said, "and with the spring, men get hot and restless. This land will not be still and silent long. Now eat your food and be on your way."

"You speak to me as if I'm a child!" he cried. "And you nothing but a wee girl in a cloak..."

She crept across the distance between them, and as she approached, he fell silent and a little scared. Close up, he'd no idea how old she was. Her skin was perfect; her black eyes gleamed. And yet there seemed something ancient in her features.

"Do as you're told, boy," she said, not unkindly. "Or the buzzards will be picking your bones clean before the sun sets on the morrow, and Macbeth, your father's murderer, set firm on the throne of Scotland for years to come."

"Why me?" he asked.

"What kind of question is this?" the girl asked.

"Why save my life when you let so many others fall?"

She reached out and touched his matted, greasy hair.

"You have something in here, child," she said. "Just like us. We look after our ain folk. We see in them such things on occasion…"

"It was your words that set this tragedy in train."

She shook her head, which was, he thought, as lovely as a strange, exotic flower.

"We plant no seed," the girl whispered, smiling. "Only water what lies there already." Her fingers played across his brow. "And the seed in you is growing now. You feel it, too."

"A line of kings, you said…"

"Is some way distant if you do not quit these hills. Eat and take the things we give you. Then leave."

He did, and one hour later, they stopped at a snowy bluff, pointing him down the path, then flitting across the sweeping white landscape like crippled crows.

◈ ◈ ◈

Two weeks later, he was at the gates of MacDuff's castle, overlooking the bright waters and white cliffs of a gentle bay. He had a beard now and better clothes bought along the journey. His mind was clear and firm—his manner, too—so earnest the thane gave him private audience without question, even though he'd never revealed his name.

"You have business with me?" the tall man with the black beard asked, perusing his visitor with a hand upon his chin.

"You know me, sir. I am called Fleance. My father was Banquo, a comrade, ally, and friend to you. Murdered by Macbeth for fear that all the world would know the treachery of the man who wears the crown of Scotland."

MacDuff was on him in an instant, hand round his mouth, hustling him into the shadows.

"Quiet, you simple fool!" he hissed.

Fleance obeyed. The older man looked at him, ever more curious. He asked some questions, family matters, the geography of Laggan, the campaigns his father had fought. Fleance answered briskly, with straight answers. These were matters his father had drummed into him since he was a child. It was the simplest test.

"You are Banquo's son, I see," MacDuff said when they were done. "Much changed. They think you dead."

"They'd have me so, sir."

"And still would. I will find you a private room here in my quarters. You are a distant nephew from the west. Here on business. Say nothing more."

"Aye," Fleance said.

"And tonight, we dine alone, son of Banquo. There's much I need to hear."

◈ ◈ ◈

It was more than a month before the royal party escaped the bewildering landscape of frozen peaks and glens. Snow had blanketed Scotland in never-ending blizzards that came roaring from the north with all the relentless ferocity of the Viking hordes. For five long weeks the train of horses and carriages had ploughed through vast drifts that were mountains in themselves, sometimes making barely a mile in the brief hours between dawn and a dismal gray sunset.

Macbeth's new kingdom had turned into an endless icy hell in which men and horses alike died trying to gain a foothold through the treacherous passes.

Toward the end of January, they finally reached the sprawling private palace that Duncan favored in Forres. Perched high on an exposed hill overlooking the inlet of Findhorn Bay, the place was built for reclusive summer pleasure, not harsh winter and the government of the land. The low arcaded buildings, more monastery than castle, invited in the wind and snow. The small harbor by the sandy spit of Findhorn was closed through ice and driven sand. Few messengers made their way from east or west, and none by boat at all. Locked in deep and silent thought, aching from a constant sense of shame, Macbeth found himself monarch of a vast white emptiness, as unknown as it was unknowable. All the effort he'd made to cement his grip on the throne now felt like powdered snow sifting through his fingers. The many spies he'd placed in households from tip to toe of Scotland, Berwick to the distant Ness of Huna, were, for the most part, useless, silent burdens upon his treasury, and those who did report said nothing that might earn their keep.

Isolated thus, his mood was to seek for proof of treachery over loyalty, and of that there came none. The locals, trapped within his power, were vocal in their fidelity, bringing food and salted fish and vegetables, when beyond the palace walls, their own bairns starved. He sent it back with thanks and orders for the common distribution of what meager provisions might be found. Lord and lady, peasant and pauper, Moray lived on dry, bony herring and rotten carrots, praying for the storms to lift. And in the arcades of the palace, Macbeth, a solitary figure, strode in silence, lost in thought, sleepless most the night, a stranger both to wife and subjects.

The dread from meeting with the sisters refused to leave him. His resolve to deal with traitors, real or suspected, remained, even MacDuff, whose true offense was no more than a slight, a lack of politeness, leaving the coronation in Scone too soon. But even if he wished to act on his slim suspicions, he saw no easy way to do so. The only troops he possessed were those around him on the Moray Firth. To dispatch them to seek out his enemies would leave Forres dangerously unguarded and show his hand to any who may be nursing treacherous thoughts of their own. MacDuff, the most obvious target of his wrath, would prove a difficult adversary, living as he did in distant Crail, far south, overlooking the Firth of Forth.

Yet Forres was a royal palace and possessed all the trappings of monarchy. In his empty hours he'd used them, found himself staring at maps of places he had barely heard of, towns, regions, and castles he had dismissed as needless when he had only been the thane of Glamis. How long ago that seemed, those clearer days when he had been locked inside the black walls of Inverness, plotting against the relentless Norsemen.

Unrolled before him by the knowledgeable Cullen, he saw the shapes of nations that had hitherto been nothing more than names from children's stories: Norway and Denmark, with their cruel and avaricious pirates; Ireland, just as bellicose; the vast spread of France and below it the Iberian Peninsula, where a strange race called the Arabs, followers of a different faith, now waged war against retreating Christian powers; and beyond that, Rome, the seat of the pope, God's person made flesh, a place for penitence and mercy.

One day, he swore, when all was well, he'd take Skena there, and side by side, they'd crawl the dirty streets like beggars, praying for absolution, putting the black shame behind them, rising with a papal blessing, refreshed, anew. He didn't care about the risk or the cost in alms. Blood dried in the end and would be washed away.

One day.

Till then…the cruel, hard season had emasculated him, as if it were an adversary itself. He had no choice but to wait and listen to nothing but the wind blowing in from across the gray expanse of sea. No news of treachery. No sign of Banquo's boy, Fleance, now thought to be nothing more than a frozen corpse lost somewhere in the Grampians, food for wolves and ravens. Macbeth wanted to believe it, but his heart told him otherwise.

That line of kings he'd seen in the grim and feverish darkness of the sisters' cave would not leave him. Nor, as some constant crumb of comfort, that other utterance: *"None of woman born shall harm you."* What else could it mean but that he was invulnerable to his enemies? That did not lessen their treachery or his hunger to seek them out.

When he stared at the map, his focus did not stay long on the foreign regions. There was a nearer neighbor of more pressing concern—England, joined to Scotland by that long and porous border that ran from Berwick to the Solway in the west. Larger, greedier, crueler, and ever more ambitious, London harbored Scotland's enemies, always. Now it clutched Malcolm and Donalbain close to its perfidious bosom, plotting to use them as puppets and bring mischief north before long. It mattered nothing to him that the monarch on the throne was the pious saint Edward. It was England's destiny to spout peace until it found the forces and the reason for war. Edward might be tottering on the throne now. But the day his successor looked greedily north would come, and when it did, Scotland would be fighting for her future once more.

These ideas would not leave him, day or night. They came, he thought, with the crown, and he was amazed that he had been ignorant of such burdens before they fell so heavily on his shoulders.

Halfway through February, the sky began to lose its heaviness. One morning, the palace woke to a line of bright blue across the horizon, brilliant behind the distant peaks. Those shivering in Forres's endless corridors remembered, finally, that summer might come again. That day, a scanty sense of hope ran through the palace, and on its back, Cullen, the head of the household guard, came to seek Macbeth, a smile on his rugged, clean-shaven face.

"We have a surprise, sir," he announced, beaming. "A gift from the loyal local populace, a monument to your bravery that will stand here as proof to it for generations to come."

"A gift?" Macbeth replied, lifting his head from the governmental papers he was fighting to comprehend.

"Rebuilding Scotland can wait a while," Cullen, a forward man, told him. He nodded toward the blue expanse of water beyond Findhorn Bay. "When we've ships and horses and a means to travel, then you can pass laws and see them followed."

Macbeth thrust aside the papers, ideas he had for courts and education, for churches and better use of money for the populace, and followed Cullen outside to a bluff beyond the palace walls.

The sun was fully out, the day glorious. A warming sense of pride rose within him as he saw the glittering expanse of the Moray Firth stretching in front of him and behind the Cairngorms, a massive range of snowy peaks, small patches of heather here and there, with the occasional smudge of red for wandering herds of deer.

This is mine, he thought, with not an ounce of selfishness. He belonged to this land, not the reverse. It was his now to cherish, to nurture and make good.

Cullen walked him out of the palace, a pack of guards always two strides behind. At the edge of the hill stood a pale stone slab seven yards high, round it a gathering of locals, a group of stonemasons, some peasants, a few local nobility. All smiling, pleased with themselves.

Macbeth walked up and gazed at the thing. The sides were carved with woven vines, after the manner of the Picts who came before. On the west was a long Celtic cross running almost the full length of the slab. On the reverse… Macbeth stepped round the perimeter and stared at the complex sculpted images carved deep into the rock. It was a panorama of warfare, like a memory plucked from his head of every battle he had ever fought now frozen in stone.

Men at war, a hundred figures or more, each scene laid upon another, cavalry and infantry, mass slaughter, individual combat, ax to ax, face to face.

And then the victims. A line of corpses, soldiers poised above them wielding swords. This was the customary aftermath of battle. The victors triumphant, the defeated beheaded in long and patient rows. Here they lay, freshly slaughtered, their skulls rolling away like cropped corn.

"A brave man who was with you when you fought the traitor MacDonwald and the Viking Sueno assisted us, sir," one of the stonemasons called, raising his hammer and chisel. "He told us how you fought the Vikings." His strong arm gestured at the slab with a proud flourish. "Here we record the victory so all may see. We'll call this Sueno's Stone."

Macbeth said nothing.

"With your permission, sire," Cullen added.

"What man?" Macbeth asked.

Yet he knew the answer before he spoke. A small and wiry figure made its way to the front of the crowd. The steward had kept himself scarce since Banquo's death. That was for the best, on both parts.

"Ah, Fergus," the king said with a sigh. "Such a sharp and active memory. I see no sign of mekilwort or beer."

The man shrugged and said, "For posterity's sake, sir, it seemed more fit we mark the fighting. Winners, losers. That's all the folk remember in the end."

All the faces watched him at that moment. He was the king. His words, his mood, affected each and every one. So Macbeth found it within himself to say a few pleasant sentiments and told himself he'd never see this bloody thing again.

Afterward, he walked back to the palace, told Skena of it as she stitched in silence in their private quarters.

"We have a legacy, then," she said without looking at him. "Where do we live next, husband? Forres is a palace for the summer. You cannot rule the kingdom from here."

"South," he said, hating the thought. "I need the lowland men. I want to know what the English have in mind. How much Malcolm's poisoned them against me."

She looked up, interested, and asked, "Glamis?"

Her home, a place she loved.

"Glamis is like this place—a palace, not a fortress. Cullen says there's a better stronghold not far away." He knelt before her, took her cold hand. "Dunsinane. You know it?"

Skena shivered and said, "A cold, wooden prison on a bleak and bitter mountain. I may as well be back in Inverness."

"When I hold all the reins of power, you'll live where you choose."

She gazed at him the way a stranger might. "We leave soon?" she asked.

"When ships can safely sail. I'll not put you through that cruel ordeal in the mountains again. The land route is for summer only. For the main force of our troops I've no other option. The court goes by ship, to Perth. Soon, when it's spring..."

He looked out of the windows.

"This will be a pleasant journey," he promised.

Fergus was there beyond the glass, staring avidly at the two of them as they spoke.

"Your henchman needs you," she said, and went back to her stitching.

Macbeth strode outside.

"You asked for news of Fleance and MacDuff," Fergus said.

Macbeth's heart fell. "You know of both?"

The steward stood there, a sly look on his narrow face. "They are together."

"Together?" Macbeth echoed with a surge of dread.

So MacDuff knows all, he thought. *What latent suspicions he may have harbored will now bear terrible fruit. My hand is forced.*

Once, he had thought kings all-powerful, men who commanded thousands on a whim. Yet now he was one, and had never felt more like a feather in the breeze, moved by forces he could neither see nor control.

"You've grown reclusive of late, sire," said Fergus, breaking in on his reverie. "I fear you're faint of heart. If so…what need have you of me?"

"Do not presume to know my mind," Macbeth retorted. "You are my servant and shall do my bidding."

"Oh, that I will, sir," he answered with a happy nod.

◈ ◈ ◈

London proved cold and foreign and friendless, though safe. Still, Malcolm would be glad to be out of England. However dangerous his position at home, there was no doubting the low esteem in which the English held the Scots. At Westminster, they had kept him alone and under guard, his men, including his brother, Donalbain, held at the Tower like foreign spies or assassins. Malcolm had been made to wait three hours for the king, who—he was told—was at prayer, during which time he was forbidden to leave the antechamber. His weapons had been taken from him for "safekeeping" and the guards had leaned on their pikes and muttered about him out of the sides of their mouths.

Edward himself, when he finally appeared, said little. The English king wore his crown throughout their meeting, which took place in the greatest hall Malcolm had ever seen, a remarkable structure of stone and stained glass adjoining the abbey itself. The Confessor sat stiff and old and pompous on his carved throne, while Malcolm was obliged to approach and kneel before him under the cavernous roof. He felt, as was intended, like a tiny, importunate insect.

The king was almost three decades Malcolm's senior and wore his royal regalia as if born to it. He was polite, even courteous, to his "Scottish cousin"—as he styled him—but evasive about lending aid. After ten minutes, he needed to consult with his most trusted advisors, and Malcolm was again banished to the waiting room and the watchful leers of the guards.

He never saw the king again. By the time his secretary returned, the thin February sun was almost down. Malcolm was escorted back to his lodgings and left there till noon the next day, when a delegation arrived with a stack of parchment and dense Latin script marked with the royal seal. He signed where he was told, wishing he had expert council on what the documents contained. Yet if English help came with harsh terms attached, that was no more than he expected. And for Edward to enforce those conditions from Westminster would require a longer arm than the English king possessed.

Malcolm thought himself no fool. He might not wear the crown of Scotland yet or own the velvet tongue and many connections of his father, but he had seen much of England on his journey from the north, and little of it was under Edward's sway. The king was hedged about on all sides by factions, by Wessex and the Mercians, by the Normans across the channel, and by the Northumbrians along the Scottish border. However much they put on this show of dominance, Malcolm guessed the pact was not as one-sided as Edward might pretend. An alliance was useful to them both, and Malcolm, who had no intention of leading Scottish troops against Edward's enemies, signed the contracts without hesitation.

Weeks later, spurred by the Confessor's support and word of growing discord back at home, he pressed northward. At York, he had met his uncle, Siward, and—more importantly—the ten thousand men promised to him by Edward. At the turn of the year he had been an exile. Now he was a warlord, leading an army strong enough to mount an invasion.

Yet what had seemed an answer to his prayers raised another problem. Malcolm and Donalbain's flight had led many in Scotland to blame them for their father's death. Even without that crime laid to their charge, Malcolm knew he had few friends among the Council of Thanes. To enter Scotland now at the head of an English army might prove... awkward.

He had sent to Ross and Menteith, to Lennox, Angus, and Caithness, but none would meet him or offer a single word of support. With Banquo dead, they looked to MacDuff to be their leader—even their king, should it come to that. But the thane of Fife would not be drawn. Three times, Malcolm had sent riders, their saddlebags full of English gold, urging him to come south. Three times, the messengers had returned, their bags no lighter than when they left.

After weeks encamped along the English border, this failure was turning worrisome. He could not sit in Northumbria forever with an army that consumed whole farms at every meal. If his forces did not strike soon, he would have to let them go. A return in ignominy to Scotland was unthinkable. There was no home for him there, no friendship, only danger. He would have to seek some miserable exile in Ireland, to live out his days empty-handed in a blasted and forgotten corner of a foreign land.

And deal there with his brother.

Camped outside Berwick, indecisive, growing desperate, Malcolm found Donalbain more tedious by the hour. The previous night, the two had argued bitterly about strategies and tactics. Malcolm was for force and impetuousness. Donalbain advised less haste and more diplomacy.

"Frightened, brother?" Malcolm threw at him in the heat of argument and drink.

The younger man flew at him, hands flailing. "I fight in an army of ten against an entire nation," Donalbain screamed. "How dare you, brother?"

"Ten?" Malcolm screamed. "What kind of fool are you? Ten *thousand*. Look beyond your door."

"Ten thousand English," his brother replied with a sneer. "I can count my Scottish brothers on two hands. And one of them is you, who follows our dead father when it comes to military matters. So perhaps I'll lose a finger there."

"You'll lose your head if you talk that way. Brother or not."

Donalbain looked at him and snarled, "We must find ourselves Scottish allies, or we're nothing more than vassals for that skinny old prig in London. An army of foreign invaders. No better than the Vikings. Worse with traitors at the helm."

A part of this was true and that was why it stung.

"We come to liberate, brother," Malcolm said. "I'll take any foreigner's soldiers if they'll help with it."

"Aye," Donalbain grunted. "And when they go home with all our riches, with the blood of our women and children on them, and Scotland laid to waste from tip to toe…

do you think our people will be grateful? How comfortable will be that throne then, brother? How secure?"

"I'll cross that bridge when I come to it," Malcolm said. He pointed out the tent, toward the icy water of the Tweed by Berwick. "And I'll cross that border when I wish."

"Best wait a while," Donalbain answered, reaching for his coat. "Macbeth lacks the cunning and the wit to be a king. Wait and his own innocence and impetuosity may send some friends our way. Or else"—he drained his goblet, then raised it in an ironic toast as he walked to the tent door—"we'll spend our days getting fat on Dublin bacon and drinking cheap poteen."

He left without another word.

◈ ◈ ◈

Fergus the steward and his three henchmen were on the first ship to leave when, finally, in the first week of March, the ice from Findhorn Bay began to clear. It was a small trader bound for the tiny port near Leuchars on the coast of Fife. The royal party would make a shorter journey a few days later, in greater vessels headed for Perth and then the inland fortress known as Dunsinane. Their trip might take weeks, with necessary calls in Aberdeen and elsewhere along the way, currying favor, establishing loyalty. Fergus was free of all these cares and knew it. There was but one objective in his sights: kill MacDuff and finish Banquo's son, as he should have done that day on the pass to Laggan.

Two of the men who traveled with him—an Inverness cutthroat and the giant with no tongue—had been with him then. The fourth was new, an Irishman who replaced the villain Banquo wounded most severely, a man murdered by Fergus's own hand not long after. He was a bloodthirsty, foul-tempered cur. The right man for this vicious job.

A week it took, with a little time for drink and whores in Arbroath's winding, sooty alleys as the captain sought provisions. After that the vessel crossed the Firth of Tay and found land at Crail, seeking refuge from the blustery gales in a tiny harbor next to a spit of sand surrounded by cruel cliffs and rocks. The captain, a tedious, pious man, dispatched his cargo and his passengers, and then sailed on to make a pilgrimage to the tiny Isle of May, five miles across the water. A saint was buried there, he said. One who'd salve all consciences, forgive—after due penance—all sins.

Not mine, Fergus thought as he listened to this brief sermon. *And still, they're not quite done.*

It was a steep walk up from the beach to the town above, with its tidy, compact castle set on the cliff top. Being a cautious man, he stopped in a tavern on the way, bought generous drinks for his men and others, ate a hearty meal, took rooms for all to spend the night in comfort. There wasn't so much money hereabouts, and he was, he said, a trader seeking business.

None looked at them much or seemed to care. The place appeared distracted. It had the febrile, nervy manner he'd come to recognize over the years, that of a quiet and peaceful people fearing conflict, close and personal. Viking raids were like the midges that swarmed over the land in summer—predictable but haphazard, a pesky drone of constant discomfort. But like midges, Vikings left once there was no more blood to suck. War was different. In Scotland it was, almost always, a civil conflict, brother against brother, town against town. In battles of this kind the rich and comfortable might find themselves penniless or worse in a single night. Fortunes rose and fell on the turn of a penny, the slash of a sword. A man like him, lowborn, an emptier of pisspots most his life, might find himself a lord with land and servants, palaces and castles, all through debt or alliance forged upon a moment's opportunity.

He watched the other three filling themselves with ale, then, when they'd had enough, put a hand over the pots and looked steadily into their eyes.

The landlord was a cheery, fat drunk.

Fergus tipped him and said, "I hear your thane's a fine and decent man."

"Oh, that he is," the publican agreed.

"I'd like to think he'd see me. Business—"

"MacDuff's just one of us, pal. He'll see any man who needs him, high or low." He squinted at Fergus's companions. "Though I'd go on your own, if I were you. Your friends"—he squeezed his nose—"have a Highland fragrance we notice in these parts."

"Alone? On these black streets at night?" Fergus asked, astonished.

"Crail's a safe and pleasant place, friend. You need fear nothing. But wait till morning anyway. The castle's empty at night, save for the thane and his kin. Business is a matter for daylight hereabouts."

Fergus thanked him. Then they made a show of yawns before ambling out back to the rooms besides the stables. One hour later, sharp knives in pockets, keen and ready for murder, they crept through the rear horse yard gate and found the path to the castle on the hill.

There were few lights there, and a single man upon the door. A porter, like him once, unarmed and cheery.

The Irishman stuck him a single deadly blow, then Fergus led the rest inside. From somewhere came the sound of voices, sharp and high and angry.

◈ ◈ ◈

That night, Ross had broken the news to Ailsa MacDuff, his cousin: her husband was flown and Fleance with him. A fearful row ensued.

"Gone from Scotland, you say?" she cried.

"There are matters he must discuss. Must clarify with Malcolm and Donalbain. Be patient, I beg you."

"Patient, cousin? What patience did my husband show? His flight is madness. Now we seem the very thing we're not—traitors to the king. And without a word to me…"

"The land is full of spies," he said. "We need caution, wisdom, fear…In times like these, a man must be wary."

She slapped his face and watched his cheeks turn red with blood and anger.

Beside the fire, Gregor, their son, a surly child of twelve, stood laughing. Next to him was the cradle with the baby, Flora, and rocking it gently was the middle child, Rose, a beautiful girl of four, with long blonde curls.

"What's so funny?" Ross stormed at the boy.

"She'd never hit her man that way," Gregor retorted. "But you…"

Rose ceased rocking the cradle and put her little hands over her ears.

"What kind of father abandons his wife and his bairn to fly to England?" Ailsa demanded. "Even a wren fights for its young against the owl. And my brave husband runs in fear at nothing more than whispers."

"Fleance—" he began.

"I never knew that boy was Banquo's son. You tell me he's the cause of this?"

"They're gone together. For diplomatic conversations. All will be well, cousin. Stay here, stay safe, and speak to no one. In a week, a month—"

"A month?" she howled.

"Be the wife," he interrupted. "Your husband's noble, wise, and judicious. He knows what's best. I cannot tell you further. These are cruel times. One man's vile traitor is another's true and loyal patriot. There's a wild and violent sea around us, whichever way one moves. Stay low, stay true to those who share your blood." He put a tentative hand to her cheek and smiled. "You are my pretty cousin and I will see to it that no harm comes to you or yours. But now"—he shrugged—"I must be gone."

"Well, thank you!" she yelled, and watched him turn his back to leave. "Thank MacDuff, too, when you see him. And say his bed will be cold and passionless should he find some reason to return to his ain folk again sometime. You bastard man…"

The little girl Rose sat down on the floor, hands clamped more tightly to her ears. Gregor shouted abuse. The baby began to bawl.

A candlestick flew at Ross's back, then a glass vase.

Briskly, he departed the room, rushed down the stairs, and out the door.

Halfway down the hill it occurred to him he'd never seen the porter at the gate.

"Crail," he said softly to himself, shaking his head as he stirred the horse for the long ride south. "Fast asleep as always. May your dreamy peaceful slumber last forever. We've wars to fight elsewhere."

◈ ◈ ◈

The child Gregor had a foul, unruly tongue, and his temper now was worse than his mother's, aggravated by the way she clung to him and hugged his head as if he were a weak, defenseless bairn.

In the cot, the baby's wails grew louder.

"Poor children," she whined, teary-eyed and trembling. "Your father's dead to us. What will we do? How will we live?"

"Like the birds, Mother," he snapped.

She eyed him and said, "What?"

"With whatever we find," he answered, tearing himself away from her, standing there, hands on hips. "Besides…"

He took out a small knife from his jacket. She stared at the thing, as did Rose on the floor. The baby's crying turned into a rhythmic choke. The blade was a present from MacDuff. Not suitable for a child.

"Besides what?" She blinked. He was dashing the dagger through the air. "Give me that thing, Gregor. It's not a toy. I don't want it near your sisters."

He stashed the knife in his belt and snarled, "To hell with my sisters. My father's not dead. Don't lie."

"Dead to me," she said.

"Then what will you do for a husband?"

"Ten a penny down the market. Give me that knife, boy!"

"If men are that cheap, buy a dozen, sell them on," he cried, laughing at her, retreating from his mother's grasping hands as they reached out for him.

"That mouth will not serve you well, child. Give me the knife!"

The boy retreated toward the door. "Is my father a traitor, then?"

"To flee this house and leave us to fend alone…yes."

"Strong words, Mother!"

"A man who swears loyalty to his family, then lies and runs away…traitor enough for me, and honest men should hang them," she said. "Gregor! Will you be still?"

He dashed around the table, teasing her, almost tripping once over Rose. Ailsa saw, to her fury, the knife was back in his hand.

"It's the honest men who'd hang, you witch," he told her.

"And why, wise child, is that?"

"Because," he replied, shaking his head as if she were plain ignorant, "there's more men out there that lie and swear than go meekly about their business, honest as the day. Strength in numbers." He flicked the dagger before her. "My father taught me that. If he were dead, you'd weep for him. Not chase me round this chamber."

"God help you, Gregor MacDuff, when I get my hands around your neck. I'll tan your arse as raw as meat and send you straight to bed weeping, that I will. Now!"

The child ran laughing to the door, straight into the open arms of a stranger there. A thin-faced man who wore a mirthless smile. There were shapes behind him, dark and tall.

On the floor, the blonde-haired girl removed her hands from her ears and placed them firmly over her eyes. For some reason Ailsa MacDuff could not fathom, the baby fell quiet, as if sensing something from within the cradle.

"Who are you?" she inquired in a soft, weak voice.

"A messenger, sent from the king. I apologize, you do not know me."

"The king?" she murmured.

"We've business with your husband. I'm sorry." He patted Gregor's head. "I heard voices from below. We'd no idea there was a…friendly spat among you."

The shapes behind him moved and three more men came fully into the light of the brands. The sight of them was unmistakable. The boy knew, too, and ran to her open arms, buried himself in her dress.

"Where's your husband?" one of them, a coarse and bearded thug, demanded.

"In no place so wicked the likes of you may find him," she replied. "MacDuff fled Crail this morning, and now I begin to understand his reasons. There's no one here except his wife and bairns, who've caused no one any offense. Does the king need our blood, too?"

The first man—the leader, she thought—not educated, but no fool, paused and put a finger on his chin.

"You tell the truth, lady?" he asked. "We're pawns in someone else's fingers. Hate us for what we are and what we do. But accept that for it's true. Our argument's with your husband, not his kin. Tell us where the traitor's fled and"—he shrugged—"I, for one, will take your word."

"Traitor! You're the traitor!" the boy cried, flying from her arms.

The knife was in his hand now, and as quick as a wild hound, he was on the biggest of them all, stabbing at the giant's stomach.

"Oh, Gregor, love," she murmured, hands creeping to her mouth, body racked with cold and dread. "I fear you've killed us all…"

The big man screamed and howled as the little dagger reached his guts. She flew to drag the boy away, but before she was there, the villain next to the wounded giant had taken out a short, sharp sword and run it clean across the child's slender throat.

The wound there grew like a wicked, gaping smile. Rose never took her hands away but now buried her golden head in her own small lap.

"My son!" Ailsa cried, hands out before her, weeping, furious, wishing she had some God-given strength to take these men, all four of them, and rip each one to shreds.

The boy spoke a single, incomprehensible word, and then the murderer upon him let the small body slip loose down to the black, cold floor.

A strong arm gripped her, pushed her to the wall.

It was him, the one who led them, sharp-featured, cunning, wily, and cruel. All these things were written in his features. And something else. A hatred for the world and everything that breathed.

"Now, that was unwise," he hissed at her, his elbow hard against her throat.

"Monster, monster," she murmured.

"We are instruments of state, love," he snapped back. "You may as well curse the cold, hard wind that brings the blizzard."

"I'll let a greater power be the judge of that."

"So be it," he barked. "I came here for your husband and that brat of Banquo's, not for you. Were your son not so hasty with his little dagger..."

She said nothing.

"Where did they go?" he asked.

Her eyes were the color of the Moray Firth in springtime.

"A handsome woman," one of the men behind him muttered.

She heard those words and stared at him.

"I'm trying to save you," Fergus told her.

"No, sir," she said. "We died the moment you crossed that threshold. Fool yourself, if that's your wish. You do not fool me. Not for one—"

The dagger rose beneath her breastbone, fighting upward in a single, furious thrust.

Her bright blue eyes never left his face. She took a short, quick breath, then spat with all the force left to her. A scarlet cloud of blood and spittle flew across his taut and snarling features.

One more thrust, another. Her eyes lost their sheen, rolled backward, dull, unfocused. Then he pulled back and let her corpse fall to the floor to lie next to the crumpled form of the child there.

"Bitch," he swore, wiping his face with his sleeve. "Bitch!"

"Macbeth will kill us," the Irish villain with them said.

The giant was on the floor, holding his belly. There was more than blood there. He wouldn't move easily again.

"Macbeth..." the man began again.

Fergus was on him in an instant. "Macbeth is mine," he barked. "I'll take no blame from him. The man is crippled with his conscience. Were it not for his prevarication, MacDuff would have been dead before the snow melted on those yonder hills. It's the likes of us that keep him on his throne, and he knows it."

"I hope to God you're right," the Irishman replied, and stared at the dead woman by his feet.

"We go to Perth to tell him," Fergus added.

"She was a pretty one."

"You'll find another in the whorehouse. Come, boys! You want the men of Crail to find us? I think they feel affection for their thane. We'll meet a pretty fate if they find us here."

The Irishman winked at him and nodded at the giant on the floor. The blood was heavier now, the wound more gaping. From his empty mouth came a series of pained clucking noises. His grim face was racked with pain and fear.

"Leave him," Fergus ordered. "He's got no tale to tell."

The girl was rocking now, making a lowing, musical sound. With it, the baby began to bawl again. Fergus nodded at the Irishman.

"Not me," the man said, shaking his head. "Not children. For pity's sake..."

"Ach," Fergus grunted, taking his bloody dagger to the bundle on the floor. "This is no world for orphans."

Then went to work with the blade.

◈ ◈ ◈

On a bright spring day, the royal boat docked in the harbor at Perth. There was a small gathering on the quayside. King and queen came ashore together, hand in hand, false smiles for those around. Couriers soon besieged Macbeth with messages. Skena listened with him to promises of loyalty couched in language that seemed formal and, on occasion, imprecise, a few diplomatic documents, from Norway, Denmark, Ireland, and France.

Nothing from England. Not a word. Spies from across the border had told of troop movements, though. An army traveling north to camp near Berwick awaiting...what? Not more men, surely. The scouts said the army—English to a man, save for Malcolm and the other puppets—was between five and fifteen thousand strong.

"They await a purpose," she said when all had left.

"What kind?" he asked, puzzled, distant now as always.

"One that will ease their scruples, let them sleep at night, secure they've acted justly."

"War's never about justice," he said bitterly. "It's about power and who should wield it. I will raise an army twice that size."

Macbeth stared at the silver coronet beside their baggage. Formality demanded he wear it when the foreign messengers visited. At every other time…She thought he'd come to despise the thing.

"When the forces arrive from Moray through the mountains," he went on, "nothing will dislodge me from this throne. I did not come so far to be usurped by those cowardly boys of Duncan and his English lackeys."

"I would rather stay in Glamis," she said with the slightest note of hope in her soft voice. "Not Dunsinane. I knew that bleak place when I was a child. The men who slew my father came from there."

"Glamis is unsafe, for now. You must be with me."

"Husband…" she pleaded. "If your confidence is so well founded, why—"

"You are the queen and will stay by my side," he interrupted.

There was someone at the door. A man who entered without knocking. The onetime porter, now the steward. A loathsome, cruel man with a heartless face. When not on some furtive business, he would hover around Macbeth like an equal, not a servant. Even Cullen, their most loyal and steadfast servant, seemed wary of him.

"I'll leave you," she whispered, and went outside.

The quay was busy with merchants. Farmers from the hills, fishermen with their catches. Traders bringing goods on small boats from north and south. Ordinary people leading ordinary lives. She envied every one of them.

There was a commotion by the fence outside their camp. Women's high voices, men shouting back in return.

She heard her name, a familiar voice. A memory from childhood.

Quickly, Skena strode over to the place where soldiers now held back a small party. Three women and their bairns.

"Lady Queen!" a woman about her age cried in that voice she knew. "Remember me! Speak to me!"

Skena pushed her way through the guards and saw them, several women, children with them, pushed and jostled by the soldiers.

"Leave these ladies alone!" she ordered.

"Madame," the officer barked back. "They say dreadful things and would cause trouble here. I beg you, do not interfere…"

"Skena! Skena! Skena!" a burly, red-faced matron at the front cried. "Remember me! Aileen from Glamis. We played together as children. You from the big house. Me from the farm."

Aileen. Glamis. The green and lovely summers of childhood.

"Of course I remember," she answered with a smile. "Why are you here? Come see us later. Not now…" She turned and gestured at the busy camp. "It's too hectic…"

The woman got down on her knees and held her hands together as if in prayer. "For all the love we shared, mistress, tell the king that none here is his enemy! I beg you. Do not exercise his wrath upon us the way he did with that poor lady over in Crail. She was a loving wife and knew nothing of what MacDuff plotted. Nor that he harbored the son of

Banquo. Do not punish the women for the sins of their husbands."

"MacDuff? Crail?" she asked.

The crowd was silent and so were the men around her.

"You do not know?" the woman asked, astonished. "And you the queen of Scotland?"

"These are riddles," Skena told her. "What—"

"Slain!" she roared. "Cut down in her home, alongside her children. A boy of twelve, a girl of four, a babe in its cot—all with their throats cut as if by a common thief."

Skena shook her head. "No," she said.

He wouldn't. Not children. Not a bairn in its cot. Not after all they had suffered themselves.

The ghost of Ewan rose in her memory. An implacable young face. One that sneered at her with hate and disbelief.

"Yes!" the woman bellowed. "Do not deny it, lady. There's not a soul here who doesn't know the truth. Spare us, please. Let them fight it out among each other. Not over the bodies of their wives and babes."

The crowd pressed further, hands reached out to her, and she tried to shriek at them, "Lies! Lies! Lies!"

And then a single silver blade flashed through the air. A dark-haired woman at the back of the pack, throwing herself forward, struggling to do her harm.

The knife caught the sleeve of her gown. Silk ripped, and through the fine fabric she felt the chill edge of pain as the sharp edge caught and tore her skin. A line of blood was soaking through the sleeve of the regal gown.

The soldiers pounced then, dragged the culprit out of the crowd, beating the rest back hard with sticks.

Skena stared at the wound, which was slight, and then at the woman thrown heavily to the ground before her.

"Why would you do me harm, lady?" she wondered.

"She was my sister!" the woman in the mud and filth snarled back and spat hard in her face.

One of the soldiers slapped her round the head with his gauntlet.

"Do not hurt her," Skena ordered. "She's not of sound mind. Take her home." She waved a hand at the others. "Take them all home. *Do not harm them.*"

They grumbled at that and shooed the mob away.

Clutching her arm, she stood there for a long and painful minute. Then she stormed back to the tent. Macbeth was there alone, head in hands, a solitary figure slumped on a chair.

She walked over and took his chin in her hand, tried hard to look into his bleak, lost eyes.

"MacDuff's wife and family," she said. "An innocent woman and her three children."

"It was a mistake," he murmured. "I asked for none of that."

"Children? A blameless wife? What kind of mistake could justify so rash and bloody a deed?"

"No more," he said, and turned away, waving her toward the door. "It was an accident. Had MacDuff been loyal, none of this would have occurred."

"And that is explanation enough? What kind of man are you?"

He rose to his feet, hand drawn back, ready to strike.

"Hit me, then, husband," she said, standing her ground. "Why should I be immune from your violence when all of Scotland feels the force of it?"

The truth struck her like the knife wound in her arm, bright and clear and terrible. There were no more words left, no feelings. What she had done, she had done for him, while he, in turn, had served her the same way. Seeking to put each other first, they had gained the crown and lost the most precious thing of all—each other. They were different people now, and quite alone.

"Be gone, woman," he ordered. "Pack for war in Dunsinane. The Confessor's army marches with Scottish puppets at its head. I will make the sea run red with the blood of these vile traitors. I will scatter their flesh and bones from Forth to Clyde. I am Macbeth and—"

"None of woman born shall harm you," she said, finishing his words.

Those words had become a circular refrain for him. A code, a hymn, to what he supposed was his invulnerability.

"If that is true," she said gently, "then you are not a man at all. And I am a widow, my loving husband taken from my arms."

He glared at her, and she scarcely knew the man she saw.

"Is there such a one?" he demanded. "The sisters spoke. I heard them."

His mailed hand had lowered, but she sensed it pushed to lash out. Skena stared at it and wondered.

"Do not blame me, husband. Or yourself. We are man and wife and made this cross for one another. Did you hold the hammer? Or I the nails? Or both, in turn?" Her head felt so light it might drift from her own shoulders. "I no longer know, nor care."

"Of *woman* born," he snarled, his face suffused with hatred.

"Then perhaps it was a blessing that our infant perished," she murmured, watching him, amazed. "For I would not wish more monsters on this world."

◈ ◈ ◈

That same day, by the sparkling waters of the Tweed, two miles from the Scottish border, the flap of Malcolm's tent opened and MacDuff walked in with Donalbain and another, a lanky youth with a wispy beard.

"Did you bring troops?" Malcolm demanded of the man who stood before him.

"I brought Banquo's son," said MacDuff. "He has a tale like yours. I listened to him. And now I'll listen to you."

"Fleance?" Malcolm asked, nodding at the young man by the entrance.

"Sir," the youth answered.

"You know what Macbeth is?"

"I saw my father slaughtered by his men."

Donalbain slammed his fist on the table. "Ours, too—the king. And this monster would cast the blame on us."

"With no small talent, it would seem," MacDuff noted. "That army of yours"—he glanced outside—"is English through and through. And for all of Fleance's earnest fears, I tell you, man…I see no proof."

Malcolm scowled at him. "You've come a long way, friend, to sit upon the fence."

"The English!" MacDuff bellowed, and pointed toward the open flap. "I am no traitor."

"And nor are we," Donalbain cut in. "Those troops will be gone the moment their job is done. Edward's old and sick. The day he vanishes into the ground the Normans will come hunting the crown of England." He nodded at the north. "Scotland is ours when we have our hands on it, and all these foreign scum can scuttle back where they belong."

"That's the way it is," his brother agreed with a nod.

MacDuff looked at them and sighed.

"It seems to me this concerns a throne rather more than it does justice for your father."

"They're one and the same!" Malcolm cried, and rose from the seat to face him. "We all thought Macbeth honest and decent. We loved him well, as did you. As did our father." He hesitated then, his voice lower, adding, "Perhaps you still feel some affection. He hasn't touched you yet. Consider yourself fortunate."

"War's a cruel, blind beast," the thane of Fife retorted. "It sweeps away the innocent as easily as the guilty. Before I watch Scotland bleed again—"

"I know you will not love me as you love him!" Malcolm retorted. "And perhaps you think me unworthy." He glanced at the youth. "Or perhaps you wish to start anew." He grinned. "Put Fleance here, a bright-eyed, blameless child, upon the throne, then pull his strings…"

The man said nothing.

"I am an imperfect sinner," Malcolm said, a little calmer. "But a king at heart."

"Others have their doubts," said MacDuff.

Donalbain stirred, but Malcolm stilled him with a glance.

"Indeed?" said Malcolm. "And what do they accuse me of?"

"Lust," said MacDuff. "Avarice. Treachery."

"These are the slanders of Macbeth's lackeys. I have none of my father's appetites. If you have witnesses to the contrary, bring them forth and we will question them together."

MacDuff looked away.

"No," said Malcolm, "I thought not. But what if it's so? What then, MacDuff? Would your delicate scruples prevent you from joining with one less admirable than your good self, even if it meant leaving Scotland to the blood-soaked fiend who wears its crown? Say it's all true. When I am king, I will take what women I please, ransack the treasury for my personal gain, and run a court full of licentiousness and riot. Yet I would not be Macbeth, and that should be sufficient."

MacDuff turned on him, his eyes flashing. "Enough!" he bellowed. "No, sir! We will not hurl one tyrant from the throne to plant another in his place, however the first one came by it. Nor risk the lives of thousands of decent men to crown a debauched villain in his stead."

Malcolm gazed at him for a long moment and then, without warning, began to laugh.

"You get carried away, man," he said. "I am not the devil they portray. But your righteous anger does you credit and makes me happier to have you cross the border beside me." He took MacDuff's arm, peered into his eyes. "You see, don't you? You're too good a man to be taken in by malicious rumor. I am the rightful king of Scotland." A glance at Fleance. "Nor will you prosper with a puppet. Follow me!" He shrugged. "And if I fail you, it's a dagger in the dark, I guess. And another coffin for Iona."

Malcolm waited for an answer, and when it didn't come, he began to worry. He could not let this man leave. If such an important lord were to return to Scotland and join Macbeth's side…

"Why do you remain silent, sir?" he asked.

MacDuff scowled at him and answered, "There are so many welcome and unwelcome things at once. It's hard to reconcile them. This world is out of joint, and for the life of me, I find it hard to know what's good, what's evil anymore."

"Go eat and drink," Donalbain said, clasping his arm. "Think on it, friend. And when you have more questions…"

His eyes caught those of his brother, and Malcolm knew they shared the same thought: these two would be kept close in a Scottish tent till they changed their minds, or became expendable.

There was a commotion at the door. A man in armor, breathless, wild-eyed, marched in.

Malcolm stared down the intruder and said coldly, "This is a private conversation…"

"Cousin?" MacDuff said, turning. "You look tired and out of sorts? What's the matter?"

"The matter?" Ross panted. *"The matter?"*

MacDuff shook his head at the spectacle of him and said, "We've been riding for a week now. Do not expect us to be current with the news."

Ross went white and removed his helmet. He tried to speak but couldn't.

MacDuff's demeanor changed. "I pray you," he said finally. "This is no time for games."

"It is a time for war and bloody revenge," the man spat back.

"Revenge?" said MacDuff. "For what?"

Ross looked at his hands and said nothing. MacDuff rose and took two steps toward him. When he spoke it was in a voice so low Malcolm barely caught the words.

"Who must seek revenge?"

There was another pause, and then Ross took a long, unsteady breath. "You," he said.

MacDuff's eyes closed and he became quite still. "My castle," he said.

Ross nodded, hung his head, and began to choke with anger and emotion. "They were looking for you," he said.

"When they realized you'd gone, they killed Ailsa, Gregor, the girl, the babe. What can I say?"

MacDuff's face creased with grief, and for a moment, he said nothing. "All of them?" he managed in the end. "You are sure? All?"

"Wife, children, servants. All that could be found."

"You know this was Macbeth?" Donalbain cut in.

"No question, sir. They came on a ship from Forres and fled back to Perth straight after. There's a vile steward named Fergus. He does the bastard's dirty work..."

MacDuff fell into a seat by the table spread with maps and sheets of troops and armaments. Tears stood bright in his eyes. His hand went to his mouth. No words emerged. Long minutes passed. The thane of Fife seemed lost to all.

"I should not have left them," he said.

"The blood's on Macbeth's hands, not yours," Malcolm told him. "Be sane, man. You cannot blame yourself. Macbeth's a murderer and will kill in his own time."

He gestured at the group around them.

"Look at us here. A man robbed of his wife and bairns. A youth deprived his father. Two sons who've lost theirs, too. And a nation their king. For what? To put a crown on the head of a villain unfit even to gaze on it from afar."

"Let your grief sharpen your sword for revenge," said Donalbain.

"Revenge?" MacDuff asked softly. "How? He has no children."

Malcolm's hand went out to touch the weeping man slumped on the chair. "Come. We need you to be a man."

MacDuff leapt to his feet and seized Malcolm by the throat. "Be a man!" he roared. "If a man doesn't greet for his family, what else is he? No better than a beast."

He was powerfully built and furious. Yet Malcolm stood his ground and, when Donalbain looked to get help from outside, shook his head.

"We're friends here, bound by tragedy," he said, unwinding himself a little from MacDuff's grip. "The blood of those we loved joins every one of us. If you will ride with us, side by side, I'll make you the general of this righteous war. A finer soldier, a better man we could not find. Nor one with more good reason to see it through."

"Fleance?" MacDuff said, staring up at the lanky youth who had come with him.

"Give me a sword, sir," Banquo's son replied. "My father told me I had no talent for fighting. So teach me. All of you. I will learn quickly. That I promise."

MacDuff glowered at Malcolm, then released him. "There is a condition," he said eventually.

"Name it," Malcolm answered.

The bleary eyes of the seated man held them all.

"When the battle's won, that creature's mine," said MacDuff. "None deals with him save me."

Then he strode outside into the bright spring day, not waiting for an answer. As Donalbain scurried after, Malcolm turned to hide his smile.

◈ ◈ ◈

It took a day to ride from Perth inland to Dunsinane, past meadows waking from the long cold winter, past verdant pastures and fields where the green shoots of a new summer's barley and wheat began to make their way out of the rich brown earth. This was her native land. Glamis was not far away, and all the places of her childhood. In her head, Skena could see the place come July, the fields full of crops and flowers, the world alive with birdsong, cuckoos and woodpeckers in the woods, larks and thrushes in open meadows.

A quiet voice inside her said she would not witness that glorious sight again. Macbeth remained unshaken in his confidence. Yet forces now moved around them, troops and teams of scouts and couriers. Less visible powers, too, the common, uncertain spirit of the people they passed along the way, racked by the nervous atmosphere of villages that felt themselves upon the brink of a great and fearful calamity. Her mind returned continually to Inverness, that night with Duncan, the earlier encounter with the witches. At some point in that chill, bleak winter, all certainties, all fixed points that set out the boundaries of the world, had tumbled to the ground. In their place came a gray and shapeless landscape where good and bad, right and wrong, seemed indivisible, brothers in arms joined in an irrational fight against the common daily round of life.

There was no fathoming this change, no explanation for it. No blame, she thought, other than the fractured nature of humanity itself.

Then they rounded the bend in the valley and she saw the grim, dark peak of Dunsinane ahead. A fortress since men walked here, back in the distant times before the Romans, before the Picts and the distant races none could name. This castle made Inverness seem graceful. Its unrelieved timber walls rose thirty feet high, surmounting the steep mound on which it sat like a circular coffin made for a race of goliaths.

She had them stop the carriage then and stared at the cruel construction on the peak ahead. No words seemed able to describe its dreadful prospect. No words seemed necessary anymore. So, silent as a mute, she let them take her up the zigzag path, past gorse and heather, past stray sheep and straggling windblown groves of rowan and blackthorn now in blossom.

Two days she spent alone in the cold, bleak room they gave her. No window, no light, for this was a place for battle or siege, not the warm and daily pleasures of company. At night she lay awake, fearful of sleep, since it brought only waking dreams—the dark halls of Inverness and then the dreadful booming of the bell. Once, twice, and then the blood on her hands, Ewan, the serving boy, drinking greedily of the drugged wine, which would kill him. She hadn't seen him do it, but her sleeping mind painted the picture clear as memory and would not let her intervene. When she realized he was slipping into sleep she tried to warn him, but Duncan was alive again, clawing at her throat despite the gashes in his chest and throat. She fought to get away, only to find herself in the chill nursery with its tiny crib, the one her husband had carved so carefully from supple ash, the first and last thing that he ever made with his own hands. The crib rocked back and forth, and though she did not want to look inside, the dream always made her.

Afterward, she woke crying, deep racking sobs that cramped her belly till she gasped with pain, surging, pulsing, wrenching stabs of agony deep as childbirth.

The sleepwalking began on the second night. She woke in the kitchens rubbing her hands as if washing them, and though she could remember nothing of the dream that led her there, she skulked back to her chamber oppressed with guilt and horror. From that night on, she insisted that a lantern burn beside her bed at all hours, a talisman against darkness of all kinds.

It didn't help.

Macbeth tried to talk her. She listened patiently to his stories, smiling, unable to think of anything to say. The English had moved beyond the border. That much she understood. Somewhere across the valley lay Duncan's old town of Dunkeld, now occupied by foreign forces along with the great green wood of Birnam that lay beside it over the waters of the Tay. They were weak and divided, and would fall like corn beneath Scottish scythes once the battle was joined.

He'd taken her hands, grown desperate—angry, even—as she listened, a distant, amused expression on her face.

Nothing changed. The bond between them, once so close and indivisible, was gone.

After that, he left her. A doctor and a nurse kept close by, day and night. The coffin of the fortress became a prison, too. And all beyond, invisible, lay the green paradise of the lowlands, a land that had enchanted her since birth.

Three days after they entered Dunsinane—or four, she could no longer recall—she went to bed early, desperate for the rest that had eluded her. Twice, she was woken by versions of those same dreams of Inverness, though now the staircase up to Duncan's chamber was strewn with the corpses of children, pale and ghastly as the owl that picked over them—not just Ewan and her own tiny infant, but the thane of Fife's as well, and others she could not name. She had to pick her way down the stairs between tiny white hands, all flecked with blood.

A third dream came to her one afternoon when exhaustion had dragged her into sleep. The children's bodies moved unnaturally, rose, and hemmed her in, muttering and pointing accusingly. She fled from them through the castle's black corridors, but they always seemed to find her, moving with impossible speed in the dark.

When she woke, shrieking, she was outside on Dunsinane's battlements, clutching her jeweled dagger. One of the sentries was staring at her with frightened eyes, his halberd held in front of him as if she might attack. Behind was another, approaching warily out of the darkness.

In the castle courtyard she saw the game of war had yet to start, though preparation was everywhere. Troops hammered to make the dark wooden walls of Dunsinane stronger, forged daggers, sharpened swords. Somewhere across the valley others did the same. The noise was deafening, and as her awareness of who she was and where returned, Skena found herself amazed that she had slept through this din, let alone walked half dreaming through the throng.

She turned, shamefaced, to the nearest guard and saw approaching the man she loathed more than any in the world—the fox-faced Fergus, porter once, now steward and much more.

He waved the guards away, then looked her up and down, not kindly. Gradually, she lowered the knife.

She spoke—the first words she'd uttered since she stepped inside this dark, grim tomb—and said, "I wish to walk, man. Here, take this." She unhooked the purse around her belt and gave him everything in it. "And let me loose."

He checked the coins, one by one, then nodded. Then he led her to the rear gate through which provisions came and opened it without a word.

A green world beckoned in the dusk beyond. Finally, she felt free.

◈ ◈ ◈

The sonorous cry of a cuckoo lured her beyond the castle. Its call kept her wandering the hillsides till darkness fell completely. It was a welcome sound after a winter that seemed composed entirely of owl hoots and the dread shrieks of eagles.

Stumbling across the perfumed heath, she heard the bird again. The gentle, two-note refrain seemed like a benison, a welcome harbinger of the summer to come, so verdant and glorious in this, her native lowlands.

The starry sky hung over her, endless and full of a pendulous, inky grace. The evening was mild, the moon so full and glorious she had no need of a brand to see her way. The fortress stood on a steep mound of the Sidlaw range to the southern side of the valley of Strathmore, which now lay before her, a broad, shallow strip of farmland set around the river Tay. On the far side rose the Grampians, the vast stretch of mountains running north almost to Inverness, bleak and bare, difficult and dangerous to cross. Beneath its dark silhouette, the bright line of the river wound toward Dunkeld and the bulging outline of Birnam wood, rising from the water's edge.

Free of the doctor and his nurses, away from the dark dungeon that was Dunsinane, able to walk alone near the gentle meadows of her childhood, she felt, briefly, close to peace. Sleep might come when she returned to the castle. Somewhere behind those high wooden walls it was possible there was a room where the night did not stir to the low, malevolent moans of terror.

The cuckoo called again, so close she wondered if she might see its darting shape against the stars.

Her foot caught in a tussock of hard grass. She stumbled, fell, then found herself turning over and over, rolling rapidly down the steep hill, past the gorse, hawthorn, and elder that marked the edge of the winding path from the vale.

She cried out, surprised by the fragile, frightened quality of her own voice, felt the breath forced from her by the impetus of her fall. Then the ground became more level, the grass softer, and finally, she found herself brought to a halt by a tussock of heather, a bewildered, pained bundle, a distant way down the incline, head hurting, fighting for sense.

One deep breath. Two. She looked up and saw the cruel ramparts of the fortress above piercing the starry curtain of the sky. It seemed tiny from here, like a child's toy, so ridiculous she wanted to laugh.

There were movements nearby. Sheep, she guessed. Or Malcolm's scouts, scurrying ever closer. She felt for the dagger in her belt, the jeweled blade that once stabbed a king called Duncan deep in his scrawny throat. The dagger that had killed Ewan and MacDuff's children.

No, she recalled vaguely. *That isn't right. Not precisely.*

The knife's handle fell to her fingers. She rolled to face whatever approached, blonde hair flying in the moonlight, spat a wordless hiss of warning from her lips, looked, and saw them—three dark shapes gathering toward her across the heath.

"Lady," said the girl in the black cloak, reaching her first, smiling, eyes as dark and opaque as Skena remembered from that freezing night by the cairns in Clava.

The slender thing bowed and curtseyed. The crone hobbled quickly over on her crutches and fell upon the grass. The third, the large one, more soldier than woman, came casually and crouched on her haunches.

"You're bleeding," the old woman declared, then hobbled across, took out a rag. Skena felt the soft brush of fabric on her forehead, snatched the material from her, looked at the fresh smear there, gingerly tested her own skin. A cut. No more serious than the scratch she'd taken from the furious woman in Perth. No broken bones. No lasting harm.

The touch of the crone disconcerted her. It was delicate, like that of a mother sadly tending a hurt child. Not the quick and sharp aggression she'd expected.

"Blood," the young one said, staring at her. "So easily set flowing. So hard to staunch." A smile. Those level, even teeth, like a bairn's before they're shed. "But then," she added, "I fancy you know that."

Her pale features rose to the turrets and walls of the fortress on the vast, towering stump of hill above them.

"It's a long climb back," the girl said with a sigh. "You think you'll manage?"

The jeweled knife was still in Skena's hand.

"Put that thing away," the big one muttered. "You think it scares us?"

No, she realized, and stowed the dagger in her belt.

"Who are you?" she asked, not wanting to know the answer.

The one on the crutches laughed and cried, "You mean…*what*?"

Skena lacked the courage to go on.

"Tell her," ordered the young one. "It's time. She has the right."

The crone came closer, stared into her face. *Beneath the grime, the wrinkles, the signatures of hate and madness, there was a woman here once,* she thought. *Perhaps pretty. Happy. Content.*

"I lived in Arran with my son, his wife, and three wee brats," the old one began. As she spoke the name of that isle, her voice took on a gentle, crooning tone, soft and thoughtful. "We cut peat, kept sheep and a still for the barley we'd malt." She snorted. "I can taste that whisky even now. All earth and smoke and fragrant fire—the finest in the west." She stared at her hands. "One day, there's men come from Ireland with malice in their faces. I says, 'We're Irish, too, a generation apart, no more. We speak the same ancient tongue, sing the same tunes. Don't you know that? Do you steal from your own?' "

Her eyes turned misty, as if seeing something distant.

"They killed the boy, then put me, his girl, and the babes in a coracle, towed it out with them on the next tide." She shivered. "The Irish Sea's a cold, gray beast. They cut the rope when Arran was but a speck above the waves. Six hours we paddled with our hands until the leather gave and that chill water took us. Still, I hear those cruel men laughing as they left. All that for six sheep and a few flasks of whisky." She scratched her chin. "Damned fine whisky, though, like I said. Just a story, lady. One more dead peasant among a multitude."

The crone stared at the tall one, who said simply, "They hanged me for taking a chicken."

The others tittered.

"I told you. I was hungry!"

"You're always hungry," the old one said, still laughing. "Even now."

There was a grunt from the woman, then she shrugged and said, "Aye. True."

The girl closed her strange, dark eyes and began to sing a short lament in a tongue Skena didn't know.

"Speak words we understand," the crone complained.

"That was Latin, you peasant," the girl scolded her. "The language of civilized men. Dead civilized men, I might add, but that's by the by."

"You know—" Skena began.

"I was the child of a fisherman from Berwick on the Tweed. Then the Romans came and wanted labor. Men who would help the emperor Hadrian build his wall. All the way from east to west, to keep the wicked Caledonians out. Fat chance, eh?"

"You're English?" Skena asked.

"I'm dead," the girl spat back at her, as if the question was ridiculous. "Only monarchs go beneath the earth with flags around them. The rest of us lie anonymous in the grave."

Skena reached out and touched her hand. It was cold, but skin and flesh and bone, as real as her own.

"You don't seem much dead to me," she said.

"They whistle us up at Samhain and we answer," the crone cut in. "Be not ungrateful. How would you have us look?"

"The Romans," said the girl, "were a curious race. Bound up in their own importance, fond of ceremony and fleeting, pompous ideas. I loved a soldier and would have been his wife were I not of lesser breeding. A heathen, not a citizen, though this was no matter in his bed. One day, he's summoned back to Rome and orders me to come. As slave, not even mistress. He had a wife, you see."

She thought for a moment, then added, "I told him I was born free by the waters of the Tweed and would live that way and die there one day, too. No matter. In his eyes—to all the Romans, with their laws and magistrates—I *was* a slave."

Her voice diminished and became that of a child.

"The first time I ran away they beat and branded me."

Her nimble fingers rolled up the sleeve of her right arm. Dark, raised numbers stood there like a wound.

"The second time they gave me to some centurions for amusement. The third..." Her eyes closed and there was pain upon her face. "They said they'd crucify me. Nailed to a cross beside that blasted wall of theirs."

Suddenly, she brightened.

"Then along comes the emperor himself. Hadrian. Visiting his troops. He hears my story, orders them to free me. Says I may go to Rome and, there, become a citizen. It was my spirit, you see, that so impressed him. My mettle made me Roman by default."

She threw her head back and laughed.

"There's a man's freedom for you, eh? Do as I say or I'll nail you to a cross of wood, to feed the carrion crows piece by piece. Oh, no. That's cruel. Do as I say and I'll take you to a foreign land, far away from your native soil, your family, the ones you love. And, there, expect your gratitude."

Her hand reached over and took Skena's arm.

"Slavery comes in many guises, lady. A woman should recognize that." She clapped her hands once. "So...the moment they loosed me this time I ran and ran. All the way to Berwick and the shining waters of the Tweed. There I threw off my Roman cloak and jewelry and walked bare as a babe into that river of mine. I still had my little knife..." She nodded. "Not as fancy as yours, but not so different. As that cold and friendly water came up to greet me, I opened my two wrists and lay there slowly bleeding, floating as best I could, feeling the seals and the salmon come by. They must feed, too, I reckon. Better I end up inside some harmless creature from the sea than trapped in the bed of a Roman bastard who thinks he owns me. Oh, that moment... sleep..."

"Sleep," Skena repeated.

The girl shuffled closer, her breath quick and excited. "Aye, sleep, and such a sleep as you have never known. As sweet and deep and dreamless as a bairn inside its mother, warm and safe." The girl cocked an eye at her. "How go the nights with you, lady?"

She didn't answer. There was no need.

"You ask yourself," the girl said, nudging her, "can this be true? Are these three phantoms haunting me across the burns and glens? Or mere hare-brained loons, their heads full of fancy and mischief?"

"The dead do not speak," Skena whispered. "They have neither flesh nor bone."

"Lady, lady," the young one laughed. "Do I dream you? Or you dream me? Or does someone, something bigger than all"—her hands swept the vast constellations above them—"this beauteous calamity, dream everything we see and more? Since no one knows, why dwell on it? Think of who you are and what you face. Think of Skena, a wee girl of Glamis. That child, I see"—her black eyes shone with joy—"a bright young thing racing through the barley in the fields, slipping her fingers across the silky golden whiskers of the grain. She's eight or nine, no more, and listens to the larks and linnets while gathering daisies, singing songs, so bright and full of life she thinks her heart may burst with girlish joy."

The woman on the ground—bruised, confused, and frightened—felt cold remembering those distant lost years, her father murdered in his home, her mother mourning, wasting away in silence. The happiness was brief, yet sweet and real.

"In my mind's eye I see this bairn," the girl went on, "and she's just like all the others, except maybe prettier. She dreams a man will marry her. A good, kind lord. And there'll be children—two, three, four. A castle in the lowlands, a family to cherish." She hesitated, as if moved by this idea herself. "Faces growing older as her own life fades. A sense of permanence, a small thing passed from old to young and then again."

Her voice hardened.

"But then the one bairn dies and no more take his place. She sees her lord turn quietly sorrowful that other, lesser men rise in the king's eyes before him, through nothing more than some shared blood or rank venality. The flaxen-haired girl who ran through the barley, so hopeful and brimming with an innocent virtue, dies slowly, day by day. And in her place comes—"

"Stop!" Skena cried. "Be not so cruel, child. I have lost a bairn, a husband, and soon may lose this kingdom we have briefly mastered—and with it, my life."

The tall one glared at her and grunted, "Which matters most?"

There were lights just visible across the valley, moving in Birnam and the wood toward Dunkeld. The English army with MacDuff and Malcolm at its head. They would not wait there long.

"Macbeth," she murmured without a second thought. "He is my soul's companion, so sweet and decent…nor is this finished. There's an accommodation to be made here. Give Malcolm the lowlands. We take chill Inverness. Or vice versa. I care not. We'll build a cathedral for his dead father. Crawl on our knees to the pope, if need be. I can send messengers, I'll…"

She stopped. They were laughing at her.

"This amuses you?" she asked coldly.

"Poor thing," the young one cried. "So wise in many ways, so credulous in others. Do you not understand? This concerns Duncan not one whit. Had you not stabbed that bastard in his nightshirt, his son would surely have had his head by now. No one suffers a single sleepless night over that dead villain except Macbeth and you, and that in such measure you might be mourning for the world itself. These are men that hunt you. They speak of vengeance and retribution, but in truth, they're moved by nothing more than hunger. For power. For land. To steal from you your supremacy, as you stole it before. As Duncan thieved the throne himself."

Her fingers strayed to Skena's shoulder, her face, curious, interested, interrupting the view of the brands and torches across the glen.

"Men! If need be, they would kill for one bare yard of barren earth. It is the victory they seek, not the prize, and they feel not one moment of conscience howsoever it is gained. Yet you two…Macbeth, impaled upon a needless guilt for Duncan, and a more solid sense of culpability for the wrong he feels he's done the wife he loves. While you, like a dark mirror, reflect the same sorrows back at him in return."

"You told me!" she cried. "At Clava you said…his…"

"Spine," the crone spat at her. "A man with spine might have stood by Duncan in his difficulties."

"A man with spine might have hacked off the heads of all his enemies and strewn them everywhere—a warning to all," the big one added.

The girl thought for a while, then said, "The will you acted upon was your own, lady. Not ours. You thought you might supplant that milk of kindness in your husband with a fierce, manly strength that came from your own veins." She sighed. "Imagine a king with both sexes in one head. Now, there's a creature. But all you created was a man twice over—a beast, I mean—and in so doing destroyed you both."

"I will barter with MacDuff..." she murmured.

"Tell him you'll bring his wife and bairn back," the hag snapped. "That should do it."

The sharp salt stab of tears pricked at her eyes. "What do you want?" Skena whispered.

"To watch. To wait. To wonder at a world in chaos," the girl said. "And hope one day you fools might learn."

She glanced upward at the grim shape of Dunsinane.

"It's a long way back," she added briskly. "This journey's run, love. Be bold and bring it to an end. Long ago, when I slipped into that river and felt that sharp knife upon my wrists, I was as you are now. Exhausted. Afraid. Yet still I found the courage. Can a queen not summon up the bravery that came so easily to a slave?"

"I die with my husband!"

"No," the girl replied. "You won't. You know what Malcolm is. You know the hatred MacDuff bears. They'll strip you naked and hand you to their foot soldiers and all the while make him watch you bleed and scream. Then hack off your pretty head with a dagger and wave it in his face. You know this, lady. Be not such a fool to think otherwise."

Skena shivered, weeping silently.

"Then they will kill him, most cruelly," the young one went on. "Not the end of a warrior in battle. They will make him kneel like a peasant and take his head. Think on what I say! You are both corpses and do not know it. All that remains is the manner of your going. Die now and he is free and full of fury, a warrior once more. Walk in his shadow like a pale, wan wraith and both of you stumble forward to an ignominious close so shameful those who come after shall shun it and speak the name Macbeth as it were a curse."

She took Skena's face in her soft, supple hands.

"From that wee bairn in Glamis to queen of Scotland is a journey of some moment. Far greater than most might dream of. Close it now with valor. A dutiful wife, dispatching her husband to a glory of his own."

Her right hand moved, slipped to Skena's clothing. The shining jeweled blade rose before them in the moonlight.

"I have been here before," her calm, still voice whispered. "I will help and sing an old song, a lullaby to pass the time."

"I fear—"

"That you'll wake later and find yourself bound to walk the earth in company such as ours," the girl said with a knowing smile. "Do not worry. This is our burden. Not yours."

"You lack the hatred," the giant said. "And the stony heart."

"Aye," the girl agreed. "That, too. Here…"

Skena cried as the blade fell upon her skin. A short cut. A scratch. A marker for the smarting pain to come.

"I will not do the rest," the young one said, offering her the dagger. "I may be many things, but not that."

So Skena Macbeth took the jeweled knife and worked with it, separating vein from sinew, one wrist then the next, and after the brief, exquisite agony, lay back in the scented heather, wondering at the beauty of the stars and sky.

The girl began to sing, an old song, one they said the Irish brought with them in their boats. It was about a wedding, a union. And something more subtle, too, an idea that eluded her, hovering out of reach as the firmament grew misty and her life eked out in a slow and steady stream, onto the peat and grass and heather of that Sidlaw hill.

By the time the sweet and breathy song had faded into silence the woman on the ground was tranquil, too weak to move, to speak.

A mouth came close to her ear, and it was, she knew, the last thing she would hear in this or any other world.

"Oh, lady," the girl whispered. "I forgot to mention. Sometimes I'm wont to lie."

◈ ◈ ◈

The following morning, Macbeth woke facedown on the hall table, among maps and sheets of troop numbers, weaponry and scheming. It was Cullen's hand that shook him. The old retainer stood close by, his face impassive, a good and loyal servant always.

"No more reports," Macbeth said with a long sigh. "These endless tallies of who stands where…"

He looked at the plain and practical man in front of him and wondered what he would make of such private and superstitious thoughts.

"I feel old this morning," Macbeth complained.

"You look fit and strong, sir."

"I said old, not feeble. Fetch my armor. We'll see off these damned traitors and their foreign friends before sunset. Go…" He nodded at the door. "I'm ready."

"There's no need at this very moment."

"If they'll not fight, we'll laugh a siege to scorn. Send out horses. Scour the countryside. Fly banners from the ramparts. Let the English know we fear no low invaders."

He didn't move and seemed, for once, reluctant to speak.

A sound came to Macbeth from beyond the door. There were few women left inside the wooden walls of Dunsinane. Those who were there seemed to be weeping and shrieking out in the courtyard.

"I had men out early," Cullen said, his head hung on his chest. "They found such a…" He glanced at Macbeth. "Such a terrible sight." The man's eyes were bleak and glassy with emotion.

"Found what?"

"Your wife, my lord." Cullen wrung his hands. "She must have slipped out in the night…"

Before the words were ended Macbeth was racing to the door. Head spinning, he dashed straight into the yard. A group of soldiers stood around a hidden burden, one man at each corner of a vast swathe of dun-brown cloth.

The nurse, the doctor, and two women of the household watched, hands to mouths, faces bloodless, tear-stained, pale with shock and fear.

Like a fallen flower, Skena lay there in the fabric, arms extended, bloody at each wrist, face drained of all emotion, life, and pain, blue eyes shorn of the light he loved.

As he knelt beside her, took her cold, dry hand, a trumpet sounded on the battlements. Men shouted, bellowed at each other, the way they did in the prelude to a fight.

"Sire, she slipped away from us…" the nurse began. "I do not know how. I cannot apologize sufficiently for this sorrowful tragedy. It affects us—"

"There is no need," he said, waving her down. "Bear no blame, no guilt on this, I pray you. I am the cause of my wife's sickness, no one else. Take all the women with you and flee this place for somewhere safer. The doctor, too. This is a fortress made for soldiers. We need no ordinary folk to hinder as we set about winning this savage day."

He let go her hand and stood to see her one last time.

"Take my wife and bury her at the church by Glamis." He looked at them. "Will you do that for me?"

They stood around, lost for words.

"I swear I lack the space for mourning," he pleaded. "Not now. I beg you…go!"

With that, he turned away and stared up at the battlements. *No tears*, he thought. This was not the moment.

Cullen, by his side, said, "Sire…there is a degree of chivalry in military matters. Were we to pass this news to Malcolm, he would surely wait a day or two…"

"Chivalry's for knights, not kings," Macbeth replied. "What's the difference? Tomorrow and tomorrow come creeping in and always will. We're fools trapped in a mechanism of our own unconscious making. Shadows strutting and fretting for one brief hour upon a stage, then heard no more. I'll weep an ocean in my heart, if the world would give me time. But not now."

He turned and gripped the old servant by the shoulder.

"Listen, friend, and understand. My life is a tale told by an idiot, full of sound and fury. It means nothing." Macbeth unsheathed his sword and brandished it before him. "Today all I have is this keen blade, and by God, those men shall taste it. None of woman born may harm me…"

He didn't like the look in Cullen's eyes. He had been a loyal servant, there for as many years as Macbeth could remember, but now the man stared at him as if he saw a madman before him.

The gate opened, the party left, a single sad shape covered by a black wool sheet carried on the cart they pushed.

"Tell me of our arrangements," Macbeth ordered.

◈ ◈ ◈

An hour Macbeth spent, speaking to every last soldier, high and low, listening to their boasts and fears, promising the earth once victory was theirs. He heard tallies of provisions, found the victualers, and was convinced the castle would survive a siege so long that those outside would starve and die of sickness long before a man within found hunger aching in his belly. The enemy would know this, surely. Each camp had well-paid informers in its midst.

When the counts of food and weapons, of water butts and horses, were done, he climbed onto the wooden battlements to survey the sweeping hills around them.

Cullen followed and, scanning the bright horizon, pointed to the lush green valley ahead. In the soft morning light, the party with Skena's body was visible close to the river, wending its way east toward Glamis, away from battle.

The archer beside him was intent on something closer. He pointed and Macbeth saw for himself—a figure creeping furtively down the heather hill back toward Birnam and Dunkeld.

"Every day we lose a traitor," Cullen said, squinting. "My vision's not so good. But his manner speaks volumes. I'll send some troops to deal with it."

Macbeth's keen eyesight followed the shape as it stole through the gorse seeking shelter. He knew that low and skinny form too well.

"Fergus," he murmured. "That man served me. If one like him should seek to flee…"

Cullen stiffened. "A deserter's a deserter. I loathe him. We're well rid of the rogue. Let me hunt him."

"Your opinion's to your credit," Macbeth replied with a shrug. "Still, he's one among many. If victory hangs on a single skinny traitor…"

"There's an army waiting here behind these walls who'll die for you. Do not insult them."

He liked this fellow more with every passing day. Cullen was too honest to do anything but speak his mind. Ignored too often of late, and that was Macbeth's own folly. "My words were thoughtless," he said, looking into Cullen's sallow, calm face. "I apologize. Yet..." He sighed. "Why would any of you wish to die for me? You, man, have a family back in Inverness. A life." He nodded to the busy yard where troops worked on weapons, finishing arrows, checking bows. "They all have. Malcolm wants me, not you. Siege or no siege, I could surrender and spare you all. Why not...?"

"That army," Cullen said, in a stern and rising voice, "is English through and through. The only Scots are the turncoats who led them across our border. You're our king, not Malcolm. As long as that crown sits upon your head, I follow you, along with every loyal man in Dunsinane."

"A fine speech," Macbeth noted. "Will your widow thank you for it?"

"If it stops some English bastard raping her in our bed, she will. Sir..." He pointed down the hill. Fergus was reaching open ground now, the line where gorse gave way to nothing but coarse grass and heather. He would be exposed for a little while until he dipped beneath the brow, then reached the straight run to the river. "That single rogue may tell MacDuff and Malcolm our dispositions. Our plans." He hesitated. "Your frame of mind."

"He may, indeed," Macbeth agreed.

"Then let me send—"

"No need." This low creature had slaughtered Banquo in the mountains that lay on the northern skyline. Murdered MacDuff's wife and children—a foul and unnecessary, unwanted deed that turned Skena's mind for good. These acts lay heavily on Macbeth's conscience, yet were nothing to the man who had performed them.

Banquo was the first—and in some ways, the worst. His childhood days with that vigorous, bold warrior would never leave Macbeth. Swirling in coracles upon the river, seeking silver salmon. Stalking ruddy stags through the passes of the Cairngorms.

"I was always the better marksman," he murmured, and walked over to the nearest archer, took his bow without a word, and three long, well-flighted arrows.

Not an easy shot. A man made a smaller target than a deer with its great antlers. And Fergus was small, too, in mind, in character, in body.

His powerful arms drew back the bow, the string and arrow notched against his cheek. Ahead, sharp in focus like a hunted animal, Fergus rose from the last patch of green and spiky gorse and began to run across the heather.

No fool, he knew this was the most dangerous section of his treacherous journey.

His narrow, angular, vicious face turned to take one last look back. Macbeth caught that expression with his keen eye and thought for a moment Fergus saw him, too, a distant figure, taut and erect, longbow in hand, stationary on the wooden battlements of Dunsinane.

The fool froze in fear, as quarry sometimes did. Macbeth let fly the arrow straight and true, then watched as it caught the fleeing man square in the neck.

"Another," he said, holding out his hand, not taking his focus once from the stricken figure below.

Notched, string taut, the muscular spring of the longbow tight in his grip.

Fergus wheeled and screeched and screamed, both hands to the wooden shaft that pierced his neck from side to side.

The second shaft took him in the chest and that was that. One corpse upon the hillside. The first, Macbeth felt, of many.

"You have a canny eye," Cullen said, impressed. "I trust you'll join us on these ramparts should the need arise."

Macbeth couldn't take his eyes off the corpse stretched out on the heather ahead, arms and legs akimbo, as if pinned to the ground by the deadly arrows.

It felt as if a part of him had died with that villainous, sly-eyed servant.

"I am not Duncan," he told the man beside him. "I fight by the side of my brave men. Perhaps…" and this thought chilled him, "it is my solitary skill."

A young and nervous sentry had climbed the ladder to join him.

"Speak up, boy!" Macbeth ordered. "Or has an English cat somehow got your tongue?"

"I come from the forward watch, sire," he replied. "Stationed in the valley."

"Well…" Macbeth sighed, rolling his hand in impatience.

"I don't know how to say what I saw…"

"Just say it, then."

"I swear, as I stood on my station, I saw the wood of Birnam move toward us. Walking as it were—"

Macbeth stared, astonished. "What did you say?"

"I swear my lord, the forest—"

"Trees do not move, boy. Do not bring me lies," the king hissed.

The boy took a step back, trembling. "No, sir. You'll see it soon yourself. Like a restless grove of trees that upped their roots—"

"No…" Macbeth whispered.

"Sire," Cullen cut in quickly. "It is an English trick. They cut the branches for their troops and hope by approaching behind such camouflage we'll fail to see their number."

The man smiled.

"A good omen, I think. If they were so many, why hide it?"

"To show us for the fools we are," Macbeth replied. "By God…"

"See!" the scout shouted. "See!"

He looked, and Cullen with him. Across the valley, like a vast green monster, the branches moved in unison, down toward the sinuous line of the Tay.

"Ring the alarm bell!" Cullen ordered. "Armor, men, and weapons. Stations all."

Macbeth was silent, watching the impossible become real in the lush and tranquil valley before him.

"No man of woman born," he whispered, not caring if they heard.

Cullen was struggling with his scabbard. His eyes were gray and rheumy. The man was fifty or more.

"I have a task for you," Macbeth said, taking his arm.

"Sire?"

"Take a horse. Find my wife's party. See them to Glamis, then go to Inverness to secure the castle. I will meet you there when this work is done."

The calm, dispassionate cast of Cullen's face vanished. "I am a Scot! I fight my enemy!"

"You are a servant and will do as I say," Macbeth replied. "Now, get you gone. I've work to do. And, Cullen?"

"My lord?"

"Godspeed."

◈ ◈ ◈

For the next two hours they watched Malcolm's army ford the river, then climb the beetling heights of Dunsinane. Horses and infantry stayed to the rear. At the front ran the green wood of Birnam, men with boughs of oak and fir over their heads, hiding themselves and whatever they brought with them.

Macbeth followed the advance from the ramparts while men alongside him brought water, oil, and fouler substances to a rolling boil in vast cauldrons pinned to swiveling frames.

Whatever those branches hid, they would be revealed once they were close enough to the high wooden ramparts of the castle.

Closer, he saw the few Scots among them, bright figures in armor, high on horseback, impudently wearing on their tunics the white-on-blue diagonal cross of the saltire, riding to and fro among the English forces, making way up the steep slopes. MacDuff and Lennox and Ross were near the front, clear and visible. Malcolm and his brother Donalbain stayed nearer the baggage train behind.

All those around in Dunsinane saw this, and catching their mood, Macbeth raised his sword and roared, "I see they are their father's sons, then! Letting others fight their battles for them. Though, even King Duncan never called upon the English to stiffen his spine..."

His voice was drowned in a deafening cheer. No one liked that family. Even the men who believed him guilty of Duncan's murder—most of those in his pay, he imagined—

saw little fault in his actions. Kings lived and died, and killed each other for the prize they craved. That was the way of the world.

He began another speech, but then an arrow whistled pass his helmet and one of the archers was there swiftly, dragging him back from the rampart edge.

"A siege," the man said. "That will be their plan."

"Not if MacDuff's their general," he replied. "He's a decent Scot. He won't waste a moment. Let him come forward. The English might want to pitch their tents and starve us out. Not him. He thinks he has good reason."

Macbeth thought of the body they must have passed on the way—Fergus, an arrow in his throat, another through his chest.

"Sire?" the archer said.

"I was distracted, friend. We should thank God they have tied us to this stake. Since we have no choice, we can only fight like bears and wolves. And will. When they come close—"

A cry went up nearby. And then a second.

Macbeth rushed back to the wall. The boughs of Birnam were now close enough the men on the battlements could see what they concealed—shields, formed like the carapace of a tortoise, the way the Romans did.

"Douse the English with the boiling oil," he ordered. "Do not cease…"

The words died in his throat. Something was rising from the line of hidden men below. Curling plumes of smoke and the distinct yellow flicker of flame.

"Oh, Cullen, Cullen," he murmured. "I am glad I let you go. These branches aren't there to hide their numbers. They're cover for their trickery. And for the fire that will bring down these wooden walls." He turned and cried to the yard, "Water! Now!"

As he watched, the line of branches opened. Behind them were great wooden engines—catapults and ballistae primed with blazing missiles. A smell rose from the ground below—oil and bitumen. Macbeth leaned over the parapet edge and was greeted by a sudden rush of sound. A great flaming ball was speeding toward them, trailing thick and greasy smoke.

He ducked back but felt the terrible impact of the catapult shot against the walls. To his right there was a burst of orange light and then a belch of foul and noxious air. He twisted away, coughing, gagging.

Still short of breath, he clung to the ramparts and watched the wall of shields below. A gap was opening in their midst, revealing archers and arrows tipped with flaming rags.

"Fire," he murmured. "And we are in a tinderbox. The English fight so many foreigners they must learn new tricks with every corpse they make."

The bows drew back, and the burning arrows flew and caught the timber walls of Dunsinane. Tongues of flame began to spread, feeding on the stinking oils they'd splashed upon the woodwork.

"I told you, man," Macbeth said, looking at the pale, shocked face of the archer beside him. Another flaming missile exploded against a corner turret and left it burning. "There'll be no siege. We fight them now and seize the day. Find me a foe who's not of woman born…"

The man with the bow shook his head and murmured a few unintelligible words.

"Find me him!" Macbeth bawled. "And then I'll feel some fear."

◈ ◈ ◈

MacDuff watched the siege equipment raining fire upon the hilltop fort. The walls were ablaze in several places, but more important was the effect the assault would have on the men inside. He could almost smell their terror and despair in the black and swirling smoke ahead. He felt the madness in himself, a deep and driving fury, at present but a smolder. Set Macbeth before him and it would leap into a cruel and deadly flame. And that moment would come.

There were partial breaches already opening in the south wall, though the heat was too intense for entry. Even at this distance MacDuff could feel it on his face, smell the stench of fire and battle and the clouds of acrid, oily smoke. He wiped his streaming eyes and watched as four catapults disgorged their fury against the walls. Somewhere inside a man ran screaming along the parapet, his clothes ablaze. The wooden decking beneath him collapsed in an explosion of sparks and he vanished from view.

All death had terrors. He had fought to keep from his mind all thought of how his wife and family had perished. Could seeing their bleeding corpses be worse than the horrors of his own imagination? He had a dread that, if he allowed them to rise in his head, their eyes would be open, would look at him accusingly.

Yet he was the one who slew them. He had been wrong to leave Fife and he would bear that cross forever. But Malcolm, snake though he was, was right. It had been Macbeth's doing, not his.

"Direct the ballistae there," shouted MacDuff, pointing.

The great oversized crossbows shifted to new targets. Moments later, they sent their blazing, spear-length bolts into the walls where the man had fallen. The timbers split and fell away, and on the fourth strike a hole appeared, black around the edges but red and molten at the center. MacDuff stared at it and thought himself looking into his own fierce and burning heart.

This was the way into Dunsinane, and he would be the first and most eager to take it.

◈ ◈ ◈

Macbeth paced the walls, sword in hand, his bow and shield forgotten. Around him, the battlements burned. His soldiers skulked and cried out. Some fled outright, some merely hid, but he walked tall, eager for the enemy's next assault.

That it would be final, he had no doubt.

He was safe, the weird sisters had said, till Birnam wood came to Dunsinane, and now that strange prophecy had come true. This sudden turn of fortune had first filled him with dread. But then the slipperiness of the witches' oracles had struck him and he found he could only laugh at himself darkly until even the men around had left him to his thoughts.

Yet the sisters had been right before, and they said that no one born of woman could harm Macbeth.

He teased at the problem in his mind. Was he supposed to be invincible to all the English rabble and those who held their leashes? Only a fool would think so. There was trickery in their language, if only he could find it. The sisters had tempted him with deceitful promises. No man was immortal, not even the fabled Greek Achilles. Dipped into the Styx, made invulnerable in every part of his body except his heel, he was prey to arrogance and cruelty. And when his nemesis came…

“The heel,” Macbeth murmured, watching the English forces wheel around, screaming for another surge.

In their vanity men focus on what they wish to hear and miss the hidden meaning, the lurking threat. The sisters' words, so clear when he had first heard them, would turn out—again—to be a kind of riddle, a twisted half-truth that would snatch his life away. But that no longer mattered, and a part of him was merely curious to see how this closing moment would arrive.

So he strode the walls, the steel of his sword held out before him like a talisman, and when he reached the point where they had broken through, he jumped down into the breach, and slew them as they blundered through the smoke.

One of them wore the rank of an English captain. A young man, but from a powerful family, if the crest on his shield was to be trusted. Macbeth confronted him in the midst of the acrid, choking fog.

“I see the king of murder before me!” cried the Englishman.

“A king all the same,” said Macbeth, gripping his sword with two hands. “One immune to such as you or any born of woman. Turn back, boy. No one will blame you for it. You can win honor with lesser men elsewhere.”

“I am the son of Siward, earl of Northumbria, and I give ground to no man.”

“Then you will die,” said Macbeth.

Sons and fathers, he thought, with a stab of sorrow. *Whatever else this day will leave me, that is one bond I will never know.*

He thought of Banquo as he parried, of Duncan, both angling for their sons. He cut young Siward's shield, gashing the family crest with such force that the boy faltered before attacking again. Macbeth pushed the lunge aside and swept his long, keen blade at the Englishman's legs. Siward leapt back, afraid now, stumbling on the charred and smoking timbers of the breach.

"Leave," said Macbeth.

"Never," cried the boy, charging wildly, his courage gone, replaced by desperation.

Macbeth blocked and stabbed once, a deep and fatal wound. Young Siward fell against him, and for a moment, Macbeth held him in his arms, as Skena had the servant Ewan and their own dead son an age ago. Gently, as the battle raged around him, he lowered the dead Englishman to the ground, then turned to face the next man to come through.

How long he kept the breach alone—or virtually, since there was still a handful of ragged old retainers armed with pikes and boat hooks in his shadow—he could not say. The flaming ballista spears had stopped as the English fought to consolidate the ground they'd taken. But soon they began again, screaming into the ruined fortress like lightning bolts in raging, murderous arcs.

◈ ◈ ◈

"To the south side!" roared MacDuff from the back of his horse. The breach there had opened up, and one catapult shot had torn a gash along the wall so deep that it ripped a tower away and reduced the rampart to smoldering cinders. The opening was forty feet across, turning wider as the battlements burned.

"Wait!" called Lennox. "We need time to order the troops. The companies on that side are our greenest men. They're not ready to storm a castle."

"This is no castle," said MacDuff. "At best, it was a fortified hill. Now it's little more than an oven."

"Macbeth's army is retreating through the back and into the woods. Malcolm says we must pursue and run them down..."

"Let Malcolm massacre his fleeing countrymen if he wishes," said MacDuff, turning his horse. "I came for one thing only—a monster's head."

Then he spurred his mount around the burning walls, scattering soldiers as he rode.

◈ ◈ ◈

Malcolm took a bite of his mealy apple and scowled. It was so difficult to get decent food away from the palace. *When this is over,* he thought, watching Dunsinane burn, *I will spend a month in Forres doing nothing but take my idle leisure.* The battle was won. The peace, such as it was, would be his to relish.

"My lord!"

It was Ross.

"What is it?"

"Word from the front, sir," said the thane.

"Sire," Malcolm corrected him.

"Sir?" said Ross, baffled.

"You call a king 'sire,' idiot," said Malcolm.

"But sir—*sire*—you have not yet..."

Malcolm took a menacing stride toward him and Ross bowed low.

"What did you come to say?" growled Malcolm.

"MacDuff is leading an assault to the south side, sire," Ross said carefully. "The breach to the north is too narrow and well defended."

"Very well," Malcolm shrugged. "Send enough after him to give his attack support. But make sure," he added, "that the north side—and the area behind the army—is secure."

Ross looked up at him, his eyes frank and his lip curling slightly. "We will ensure," he said, "your highness comes to no harm."

◈ ◈ ◈

Even the keep was burning now. Macbeth could see the smoke rising from the summit. All around him, the perimeter wall was fractured and crumbling. A dwindling band of troops remained to fight on; though, in his heart, he knew there was nothing now left to defend.

He turned toward this last stronghold, the tip of his sword trailing in the dust and ash as he climbed the ramp. This was no impregnable stone mansion like the place he'd cornered MacDonwald in Lochaber. Just a squat wooden tower on the highest part of the hill, the upper stories reachable only by ladder.

Macbeth sheathed his sword and began to climb.

For all the noise of battle outside and the steady crackle of flame, it was eerily quiet within. No one was fool enough to take shelter here. They had all gone out to fight or flee. The air was hot and thick with smoke and sparks, the timber old and fragile.

Somewhere below, he heard a crash. The tower itself seemed to shudder, and as he paused to listen, he caught an angry, fearsome shout on the scorching air.

"Macbeth!"

He knew that voice of old.

Turning on the ladder, he caught a glimpse of the chaos around him. Burning wood, screaming men, horses slain in the yard below. And a man in armor staring up at him, visor raised on his helmet, eyes black with fury.

MacDuff.

He held his sword aloft—in threat or greeting, he knew not which. Then, shutting his eyes against the smoke, Macbeth gripped the rungs of the ladder and began to climb again.

◈ ◈ ◈

MacDuff found no opposition in the tower base and, slowly, doggedly, began to take the rough stairs, then the ladder to the topmost levels. Halfway up, he caught the sound of someone walking on the wooden floor above him, a measured, purposeful stride.

He'd no need to know who this was; though, again, he called the name. This would be no pursuit in stealth. He wanted Macbeth to know he was hunted and by whom. On the last of the tower's indoor floors, he paused to catch his breath and look about him. The trapdoor in the ceiling was left open, as if inviting him to enter. Sword in hand, MacDuff made his awkward ascent up the last few rungs, bracing himself for a hacking attack as soon as his head came out into the air.

It never materialized. He clambered out into the crude open cabin, where the wind blew the smoke and fragments of burning tinder around in a swirling cloud. A single man was there, seated on a rough watchman's chair as if it were the throne of Scotland itself.

Macbeth's sword was across his knees. He was cradling his shallow battle crown in his hands, considering it.

"I imagined it would be you," he said, not looking up as MacDuff strode toward him. "Go back. Rejoin your men. I have too much blood of yours upon me already."

"You think I will let you live?" MacDuff demanded.

"Unless you were not born of woman, you shall not have the choice. Go. Survive. I stay here. This tower will not last much longer."

"I am owed more than that!" MacDuff bellowed. "You will not burn like some king upon his pyre. I will kill you for the bloody traitor you are and cast your body to the dogs."

"Traitor?" asked Macbeth. "I wear the crown of Scotland. You gave it me in Scone. I am still king, and you—with your English invaders—are the turncoats."

"Treachery is not confined to kings and nations," said MacDuff, stepping forward, his jaw set, eyes blazing. "You are a traitor to friends, to family," he said, voice cracking. "To all that our people hold dear and true."

There seemed no rage, no fury or fear, inside the man before him. Instead, Macbeth seemed to listen, and at last, he looked away, his face sad and distant, as if thinking of things from long ago.

"I live a charmed life," he said, though the voice was bleak, bitterly amused. "Three witches told me. None can harm Macbeth. No man born of woman."

MacDuff frowned. "Then despair," he said. "No woman gave birth to me."

The man on the chair looked at him then, his face unreadable, his eyes full of strange, intense emotions, the last of which—if MacDuff had to name it—seemed a kind of desperate longing.

"That is impossible," he said.

"There's a story," said MacDuff, "about Caesar and the manner of his birth. Perhaps you've heard it?"

Macbeth continued to look at him, saying nothing.

"My mother took sick a month before I was due," said MacDuff. "The doctors tried to save her but…The moment she was dead they cut her open and tore me out, squealing, as they did with the Roman."

For a long moment, neither spoke. The wind had died to nothing and there was a curious, empty calm in the hot air. The battle below seemed over. Beyond the sounds of the fire, there was nothing but the breeze that carried on it the faint cries of dying and wounded men.

Then Macbeth began to laugh. It was a long, slow, mirthless sound that raised the hair on the back of MacDuff's neck.

"You think this funny?" he asked. "You'll die upon my sword and I will take your head, as once you did MacDonwald's."

"The wheel is come full circle," said Macbeth. He rose very slowly, setting the battle crown upon the chair. He gave the thing a long look, then turned and slowly drew his sword.

"I do not fear you," MacDuff lied. He had seen Macbeth in battle.

"You're no fool, man," said Macbeth. "Of course you do. But anger is as good as courage. Lay on, MacDuff. Lay on."

The first charge came, shield first, MacDuff's sword lancing over its rim. Macbeth deflected the strike and stepped to the side. The roof of the burning keep was cramped and its surrounding flimsy wall just three feet high. MacDuff deflected Macbeth's cut, then slashed wildly with his blade. His foe swung down his sword to catch the blow, then kicked back hard, sending him stumbling against the wall, headfirst over the sickening height below.

They both felt the tower sway at that moment. It would not last much longer.

MacDuff steadied himself and came lunging and cutting, forcing the man before him to give ground, sweating, his face half black with soot. He pressed home the attack, driving the king back so that he tripped against the open trapdoor. Then he heaved at him with the boss of his shield and Macbeth sprawled into the corner.

A moment's breathless pause. The man on the ground gathered himself to spring and MacDuff braced, his sword lowered, aimed like a spear.

With a great cry, Macbeth leapt forward, but his breast was bared. In that brief moment, MacDuff stabbed once and knew that it was over.

◈ ◈ ◈

A single deep breath of sharp, cruel pain. The stricken figure slumps against the shallow wall and finds his vision retreating to a diminishing tunnel, yet clearer with each desperate passing second. His hand goes down to feel the wound and comes back crimson from his guts.

An image rises in his memory: the stone they built for Sueno outside the palace in Forres, the line of kneeling warriors, heads taken by the sword like barley cropped with a farmer's busy scythe.

"Aye," he murmurs from the floor, "I bleed, too. You see, man of Fife?" His voice goes lower. "But I do not leave this foul stage stooping."

The figure opposite is dark and distant. Macbeth marvels at the stain and rubs the crimson between his fingertips. His head tips back into the empty space beyond the shallow wall. He gasps and chokes on the smoky air, then stares beyond the carnage and the cries of dying men.

The day is bright and beautiful. Red kites hover overhead. The purple heather crowns the distant Grampians beyond the wide green valley and the sinuous snaking line that marks the river. In the verdant land before him, that wild and savage paradise, stags roam, hares box, and salmon leap for joy and freedom, daring bold men to seize them from their glittering, icy burns, for that's his destiny and always will be, to lust for the shiny prizes men covet and wish to own before all others. Somewhere close, he wooed his wife and first lay with her amid the meadowsweet and buttercups, a memory that now bites more keenly than any blade a furious foe might wield.

This sight, these recollections, fire him with such inward anger and regret.

Unarmed and bleeding, he rises this one last time, confronts the man before him and his gleaming, swinging sword, throws strong arms wide, and bellows in a bold, defiant roar, "This precious realm was mine!"

To squander, croons that low, interior voice he first heard the night in Inverness he crept to Duncan's chamber, dagger in hand.

"My love," he whispers. "I did all this for you. For us. I am so truly sorry."

There's a rushing sound in his ears, like a falcon cutting through the air as it swoops toward its prey. And then that lustrous great green world beyond is spinning round and round before him, its bejeweled peacock colors fading slowly with his agony.

◈ ◈ ◈

The river flows red like a vein through the land, bleeding to the sea. Hawks and crows swoop upon the carrion lying scattered on both banks. Wild dogs and foxes, all the hidden ravening vermin of the fields, come out to feed on the crimson carnage strewn over grass and heather, thistle and gorse. The victors stagger around drunk on arrogance and beer; the losers lie slain or fettered in chains if any think them worthy of ransom. In the ragged camps of Malcolm and MacDuff, weary soldiers slowly settle in for the night, too tired, too full of trepidation to speak.

At the foot of the steep slope beneath the charred remains of the wooden fortress Dunsinane, three dark shapes whirl and skitter, cloaks flying, past the corpses of man and animal, like three black crows scavenging for meat. They grow larger, becoming the last things alive possessing energy at the end of this long and bloody day.

Then they stop by a burn aflood with water the color of a babe fresh from its mother's aching womb.

"Ach! Poor man! Poor man!" the youngest cries. "Here! Here!"

They crowd together, and then the young one reaches gently down and, from the stream, retrieves the bloodied head, hair matted and dripping, lips black, eyes open, blank and staring.

"Oh, sir! Oh, sir!" she whimpers and the tears start in her eyes. "It was a majestic visage. Too splendid for a thane. And now…oh…"

Indignant, she holds the thing for them to see, and neither crone nor brute knows what to say. Her eyes are streaming, full of grief and pain.

"We'll need a cart," the big one grumbles. "I cannot carry a man so large all the way cross Scotland."

"Find one, then," she orders, sane again, and places the severed head next to the savaged torso the giant has lugged here, staring at the grim and fearsome sight.

An eagle cries. A shape approaches.

She is not of a mind to turn for a moment, and when she does, she sees Fleance there, a skinny, trembling figure, with wispy beard and shabby armor, bloodstains upon it. His face is set in angry fright, and his sword quivers before him.

"Fleance lives," the crone says, seating herself on a tussock of heather. "Let all the world rejoice."

"Yet," the girl adds, cocking her strange head, opening her black eyes farther, "he is different now. I feel it." She stares at them. "You?"

They think for a moment, nod their heads.

"I slew a man!" he screams, wild eyes damp with tears. "Some…poor soul wounded in the side. I watched him trembling and thought he meant me harm."

"There's courage," mutters the crone. "Still, it's a start."

"Silence!" The sword wavers. "You promised me…"

"What?" the girl says, standing to face him.

"A throne. Some elevation."

The big sister throws her head back and laughs like a taproom drunk. "All hail, Fleance," she cries. "Hail monarch of the piss pot. King of the kitchen hearth."

A juvenile look of anger distorts his thin, gray face. He waves the sword and shrieks, "I'll slay you all, then, and do the world a favor."

With a single slender finger, the girl reaches out and touches the bloody blade.

"Do it, then," she says, smiling. "You may as well murder the weather or the ocean. We are mere bystanders in this tale..."

"You are the cause!"

She laughs and places her hands on her skinny hips.

"Now, is that so? Had your father kept his counsel, Macbeth here would have reigned for many years, trying to swallow his guilt, perhaps, but a king with good intentions."

"Better than Duncan," the crone cuts in.

The tall one stares down the field, across the bloody landscape, toward the sprawling English camp and mutters, "Better than that foul son of his shall be."

The girl touches the silver crucifix that hangs over his armor on a chain.

"It was Banquo's greed that brought about his end, as it was Macbeth's ambition that engendered his. Men and monarchs make uneasy bedfellows. Both desire the other, but neither wishes to countenance the cost. Slavery on one part. The heavy burden of a people's manifold sins on the other. There is a reason you slay your kings with tedious regularity." Her fingers leave the cross. It clatters noisily against his chest. "And always have. This god you pray to gave the world his only son and still you slaughtered him, the greatest king of all. Do not lay the blame for your savagery on the likes of us."

Trembling, he watches. She comes so close his rank and nervous breath assail her flaring nostrils.

"But tell us, Fleance. You have a rare gift. The dreams. That faculty we share. Peer into the shadowy future. Tell us what awaits you there."

"I cannot!" he weeps. "I cannot..."

They say nothing, waiting.

"I slew that man and felt the strangeness leave me as if some bird had flown. I see..."

"Nothing," says the big one. "It happens."

The child glowers at the shambling figure in front of her, then spits full in his face. "So nature gives you a third eye, boy, and all you can do is blind it with your timid rage." She nods at the troops along the river. "Go join the rest of them. You're a pawn, a puppet, nothing special to us now."

"A line of kings, you said..." he whines, wiping away the spittle.

"One day!" she laughs. "And that's a miracle. I will waste my breath on you no more. Know this: your mother's dead, your uncle's thieved your land in Laggan, Malcolm loathes you, and MacDuff, though decent, sees his dead wife and bairns each time he sets his eyes upon your bony frame. There's nothing here for Banquo's son but death and misery." She glances at the distant camps. "As there is for them."

The crone points a crooked finger at him.

"Go south and west, boy. To Wales and the court of a prince called Gruffydd ap Llywelyn. There, marry his daughter and take the name Steward, for that is what, in truth, you'll be."

The big one grunts, "And die a lowly, insignificant death, knowing none of those who follow you to greatness will remember the cowardly boy who sired them from a distance."

He shakes with the impotent fury of a child, stabs the sword at the severed corpse before them. "And what of him? You scoop up this murderer's remains as if they're holy."

The girl gazes at the bloodied torso and the head with blackened lips. "Macbeth, Macbeth," she sighs. "Our fleeting king. You had the heart but not the stomach. Half a monarch, then, which is better than most of who went before and those who will soon follow. We take him to Iona to be buried in the place he merits. The graveyard where our kings have lain since men first walked this land."

He stares at them, aghast. "He was a monster!"

"He was a man!" the child retorts. "Who, had the die turned differently, would have been the most just and well-loved king this nation's ever known." She strikes him on the face; he whimpers. "You are not fit to stand in his shadow. Be gone. This is no place for fools who've thrown away the single curious talent they owned. Be"—her arms shoot out, and she seems, for one brief and terrifying moment, to fly in some great black cloud before him—"gone!"

Still, he stands and shouts, "The sisters of Iona are holy, blessed creatures, saints who've served this land for centuries. What use have they for black-hearted crones like you?"

The silence chills them. First, the young one laughs, then the others. And all are wracked with mirth now as they weep and shake their heads.

The oldest rises on her crutches, comes round, and takes his arm. "We three are sisters of Iona, sonny," she says. "We birth kings and we bury 'em. Now get your scrawny arse hence before our patience fails."

They watch him limp and stumble round the ragged hill of Dunsinane.

"A cart," the burly sister says. "I long for home."

"For sleep and silence," the old woman adds. "For peace."

The girl's eyes will not leave the camp below her, with its fluttering flags and drunken men, crowing about their prowess in the field.

"Peace?" she murmurs. "*Peace?*"

Haughty and as stupid as a peacock, he struts around them, monarch and coward, oblivious to their truculent, wary mood.

She points across the vale with her long finger, fixing her eye on the lanky, swaggering figure there. "Malcolm, Malcolm," the child says in a low, hard whisper. "I never met a man I liked called Malcolm."

Authors' Notes

The Play

We first came to this story—like most readers will—through Shakespeare's version of it, and while ours deviates in certain crucial details, much of what we have done is more about embroidery of the play, filling out what is passed over there and occasionally bringing a different perspective to the events and people that comprise Shakespeare's account. It makes sense, then, to begin this reflection on our own work with a consideration of the play.

The play was probably written in 1606 or 1607 for the theater company known then as the King's Men. We know that it continued to be staged for several years, but the first printing seems to have been for the 1623 collected works of Shakespeare known as the First Folio, which was compiled seven years after the playwright's death. The play is short for a tragedy, and it contains elements almost certainly not written by Shakespeare alone, probably the result of either collaboration with or borrowing from Thomas Middleton, another playwright who also worked for the King's Men. This is not unusual for the period, but it does raise questions about whether Shakespeare wrote material for the play that did not appear in the Folio text. There is no evidence for such lost material, so it is fruitless to speculate on whether the play was rethought or censored in the seventeen years or so between its composition and its publication.

Censorship is a possibility, however, because the play as it stands is so clearly topical in its politics. King James I, who had assumed the English throne upon Elizabeth's death in 1603, was a Scot who traced his lineage through Banquo.

He believed in witchcraft and had written about personal encounters with people he believed had magical abilities, and he was fierce on the idea of kings as the right hand of God. In one of his published works he makes it clear that a legitimately crowned king cannot be removed by his people, regardless of his tyrannous actions. Rather, the tyrant must be left to the judgment of God.

Shakespeare's *Macbeth* raises all of these issues; though, as is usual with Shakespeare, the play's final position seems uncertain, and we think the old idea that the play was a compliment to James is, at best, inadequate. Shakespeare's Banquo is carefully washed of his historical complicity in Duncan's death, but Fleance, through whom James was descended, is pointedly left off the throne at the end of the play. Most problematically, Scotland is only reclaimed from Macbeth through the regicide James would surely have deplored. The English were skeptical of their imported king whose Catholic mother, Mary, Queen of Scots, had been executed by her English cousin Elizabeth for plotting against England with Spain. James's own behavior didn't help, and if there's a picture of him in Shakespeare's play, it might be the portrait of debauchery sketched by Malcolm in his curious test of MacDuff. Regicide, it should be remembered, was in the air, not just in the assassination attempts that Elizabeth and James survived, but in the formal trial and execution of James's son, Charles I, on the charge of tyranny thirty-five years later.

For all its political weight, however, subsequent periods came to see *Macbeth* as a primarily domestic play, one driven uniquely in Shakespeare by the terrible collusion of a husband and wife. For the theatrical medium, which was not capable of representing large-scale conflict, the focusing onto the central couple is, perhaps, inevitable, as perhaps is the misogyny that drove much of the interpretation of Lady Macbeth. For many, she was the demon at the story's core, the driving force that (like the witches) somehow absolved Macbeth of culpability. More recently, productions have found in her a new complexity and a crippled sense of loss speculatively deduced from her childlessness. Scholars have come to see the play as crucially about gender, a play in which masculinity is defined by violence and aggression, femininity by a doomed and grieving passivity, and between these two extremes are the sexually ambiguous witches with their beards and Lady Macbeth, who tries—and, it seems, ultimately fails—to rid herself of the weakness she sees in her sex.

Shakespeare's Sources

Shakespeare rarely invented plots. He drew heavily on sources that he tweaked and augmented to suit his purpose, and Macbeth is no exception. His primary source was Raphael Holinshed's *Chronicles of England Wales* (1587) in which he found not just the story of Macbeth, but also the story of King Duff, who was slain by Donwald, from which Shakespeare also seems to borrow. The historical Macbeth, according to Holinshed, slew Duncan in a dynastic feud, aided by Banquo, after which he became not just a successful king, but a good king for over a decade before lapsing into paranoia and tyranny. Shakespeare condenses the action for dramatic effect so that the play feels like it spans no more than a few days or weeks, each act having significant consequences that escalate the tension and move toward the play's dreadful climax. Because of his condensing of events, much that Holinshed raises has to be left out. One key instance is that Shakespeare collapses into a single reported battle the two separate encounters with MacDonwald and Sueno. The latter encounter, against the Norwegian king's army, is sketched in Holinshed much as we have rendered it here, Macbeth's advantage achieved by the secret drugging of Sueno's army with the mekilwort (deadly nightshade), which grew thereabouts.

The "Real" Macbeth

We have only a hazy picture of the Scotland of the eleventh century. There is little doubt it was a wild and savage place where the crown was passed from one warlord to another, often on the basis of power and brute violence. Scandinavian powers laid claim to the northern parts of the country and frequently raided those areas they failed to control. Savage vendettas between rival clans were commonplace and bloody.

While we may be uncertain of much detail, it is clear that Shakespeare's portrayal of Macbeth—which has now become, in some ways, the man's historical record—is grossly inaccurate. This may be for purely dramatic reasons, but whatever the reason, the play's portrayal of Macbeth bears little resemblance to what scant facts we possess.

Macbeth—Mac Bethad mac Findlàech in Gaelic—was born in 1005 and died in 1057. He was the son of the "mormaer" (a kind of regional king) of Moray, a region covering Inverness, parts of the Great Glen, and other surrounding areas beyond the borders of the modern Moray Council in Scotland. Macbeth's father was murdered in 1020, probably by relatives later killed by Macbeth, who then became mormaer himself. As a member of the Moray "royal" line, he was involved in Scottish politics from an early age. In 1031, he attended a meeting between then Scottish monarch Malcolm II and England's King Canute.

Three years later, the despotic Malcolm died—perhaps murdered—at the age of eighty in Glamis. He was succeeded by his own son, Duncan, not the gray-haired ancient of Shakespeare, but a young and inexperienced man of thirty-three. Macbeth was listed as Duncan's "dux," or lord, suggesting Macbeth, who had a royal claim of his own, was a principal supporter.

In 1039, Duncan led a Scottish army south into England in a disastrous expedition that ended in defeat in Durham. After relations between he and Macbeth worsened, the young king then unwisely led a second expedition north the following year, to attack Moray. He was killed in battle, not in bed, near Elgin in August 1040, and Macbeth was crowned king of Scotland at Scone shortly afterward.

Macbeth spent seventeen years on the throne, a period some Caledonian historians say was the most peaceful and prosperous of medieval times. There are no contemporary records that paint him as a tyrant. In 1050, he made the long and dangerous journey to Rome as a pilgrim, a sure sign that he felt confident of his political strength at home. Four years later, however, an invading English army defeated Macbeth's forces at Dunsinane. Macbeth escaped and returned north to Moray. There, Malcolm's forces attacked him three years later, finally hunting the king down at Lumphanan, near Aberdeen, where, several chroniclers claim, he was beheaded by Malcolm himself.

It was Macbeth's son or stepson Lulach, however, who was crowned king of Scotland at Scone the following month, only to be assassinated by Malcolm's agents the following March. His murderer finally ascended the throne as Malcolm III, reigning for thirty-five years until, in 1093, he was slain during an expedition into Northumbria. He was succeeded by his brother Donalbain (Donald III), who spent a year on the throne before being killed by an invading English army led by his own nephew, Edgar.

Of all Scotland's eleventh-century monarchs, only Edgar was to die of natural causes. He is buried in Dunfermline Abbey. The remains of Duncan I, Macbeth, Lulach, Malcolm III, and Donald III were all, after various journeys around Scotland, interred on the island of Iona.

Where We Diverge from Shakespeare and History

In approaching this project, we tried to keep a few ideas uppermost, not least of which is that our book, like a stage production or film of the play, must be a new artistic product in its own right and not simply a slavish "translation" of Shakespeare's original. We have done what Shakespeare did, adapting and rethinking his source text to suit what he thought interesting or effective, a practice followed by any subsequent staging of the play. There can be no "straight" or definitive production that grows out of nothing but the playwright's words, performance being generically different from the script, which seems to originate it, or all stagings would be the same.

We, too, had to face up to a shift in genre—in our case, from play to novel. These two forms build meaning differently, they communicate differently, and they act upon the imagination differently. And while we could have simply tried to fill in the blanks inevitably left by a play script (what characters look like, what they can see around them, and so forth), this seemed inadequate. We wanted to make real use of the novelist's ability to represent more than dialogue, and to do so in a language readers would find more approachable than Shakespeare's, but we also did not want to simply render a pale imitation of the play. We wanted to wrestle with it, tug at it, mold it, and even, from time to time, tear it. Though we bow before Shakespeare's genius and freely acknowledge that nothing we have done here could have existed without his words as a starting point, we wanted to make the story—not the play, but the story—our own.

So we expanded the initial battles to show a Scotland under siege, a Scotland saved by the courage and heroism of the man who gave the story its name. We gave his wife a name pulled from the records of ancient Scotland, because we liked the sound of it and because we thought it suited the woman we had started to build. Most importantly, we decided to like the Macbeths, not to excuse their actions, but to try to explain them, to afford them an inner life that went beyond whatever the play could tell us, and then to watch them make a series of bad choices that escalate till they are dragging tragedy at their heels. We kept the porter (though we nearly cut him) and made him an icon of Macbeth's journey and decline. We painted the witches in ways quite different from the play, making them central but—we hope—at least as enigmatic, striking, and unsettling. We make no apologies for any of this. We have not violated Shakespeare's play, as the playwright would (we're sure) be the first to admit. We haven't destroyed it. It's still there for you to read and enjoy.

The Scottish Locations

Did Shakespeare visit Scotland? The truth is…no one knows. City annals in Perth record a visit by an English theater company in 1599, possibly at the invitation of King James VI (shortly to be James I of England, too). This was probably the same group, later known as the King's Men, that Shakespeare had worked with for most of his adult life. James I was a great fan of the company, giving them a royal patent in 1603 that named them the King's Men. The first player named on that charter, Lawrence Fletcher, is cited in the Perth records. But there is nothing to indicate that the second name, Shakespeare, was among the company traveling north.

Nevertheless, there is a strong tradition that Shakespeare did, indeed, visit Scotland and, there, gathered inspiration for future plays. Some authors have even suggested that he preceded Dan Brown to the famous Rosslyn Chapel and Castle as a guest of the St. Clair family and visited Glamis Castle along the way. They cite the bucolic paradise pictured in *As You Like It* and its key character, Rosalind, as evidence of the links. Did Shakespeare also pick up threads of the darker story that would become *Macbeth*? One can only guess, but whether through reading history books such as Holinshed's or through personal acquaintance, he certainly had a grasp of Scottish geography.

In our interpretation of the story, we have placed much of the tale in the Moray area, running from Forres to Inverness and then to the western reaches of the Great Glen in Lochaber, where our version of the story begins. Anyone wishing to find traces of the real Macbeth in modern Scotland will be sorely disappointed for the most part.

Though historians may acclaim him as one of the nation's greatest kings, the public perception is largely shaped by Shakespeare's fictional portrayal. The ancient castle of Inverness has long been lost, and its Victorian replacement, by the river, is probably not in the same position.

A few miles from Inverness, beyond the bleak battlefield of Culloden, lie the Balnuaran of Clava, a set of prehistoric burial cairns half hidden in woodland. They do not feature in Shakespeare any more than our invented meeting between the witches and Lady Macbeth. But anyone hunting the atmosphere of Macbeth in the Highlands will surely find it here. A little farther east, Forres, cited as a royal palace by Shakespeare and here, has no great remains from the eleventh century, though it does possess Sueno's Stone, which features in our version of the story. An imposing and bloodthirsty monument that probably predated Macbeth, it now stands protected in a glass case on a hill at the edge of this small, pretty town.

Glamis Castle is a popular destination, for its beautiful building and royal connections, though the links with Macbeth are, frankly, flimsy. Scone, not far away to the southeast, is still visibly part of the story of Scottish kings. The "moot hill" or "hill of credulity" can be seen in the grounds of Scone Palace. Scottish monarchs were crowned here from the ninth century on. A replica of the Stone of Scone marks the site of the original today, in front of a small Gothic chapel. The last monarch to be crowned on the site was Charles II, who took the throne of Scotland in 1651, nine years before he was restored to the English throne.

Fifteen miles north lies the charming old capital of Dunkeld, which Duncan used as a base. On the outskirts lies Birnam and its wood, still green and leafy, and an ancient hilltop fort. Duncan's father, Crinan, was abbot of Dunkeld and was killed by Macbeth when he rose up against his forces after Duncan's death. Malcolm's use of branches from the wood for camouflage is taken straight from the pages of Holinshed.

Dunsinane is thirteen miles as the crow flies from Birnam, but more like twenty by circuitous roads. It is, as befits the story, a bleak spot, a bare, lone crag rising to 1,012 feet above the hamlet of Collace. It's a stiff and steep walk to the top, once the site of an ancient fort going back to the Iron Age. Shakespeare's Macbeth died here. The real-life Macbeth survived for another three years before succumbing to Malcolm's forces close to Aberdeen.

Which one is more real? Stand breathless on the summit of Dunsinane, listening to the wind whistling, gazing across the valley of the Tay toward the green forest of Birnam in the distance and you can only wonder.

About the Authors

Photograph by Bill DeLoach

British-born author A. J. Hartley is the Russell Robinson Professor of Shakespeare Studies at the University of North Carolina-Charlotte and works as a scholar, screenwriter, dramaturg, and theater director. In addition to seven best-selling novels, he is the author of *The Shakespearean Dramaturg*; an upcoming performance history of *Julius Caesar*; a book on Shakespeare and political theatre; and numerous articles and book chapters. He also edits the performance journal, *Shakespeare Bulletin*, published by Johns Hopkins University Press. He is married with one son and lives in Charlotte.

Photograph by Mark Bothwell

David Hewson is the author of seventeen novels that have been published in twenty different languages. His first book, *Semana Santa*, was transformed into a movie, and his nine-book, Rome-based Nic Costa series is currently in development for television. Before devoting himself full-time to writing, he worked as a journalist for the *London Times*, the *Sunday Times*, and *The Independent*.